Unguilded

Jane Glatt

Unguilded

Jane Glatt

TYCHE BOOKS LTD.

Unguilded

Published by Tyche Books Ltd.
www.TycheBooks.com

Copyright © 2015 Jane Glatt
First Tyche Books Ltd Edition 2015

Print ISBN: 978-1-928025-25-2
Ebook ISBN: 978-1-928025-26-9

Cover Art by Artist: Niken Anindita
Cover Layout by Lucia Starkey
Interior Layout by Ryah Deines
Editorial by M. L. D. Curelas

Author photograph: Eugene Choi
Echo1 Photography

This book was funded in part by a grant from the Alberta Media Fund.

Contents

Dedication

I want to thank my mom for gifting me with a love of stories.
She always has a book close by.

Chapter one

"HURRY!"

Kara Fonti scrambled up the narrow stairs after her mother. "Which room is yours?"

"Here." Kara brushed past her mother's rigid figure to the small door at the end of the hall. She opened the door, revealing an even steeper set of steps. "Be careful," she told her mother. "The ceiling is low." Uneasy, she paused on the stairs. Her mother had wanted to see her room—to watch the sunset, she'd said—but Kara didn't think she'd travelled so far for a view.

"Keep moving," her mother said, her hands firm on her daughter's back.

Kara stumbled up the half dozen stairs that led to her room, ducking to avoid the low ceiling.

Kara's room was the smallest in the house, barely large enough to hold her pallet and small desk and chair. The low sloping ceiling had been perfect for the eight-year-old Kara, the Kara who'd held such promise, the Kara they'd all had such hopes for.

Now she could only stand up straight when she stood at the foot of her bed. At sixteen, she'd outgrown her room—and everyone's hope.

Her mother, Arabella Fonti, frowned and, with eyes so dark they looked black, scanned the cramped space. With more grace than Kara had ever managed, she glided to the chair.

"So," her mother said as she settled herself. "You've failed again."

"I'm sorry, Mother," Kara said, gazing at her feet. She was used to the shame of failure—or so she'd thought before she'd had to face her mother.

"Don't call me that," her mother snapped. "You may call me Donna Fonti or Donna Arabella."

"Yes, Donna," Kara said. Her mother had come to visit—for the first time ever—but it wasn't out of love.

Arabella Fonti was even more beautiful than Kara had imagined. She was tall, although not quite as tall as Kara, and her long black hair gleamed against pale, smooth skin. Her mother turned her head and in the sunlight that streamed in through the small window, her eyes flashed a deep purple.

Resigned, Kara looked down at the smooth orange tiles of the floor. Her mother was here—filled with disapproval and disdain—because she'd failed the test, again. And now that she was sixteen she had no more chances.

"Now I have to come back here, to the villa I'd hoped to never set foot in again." Arabella glared at her, and a purple mist swirled around her angry features.

"I'm sorry," Kara repeated.

And she was. Every year since she'd turned eight she'd waited for the Guild Tester to come. Every year she was sure that *this* year would be different—*this* year her talent would show itself. Instead, every year the Guild Tester left in a shimmer of blue with a promise to return next year. And Kara was left to deal with the disappointment of her father and the bitterness of his not-quite wife.

"You're sorry," Arabella said.

Kara flinched at the venom in her mother's voice.

"Guild Law meant I had to bear a child before I could leave this villa—I had to leave someone with potential behind." Arabella frowned and shook her elegant head. "I thought my talent strong enough to breed true, and Banio Fonti agreed to raise you and let me leave. I should have chosen someone other than him—there is no magic in his family. So you are your father's child—without magic—but *my* problem."

"Papa always said he married you because you were so beautiful," Kara whispered.

He *used* to say that, when Kara was little and still had hope of finding her talent. He'd stopped saying it when he met Noula. Noula, who was bitter because Kara's mother had everything she didn't—magic, beauty, and legal marriage to Banio Fonti.

"Pah," Arabella said. "I had the strongest magic seen in this villa for generations and my father was Villa Primus of Mage Guild. I know exactly why your father married me."

Kara knew too. Because of his marriage to Arabella, her father was an important man in Villa Larona—Guild Secundus in the villa's Mage Guild. He had no magic of his own, but a marriage—even in name only—to a strong Mage and a daughter who would inherit her mother's talent was enough in this small villa.

At least it had been.

"We don't have much time. Get some clothes together," Arabella said. "You're leaving."

"What about the guild?" Kara asked. "And Mage Guild Secundus Valendi?" By right of Guild Law, Mage Guild would determine her fate. Before today she'd assumed that the villa Guildsmen would make the decision—then her mother had arrived with the second most powerful man in Mage Guild.

Though she had no magic Kara could still be useful to the guild—she'd assumed they'd want her to continue teaching. But in the two weeks since her final failure, Noula, more malicious than ever, had taken great pleasure in telling Kara that her only use now was as a breeder. Her mother was a powerful Mage, someone would take her, Noula taunted, some old man willing to feed and house her so he could bed her and get children on her in the hopes that at least one child had magic.

I would rather die, Kara had thought, never expecting it to come to that. Then she'd met Mage Guild Secundus Valendi. He'd stared at her so intensely that she'd had to suppress a shiver. And admit that Noula was right. Mage Guild would use her as a breeder—*Valerio Valendi* would use her as a breeder.

"I'll deal with the guild and Valerio Valendi," Arabella said. "Pack your things."

Kara knelt by the trunk that held her extra clothes. Her mother's steady gaze made her jumpy, and she fumbled as she opened the chest. She scooped the contents into a pile and stuffed everything into a small pack. It wasn't much. Her winter stockings, a skirt that was too short, a faded blue shirt, a second set of smallclothes, and an old pair of her father's trousers, threadbare at the knees, which she wore while tending the herbs.

"Do you have any guilders?" Arabella asked. "Jewelry?"

Kara shook her head. As the years passed and she continued to fail her test, fewer items of value had been given to her.

"Nothing? I thought you were teaching the younger ones?"

"Noula has Mage Guild pay her directly," Kara said. "To cover the expense of keeping me."

"That *donnina*," Arabella said. "Here." She untied a small bag from the belt at her waist. "It's not much. You'll have to earn your own guilders as soon as possible."

"Where are we going?" Kara asked warily.

"Not we, you," Arabella replied.

Kara's skin prickled. Her mother wasn't going to *take* her away—she was going to *send* her away.

"Where? Will the guild approve?"

"Leave Tregella and go to Wulmar, or maybe Terenia," Arabella said. "Of course the guild won't approve." Her mother smiled a small, tight smile. "But I will give them no choice. Time to go. We only have a few more moments before someone comes looking for us."

Kara didn't move, couldn't move. Leave the country, leave the guild? She'd never imagined such a thing. Living outside of the guild was as good as being dead, wasn't it? But living as a breeder would be *worse* than being dead.

"Come," Arabella said. She put her arm around Kara's shoulder. "It will be a great adventure. Besides, if you stay with the guild when you have no magic you will become a woman such as Noula."

Kara shook her head. Become like Noula? Powerless and bitter? Never.

"The guild is intrigued with *my* power," her mother continued. "They plan to pair you with a powerful Mage to see if my magic will be inherited by *your* children."

Kara closed her eyes. It wasn't much of a choice, but it *was* a choice.

"I'll leave," Kara said. "If you're sure they won't let me stay here with Papa and teach." She knew they wouldn't let her—Valerio Valendi wouldn't let her—but she had to ask. The safe life she'd assumed would be hers seemed so far away now.

"No," Arabella said. "The guild will not allow that. Besides, now that you're an adult, my marriage to Banio Fonti is no longer necessary."

Her mother's thin smile chilled Kara. Her father would be stripped of his high position in the guild and given another, lower role. Kara's laugh was sharp and bitter.

"You find this amusing?" her mother asked.

"Noula will finally be able to marry Papa," she said, her eyes on the floor and her expression blank.

"I doubt he'll have her. Banio used marriage once to gain status—I expect he will try that again. Noula will be at Mage Guild's mercy just as we all are."

Numb, Kara let herself be steered toward the door. She had no pity for Noula. Overly proud of being the not-quite wife of the Villa Mage Guild Secundus, she would find few friends among those who were to decide her fate.

"You cannot go out the front door," Arabella said. "I saw the little bridge that connects the second floor to your neighbour's house—you will leave that way."

Kara stumbled on the top step. "What will I do?" She clutched her pack against her chest as if to slow her racing heartbeat. She knew it was better than staying, but she was afraid all the same.

"You will teach," Arabella said calmly. "Mage Guild has educated you far beyond most people. You will find a place."

Kara could only stare at her, at the woman who had given birth to her but had not raised her. And who now was telling her to leave the only home she'd ever known. But she was right. Kara didn't have a place—at least not one that she wanted. Not in the guild, not in Villa Larona, not even, so it seemed, in Tregella. Did she belong anywhere? She did, she had to believe that, but it was up to her to find out where.

"You will be fine," Arabella said. "Here." She slipped her silver bracelet off a delicate wrist, unpinned the matching brooch from her scarf, and shoved them into Kara's hands. "Take these. Now go."

Kara took a steadying breath and stuffed the jewelry into the bottom of her pack. With her bag slung over one shoulder, she grabbed her shawl from the peg by the door and wrapped it loosely around herself. She descended the stairs, pausing at the bottom to look up at her mother.

A purple mist wafted around Arabella and Kara reached a hand toward it. It circled her mother gently, in contrast to the grey-black cloud that had pulsated threateningly around Mage Guild Secundus Valendi.

It took all of her will but she turned and ducked out into the hallway. Nothing about her first—and likely only—meeting with her mother had been what she'd anticipated. She hadn't expected love, exactly, but perhaps a measure of regret for the babe she'd been forced to leave behind. Instead, all she'd felt from the woman who'd given birth to her was indifference.

The hallway was dark. She and her mother had sat through one of Villa Larona's spectacular sunsets, and neither of them had noticed. That was the reason they'd given for their trip to Kara's room in the first place—so Arabella could see the sun paint the sky before it dipped behind the mountain. Now that it was dusk the others would be expecting them downstairs.

In the small alcove Kara eased open the window and stepped out onto the narrow whitewashed bridge that spanned the cobbled street.

It had been years since she'd used this bridge—as a child she'd spent hours on it, lying flat and peering over the edge to spy on villagers below. That was before Noula had come to live with them, before she'd been forbidden to spend time with their neighbour, Donna Jonella. The kindly widow had been ancient even then and, unlike her own family, she'd always made Kara feel wanted.

Kara reached up to the handle and gently lifted the latch of the small door that led into Donna Jonella's house. She cocked her head to listen. There was no sound from within the house so she shouldered aside the door and crawled inside.

The upstairs hallway was dark and dusty as though it had not been used for a long time, and Kara quickly made her way to the stairs. She crept down, her feet silent on the smooth tiles. At the bottom she paused to orient herself.

There. A sliver of light outlined the kitchen window.

A cough came from the main room, and Kara froze. Donna Jonella was sleeping downstairs. Careful not to stumble into furniture, Kara glided a foot forward. One more gliding step and she was in the kitchen with its stale odours of cooked onions and garlic.

A small knife glinted on the counter, and she grabbed it and put it in her pack. She felt a twinge of guilt at stealing from a woman who had always been kind to her, but she forced it aside. Donna Jonella likely had other knives, but this one could be the difference between Kara living or dying.

She eased the door latch up out of its bracket and stepped outside into the night.

In the dim moonlight the neglect of the curved, white adobe wall that sheltered her from the street was evident. Tufts of grasses sprouted from the white-washed walls, and large sections had crumbled, leaving clumps of dried clay scattered on the ground.

She reached out and dislodged a small piece of adobe. The wall was in such poor repair that she should be able to climb it. She glanced at the path that led to the street out front. It would be better if she didn't have to pass her father's house. She might be missed by now, and someone could be looking out the window.

Kara stuffed her shawl into her pack and placed one shoe on the crumbling wall, shifting her foot from side to side until she found a solid foothold. She reached up, grabbed a tuft of grass, and tugged hard. It held. She pulled herself up and peered over the top of the wall into another small, much better kept, garden. It was empty so she swung first one leg over, then the other. Fingers digging into the crumbling adobe, she lowered herself as far as she could before she let go. She landed in a heap at the bottom, and quickly untangled her skirt, and got to her feet. No faces peered out the curtained window, and no raised voices broke the silence as she ran from the garden to the street.

ARABELLA SAT IN the small room until she could no longer hear any sounds from the second floor. The girl—even to herself she refused to call her daughter—should be well away. She smoothed a hand along her skirt. She would have to manage Valerio Valendi now. She smiled. They had grown close during the journey to this Gyda-forsaken villa—just as she'd planned. Her smile faltered. She hadn't expected the Mage Guild Secundus to be so obviously interested in the girl.

She'd told the truth—Mage Guild *was* intrigued with her bloodline. There was no history of such power in Villa Larona or in either of her parents' families. That was why, even though she found her magic early, she was an adult before the Guild realized just how strong her talent was. And then only because *she* made the bargain with Banio Fonti that let her leave the villa and travel to Rillidi.

"Donna Fonti?" a woman's voice called up from the second floor. "Kara? Are you there? The Mage Secundus is asking for you."

Banio Fonti's woman. She'd let her call again, call for the woman who had the title she longed for.

"Donna Fonti?"

"Did the girl not return?" Arabella asked. "She left the room a few moments ago. I wanted to watch the sunset in peace."

"She did not return to the main room," was the worried reply. "I'll see if she's in one of the rooms on this floor."

Arabella stood and carefully smoothed her skirts before stepping over to the stairs. She heard doors open and close on the floor below her and then a muffled sob as the woman of the house realized that she had to relay bad news to the Mage Guild Secundus. Kara Fonti was gone.

Arabella descended to the main floor, wrapping her scarf around her shoulders. She shouldn't have given the girl her jewelry, she realized. That had been a mistake. Now she had to make sure the girl had time to get far enough away that she—*her body*—was never found.

"Arabella."

"Secundus." Arabella inclined her head. "Have you made a decision about the girl?"

It hadn't mattered to her who the Mage Secundus decided to breed the girl to. Until she saw the way he'd looked at Kara Fonti. She could not let him have her.

When she'd arrived on Mage Guild Island all those years ago, others her age had been Journeymen or full Mages. But she'd had a formidable talent as well as beauty and charm, which she'd used to secure the best mentors she could. She'd never had a mentor as powerful and connected as Valerio Valendi, though, so she'd told the girl to flee. She would not allow a talentless girl to interfere with her plans.

"It seems she has disappeared," Valerio Valendi said. "What did the two of you discuss?"

"Our shared disappointment," Arabella said. "And the consequences—for both of us."

"Ah yes, you will need to find another Mage for the villa. Unless you plan to return?"

"I already have someone in mind," she replied. Since the child she left behind had no magic, Guild Law demanded she find a replacement. "A minor talent, but enough to make him Villa Secundus."

"I see." Valerio's voice held amusement. "A position that is currently filled by your husband."

"Yes." She lifted her chin and met his steady gaze.

"And the girl, you do not know where she went?"

"No." Arabella dropped her eyes. "She said she was going downstairs. I assumed to rejoin all of you."

"Which she did not do," Valerio said. "I have searched the house magically, and she is not here. Come and sit. We must discuss our options."

Arabella followed the Secundus into the small living room. He had taken her at her word—or at least he hadn't challenged her. He'd even been amused.

Arabella's current position within the guild was already precarious. Now that it was certain Kara Fonti had no talent, she needed both a political alliance and to bear a child with potential. Valerio Valendi was a powerful Mage—ambitious and ruthless— which made him very dangerous. But he was a man. And, she thought, not immune to her charms. A child of theirs *must* inherit power. But if it didn't she would still have years before it was known, years in which—with Valerio's support—she could establish and strengthen her position within Mage Guild.

KARA MADE HER way down through the villa. Down steep rock stairs hacked out of the mountain, worn smooth by torrential rains and decades of use. Down winding, narrow alleys where she hugged walls and hid in shadows. Down past the high square where the weekly market was held and Merchants sold goods that had been dragged uphill by stocky burros, cousins to the animals that roamed free on the mountain. Down through the lower villa, where the wooden doors were set two steps above the cobbled lane to safeguard against flooding. And finally, down to the lower square that was enclosed by warehouses on two sides and stables on a third.

The cobbles ended. The dirt road that stretched out into the valley had been hardened by animals and wagons over long years of use. This road would take Kara out of the villa she'd spent her whole life in, out of the only life she'd known. As her mother suggested, she would leave the country. But she'd have to get to Rillidi, the port city, in order to do that.

Firelight lit the handful of people still in the square—probably Merchant Guild delivering goods for trade. They huddled in chairs that ringed a small table, and hushed laughter drifted her way.

Kara glanced up at the shining white walls and dark roofs of Villa Larona. She clenched her hands, trying to slow her breathing and push away her apprehension about walking out of the villa and into the darkness of the valley.

She'd had no chance to think since leaving her father's house. She needed to sit for a moment before she walked away from her life.

She slipped through the half-open door of a stable. The air carried the earthy odour of animals and something big moved nearby—large feet shuffling straw. There was a snort from a stall along the far wall, but no voices. Kara crept down the aisle, her shoes scuffing the dirt floor.

A large brown head swung out over a stall door and into her path, and Kara stopped, startled. Huge brown eyes stared at her, and then the horse snorted softly. Kara reached a hand out, but paused when she saw grey-black mist snaking along the horse's neck. She stepped closer to get a better look, but the horse backed up into the stall.

"I'll check the nags and be right back," a voice said from just outside the stable. "The Mage Guild Secundus will have my balls if anything happened to his horses while I was playing cards."

Kara held her breath and glanced around. She couldn't be found, not in here. She eased the stall door latch up and crept inside. The horse, mist swirling along its flanks and neck, pawed at the straw. Kara tucked herself into a corner at the front of the pen, shrinking away from the animal.

Muffled footsteps came towards her as the stable hand walked down the row of stalls, muttering to himself. When he was even with the stall she was in, the horse snorted.

"What's got you spooked, big man," crooned the voice. "Though if I had that Mage on my back I might be a bit uneasy too." He chuckled. "That other Mage though, I'd not mind to take a ride on her. She's a fine one."

Kara held her breath and tried to sink farther into the shadowed corner of the stall. Straw poked at her through her shawl, and her skin itched, but she ignored it, praying for the stable hand to stay on the other side of the door.

"You're fine, so settle down," the voice said. "Got a card game waiting."

Solid footsteps headed away from her, and Kara took a shallow breath. Her heart pounded as though she'd run all the way to Primus Diallo's house, at the very top of the villa.

A shout, followed by laughter, filtered to her through the open stable door.

"Coming, coming," the stable hand's voice replied, farther away from her now.

Kara stood and peeked over the rough wood of the stall—the door shut, muffling the noise from the square.

She was safe, for now. She leaned against the stall and slid to the ground, her legs suddenly weak. She would not cry. Nothing was ever gained by feeling sorry for herself. She'd learned that when Noula had moved in. Besides, wherever she ended up, it couldn't be worse than the future Mage Guild had planned for her.

Kara wiped her hands on her skirt and looked up. The horse eyed her from the opposite corner, the grey-black mist still swirling around it.

She frowned. She'd first seen mist like this when she was eight and the Mage Guild Tester had come for her initial test. A faint blue cloud had enveloped him, and Kara had been delighted. She'd thought of him as the Blue Mage, though she'd been too shy to mention it. The blue was similar to the colour of the columbine flowers that grew on the side of the mountain so Kara picked flowers for him each visit. When she turned thirteen, Noula had forbidden it. It wasn't seemly for a young woman to give a grown man flowers, she'd said. By then the Mage Guild Tester's visits caused so much anxiety that she'd stopped wondering what caused his blue mist.

Then her mother and Guild Secundus Valerio Valendi had arrived—and like her tester, they had their own swirls of mist.

Kara had hoped to ask her mother about the mists when she'd asked to see the sunset, but Kara had forgotten about it once her fate as a breeder had been confirmed.

She stepped a little closer to the horse. The mist eddied away from her, as if blown by a gentle breeze. She blew out softly, but the mist didn't react. She lifted a hand, and the mist swirled away from her fingertips.

According to the stable hand, this was Mage Guild Secundus Valendi's horse—and the mist was the same shade of grey-black that surrounded him. Had his mist, whatever it was, somehow rubbed off onto the horse?

She wished she'd asked her mother. Kara paused. Maybe it was better this way. Being able to see the mist might prove that she had enough magic to be promising as a breeder. It wasn't a sign that she had real magic—the Mage Guild Tester had been very clear about what to expect when her magic *found* her.

"It will feel like a soft wave has washed over you," he'd said. "And for a moment your head will feel so light that you won't believe your feet are still on the ground." There had been no mention of coloured mists.

"What does this do to you?" Kara whispered. She placed her hand on the horse's nose.

It snorted and backed up a bit, just out of reach, the skin on its neck twitching.

Kara reached out again, this time to the horse's neck. Again the mist retreated from her hand. She stroked the warm brown hide, and the horse leaned into her touch. The mist eddied away from her hand and bunched up along the animal's back. Kara plunged her hand into the middle of it. The mist around her hand started to change colour, going from grey-black to white. Startled, she snatched her hand away.

Slowly, the mist continued to whiten. Was this the horse's natural mist colour? Did horses naturally have mist? She'd only seen one other horse in her life, the dappled grey that had belonged to the Mage Guild Tester, and there had been no mist swirling around it, not even the blue of the Mage who owned it. But Secundus Valendi was the second most powerful man in all of Tregella—his magic would be very strong. Had riding the horse transferred Valendi's mist to it, or had he somehow deliberately put the mist on the horse?

She glanced into the other stall—there was no cloud of violet surrounding her mother's horse. Was Valendi's magic that much stronger than Arabella Fonti's? Kara shivered. Her mother was the strongest Mage seen in this part of Tregella in generations, how much more powerful was the Mage Guild Secundus?

She examined at the horse. The mist, now a white cloud, gently swirled around the animal. Had it thinned out? Yes, she could see through it to the horse's hide. As she stared, the mist faded until not a trace of it remained. The horse snorted and shook itself, its skin quivering from neck to tail.

Kara stepped away and pressed herself against the rough wood of the stall door. The mist was gone. Because of her—because of whatever she'd done to it when she'd petted the horse—the mist was completely gone.

The horse took a couple of prancing steps towards her and tossed its head. Could it feel the difference? The animal tossed its head again. She didn't have any more time to worry about this— she'd already been inside the stable too long.

Kara eased open the stall door and slipped out into the aisle. She latched the door and crept towards the stable doors. Her pack firmly settled on her back, she pulled her shawl over her dark hair. Carefully she tugged open one tall door. The group was still in the lower square, their quiet conversation a steady murmur in the still night.

With a deep breath, she rounded the corner and headed behind the stable, out of sight of the square. When she reached the road, she looked back, once, before she hurried off into the night, towards an uncertain future.

Chapter two

It was just before dawn, and Arabella stood in the doorway, staring out across the rooftops and down towards the valley floor. Banio Fonti—her *husband*—hovered behind her.

"A search party is not required," Arabella said sharply. "The Mage Guild Secundus will handle this."

"But I feel some responsibility," Banio stuttered. "That our daughter should prove to be so defiant."

Arabella turned her head and stared at him. "I gave her to you to raise," she said. "So I do not share your responsibility." She turned to the valley vista, watching the line of shadows retreat as the sun rose over the mountains. "Valerio Valendi has agreed to deal with the child. He has already sent a spell to find her." *And kill her.*

It had taken some time to convince Valerio, and she'd had to play the grieving and reluctant mother, but her years within Mage Guild had taught her how little men understood women, and how readily they believed in a mother's love.

Noula was another matter. After her initial distress at not being able to find the girl, she'd had the impudence to ask Arabella what she had said to her. Noula would not question her again—not if she wanted her own child to live. Because a mother's love *did* exist, for some. For Noula's son, apparently.

She stepped back, forcing Banio to scuttle out of her way. How she longed to be out of this Gyda-forsaken villa!

"I will see the Villa Mage Guild Primus," she said.

"Yes, Donna," Banio replied. "But it is early. He may not yet be awake."

"Wake him!"

"Of course," Banio said.

A smile curved her lips as he half-bowed. He had been so smug all those years ago, when he'd had the power to allow her to escape this villa. Now *she* had all the power.

"What should I tell him you wish to discuss?"

"Our marriage," Arabella replied. "I want it ended."

"End our marriage?" Banio's voice was a whisper.

"Yes," Arabella said. "With the child gone, so is the reason for our marriage."

"But . . ." Banio shut his mouth. He dropped his eyes to the floor, and his shoulders sagged. "I may lose my position within the guild."

"A position you have because of *me*—because of *my* sacrifice."

Banio's eyes met hers, and she saw defiance in them.

"You would contest me on this?" she asked softly. "Remember who I travel with. I could have you sent somewhere else." She had hated growing up here—couldn't leave fast enough—but there were worse places within Mage Guild. Even if he lost his current position, Banio could salvage a higher rank here than he would somewhere new—where he wasn't known. He looked away, and she smirked.

"I will bring the Villa Primus at once." Banio's gaze dropped to the floor again, and he bowed formally as Arabella swept from the room.

She heard the front door open and close even before she'd reached the small sitting room. Valerio's spell would take care of the girl, and with her marriage finally dissolved, she would finally sever all ties to Villa Larona.

THE NIGHT HAD been cold, much colder than Kara expected. Nearly dawn now, the frigid wind still whipped across the valley and right through her woolen shawl. She pulled it tighter and tucked her chin into her chest.

The road followed the winding path of the River Dag, and the rushing rumble of the water sounded dangerous in the gloom. Shadowy willow trees lined the river, their limbs swaying and swishing in the wind.

She'd stopped once to quench her thirst, stumbling through the night to crouch at a wide bend in the river, scooping up the icy water with one hand. Her fingers never felt quite warm after that, even when tucked inside her shirt, next to her skin.

She glanced behind her—the road was empty—there were no signs of pursuit. Lights from houses in Villa Larona dotted the mountainside and there, near the top, a light that might be her father's house.

She imagined her mother, beautiful and implacable, and Papa trying to hide his fury. And Noula—angry, bitter Noula—forced to keep the tea pot full and serve the woman who was taking away what little she had.

Kara shook her head. Noula deserved it. The woman had made her feel unwanted, an outsider in her own home. And Papa had allowed it. All he cared about was his status—status he had because Kara was a potential Mage and the granddaughter of the Villa Mage Primus. But Grandfather died and Kara never found magic, so her use to her father vanished.

She felt numb, both physically and emotionally, as she trudged along the road. Would the searchers carry lights? Would she be able to see them coming for her?

If she were caught, Mage Guild would take her to Rillidi and pair her with someone with more magic than anyone in Larona had. She would have no choice in the matter—old men would decide who she bedded, who she lived with, how many children she gave birth to. She would never have her own place or anyone who cared about *her*. Except for any children she bore—children who might end up like her, with no magic, no choice, and no real place in the world.

Kara stumbled on a rut in the road, remembering the way Mage Guild Secundus Valendi's blue eyes had appraised her when they'd met. She would never be able to refuse such a powerful man if he decided to father children on her.

She tightened her shawl around her shoulders and shivered, her eyes on the road, watching one foot shuffle forward, then the other, over and over and over. Her breath puffed out in a cloud, and she clutched at her shawl.

Now that it was dawn she could see the road. The sun kissed the top of Villa Larona, and the white houses at the summit sparkled against the clear blue of the sky. She had hoped to make it as far as the fork where the Larona and Mountain roads met before dawn came, bringing the expected search party. But she was still hours away from safety.

Searchers would assume she'd go to Rillidi. There was no other possibility for her—other villas were too small for her to hide or disappear in. Villa Merchant was the closest villa to Larona, and from there it was a short ferry ride to Rillidi. That was the route everyone would expect her to take—the route that would be most closely searched. So that was the route she didn't dare travel.

No, she would take the longer, more difficult road that wound through the Zaltara Mountains. It meant days, even weeks of travel, but eventually she'd get to Rillidi Port and find a ship that could take her away from Tregella. Her mother's guilders and jewels would be enough for that, she hoped.

Fear shuddered through her, and she stumbled and almost fell again. *Stop it*. She would not be afraid! She would turn her fear into anger—anger that she had no good choices in life, anger that the guild that should protect instead would use her. But it was harder to bury her fear with anger when she was tired, and her feet ached after a long night of walking, and Mage Guild would be pursuing her soon.

It was now too light to risk being caught on the road. She looked left, up the mountain to a line of pine trees that traced a ridge not more than a mile away. If she could make it there she could find a place to hide—a small cave or crevasse, maybe even a thicket of brambles.

Kara stepped off the road. Dew from the long grass dampened her skirt and her shoes. She trailed a hand along the plants, wiping cool, wet fingers over her dusty face.

It was uphill, and the closer she got to the ridge, the steeper the incline became. Halfway up, the slope became rocky, and she had to scrabble, grabbing at the tough dry plants that clung to the hillside. Again and again she checked over her shoulder, praying that the valley road would remain empty of riders.

It took her an hour to reach the top of the ridge. Her hands were covered in scratches, and the wool of her shawl had pulls and tears. Her tongue felt thick with dirt and dust and exhausted, she lay down in a pocket of tall grasses. Just a few minutes rest, and then she'd be on her way. Later she'd find some water, find one of the mountain springs or small streams that fed into the Dag, and search for something to eat.

Something was tickling her nose. Kara turned her head. Now her face itched. She lifted a hand to swipe at it. If Osten was teasing her while she slept again she'd make him sorry. He was becoming as mean-spirited as his mother. She shifted, and grass rustled.

She opened her eyes to the glare of the sun high overhead. It wasn't her bed, it wasn't her house, and it wasn't her half-brother teasing her—it was tall grasses, bent over by the wind, caressing her face.

She lay there for a few moments, trying to figure out how long she'd slept, trying to decide which way to go, trying not to let her fear and despair overwhelm her.

A few hours, that was all. She brushed a wayward tear from her cheek and sat up. Her shawl slipped from her shoulders, and the heat of the sun warmed her arms and neck.

She shielded her eyes and looked out over the valley. There was no sign of anyone on the road. Could they already have passed? Could she be safe up here, near the Mountain Road?

She licked dry lips and ran a hand through her windblown hair. No matter where her searchers were, she needed to find water. She grabbed her pack, slung it across her shoulders, and glanced out over at the valley. And froze.

What was that? She squinted. A dark mass flowed along the road, its shape uneven and so thin in places that she could see through it. When it reached the point where she'd left the road, it followed her path up the hillside.

Is it tracking me? She glanced around in panic. She had to hide—but where? And how? She stared at the mass as it came her way. The colour—that dark, grey-black—was the same colour as the mist on Mage Guild Secundus Valendi's horse.

Shaking, she sucked in a breath. Was it magic? Was he searching for her with a spell? She'd assumed that her pursuit would come in the form of riders—she should have realized that a Mage as powerful as Valerio Valendi would use magic.

She stood on the edge of the slope. The dark cloud flowed

towards her too fast—she would not be able to outrun it. And it *was* a mist, Valerio Valendi's mist. Could she do what she'd done to the mist that had swirled around the horse? Disperse it, or dissolve it or . . . *Gyda, what did I do?*

She had made that mist disappear, Kara knew that for truth, but she didn't know *how*. And she hadn't done it on purpose.

She took a deep breath and squared her shoulders. Either the mist would do whatever it was sent to do or she would make it disappear—watching it come for her wouldn't change that. She might as well search for water.

The twisted willow tree was out of place amongst the pines and hardy bramble and arbutus bushes. Kara stepped under its leafy canopy and peered past the gnarled trunk. Water bubbled up out of the soil into a shallow pool before it seeped into the ground. Her feet sank into the lush, green grass that grew around the spring.

She knelt by the spring, her knees instantly becoming damp from the saturated soil. She'd just dipped her hand into the water for a second sip when the nape of her neck tingled.

She turned around. It was here—the mist. The grey-black cloud glided across the sloped path towards her. She blew out a big breath, trying to dispel her fear. Then it was on her. She closed her eyes as a cool film settled on her exposed skin. *Go away, go away, go away!* Her damp skin warmed, just a little at first, then more, until it felt like a slight sunburn. She opened her eyes to find herself engulfed in a white haze. The white thinned, and in a few moments it had faded completely.

The sun shone down from a clear blue sky, and not a trace of mist remained. Had it truly been a spell? If so, would Valerio Valendi know it was gone? Would he realize that she'd done— *something*—to get rid of it?

She didn't know exactly what she'd done, but she was still alive and free. And she still needed water—and food if she could find it. Worrying about Valerio Valendi and his magic wouldn't help her with those tasks.

Like all children in Villa Larona, she'd spent time on the mountain slopes gathering wild fennel and the dark purple mountain berries. Adults climbed higher, up to the tree line, to gather the cones from the stone pine trees. The seeds were hard to pry out, but worth the trouble.

Kara shaded her eyes and stared up at the hillside. A scraggly stone pine tree clung to the side of the mountain above her, a few cones dotting its branches. There wouldn't be much, but it should help to ease her hunger.

BY THE TIME Kara crossed the rutted tracks of the Mountain Road, her fingers were stained purple from berries, and her shawl, tied and slung over her shoulder, held more than two dozen pine cones. The road stretched ahead, the earth bare where countless wheels had passed. Tall grasses swayed between the wheel tracks.

On her left, the mountain sloped skyward; on her right, it fell away towards the valley floor. Scrubby pine trees partially blocked her view of the valley, and brambles and myrtle plants covered the ground at the edge of the road.

She shifted her shawl and started forward. It was beginning to cool down, and she was thirsty again. The River Dag was below her, too far for her to reach before dark. Not that she wanted to head to the valley—but if she didn't find another spring or stream she wouldn't have a choice.

When she'd climbed the stairs to her room, she'd been nervous about what her mother wanted, worried about her future—but she hadn't expected to leave her life behind with not much more than the clothes she was wearing.

She didn't think Arabella Fonti had come to Larona planning to help her daughter run away—she didn't think Arabella had given her that much thought. Arabella certainly hadn't brought anything to help her daughter when she'd visited her room—she just happened to have a few guilders and some jewelry at hand. So why had she told her to run?

Kara rounded a bend and stopped, surprised. Two burros stood in the middle of the road, facing her. One snorted and shook its head, while the other browsed on the tall grass. They appeared well-fed with smooth grey coats and white noses that were clean and dry. While Kara tried to see if there were any halter marks on their heads, one burro eyed her warily, its ears swiveling from side to side.

She took a single step towards the pair.

"Hello," she crooned. "Are you owned by anyone?"

Was someone out here with them? This close to Larona anyone she met might recognize her. But she needed water, real food, and a blanket to keep the chill of the night away. She was willing to risk being recognized in order to have those things.

The wary burro edged away from her. The other one raised its head slightly and eyed her before it resumed tearing at the grasses that grew between the ruts in the road. Maybe the one eating had escaped captivity? *Like me.*

She took another step forward, and the anxious burro backed into the calm one. With a snort, the calm animal stared at her, as if to make sure she understood that it did not appreciate being disturbed.

"Hey!" Kara said. "You don't own the road." She waved her arms, but the burro ignored her.

She tried to remember if wild burros were dangerous. Villa Larona owed its existence to the burros, but they hadn't been part of Kara's daily life. Maker Guildsmen trained burros for use on their farms or sold them to Merchant Guild to transport goods. Even in Larona the different guilds kept to themselves, so Kara hadn't had much contact with anyone not Mage Guild. She'd bought the odd item from a Merchant, but that had been rare since Noula had all of Kara's money.

The calm burro rubbed its head along the back of its companion, scratching an itch or dislodging a fly. It barely seemed to notice Kara so she took another step closer. If it was tame, could she ride it? The children of the Maker's Guild rode them up and down the lanes of Larona. Surely she could do it too? And the burros might help her find water!

The animal seemed sweet and gentle. Kara took another step. The horse had enjoyed it when she'd rubbed its nose, maybe the burro would too. She reached out her right hand.

The burro's ears swiveled forward, and it stretched its head towards her. Teeth clamped down on her hand.

"Ow!" She snatched her hand away and stumbled backwards. "Gyda! I didn't hurt you."

The burro she'd thought was so calm bared its teeth and brayed.

Kara's fingers were red, and the skin was broken on the middle finger. Blood oozed from the wound. She winced when she stretched her hand and carefully bent each of her fingers. They all worked, thank Gyda. Nothing seemed broken. She glared at the burros, and they steadily stared back.

"Get going." Kara cradled her hurt hand to her chest and waved at the animals with her other one. "You better take me to water. I need to clean my hand." She didn't really expect the burros to lead her anywhere, so she was surprised when they ambled away.

The burros were slow—too slow for Kara to feel safe, even on the Mountain Road.

The road was perched on the mountainside with steep slopes both uphill and down, makingit impossible to pass the burros. The search party could be on her any minute, but she was afraid to get any closer to the burros—at least one would bite, and they both might kick.

She picked up a clump of dirt and tossed it. It hit the ground behind the trailing burro and disintegrated in a cloud of dust. The animal eyed at her with disdain, but it didn't move any faster.

WORRIED, KARA GLANCED behind her. The road was still empty. She'd been following the plodding burros for over an hour, and her hand throbbed, her throat felt like it was coated in dust, and she was afraid that those searching for her would catch up.

Suddenly the two grey rumps left the road and dropped out of sight behind a rocky outcrop. Were they heading for water?

She leaned against the rock and peered down a narrow dirt path that wound through desiccated bushes and past a rock ledge. Beyond, the valley spread out below.

From this distance, Villa Larona was just a smudge of white clinging to the side of the mountain. Nothing moved along the thin ribbon of road, but that didn't mean they'd given up looking for her. She focused on the trail—her immediate need was for water, both to drink and wash her wound.

Cradling her injured hand, she worked her way down the steep track to a small glade. It was little more than a ribbon of green and a few stunted willow trees. But—thank Gyda—a shallow stream trickled through it. The burros drank with front feet planted in the water. When they finished, they started cropping the grass that lined the bank.

Kara warily edged around the animals, giving them a wide berth, and stopped a few yards upstream. She knelt and gulped the cold, clear water, letting her injured hand dangle in the swift flowing stream until her skin tingled from the cold and she no longer felt the hot, aching pain.

She pulled her hand from the water, hardly daring to look. It was swollen and red, and the edges of the wound were raw and seeping. She stared at it, praying that it wasn't infected, praying that she'd cleaned it in time. She folded her damp hand against her body. For now, there was nothing else she could do for her wound.

By the time Kara had pried the last stone pinecone open and eaten all of the tiny brown seeds, the sun was sinking towards the far range of mountains, and half of the plain below her was shadowed in darkness.

She flexed her hand and winced.

Her journey had already been impossible, but if her hand was infected, in this heat, without treatment, an infection could easily get into her blood. If that happened, she'd only live a few painful days.

She brushed her left hand across her eyes. She would not cry, she would not! In the morning, when it was light, she'd find what she needed to treat her hand—she *had* to. She was not going to die on this mountain.

She looked out towards Villa Larona—the buildings at the top of the mountain glowed in the late day sun. If she did die, none of them—no one she called family—would care. Especially not her mother.

The burros had long ago ambled off west, following the stream as they browsed. Kara leaned against one of the willow trees, wrapped her shawl around herself, and fell into a restless sleep.

ARABELLA DISMOUNTED AND handed the reins to the Guildsman who stood waiting. The ferry wasn't due to dock until late this evening, and it wouldn't leave until morning. She planned on taking full advantage of her time with Valerio Valendi.

"We need rooms," Valendi said to the man who hovered at his side.

A Merchant—Arabella recognized the guild patch on his jacket.

"Yes, Master Mage," the Merchant said. "Right this way."

"It's Mage Guild Secundus," Valendi replied as he swept past the man.

Arabella paused long enough to see the man's ruddy

complexion pale as he realized just how powerful his guest was. She smiled and nodded as she stepped past him, following Valendi into the small inn. One day men would tremble in fear of *her* power, she promised herself. But for now, she must follow another.

Valendi was already seated at the best table, and a Server was scurrying towards the bar, waving her hands to catch a fellow Guildsman's attention.

Arabella calmly sat down.

"I've ordered tea," Valendi told her. "If you want anything different, you'll have to order it yourself."

"Tea sounds lovely," Arabella replied. She smiled gently and ducked her head. After the dusty ride, she would have preferred a cold lemon drink, but she wasn't going to challenge Valendi on anything as minor as his choice of refreshment.

"You look troubled, Mage Guild Secundus," Arabella said. "I hope it wasn't anything I have done?" Valerio Valendi believed the girl had left Arabella alone to view the sunset. At least, he *seemed* to believe her. But a man didn't rise to such prominence without being able to read people. She bit her lip and lowered her gaze.

"What? Oh, no." The Server placed the tea pot and cups on the table, and Valendi scowled until she left. "My spell has not yet been activated."

"The one you sent after . . ." Arabella hesitated. She didn't want to remind the Secundus that it was her daughter he'd sent the spell after. "The Mage Guild runaway?"

"Yes. The runaway." Valerio Valendi glanced at her. "She couldn't have gotten very far, and yet my spell has not been triggered."

Arabella leaned forward. "How could that be?"

"It's possible I was too specific," Valendi said. "The spell might have found her but not recognized her as the target."

"Or, perhaps she has already succumbed to some other . . . misadventure," Arabella said. It would be just like the girl to die before they could get proof. "By all accounts she had neither the skills nor the supplies required to travel on her own."

"Perhaps," Valendi said. "Before we board the ferry in the morning, I will execute another spell. We cannot allow a runaway to remain free."

"Of course not," Arabella said soothingly. She picked up the tea pot, filled a cup, and pushed it towards the Secundus. "Until then, why don't we enjoy our tea?"

Chapter three

Kara bolted awake.

"Gyda!"

Agony radiated from her wounded hand—she must have jarred it in her sleep. She whimpered, lying still until the pain subsided to a steady throb. Gently, she pulled her shawl off her hand and held her finger up to her face. Even in the dim light of pre-dawn she could see that the wound was infected. She crawled over to the stream and dipped her hand into the cold water. A few moments later, her pain numbed, she sighed and stretched out along the bank. The sun peeked out from behind the mountains, and a kestrel twittered as it flew overhead.

She dragged herself to her feet. She had to get moving. She was probably still being pursued, and—even more pressing—she had to heal her hand.

She'd learned the non-magical healing arts, of course, had even taught them to the younger Mage Guild students in the villa. Garlic, basil, calendula, any of them would reduce the infection. She knew what they looked like—she'd grown them in pots on the windowsill of the school. But she wasn't sure if they grew wild, here on the mountain.

She closed her eyes, fighting despair. *Stupid burro—stupid me!*

Villa Merchant had a Mage Healer—she could be there by

sunset—but then she'd be caught. Mage Guild would still be searching for her. If she wanted to survive, she needed to find the plants and treat herself.

It took less than an hour to search the glade and the path that led up to the road—but there was nothing to help her wound.

She settled her hand against her chest and studied the few scrubby plants that grew beneath the pine trees on either side of the road, but they were dry and brittle, nothing like the bright greens of the pots of healing plants.

She didn't want to turn back for Villa Merchant, but would she rather die than become a breeder?

She looked behind her, back the way she'd travelled. Life was there—but not a life she wanted. She looked forward and shivered despite the heat. She was afraid of what lay ahead—her wound could kill her, pursuers might catch her, or Valerio Valendi's mist—his *spell*—would do whatever unpleasant thing it had been sent to do. But she couldn't—*wouldn't*—become a breeder.

KARA'S MOUTH WAS dry and her finger throbbed. Despite the early hour, the hot wind that blew down the mountain offered no relief from the heat.

The ground was hard and rocky where she stood, but when she peered over the edge, she could see green bushes. She had to hope it was another stream or maybe a spring.

She pulled the shawl off a finger that was so swollen she could hardly move it.

With her skirt tucked into her waistband, she carefully made her way down through scraggly trees. Her foot caught on a root, and she reached out with her right hand to steady herself against a tree.

Pain shot up her arm with a brutal intensity.

"Gyda!" She cradled her hand against her chest and sucked a breath in through gritted teeth.

The wind direction must have changed because the sound of rushing water reached her now. Kara closed her eyes in relief—there was a stream.

Gingerly, with her right hand tucked against her chest, she made her way towards the sound of water.

The banks of the stream were steep, and at some point in the past, the flowing water had been strong enough to undercut them. Now the water flowed slowly over the rocky streambed, leaving a wide, muddy flat between the stream and the overhang.

Kara slid over the bank, dropped to her knees, and plunged her injured hand into the water. The relief was immediate, and she slumped onto her hip, her damp skirt bunched up around her legs. Exhausted, she rolled over and scooped some water into her mouth. When her hand was numb, she pulled it out of the stream.

She walked along the muddy flat, hoping to find a useful plant—medicinal or edible—but if she passed one, she didn't recognize it in the waning light.

Well past where she'd entered the stream, she found a gently sloped bank and climbed up onto dry land.

She was in a small glade—tall grasses waved in the breeze and a young willow tree grew a few yards away. Too tired to even make it that far, Kara simply lay down where she was, her wounded hand cradled against her chest. She could feel the heat from her infected finger through the heavy cotton of her blouse.

She should get up, she should find something to eat, and look for garlic or calendula to help reduce her infection. Instead, she fell into a troubled sleep, giving the threat of pursuit only a single, fleeting thought.

SOMETHING WET AND warm dribbled onto her cheek. Kara reached her left hand up and wiped. *Yuck.* Whatever it was, it smelled. She rolled over, trying to get away from the sticky slime.

She felt hot breath on her neck, and something tugged at her blouse.

"What?" she muttered and pried her eyes open. The sun was bright—it was almost noon she guessed, and she was sluggish and feverish, and her finger ached. She looked over her shoulder at a burro.

"Gyda, go away."

A white muzzle—slimy with green drool—hovered over her. Big brown eyes watched her with friendly interest, but wary of the burro's teeth, Kara rolled away. The burro, of course, followed.

"Go away!" she yelled.

The animal lowered its head and nudged her chest, leaving a trail of green ooze on her blouse.

Getting to her knees, Kara whipped her shawl off her shoulders and waved it at the burro, which nipped at it. She cringed at the sight of the burro's teeth and snatched her shawl away. She edged farther away, but the burro followed.

Keeping her sore hand tucked to her side, Kara got to her knees. She dragged her left hand along the ground, picking up dirt and twigs and a few pebbles.

"Go. A. Way," Kara said. She threw the handful of dirt at the burro and scurried backwards as fast as she could.

The burro snorted and stepped away.

"Hey! Zayeera didn't hurt you."

Startled, Kara looked past the burro. A blocky man of middling height strode towards her, a scowl on his face. He grabbed the harness on the burro and pulled it close.

"What's wrong with you?" he shouted. "She's just curious, is all. And there you go trying to blind her."

"Sorry," Kara mumbled. She edged away from him. "I didn't mean to hurt it. I just wanted it to leave me alone." She held up her injured hand. "A burro bit me, and I thought it might have followed me." She reached behind her with her good hand, searching for rocks. She'd throw them if the stranger came any closer.

"Oh, you got too close to a wild one, did you?"

The man took off his battered hat and rubbed a hand across his close-cropped hair.

"Not surprised it bit you, but it wouldn't follow you. They don't much like people." The man took a step closer and peered at her hand. "That's a right nasty bite. Maybe you should see a Mage Healer."

"Um, yes." Kara backed away from him. Why was he here? Had he been sent after her by Mage Guild? She eyed him—his shirt was bare of guild patches—but that didn't mean he wasn't guild.

"Nearest one is in Villa Merchant," the man said. "In that direction." He nodded towards the valley.

"I just need a few herbs," Kara said. "Maybe you have them to spare?"

"Me? I'm no Merchant Guildsman you can buy things off of. And I got no reason to cross the guilds like that neither."

"No, sorry, I didn't mean . . ." Kara's voice trailed off.

She *had* meant that, hadn't she? All she wanted was something to help her infection. Was that wrong? Should the guilds, even way out here, determine what she could and couldn't do?

"It's just . . ." She shrugged. "It's just that I know what I need and what to do with it. If you could spare some garlic or basil, or if you have calendula? Or if you spotted one of them in your travels, you could you show me?" She didn't trust him, but she was desperate. She felt feverish—a sure sign that the infection was spreading.

"I might have some garlic," the stranger said. He rubbed his head again before shoving his hat down on his head.

Now that his eyes were shaded Kara wasn't sure what she was reading in them. After staring at her for a few more moments, the stranger seemed to make a decision.

"I won't ask how it is you know some healer tricks, but I will help you. With one condition."

"Yes." Kara's relief was tempered with suspicion. "What is it you want in return?" She didn't have a choice. She would have to pay his price—whatever it was.

"You show me what you're doing."

Kara peered up into the shadowed face.

"In case my burro ever gets a hurt," the man said quickly. "Not sure a Mage Healer would even look at her."

Did he know what he asked? His mouth was a tight, thin line. He knew. Guild knowledge belonged to the guild—to give it to someone outside of that guild was a greater crime than running away. Betraying Mage Guild in this way could be death for both of them. But her life depended on treating her infection.

"I'll show you," she said. "I know other remedies as well."

"All right," was the reply.

"Thank you," Kara said. "I'll need hot water." She stopped herself from commenting on how dangerous this was. They both knew they were breaking Guild Law, so there was no reason to talk about it.

Again Kara looked up into the shadowed face. The stranger pushed his hat back on his head, and she held his solemn gaze for a few seconds before he nodded.

"I'll get your water," he said. "I'm Mika Gianetta. A traveler. Let's get you set up closer to my wagon, and then I'll find what you need."

Kara followed Mika to the far side of the willow tree. A small two-wheeled cart, its two wooden poles empty of the burro, sat there. The wood was grayed and weathered, and a dusty once-white tarp covered the basket of the cart.

Mika strode to the cart and flipped up the tarp. After a few minutes of rooting around, he dropped some items onto the ground.

Kara sat and leaned against the trunk of the willow, her eyes tracking Mika as he set about making a fire. She needed his help—that was all. She would trade a few simple healing tricks for his herbs—and a meal—she would dearly love some real food—but then they would part.

Once he had a fire going, Mika took a battered metal pot down to the stream to get water. The wet pot sizzled when he set it amongst the flames.

"Here you go, Donna." He handed her a cloth-wrapped bundle. "There's some garlic in there. And there might be something else useful to you as well."

"My name is Kara," she said as she took the bundle. "Sit down, and I'll show you what I'm going to do with the garlic."

Mika sat down on the ground, and Kara unwrapped the bundle of what seemed to be all of the man's cooking herbs. She plucked a half bulb of garlic from the pile of herbs. She pulled out her small knife, quickly separated a clove, and sliced through it.

"You put this on the wound," she said. She placed half of the garlic, flat side down, on her wound. She sucked in a breath. "It stings, but the garlic will stop the infection."

"So I'll need to make sure Zayeera's tied up tight."

"Yes," Kara agreed. She could keep up the pretense that this would only be used for the burro too, if that's what Mika Gianetta wanted.

"Every half hour I will cut a thin slice from the garlic. I'll put the fresh end on the wound until this half of the garlic is gone." She adjusted the garlic on her wound so it would stay there. With her left hand she sorted through the contents of the bundle. There. She lifted out some dried basil.

"The other half of the garlic will need to be crushed." She looked over at Mika. "I may need your help with that. Once the water is boiled, I'll steep a handful of basil leaves with the crushed garlic. Once that cools, I'll use some of the water for a compress on the wound. The rest I'll drink."

"That sounds easy enough," Mika said and nodded.

"Yes," Kara replied bitterly. "It's not as though it's magic." And then she realized what she'd said, what that small statement told her companion about herself. She looked over at Mika, who had a thoughtful look on his face.

"But there's many who'd like us to think so," he said. "To their shame, I'm thinking. To my mind this simple procedure could save . . . burros a lot of pain and suffering. Save lives, even."

"That's true." In her old life, Kara had never thought of it that way—that Mage Guild hoarded these basic cures despite the suffering it caused. The most powerful ways to heal required magic, but there were also a lot of simple poultices and salves that took nothing more than knowledge. She'd always assumed that anyone could access a Mage Healer—in the last few days she'd found out how wrong she'd been.

She tamped the garlic down on her finger. It stung as the wound oozed again. Mika busied himself with his wagon, pulling out a hook to lift the pot along with an oiled bag and a folded piece of cloth.

"Here."

Kara started and opened her eyes. Mika had placed a flat, wet stone down on the ground in front of her.

She must have dozed off. Even though Mika was a stranger and she had powerful people trying to find her, she'd been too drained to stay awake. But if he really was a simple traveler, then she had nothing of value to him except for her knowledge.

"I'll get the pot." He turned and went over to the fire. Using the hook, he carefully snagged the wire handle of the pot and pulled it out of the fire. The rock hissed when he set the pot down on it.

Mika sat down beside her. "I expect this is cleaner than anything you got." He handed her the cloth.

Gratefully, Kara took it and unfolded it. She let the garlic drop off her hand and dipped a corner of the cloth into the water. Gritting her teeth, she dabbed her wound. Blood and pus seeped onto the cloth. She dipped a fresh corner into the pot and then placed it on her wound, holding it in place with her left hand.

"All right," Kara said. "Now I'll add the basil." She held the basil leaves over the pot and crushed them, one handed. "You can mash up the garlic and put it in as well. Use the flat of a knife and a small rock," she instructed when Mika hesitated.

Almost immediately the odours of garlic and basil wafted from the pot. Kara found her little knife and sliced the garlic so that there was a fresh end to place on her wound. That done, she leaned against the tree and closed her eyes.

Mika rustled around, but she was simply too weary to be concerned about him. She'd know in a few hours if her treatment had reduced the infection. If it had, then she'd worry about Mika—and what she wanted to do next. And if the infection wasn't reduced . . . well, Mika would be the least of her problems.

"You look like you could use something to eat," Mika said.

Kara opened her eyes. He held a chunk of white cheese and some dark bread out to her, and she almost wept at the sight.

"Thank you." She clumsily grabbed the food with her left hand. "I can pay." She made herself take a small bite of cheese and chew slowly, savouring the tangy sharpness. "I have guilders." She had hoped to use them to secure her future—passage on a ship maybe, or to buy a place in a foreign household—but she had to get to Rillidi Port alive.

"Pah. You can't be going around saying you got guilders," Mika said. "That'll get you trouble." He eyed her. "*More* trouble. Only Guildsmen can use them. Which I think you're not."

She ducked her head, not willing to say it out loud to someone she had just met. She bit off a piece of bread. "Is it illegal for non-Guildsmen to buy anything with guilders?" she asked. Had her mother known? If she hadn't expected Kara to be able to use the guilders, why had she given them to her? Or had she *wanted* Kara to be caught trying to use them?

"Illegal to even have them, though there's some'll take a risk." Mika wiped his hands on his pants. "Not out here though, only in Rillidi. That where you're headed?"

"Yes," Kara replied. She didn't want him to know her plans, but she couldn't think of another believable destination. Besides—she would only be there long enough to find a ship to take her away from Tregella.

She'd finished eating and had settled against the tree when she had a thought and sat up, scanning the glade. "Did you see a pack?" She wouldn't have to worry about guilders if she'd lost her pack—she peeked up at Mika—or if it was stolen. Her mother's jewelry was in the pack. Surely it wasn't illegal to trade that?

Would those two items even be worth enough to buy passage on a ship?

"Zayeera found it." Mika stood up and walked towards the wagon. He lifted the tarp and pulled her pack out. "Sorry, there's a bit of burro drool on it." He dropped it at her side.

"Then it matches me," Kara said. She opened the pack and closed her hand on the jewelry. Still there—Mika hadn't stolen it, at least not yet. She pulled out her clean shirt and her father's cast off trousers—they would be much more practical than a skirt. "I'll be back in a few minutes."

Away from the river and just into the trees, she found a private spot and relieved herself before donning the fresh clothing. Her body was still filthy, and her hair was tangled and matted, but eating real food and wearing clean clothes made her feel almost normal.

"You look better already," Mika said when she returned. He sat down across from her. "Even without this brew." He gestured to the pot of steeping herbs.

Cautiously she felt the side of the pot. It was cool enough to drink.

"I feel better, thanks." She sat down again. "Do you have a cup I could borrow? I'm badly prepared for a journey."

"Sure." Mika pulled a chipped clay mug from his own pack. "I hardly ever use this, you can keep it."

"Thank you," Kara said, grateful that Mika hadn't commented on her lack of supplies—no food or even a way to carry water. She took the mug and dipped it into the pot—she would keep it, it was far too useful for her to refuse such a generous gift, but she was starting to worry about just how much she owed Mika Gianetta. Besides some healing tricks, how would Mika expect her to pay? Quickly she downed the pungent liquid.

Kara recut the garlic and placed it on her wound. Soon it would be time to apply the compress.

"Burro bite, you said?" Mika asked. He peered at her hand, and she lifted the garlic to show him the weeping wound.

"Yes, and it hurt."

"They don't usually bite," Mika said.

"I thought it was tame," Kara explained. "It wasn't afraid of me, and I thought I could catch it and ride it."

She smiled in embarrassment. Saying it now, like that, it

sounded ridiculous. Mika must have thought so too because he whooped with laughter.

"Burros are the most stubborn creatures Gyda put on earth," he said. "They don't scare easy, and you can't make them do anything they don't want to."

"I know that now," Kara said. "Even after one bit me, they weren't in a hurry. They did finally lead me to a stream, but if I'd been able to clean my finger sooner it might not have become infected."

"Burros have their good points," Mika said. He shook his head and leaned back on his hands, his hat tipped forward against the afternoon sun. "But doing anything in a rush isn't one of them."

"I can tell you how to make another salve," Kara said. "Let me know what ails your . . . burro the most. You've helped me a great deal, but I don't want to keep you."

She turned to look uphill at the pine trees that dotted the slope. She didn't know if she could trust Mika, but she didn't want him to leave, didn't want to be alone again. This trip, going to Rillidi Port to board a ship for another country, seemed foolish now.

"I'd rather strike a different bargain," Mika said. "I know you're Mage Guild. Or at least you were."

Shaken, Kara met Mika's gaze. "I can't go back," she said.

"I won't hand you over," Mika said. "I *hate* the guilds, but I can help you—make a trade. But not for healing skills." He frowned. "I'll take you to Rillidi Port if you'll teach me to read and write."

"Won't healing be more practical?" Kara asked. "And safer?" Knowing a poultice or two wouldn't necessarily attract Mage Guild's wrath, but this? They would definitely kill both of them.

"Or the knowledge I can read in books might save me," Mika said.

"You have books?"

"I'm a traveler—I've come across all sorts of unusual items," Mika said.

"What you're asking for is dangerous," Kara said. "For me to teach and for you to learn. The guilds . . ."

"Guilds!" Mika said. "I told you I hate them. And I'll risk much in order to gain what they want to keep from me."

"It's my risk too," Kara said.

"Yes," Mika agreed. "But you already showed me the poultice."

Kara sighed. That *was* enough for Mage Guild to put her to death—would teaching Mika to read and write make that death any worse? She didn't trust Mika—but neither could Mika trust her.

"All right," Kara said. "You take me safely to the port, and I'll teach you as much as I can while we travel. And you must promise to keep me safe from the guilds."

"I'll do what I can," Mika said. "They don't like our kind much—unguilded. We keep to ourselves, and for the most part we aren't bothered."

"Unguilded," Kara said. She'd never heard the term. "Were you ever a Guildsman?"

"Me, no. But there's lots of us who were. Them that have left guilds are more shy about strangers, though."

"With good reason," Kara said. The guilds didn't like losing people. In her case—unless they found out she'd shared Mage Guild secrets—she had enough value that they would probably let her return. For others, it could mean death.

"Then we have a trade," Mika replied softly. "I'll take you with me to Rillidi, and you'll teach me to read and write."

"And help me stay away from the guilds," Kara added.

"Yes," Mika replied. "Although along the way I might have to introduce you to some unguilded."

She nodded. She would like to meet some who lived outside of the guilds. It gave her hope that she could live that way too. She paused. "Someone very powerful has been looking for me."

"It's always dangerous for unguilded," Mika said slowly. "That's why I keep to the Mountain Road. Besides, some things are just worth the risk."

"Yes," Kara agreed. Running away *had* to be. Mage Guild would have consigned her to a miserable life bearing babies for men she didn't have the right to refuse. And if none of her children showed magic, she'd have to live with the horror of knowing she'd brought *her* children into the exact same life. She wouldn't do that. It *would* be better to be dead. And if she was caught teaching Mika, Mage Guild would make sure she was.

"I'll need some supplies," she said. "Books, pencils, paper to write on."

"I think I have what's needed," Mika said. "It's always been a hope, reading and writing." He looked down at his feet, a blush on his neck. "Sometimes at night I take out a book and pretend I can read it, pretend I know what the words say."

"Are you sure you want to know the truth?" Kara asked. "The truth can be a lot more ordinary than what we imagine."

"I want to know," Mika said fiercely. "I want to know what others have tried to keep from me, ordinary or not."

Kara nodded. "I'll start later today."

ARABELLA SMOOTHED A hand along her hair and smiled at her reflection. It was late morning, and Valerio had just left for his own room.

She dipped a cloth into the basin of water and gently patted her face. There was no need to enhance the blush on her cheeks—Valerio had proven to be quite . . . athletic. She tossed the cloth onto the washstand, placed her hands on her stomach, and whispered a small spell, the warmth from her hands spreading to her belly. She would know in a few days.

She quickly dressed and packed her bag. After a night spent pleasing the Mage Guild Secundus in bed, it would not do to displease him out of it.

He greeted her warmly when she stepped into the main room, and she had to suppress her triumph when he stood and pulled her chair out for her.

Arabella settled in beside the second most powerful man in all of Tregella and smiled demurely as he poured her tea.

"The ferry leaves in half an hour," Valerio said. "I will create the spell after we eat."

"Would it be too much to ask to watch?" Arabella said. "I do of course know how to create seeking spells, but none quite this . . . directed." She didn't want to watch, she wanted instruction. Valerio Valendi was well-known as a powerful, yet subtle, Mage—no doubt his killing spells were finely crafted. She would dearly love to know his technique.

Valendi stared at her for a few heartbeats, and Arabella wondered if she'd made a mistake. He would mistrust her if she pushed him too quickly. Finally he nodded.

"I forget that you came to Rillidi late and did not have the same opportunities to learn that others had," he said. "Of course you may watch."

Arabella smiled and nodded, trying to hide her relief. "Thank you, Secundus."

"Arabella. I think that after all we've . . . shared . . . you should call me Valerio, don't you?"

"Thank you, Valerio," Arabella replied. "I would like that."

"Yes, I was sure you would," Valerio said.

A Server brought a plate of bread and butter, along with some fresh fruit. Arabella tried to judge Valerio's mood, but he simply ate in silence, ignoring her. Had he meant that last comment as a warning? Had he seen through her efforts to get close to him? She nibbled on a piece of melon, her appetite gone. He glanced at her, and she smiled brightly until he looked away.

Valerio pushed his chair away from the table and stood up. "It's time," he said and strode away, forcing Arabella to hurry after him.

He knew. He knew she'd been manipulating him. She slowed and smoothed her hands across her dress. So. She should have expected that the Mage Guild Secundus would not be so easy. And he didn't know, he'd *guessed.* Because she'd given herself away. And now she had to make sure he didn't know the truth—that she'd ordered her daughter to run, knowing that the guild would kill her.

"Valerio," she called after his retreating back. He paused and allowed her to catch up to him, but he didn't turn around.

"I apologize for my clumsiness," she said. "As you mentioned, I did not come to Rillidi until late. My peers were much further ahead of me in so many ways."

Valerio turned to face her. "And now?"

"I am still paying for my lack of experience," she said. "I want to change that." She lifted her chin and met his gaze. "But I need the right mentor."

He smiled, and she knew she had him. But that thought didn't comfort her.

"A mentor," he said softly. "What else do you want?"

"A child. I need a child—one with magic."

"Or at least the potential for magic," Valerio said. "It will be a decade or so until it's known for certain. What do I get in return?"

"Me," Arabella said.

"I've had you," Valerio said. "What else do you offer?"

"I know things about certain members of council, things that would help you control them."

"I find that hard to believe," Valerio said.

"I have no connections, but I do have some . . . talents," Arabella said. She lifted a hand and caressed his face.

Valerio grabbed her wrist and pulled her close. "Yes, you do." He stared at her, then shook his head and laughed. "I believe that you *have* been able to gather some secrets. All right. I will be your mentor. But we must keep it a secret."

"Only until I am with child and can no longer hide it," Arabella countered. "The father of my child must be known."

"So I can protect you from your enemies?"

"So that they know my child will be powerful."

"Our child," Valerio said.

"Our child," Arabella agreed.

"Come, the Servers will take care of our bags and mounts. We have magic to do."

"Yes," Arabella. She let her hand rest for a moment on her flat stomach before following Valerio Valendi towards the ferry dock. They had magic to do—a spell to ensure that her child was born without a living sibling.

KARA PURSED HER lips and lifted the compress off her finger. The wound was still a little swollen, but she thought most of the infection had been drawn off. She prodded it with a clean finger and flexed her right hand. She felt only a twinge of pain.

She was lucky, thanks to Mika. She was still wary of him, but she thought he was telling the truth—he was willing to risk much to learn how to read and write. Without his help she could have lost her finger—or even her life—and as long as she had something he wanted, she thought she could trust him to help her.

She wondered if she could get more from Mika than safe passage to Rillidi Port. He was part of a world she'd never even heard of, a world where people weren't owned by their guild, weren't at the mercy of the guild's wishes and desires. If she could become part of that world, she could choose the type of life she wanted. She might even be able to stay in Tregella.

Her problem, Arabella Fonti had called her just before she'd told her to run away. Now Kara wondered if she'd hoped the daughter she'd never wanted wouldn't survive the trek to Rillidi.

Thoughtful, she stared into the fire. What problem was solved by Kara running away? Not Papa. Her mother had said she was going to divorce Papa. Arabella didn't care about the daughter she'd born, so she likely cared even less about the man who'd fathered that child.

Was she somehow a threat to Arabella's position within Mage Guild? She would expect her mother's reputation to diminish with her daughter's escape, but maybe having a daughter without magic was worse. Kara running away didn't change that, but it did mean she wouldn't be around as a reminder.

The guild wanted more Mages—it was a Guildsman's duty to have children, talented children. But in all her years in Rillidi, her mother had not born another child. Did a Mage without talented offspring lose status? Would Arabella Fonti need to bear another child since her only child had no magic?

Even if she did, that didn't explain how her own disappearance benefitted her mother. Perhaps she really did want the best for her? Kara shook her head. That's what she *wanted* to believe, not what she *could* believe.

"Here," Mika tossed a blanket to the ground beside her. "It'll get colder once the sun goes down."

"Thank you," Kara said. She was grateful to have more than her tattered shawl. She knew too well how cold it could get at night.

"And I brought some books." Mika held out a battered volume. A second one was tucked under his arm. Kara took the book from him and set it down in front of her.

"Navigation: Charting a Course Using the Sun and Stars," she read. She opened it to the first page. "It shows how to determine where you are based on the sky. I've heard of this, but it's not something I've been taught. It's a Guider Guild skill."

"That would be useful to a traveler like me," Mika said. "The man I got it from said it was the story of Gyda—how she came from the heavens to show the First Guildsman the Way. There are pictures of the heavens, and Gyda's star."

Kara flipped through the book until she found a series of drawings of the night sky. Sure enough, Gyda's star was identified.

"Yes, but the pictures show the sky as you'd see it in different seasons." She turned the page. "See," she put the book flat on the ground, and Mika leaned over her shoulder to look. "This is the sky in early summer, like now." She flipped to the next page. "And here it is midsummer. See how Gyda is lower in the sky?"

"I never noticed that before," Mika said. He stooped and gently turned to the next page. "And this drawing?"

"This is early harvest." Kara turned another page. "And late harvest." She smiled at Mika. "As long as you know the season you can determine where you are, more or less."

"I've been lost a time or two since I had this book. If only I'd known what it held," Mika said. "No wonder they don't want us all to read. They'd lose their power over the rest of us." He picked up the second book. "Imagine if I had that first book and then this one showed where fresh water was? I could go somewhere new and wouldn't need a Guider to tell me what routes were safe."

"I'm sure Guider Guild has water sources marked down," Kara agreed. She could have used knowledge like that in the past few days, instead of praying for burros to lead her to water.

"Yes, they would," Mika said bitterly. "Hoarding what they know so's their guild can manipulate the other guilds, letting us regular folk suffer. People lost 'cause they can't afford a Guider—children without shoes 'cause Maker Guild hasn't bothered to send anyone to their town—houses letting the rain in 'cause no Mason's willing to fix it. And Mage Guild," he sent her a sideways glance. "That's the worst of them all. They let sick people get sicker and die 'cause there's no Healer close enough, or cheap enough. If you're not guild, you're nothing, and if you are guild, you better be important. It's all just people looking out for themselves. Nobody cares about their neighbour, their friends, or even, sometimes, their family."

"True enough," Kara agreed, thinking about how her own family had treated her, how they had used her—even planned her birth—in order to gain status within Mage Guild. And what her fate would have been had she not run away.

"Anyways," Mika said. "The two of us aren't going to change how things are done. You promised to teach me how to read some." He sat down beside her and held out the second book. "No pictures in this book. I got no idea what it's about."

"*First Guildsman, the Teachings of Paolo Santonini*," Kara read. "It must be a history of how the guilds started." She looked over at Mika. "Are you sure you want this? I can't guarantee that you'll be able to read either of these books any time soon—I can only give you the basics." She paused. "I could show you another healing poultice, instead."

"No," Mika said. "You said you would teach me to read and write." He frowned at her. "Why are you trying to get out of this trade?"

"I'm not," Kara said. "I agreed—I *promised*—to teach you and I will. I just . . ." She looked away. "I don't know you. You could be planning to hand me over and collect a reward from Mage Guild."

"Could be," Mika said. "But if I was, do you think I'd ask you to teach me to read? Gyda, if Mage Guild found out I knew the healing trick you already showed me, they'd kill me. And you and I both know they would be able to find out."

Kara met Mika's solemn gaze and nodded. If Mika did betray her, she would have no reason to keep the healing poultice a secret. Mage Guild wouldn't believe her, but they would get the truth out of Mika—either by magic or torture.

"All right," Kara said. She was as satisfied as she could be. Mika had just as much to lose as she did if they were caught. "Which would you rather start with, letters or numbers?"

"Numbers?" Mika said. "You know numbers too? I wasn't even hoping for that."

"I can't do the calculations Masons need to build a house or a bridge, but I can do simple addition, subtraction, and multiplications," Kara said.

"Nothing simple about that," Mika replied.

"All right." Kara picked up a stick and smoothed the dirt in front of her. "We'll start with numbers."

The rest of the afternoon was spent with their heads together, scratching numbers in the dirt.

Chapter four

A BURRO BRAYED close by. Kara jerked awake, her heart pounding. It was just after dawn, and the sky was lightening over the mountains. The burro, Zayeera, still tied to the wagon, pawed at the ground and shook its head. She sat up and rubbed the sleep from her eyes. *Was that fog?* She blinked and peered towards the burro. Not fog—a dark grey mist swirled along the ground. It looked exactly like the one she'd seen that first morning, when it had followed her up to the ridge. The mist eddied around the burro, and the animal lifted its head and brayed.

"Stop yer racket," Mika growled. Zayeera brayed again, as if in response, and Mika rolled out of his blanket and sat up. "Gyda curse that burro. Can't a body wake with the sun instead of the screeching from an ungrateful, lazy animal?" He turned to her. "Sorry, she doesn't start every day this way."

Kara was so focused on the grey-black mist that she barely heard what he said. The mist surrounded and then swept past the agitated burro before it crossed the small clearing towards them. She tried to make herself feel small. *I'm not here, I'm not here,* she repeated in her head, over and over. The mist parted and flowed around her without touching her before it enveloped Mika.

"Brrr, there's a bit of a chill in the air," Mika said. He stood and shook out his blanket, the mist swirling around him. "Might as well get moving, seeing as we're already awake." The grey-black mist eddied at his feet and then it moved off, following the river.

Magic, Kara thought, from Mage Guild Secundus Valendi—the mist was his colour. Mika hadn't been able to see it, but he'd felt it. And the burro—Zayeera had reacted to it.

But why hadn't it touched her? She was certain that she was the one the magic was looking for, yet it had gone *around* her. This was completely different from when she'd seen the mist that first morning—when it had changed colour and dissipated. What had happened? Had the spell reacted to her in some way? Did this mean she had magic after all?

For a brief second her heart soared. Magic, what she'd always wanted. She would be someone of consequence in the Mage Guild, someone important. And her mother would have to pay attention to her, finally.

Kara's shoulders slumped. She did not have magic. She'd failed the test for years, and neither Mage Guild Secundus Valendi nor her own mother, two very powerful Mages, had sensed any magical abilities in her. She had to stop hoping every time something odd happened. She was too old to believe in children's tales of happy ever after. She had to face her reality. No magic, no guild status, no safety, no security. All she had was her wits and her guild-taught skills. That would have to be enough for her to have a decent life. She would *make* it be enough.

Kara shook out her borrowed blanket and folded it. "I'll just wash up," she said as she moved towards the river. "Then I'll be ready to leave."

"Good," Mika said. "I'll get Zayeera hitched up to the wagon. I've some hard bread we can tuck into as we walk."

KARA RINSED HER finger in the cold stream before inspecting it. There were no signs of infection, and the skin was a healthy pink. She crooked her finger—it moved smoothly with just a spasm of pain. She wrapped the wound in a bit of clean cloth and stood, wiping her damp hands on the loose trousers she wore.

She felt good today—better than she remembered feeling for a very long time. And it wasn't just that her finger was on the mend.

She'd been living with the burden of failure for so long that it took her a while to realize that what she felt was relief. No more conversations explaining what she couldn't do, no more accusing glares from Noula or her father, no more worrying and waiting for her mother to come and see her disappointing daughter. All of that was behind her.

As uncertain as her future was, she had a chance to decide who *she* wanted to be. She was no longer Kara, the Mage without magic—now she was Kara the teacher who could read, write, and do sums. Skills that had value, as Mika had confirmed.

Kara climbed up from the river and looked out across the valley. A great adventure, her mother had called it. Now she was beginning to believe it.

KARA WIPED HER sleeve across her forehead. The Mountain Road wasn't much more than a trail right now—she doubted that anything bigger than Mika's burro cart could actually travel on it. The road stubbornly hugged the edge of the mountain, and below, rock striated with browns and tans and deeper lines of grey stretched down for hundreds of feet. The valley floor far below was lush and green where the silver glint of the River Dag snaked. The mountains across the valley were blurred by the heat of the afternoon sun.

Two days they'd been walking. Two days of endlessly putting one foot in front of the other. She'd come to appreciate the slow, steady pace of the burro. It kept to the same rate, hour after hour, uphill or down, persistently eating away the miles.

They were far above any streams now, but Mika had traveled this road many times and knew where the springs were. Last night they'd climbed off the road—up past the tree line—to a well-used campsite. They'd had little fuel for a fire, and the trickle of water that ran down between two large rocks had left a metallic taste in her mouth, but she had slept soundly. In the morning she'd woken to the snorts of three wild burros nose to nose with Zayeera. Mika had been delighted with the company, but Kara had worried that they'd kick or bite.

She and Mika had settled into a reasonably comfortable companionship. Neither trusted the other, not completely, but Kara *did* trust that Mika would keep his promise and take her all the way to Rillidi Port.

"We'll camp soon," Mika said. He offered her his water skin.

"Thank you." Kara took a sip. Since she didn't have her own water skin, Mika had taken to handing his to her whenever he drank. She appreciated not having to ask.

"Can we have a fire?" she asked. They'd been above the tree line since last night. She looked down onto the tops of the scrubby mountain pines that grew below the trail.

"Probably," Mika replied. "We'll be heading downhill soon. Tomorrow we reach the bridge."

"Broken Burro Bridge," Kara said and shivered.

She'd heard about it, of course, the highest bridge in Tregella. The gorge it spanned was very deep, and the rock face was sheer, so she'd read. Mika was the only person she knew who had actually been across it. Her Mage Guild Tester had avoided it by keeping to the valley roads.

"It's safe?"

"Aye, Mason Guild makes sure," Mika replied. "We'll need to watch for a work crew. Sometimes they don't appreciate that their hard work helps unguilded."

"Would they stop us?" Kara asked.

"Not if we don't give them a reason to," Mika said. "Keep quiet, and let me talk to them."

Kara handed the water skin back to Mika. He'd been across the bridge many times, he'd said. She had to trust that he could get them across—she had no choice.

Mika pulled on Zayeera's harness, and the wagon picked up speed. Kara fell in behind it and pulled her shawl over her head.

Mika was pleased with their trade—Kara didn't think he was pretending. He'd been traveling with books he couldn't read— books that he desperately wanted to read. He would keep her safe.

KARA FOLLOWED THE wagon around an outcrop of rock and stopped.

Ahead, the world fell away.

The usual scrubby trees and dry grass led up to the edge, and then there was nothing but sky, as though she could step directly out into the brilliant blue morning. Earth and rock, scoured by years of wind and rain, formed ledges and layers as far down as she could see. The road wound down and away, following the edge of the rock face. Here and there determined trees and shrubs clung to the side of the rock. Dry branches lashed back and forth, buffeted by the hot wind.

"It's a sight, isn't it?" Mika stood to one side, holding Zayeera's halter.

"Yes," Kara agreed. "If you dropped something over the edge, I think it would fall for days."

"Don't go doing that," Mika said and scowled. "One single pebble from way up here could turn into an avalanche down at the bottom. If it causes trouble, the Masons would know it were us. Then they'd never let us cross on the bridge."

"I wasn't going to do it," she said quickly. She had no intention of getting closer to the edge than she needed to.

"Good." Mika nodded. "Then let's keep moving. We still have a few hours before we get to the bridge."

An hour later, Kara was still awed by the scenery—as the road descended, one spectacular view followed another. The blue sky lightened as the sun climbed higher, and a few clouds shrouded the distant mountains. Mika called a halt at midday, dividing up some hard journey bread and passing the water skin to her. Once she'd drunk her fill, she passed it back to him.

"Going down's almost harder on a burro than going up," Mika said. He pulled out a chipped bowl, filled it with water, and shoved it under Zayeera's nose. The burro sniffed once then started lapping it up.

"Is that why you're holding onto the halter?" Kara asked. Up until now Mika had walked in front of the cart, not beside it, and had let Zayeera follow him without a lead.

"Partly," Mika replied. "Zayeera knows she's got to keep that cart under control. I'm there in case she gets spooked." He looked over at her, his face serious. "It's not a good idea to be in the path of a cart on the way down. If a cart got away from a burro on this type of trail and the burro was smart, like Zayeera here, and knew the terrain, she might be able to outrun it and not have it pull her over the edge. But anyone in the way would get trampled." Mika wiped a sleeve across his forehead. "Or worse. I once saw a man jump out of the way of an out of control burro only to slip over the edge." Mika's face was still and hard. "The burro and cart were fine, but we never did retrieve his body. Too far down the rocks. We knew where he ended up by the vultures and crows, though."

Kara stared down the winding road and out over the edge. It

was a long way to fall, a long time knowing that you were about to die, knowing that you couldn't be saved. All the while praying to Gyda that you died quick, before the birds came. She shuddered.

A few switchbacks later, Mika stopped again. He pulled Zayeera off onto a flat area and tied her to a stunted pine tree.

"Stay here," he said. "We're close to Mason Guild's camp." Then he disappeared around a rocky outcrop.

KARA WIPED HER shawl across her forehead and sat down, her back against the slope of the mountain.

Mika hadn't said how long he would be. If he hadn't left the cart, she would have worried that he'd decided learning to read wasn't worth the risk of being caught with her.

She gazed out over the valley—it stretched out below her, browns and russets and a ribbon of green that followed the path of the river. She lifted her hair off her neck to let the warm breeze dry her sweat-soaked skin. The sun beat down on her face, and she closed her eyes.

A boot scuffed a rock beside her, and she started. She must have fallen asleep. Even without opening her eyes she could tell that the angle of the sun was different.

"Did you see any Masons?" she asked.

"You could say that," said a strange voice.

Kara's eyes flew open. A man stood over her, his face a shadow. He leaned down and grabbed her arm and yanked her to her feet.

"Your friend told us you were here," he said. "Didn't say it but I know what you are. Runaway." He spat the word at her, his lip curled in disgust. "Bet there's a guild favour for us when we return you to your guild."

Mika had told them where to find her! She stared at the stranger, trying to figure out if he was telling the truth, that Mika hadn't told them she was a Mage Guild runaway.

He was younger than Kara had first thought—not more than a couple of years older than her. But he was thin and hard and dry, like an old man. Poor then, not well connected within his own guild, so a guild favour could be the making of him. His blue eyes glittered in his pinched and tanned face. She fought the urge to cringe from the way those eyes traveled over her body.

"Maybe we get a chance to have some fun before we hand you over," he said. "A pretty one like you." He leaned close and let his free hand trail along her cheek. His breath was rank, and two of his front teeth were broken and black.

"If you do, then you better not hand me over at all," Kara said, her head up. "Mage Guild won't want me if I've already been bred to such as you." She almost laughed when he flinched away from her. But his surprise told her that Mika hadn't told him her guild.

"Mage Guild you say." His grip on her arm loosened. "How do I know you're telling the truth?"

"I am." Kara shrugged. "Mage Guild wants to breed me to a Mage to see if my children have power. If you get me with child, or ruin me for breeding—Mage Guild won't like that. I doubt Masons would protect you against the Mage Guild Secundus." Gyda, would fate be so cruel that in running from forced mating she would be forced anyway?

"I'll think about it," the man said. "Meantime you're coming with me." He dragged her over to the cart. After rummaging one-handed through the contents, he found a piece of rope and tied her hands to the rear of the cart.

"I could just get rid of you. After." He nodded his head to the edge of the cliff.

Kara's heart constricted. *Not over the edge, Gyda, not that.*

"They'd know," she said. "They would find out by magic."

"Do you think I'm stupid?" The man yanked on her bonds, and she stumbled forward. "They have to know where to look, don't they? And who'd look here? Broken Burro Bridge is near enough to the end of the world that no one comes here unless they have to. I've never heard of a Mage setting foot near the bridge. Why else would I be out here?" His voice held an age of bitterness. "If we could get a Mage up here, they could put a spell on the bridge. No need for Masons to spend day after day, year after year, tending a bridge that mostly gets used by thieves and *ruffianos.*" He turned and spat on the ground. "It's a waste of my life, is what it is. A waste of my life."

He untied the burro from the tree and set off down the road, the cart and Kara trailing behind him.

The road wound gently downward. As they walked, her captor muttered a litany of evils done to him by everyone he'd ever known. Kara kept her head down and her eyes fixed on the cart in front of her, trying to push down her fear.

She'd been terrified when he'd calmly suggested that he'd rape her and toss her into the gorge. This was not the proud Mason Guild she'd read about in her history books, the guild the First Guildsman had established to create order out of chaos. No, this man, this *Guildsman*, was loathsome. Mika, who lived outside of Guild Law, had treated her with respect and decency. This Guildsman had threatened her and tied her up like an animal.

"Gilson," the man called when they rounded a bend in the road. "The unguilded was telling the truth. A burro, a wagon, and a girl."

The camp was small and looked like it had been there forever. A wooden cabin, weathered to a silvery grey, stood in a clearing. Mika was tied to a tree close to the cabin, near an old fire pit. He looked up, and when she met his eyes, she saw regret. Kara nodded. She was glad to see he was safe, at least.

"Gilson," her captor called out. "Where are you? Did you hear what I said? Come look at our prize. She's a pretty one."

A second man—Gilson—came out of the cabin. He was small, one of the smallest men she'd ever seen, not much higher than her shoulder. His skin was as dark as tanned leather, and his bushy black beard and hair were matted and tangled.

"I heard you," he said. He glanced over at her and then ducked inside the cabin.

"Damn crazy *ruffiano*," her captor swore. "Can't he see that I could use some help? It's not like we usually have prisoners to tend to." He steered the burro across the clearing and tied Zayeera to a small tree opposite the cabin.

"Gilson." Her captor headed towards the cabin. "We need to talk about this, about what we're going to do with these two."

Gilson leaned out the cabin door.

"What's to talk about," he said. "We're taking them over to Villa Grana and the Mason Guild."

"I know, but she's mighty pretty. It'd be a shame to hand her over without us having some fun."

"What did you say?" Gilson stepped closer to the other man and glared up at him. "Ranit, if you touch her then you better watch yourself from here on in. Might be that one day you'll stumble and just fall off the edge. And no one here but me to tell the tale."

"You're crazy," Ranit said, but he backed up a couple of steps. "You're siding with her? I'm a full Guildsman. She's nothing—a runaway. No guild, no family, no use. Who would care what happened to her?"

"Me," Gilson said. "'Cause what you're talkin' about isn't right. We're taking them to Grana. Unharmed and untouched. Let the guild sort out if she's a runaway and if the other one helped her. Now make sure they get some water. The burro too." Gilson went back inside.

"He'll toss me over the edge?" Ranit grumbled. "I'll toss him. Just wait. Just wait."

Ranit continued to mutter even as he followed Gilson's instructions. He held a waterskin and let Kara take a few sips before taking it to Mika. He poured what was left into a bowl for the burro.

Kara, her hands still tied to the wagon, slumped to the ground. She tried to shelter in the shadow of the wagon but was only able to get one shoulder out of the sun. Zayeera brayed, and then the wagon was tugged forward, and she was dragged onto her knees.

"Stop moving," Kara said.

"She's just trying to reach some grass," Mika said from across the clearing. "She'll move again once she's eaten what she can reach."

The wagon lurched again, and her arms were pulled tight. "At least someone gets to eat."

"Zayeera will always look out for herself." Mika's voice held a hint of humour, and she wondered at his acceptance of the situation.

"Be quiet," Ranit barked. He was scraping ashes out of the fire pit. The wind caught some, and they flew up into his face. He coughed and rubbed his eyes.

"Gyda curse this stinking camp." He stomped on the ashes, flattening them down. "And why do I always have to get the wood?" he muttered. "Just 'cause I'm a Journeyman and Gilson's a full Mason don't mean he shouldn't have to do his share."

He kicked at a clump of dirt as he headed into the trees but came into view a few minutes later with some cut logs stacked in his arms. He dropped them to the ground beside the fire pit.

"Let's go."

Kara turned to see Gilson stooped over Mika. He untied him

from the tree and herded him towards the cart.

"Ranit, you lead with the burro. I got the unguilded," Gilson said.

Ranit dusted his hands on his pants and glared at Gilson. "What's the hurry all of a sudden?"

"We need to be over the bridge before sundown." Gilson looked up at the clear blue sky. "A wind is coming in tonight, a strong one. Can't be on the bridge when it hits."

Ranit eyed the sky, his face worried now. "A quick pace then," he said. "To get us there in time."

Kara was on her feet by the time he'd untied the burro. He set off down the road, Zayeera, the cart, and Kara trailing behind him.

Chapter five

RANIT WALKED AS quickly as Zayeera would allow, tugging at the burro's halter. He swore at it when it kept to its steady walk.

Kara tripped over a rock and fell to her knees—her arms stretched out, and the ropes dug painfully into her wrists. Ranit turned and screamed at her, his face contorted with fury.

Once she regained her feet, she tried even harder to stay upright. Gilson would be angry if Ranit hurt her, but he was a few steps behind them, with Mika. An enraged Ranit could push her off the road and into the gorge before the other Mason had time to react.

In some places the road cut right through the mountain, while in others it seemed to lead straight over the edge before turning sharply to hug the mountain.

And always the road led them down.

They'd been walking for close to an hour. Kara kept her eyes straight ahead, focused on the steady up and down of the burro's rump as it calmly pulled the wagon, rather than on the sheer drop that was always just a few feet away from her.

In Grana, Mason Guild would send her back to Mage Guild. If she told them she was Maker or Merchant, would they send her to another guild? She'd read their histories—she might know enough about them to fool Mason Guild. It might give her a chance to escape before they realized their mistake.

The wagon lurched. Pain shot up her arms, and she was pulled forward. Kara pulled against the rope, concentrating on her feet. She blinked, trying to keep the sweat from running into her eyes.

Suddenly there was a loud crack, and Zayeera brayed and bucked. Mika shouted, and the cart surged forward. Kara's arms stretched out, and she stumbled and broke into a run—desperately trying to stay on her feet as she was pulled, faster and faster, down the mountain road.

The burro's ears flattened against its head. Then the cart butted up against its rump. With a squeal, Zayeera stretched her neck and ran, staying in front of it.

Frantic, Kara pulled on the rope, trying to slow the careening cart and keep it from overrunning Zayeera. The burro bumped into Ranit. He teetered on the edge, before slowly, horrifyingly slowly, tumbling into the gorge, his scream fading as he dropped from her view. Then she was past him, and Kara couldn't spare another thought for the Mason.

Zayeera turned sharply, and Kara pulled with all her strength. For one terrible moment the left wheel of the wagon hung over air, then it jerked back and landed on solid ground.

Looking past the burro's head, Kara saw another sharp curve in the road. Anticipating it, she pulled hard to the right, keeping the wagon on the road. Down and down they went, turn after turn, until she thought her arms would be pulled from her shoulders. Her wrists ached and were slick around the ropes. Blood or sweat, she didn't care, *couldn't* care, as long as they stayed on the road, as long as they didn't tumble over the edge like Ranit. She ignored the pain in her shoulders, in her wrists, in her chest as she tried to gasp in enough air to keep running, always running, burro and woman, running to stay alive. Barely, they stayed on the road—stayed in control just enough to navigate the next sharp turn, the next narrowing of the path.

Kara was so intent on remaining on her feet that it took a few moments for her to realize that the sound of her footfalls had changed and that they were, thankfully, finally, slowing.

The cart stopped.

Heaving, Kara leaned against the wagon and stared at her hands. Her wrists were raw where the rope had cut into them, and her legs felt limp and heavy. Thank Gyda she'd been wearing her father's old trousers—she never would have managed the turns in a skirt. Hands shaking, she looked up from the cart.

They were on an impossibly narrow bridge. The wooden planks underfoot felt solid enough, until she realized that they were held up by ropes that stretched off into the distance. Zayeera snorted and tossed her head, then rubbed one cheek against the rope handrail.

"No," she called softly to the burro, her voice trembling with fear and exhaustion. Could the burro's movements tip them? Could they have survived the race down the mountain only to plunge into the gorge anyway? She studied Zayeera, who stood calmly between the traces of the cart.

Kara took a deep breath. *This* was Broken Burro Bridge. She and Mika had *planned* to cross it. It was safe. Mika had been over this bridge many times. *Zayeera* had been over it many times.

Carefully she twisted to look behind her. They were more than a third of the way across, and there was no way to turn around. The only choice was to go forward.

"Zayeera," she called. "Keep going." Even if Mika and Gilson were able to catch up, they wouldn't be able to help. No one could squeeze past the cart.

A strong gust of wind shook the bridge, and Kara shivered, remembering Gilson's warning about not being on the bridge too late in the day. She had no idea how far behind Gilson and Mika were. Would they even be willing to brave the wind-blown bridge to save her?

"Come on, Zayeera," she crooned. "Time to move." She leaned over the cart.

She would *not* die here. Not after escaping Mage Guild, not after finally seeing a way to make a life of her own.

She shoved the cart forward. The burro brayed, but didn't move.

"Come on, burro," Kara yelled. "Move!" She shoved again, and this time the burro took a few steps forward. Kara lowered her shoulder to the wood of the cart, and braced her feet against the planks of the bridge, and pushed with all her might. The cart skidded forward, and she almost sprawled. The burro took a step, then another. Kara grabbed the wood of the cart and pulled herself to her feet, leaving smears of blood on the once-white tarp.

"Good Zayeera, good burro."

Two long ears flicked towards her as the burro plodded slowly forward.

"We're halfway across, good work," she said.

They were going slightly uphill, heading to the far end of the bridge. A gust of wind buffeted her, and she felt the burro pause.

"Keep going. That's a girl."

The cart inched forward in the late afternoon sun, and the wind howled through the gorge below them. Kara kept her eyes forward, staring past the flattened ears of the burro to the solid ground she could see ahead. She didn't want to see how far the drop was—didn't want to think about falling or about Ranit slipping over the edge and being alive, broken and bleeding, somewhere below. She simply concentrated on that patch of solid ground ahead of them—taking one step after another toward it.

Then they were there. The wheels bumped when they left the bridge, and then Kara's feet were on dirt and windswept rock.

Weak with relief, she collapsed against the back of the cart. She'd stay here until Gilson and Mika arrived. The other two couldn't cross the bridge until the wind died down but she could wait—all night if she had to.

Unfortunately the burro had other plans—Zayeera started down the road.

"Stop!" Kara yelled and pulled on the ropes until her wrists flared with pain. The burro ignored her and continued to plod down the gently sloped road. All Kara could do was trudge along behind the wagon.

ARABELLA PACED HER salon. It had been a few days since she and Valerio had returned to Mage Guild Island, and she had not seen him. She was worried that he had—not forgotten her, no—but had decided she was of no use to him. She'd sent a note this morning, inviting him to dine with her, and had spent the remainder of the day fruitlessly waiting to hear from him. She'd had her Server clear the ruined supper an hour ago.

She hated waiting for others, hated being dependent on someone else for her well-being. She settled into the plush chair she used for reading and took a deep, steadying breath. If her plan succeeded, then Valerio Valerian would be the last man she had to appease in this way.

For now, she had to wait, she had no choice. And she must appear calm and unconcerned when he did contact her. And he would, eventually.

"Annya," she called to her Server. "Prepare my bath." Yes, calm and unconcerned, that was how she had to play Valerio Valendi.

He'd agreed to align with her—mentor her, father her child, teach her the skills—both political and magical—she was lacking. In return she would be his—she would do as he asked, whatever he asked. He hadn't said it—he hadn't had to—but she knew she was agreeing to kill for him, if that's what he required.

And she would do it. She would do anything to keep herself out of the workrooms. She'd been sent there when she first arrived on Mage Guild Island, before she'd managed to secure an Apprenticeship. The council had wondered if she was too old to learn, if she would ever be able to use her magic to cast spells.

She'd spent two horrifying days amongst the drudges, her power being drained away while she sat in a stupor. After the second day, she'd approached a minor Mage and struck a bargain. She would do anything he asked of her—including sharing his bed—if he took her on as his Apprentice.

In the bathroom she slipped out of her gown and into the deep tub, relishing the warmth that enveloped her. Annya had added a drop of vanilla to the water, and Arabella breathed in the scent and closed her eyes searching for the calmness she needed to endure the wait for Valerio.

"Such serenity."

Startled, Arabella opened her eyes to find Valerio Valendi perched on the edge of her tub. Forcing herself to stay still, she smiled up at him. "I apologize for not greeting you formally."

His eyes drifted from her face to her submerged body, and he smiled. "No apology necessary." He reached a hand out, dipped it into the water, and traced a finger along one nipple. "In fact, I can't recall a more pleasing greeting."

"You are welcome to join me," Arabella said. "Or if you prefer me dry, you can hand me a towel."

"Unfortunately," Valerio sighed. "I do not have enough time to enjoy the benefits of our agreement tonight. I came to tell you that Primus Rorik has agreed to formally nominate you to a seat on the council tomorrow. I still need to secure two other council members to champion your nomination, which is why I cannot stay."

"Tomorrow," Arabella repeated. "What must I do?"

"Speak up for yourself and convince the council that you are both ready and needed," Valerio said. "You *will* be accepted, but do not disappoint me."

"I won't," Arabella assured him, sitting up in the bath.

"See that you don't." Valerio's gaze lingered on her breasts before he stood. "Perhaps I'll make an effort and return when my business is completed."

"Yes," Arabella replied breathlessly. "I would show you my gratitude."

Arabella sat in her bath until the water turned cold. *Mage Guild Council!* She hadn't dared to hope for so much so fast. She reached for a towel and stood, letting the now cool water sluice off her. Mage Guild Council! She clenched her fists as goosebumps dimpled her arms.

She wrapped herself in a robe and padded to her bedchamber. Would Valerio return to her tonight? A child—their child—was less important now that she would be on the council. She would have her own power. Valerio would use that as well—she was certain that it served his purposes more than hers—but being a member of council granted her security beyond Valerio's patronage.

The position was for life—only death or promotion to a higher office opened up a seat. Idly, she wondered who had died—or more probably, who had been killed—in order to make room for her.

She didn't care, not really, and it would be better if she didn't know who she was replacing when her name was announced. There would be speculation about why she was chosen, and she needed to be genuinely unaware. Would they use magic on her? She could not discount it.

She draped her robe across the end of the bed and slid between the bed linens. As she drifted off to sleep, she thought about the arguments she would make to convince them that she was a good choice. It had been a long time since a woman had sat on the council, and even longer since someone not born in Rillidi had. She smiled. Being from that Gyda-cursed villa might actually help her. And then she would forget she had ever set foot there.

EXHAUSTED, KARA ONLY noticed the lengthening shadows when it was too dark to see the path. She raised her eyes from her feet. Above, the peaks of the mountains were still bathed in sun, glowing pink at the end of the day. At eye level, trees bordered the road allowing no room for them to step off the edge of the mountain in the dark. Although at this point she was so bone-weary that she wasn't sure she even cared.

She didn't know how the burro kept going, *why* it kept going, but it had managed to get them down the mountain and across the bridge alive. It had been about five hours since they'd left the bridge, and Zayeera seemed to be heading somewhere.

Kara jerked alert when the cart took a sharp turn and headed down a steep hill. For a moment she was again on that headlong rush down the mountain, trying to control the cart. Then she realized that Zayeera had taken them off the main road.

This track was much narrower, and the pine trees brushed against the sides of the cart as they travelled through the dark. Eventually the road flattened out, and a cool breeze ruffled Kara's hair. She smelled the damp earth and lush grass before she heard the rush of water.

The burro didn't head to the river. Instead, it stopped in the middle of a clearing and brayed.

Kara's legs ached at the sudden inactivity, and she rested her head against the wood of the cart as Zayeera continued to bray, over and over again.

She heard a muffled voice, off to her left, and then a door slammed. The sudden glare of a lamp made her eyes water.

"What in Gyda's name is going on?" The voice was male and clearly wary. "Mika, is that you? I recognize that degenerate burro you're so fond of. I wasn't expecting you until next week."

The lamp moved towards them.

"Mika?" the voice was more uncertain now. "Where are you? Gyda, what happened to Zayeera? She looks done in."

"Help," Kara croaked. The word, scarcely a whisper, barely made it past her cracked lips. "Water."

"Mika?"

The light nearly blinded Kara, and she blinked, trying to see past the light to the man who held it.

"Gyda, what happened? Who tied you to the wagon like that?"

Kara felt hands on the rope that bound her raw wrists. She sucked in her breath as the ropes were peeled away. Free, finally, she slumped to the ground. She felt a dribble of cold water against her lips. She licked her lips and opened her mouth to let the refreshing liquid run into her parched mouth.

"Not too fast there," the voice soothed. "Slow and steady. You want to keep it down."

"Zayeera," she said. "Make sure she's looked after."

"I will, don't worry."

A cool cloth was placed on her forehead, and she sighed. "Good," she mumbled. "Gyda-cursed burro saved my life."

The last thing she heard before she collapsed was a low rumble of laughter.

Chapter six

KARA AWOKE IN agony. She sucked in a breath and lifted her wrists off her chest. When the pain finally subsided to an aching throb, she opened her eyes.

The bed she lay in was in a small room with walls of rough-hewn wood. The sun streamed in through a high, square window and pooled on the closed door across from her. Muffled sounds of movement came from beyond the door.

The bed coverings were faded blue cotton, threadbare in places, but the tight weave felt soft against the skin of her arms. Her wrists were wrapped in clean, white bindings.

A small table was wedged between the bed and the wall—a clear glass of water perched on it. She eased herself up, leaned against the wall, and carefully gripped the glass between both hands. She remembered the admonishment of last night and sipped slowly, taking a break in between each sip to savour the clear water. Finished, she gently placed the glass back on the table and closed her eyes.

"You're awake," a voice said.

Kara's eyes flew open. A man stood in the open doorway. In mid-life, with a little extra flesh on him, his head almost reached the top of the door frame. Short salt-and-pepper hair capped his head, and his gray beard was neatly trimmed.

"Yes," Kara said. "Thank you." She looked around the room. "For everything."

"I'm Allon," he said. He crossed his arms over his chest and leaned against the door frame. "And you are?"

"Kara."

"All right." Allon took one step into the room. "Kara. What happened to Mika, and why were you tied to his wagon?"

His eyes narrowed, and Kara swallowed. He had saved her, given her water and tended to her wounds, but at the moment he did not look like a friend. At least not hers.

Kara took a deep breath. She had no idea what had happened to Mika, no idea if she would ever see the traveler again. But Mika's friend Allon had helped her.

"I met Mika a few days ago." She paused and looked down at her hands with her bandaged wrists and scarred finger. Less than a week from home and her hands would never be the same. She met his gaze. "I'd just run away from my guild, and I wasn't prepared for the road. Mika helped me."

"Why?" Allon asked sharply. "What do you have to trade? Mika wouldn't take a risk like that unless he felt it was worth it."

"He would help me get to Rillidi, and I would give him some simple healing remedies."

"Healing remedies," Allon repeated. He uncrossed his arms and took a step into the room. "A few remedies wouldn't be enough for Mika to take such risks. What else?"

"I also offered to teach him to read and write," Kara said.

Allon's shoulders sagged, and he seemed to deflate. "Mika couldn't walk away from that trade, no matter how dangerous." He eyed her, his eyes half-closed. "Mage Guild." It was an accusation.

"Yes," Kara agreed.

"They found you," Allon said. He raked a hand through his hair. "How long ago? Mika won't be able to keep secrets from Mage Guild, but we might have time to get away."

"No," Kara said and shook her head. "No, it wasn't Mage Guild. It was the Masons. Yesterday, just before we got to the bridge."

"Thank Gyda," Allon said. He exhaled one long breath and closed his eyes for a moment. When he opened them, he nodded. "I might be able to get Mika back. Just yesterday?"

"Yes. There were two Masons." Kara looked out the window.

The sun shone brightly, and she could see the top of a willow tree swaying in a gentle breeze. It was only yesterday. The day had been so tortuously long it seemed like it happened days ago.

"There's only one now, though." She turned back to Allon. "One Mason tied me behind the cart, and he took Zayeera's lead in front. The other Mason, the little one, he walked behind with Mika. Halfway to the bridge there was a noise—a rock falling into the gorge, maybe—and Zayeera bolted. She bumped into the Mason. He . . ." She paused and shuddered. She could still see him, arms flailing as he lost his balance. "He went over the edge."

"Let's hope he died quick," Allon said, a grim look on his face.

Kara nodded before she continued. "The cart just kept going. Zayeera mostly kept it on the road, but when it started to swing out over the edge, I was able to pull it back." She laid one arm over her eyes, trying to forget those heart-stopping moments when she didn't think she'd be able to keep them from tumbling into the gorge. "We were part way across the bridge before we stopped."

"Gyda. I know that road well. It's lucky you didn't go over."

"Lucky," Kara repeated. She dropped her arm onto the bed.

"Aye." Allon rubbed his beard. "And determined. I know that burro is, and I've seen your wrists. The ropes bit deep. How far from the Mason's cabin were you when Zayeera bolted?"

"We'd been on the road for about an hour," she replied. "Maybe less."

"You think Mika is all right?"

"Yes," Kara said. "Before Zayeera decided to drag me here, I was hoping they would catch up with me on this side of the bridge. The Mason who is with Mika, he said he expected a wind towards evening, one that would make crossing the bridge dangerous."

"Good," Allon said. "I've got time."

"For what?"

"To get Mika. They won't have crossed the bridge until this morning. It's six hours from the bridge to the trail that turns down here—I have time to meet them."

"The Masons were taking us to Villa Grana to hand me over to the guild."

"Yes," Allon nodded. "To hand *you* over. The Mason who's left, that's Gilson. He won't find the cart, so he'll assume you've gone over the edge. He still needs to go to Grana to report the deaths of you and his fellow Mason, but the only charge against Mika would be helping a runaway, and Gilson's going to assume you're dead." Allon smiled. "Gilson doesn't much like people, even his fellow Masons up in Grana. The less he has to explain to them, the better he'll like it, so I think he'll let Mika go." He turned to leave, then looked at her. "I've bread and cheese in the cupboard by the pump, and I'll bank the fire. Make tea if you want. I should be back by dusk."

"With Mika," Kara said.

"Gyda willing," he agreed. Then he was gone.

WHEN KARA WOKE again, she was warm from the sun that streamed in through the window.

She stretched, enjoying the feel of the soft bed under her. After yesterday, she couldn't even find the energy to be worried, although she knew she should be.

She was warm and safe—at least until Allon returned.

If her bladder hadn't been painfully full, she would have gone straight back to sleep, but some things were required no matter how tired and battered a person was.

Her pack was on the floor, tucked beside the bed. Allon must have found it in the cart and realized that it belonged to her. She shook her head, grateful for his thoughtfulness even when he believed his friend to be dead. Quickly she donned her last clean skirt and blouse.

She walked through the cabin and straight outside toward a small outbuilding. A few minutes later, her immediate physical needs taken care of, she wandered the clearing.

The cabin sat in the middle of a small meadow. On the far side, a row of willows lined the river, and across from her three burros ambled around a small fenced-in area, their heads down as they cropped grass. She recognized Zayeera. The burro seemed recovered from yesterday's ordeal, but Kara said a little prayer to Gyda anyway. She'd spoken the truth last night—the burro had saved her life.

She sat on the top step of the cabin's porch, facing the garden and a few weathered buildings that were scattered around the meadow.

She breathed in the sweet air and closed her eyes. The warmth of the sun on her face had her yawning and craving the warm bed, but she couldn't slip back into bed no matter how exhausted she was. She had to see to her wounds.

Rummaging through the cupboards in the cabin turned up a bulb of garlic. Now she needed water. She studied the pump and shook her head in wonder. No one in Villa Larona, not even the Villa Primus, had such a luxury. You fetched water from the pump in the square or caught rain in barrels; you didn't have a pump in your own home.

She set the full kettle on top of the wood stove before filling a bowl with water. She eased her wrists into the bowl to let them soak for a few minutes before lifting the end of the damp dressing on her left wrist and gingerly unwrapping it.

Kara lifted her arm and inspected her bare wrist from all angles. There was a circle of raw flesh where the rope had rubbed her skin, and purple bruises covered her forearms. On the outside of the wrist the wound was deeper, but no tendons or bones were exposed, which was what she'd been most afraid of. She'd have scars, of course—carefully she flexed her wrist—but she didn't think the way her wrist functioned was affected. When she unwrapped her right wrist, it was in much the same condition. Relieved, she set about steeping some garlic in the boiled water.

She rinsed out the dressings and let them soak in boiled water for a few minutes. Sanitized, the cloth then went into the brew. After a few minutes, she squeezed out most of the moisture and re-wrapped her wrists. It wasn't as neat a job as Allon's, but the wounds were clean and disinfected.

Her stomach rumbled, reminding her that she had yet to eat. She found the bread and cheese Allon had left out and ate quickly, washing her meal down with another glass of water. Exhausted, she went to bed.

IT WAS AFTER dusk when she woke again. Kara stumbled around the dark cabin until she found and lit the lamp that sat on the kitchen table. She was picking at another piece of bread, wondering if she should do anything about the burros, when she heard a call from outside.

She took the lamp and opened the door. The light spilled out across the meadow, illuminating the two approaching figures.

"Kara," Mika called, waving. "You *are* alive. And Zayeera too. I almost didn't believe Allon. " Mika reached her side and grinned. "We were sure you'd both gone over the edge. Gyda's own luck, that's what it was. She was looking out for you."

"Maybe Gyda was looking out for the burro," Kara said. "I just happened to benefit too." Kara relaxed. Mika seemed genuinely glad to see her alive.

"As I'd hoped," Allon said. "Gilson wasn't keen on keeping Mika, seeing that you're dead."

"Gilson's a good sort," Mika added. "He would have let me go earlier, except he didn't want to leave me without food and water." The sidelong look Mika sent Allon was full of amusement. "He didn't know I had a friend living close by."

"He was plenty surprised when I came strolling up the road," Allon agreed. "Come on, let's get inside. I could use some food and a drink."

"Yes," Mika said. "I've missed your beer."

"Just my beer?"

"That's all I'm going to admit to," Mika replied with a laugh and led the way into the cabin.

Mika lit another two lamps before stepping into the bedroom, closing the door behind him.

From a shelf under the pump, Allon pulled out a large jug and poured frothy, golden liquid into three earthenware mugs. He handed one to Kara. The mug was cool in her hand.

"It's not fancy," Allon said. "And it's warmer than I prefer, but short of dragging the jug from the river every time I want a drink, it'll do."

"What he's saying," Mika said as he joined them, "is that he's too lazy to keep it cold. Even for guests." Mika had changed into a loose, woven top in a blue that accentuated the colour of his eyes. He picked up a mug and took a long drink.

"Better," he said. He held out his mug, and Allon refilled it. "I suppose it's time to tell Kara."

"Tell me what?" Kara asked. Were they going to send her on her way? The worry she'd ignored all day hit her with full force.

Allon and Mika exchanged a long look before Allon nodded.

"Kara," Mika said. "Allon and I are married."

"You are? But . . ." Kara was shocked. Two men, married? Was that why they were unguilded? And then she saw what she hadn't noticed before. Mika's face was clean shaven, had always been clean shaven, despite days on the road. "You're a woman!"

"Yes," Mika agreed. She leaned into Allon who wrapped an arm around her. "It's dangerous to be a woman alone on the road."

"So I've learned." She thought about the Mason—if he'd been the only one at that cabin he would have raped and killed her.

"I won't let her go unless she's dressed as a man," Allon said. "And she promises to stay away from people." He shook his head. "But she had to help you."

"Not help," Mika interjected. "*Trade*. There's a difference. So." Mika paused. "I've told you my secret."

"And you know mine," Kara said.

"Mage Guild runaway," Allon said.

"Yes," Kara agreed. She'd already told Mika someone powerful was after her. She didn't have to say it was the Mage Guild Secundus, did she?

"You still have something I want, Kara," Mika said. "Will you stay here with us until you've taught me to read and write? I'll take you to Rillidi after."

"You should stay off the road for a while anyway," Allon said. "Wouldn't want anyone from Grana to recognize you as the runaway who was reported dead."

"It would allow time for Mage Guild to get word," Kara said. "Yes, I'll stay. A few weeks, maybe a month." She tried to keep the relief out of her voice, but the look on Mika's face showed that he . . . no, *she* understood.

She took a sip of her almost forgotten beer. It was cool and slightly sweet. She felt a little knot of tension in her shoulders dissolve. Mage Guild would believe she was dead! And if they were no longer looking for her, she didn't have to leave Tregella. She could even make her new life in Rillidi. Kara smiled, her first full smile since she'd left her mother in her room in Larona.

"I think she likes the idea of being dead," Mika observed.

"Yes." Kara gulped her beer and held her mug out for more. "If I'm dead to the right people."

"You did well," Valerio said as he handed her a glass.

"Thank you," Arabella replied. She sipped her drink and smiled. It was very fine—and expensive—Seyoyan mead from the southern islands. Proof that Valerio truly was pleased with her performance.

"Yes, very persuasive," Mage Guild Primus Rorik said. He lifted his glass and saluted her. "You even garnered a vote not paid for."

"Castio would vote for anyone wearing a skirt," Valerio said. "I was expecting him to vote our way." He sat on the settee beside Arabella.

"But not depending on it," she said.

"Only a fool depends on a fool," Valerio said. "Castio has been on council long enough to realize he won't advance further, and he's bored. That's what drives him."

"Then I'll have to . . . excite him," Arabella whispered to Valerio.

"I'm sure you already have," Valerio replied softly.

"Castio is a fool," Rorik said. "But he's not stupid. You need to handle him carefully."

"Of course, Primus," Arabella said. Her opinion of the Primus matched his of Castio—a fool, but not stupid. She would have to handle him carefully as well.

"I must be off," Rorik stated. He stood up, drained his glass, and set it down on a table. "I can't spend too much time with the newest council member—she has plenty of time to make her own enemies, she doesn't need mine." The Mage Guild Primus nodded and left the room.

Once the door was closed, Arabella reached a hand out and stroked Valerio's arm.

"I am glad that you are pleased with how I handled the nomination," she said. She sipped her mead, meeting his eyes over the rim of the glass.

"You exceeded my expectations," Valerio said.

He set his glass down and leaned over her. Arabella licked her lips. His pupils dilated, and his breath warmed her face. She moved her hand from his arm to his lap, and he sucked in a ragged breath.

"I have news," he said as his hands found their way under her skirt, shifting the cloth out of the way. He dragged her on top of him, and they both fumbled with his trousers. Then he was free and in her.

"What news," Arabella gasped. She rocked on top of him,

pulling him in.

"The girl," Valerio panted. "The runaway. My spell was successful."

Arabella cried out in pleasure, and Valerio tensed, then relaxed, spent.

Arabella leaned her head against his chest and closed her eyes and smiled in contentment. She would bear his child—and it would be an only child.

Chapter Seven

"WHAT ABOUT THESE ones?" Kara asked, pointing at a clump of small, brown mushrooms that were growing on the side of a fallen tree.

"No," Allon said. "Stay away from anything small and brown. They're almost all poisonous. You want the bigger white ones."

Kara and Allon were just a few steps into the woods beyond the clearing.

Kara sighed and straightened. "Will these kill right away?" She knew of more than one herb that would induce vomiting—if ridding the body of the poison was what was needed.

"Within minutes," Allon said. "So I've heard."

Kara nodded and stepped past another tree.

The three of them had quickly fallen into a routine. Mornings were spent on chores: tending the garden, caring for the burros, washing the laundry in a big tub of water pumped from the kitchen—all of the menial tasks required to run a household.

Afternoons, when the sun beat down and the wind blew hot and dry from the top of the mountain, they headed down to the shaded banks of the river for lessons. Kara taught Allon and Mika to read and write. In return, Allon showed her where and when to gather the plants and herbs she needed to make her potions and poultices, as well as what was safe to eat.

"Kara," Allon called.

Kara looked over and met his steady gaze.

"Mika didn't ask, but I will. Why did you run away from your guild?"

Kara moved to face him, leaning against a tree. Allon didn't look angry, or upset, but that didn't mean her answer couldn't change things. Over the past week she'd learned that there wasn't much Allon wouldn't do to keep Mika safe.

"I have no magic," Kara said.

"There are many in Mage Guild without magic—especially out here." Allon crossed his arms, a frown on his face.

"My mother has magic, enough that Mage Guild is . . ." She paused. "Curious to find out if it skipped a generation."

"So they want to see if your children have talent," Allon said. "That's the case for every child born into every guild."

"Yes, but Mage Guild didn't plan on leaving it to chance," Kara said. "They were going to choose which Mages fathered my children."

"Mages," Allon said. "You think there would have been multiple fathers?"

"Yes," Kara said. "And none of my choosing."

"So you ran from having children forced on you," Allon said. "I understand."

"No," Kara said. "You don't. I ran from knowing that if my children did not have magic, they would have even fewer choices than I."

After their talk, Allon seemed to relax, and the next few weeks were some of the most contented of her life. She felt safe and if not loved, at least trusted and respected by her hosts.

The wounds on her wrists healed, leaving thick scars that faded to a soft pink. If she'd been vain, she might have tried to fashion bracelets to cover and distract from the scars, but she didn't worry much about how they looked. She *was* dead, after all.

The thought of that, the idea that she may have outwitted Mage Guild, left her feeling both relieved and nervous. Had Mage Secundus Valendi heard of her death? Is that why she hadn't seen any more of his mage mist spells? Her mother, no doubt, was pleased. After all, Arabella Fonti's problem was now permanently solved. But still, Kara knew she couldn't stay much longer. She had her own life to make—and she could be repaying her hosts' kindness by putting them in danger.

Finally it was time to leave. The days were getting shorter, and the sun was weak, even in the middle of the afternoon. Kara had picked and dried enough herbs to make potions and poultices to stock both the cabin and the leather pack Mika had given her. With her few bits of clothing, her knife, and a few other utensils that could be spared from the cabin, Kara had some traveling gear, at least.

And Mika needed to get to Rillidi and back before the fall rains made traveling the Mountain Road too dangerous.

"Are you sure you won't stay?" Allon asked. He was struggling to harness a reluctant Zayeera to the cart. "At least over the winter?"

"Thank you, no. I need to find my own place in the world," she said, repeating what her mother had told her, what felt like a lifetime ago. And it was true. Her mother may have had her own motives for setting her daughter on this path, but Kara had embraced it as her own. "I wish it could be here, but it's not."

"I understand," Mika replied. "We all must find our own place, or person." She glanced over at Allon, and the two shared a smile. "I'll help you settle in Rillidi. Some unguilded on Old Rillidi Island owe me a favour."

AFTER THE SERENE days in the meadow, traveling was almost unbearably tedious. Mika kept them to a steady pace, and both women and burro settled into it, although none of them were in good spirits.

In the mornings, they rose with the sun. Mika would tend to the burro while Kara cleaned up the camp. The morning meal was water and a piece of hard, salty cheese. An unguilded man made the cheese from the milk of half-tamed mountain goats, Mika said. There was a partial round of it in the wagon, and Kara's task was to slice off a chunk for each of them.

Lunch was a piece of journey bread that Kara had helped Allon bake before they'd left the cabin. And whenever Kara spied mountain berries lining the road, they paused while she stripped the fruit off the bushes, although there was never more than a handful for each of them.

Each evening Mika led them off the road to a campsite she

knew. With access to a spring or stream, the camps weren't evenly spaced, so they didn't stop at the same time every day. On days when they set up camp early, Kara would continue with Mika's lessons.

On the fourth day after leaving the clearing, they passed the road to Villa Grana. From here the Mountain Road was wider and more heavily rutted. Wagons loaded with ores from the Grana mines used this road, Mika told her.

Two days later, Mika led the burro and cart off the road and along a narrow path. The mountain pines arched over the rutted track, shielding them from the afternoon sun.

"A farmer lives down this way," Mika said. "I trade with him." She looked over at Kara. "I wasn't going to stop, he won't like me bringing you along, but he might have news of Rillidi." Mika frowned. "The road's quiet for this time of year. I don't much like it."

An hour later they rounded a bend in the path, and a meadow came into view. Much like where Mika and Allon lived, there was a small cabin and a couple of smaller out buildings. No smoke rose from the chimney, and two burros huddled miserably in a small fenced-in field. The animals raised their heads, and one brayed loudly.

"I don't like this," Mika said. She handed the lead to Kara. "You stay here." She walked to the edge of the trees and paused to stare out. After a long look, she started to jog towards the cabin.

Now both burros were braying. Zayeera answered, and Kara had to tug hard on the lead to keep her from going to them.

Mika reached the small window on the side of the cabin and peeked in. Her shoulders slumped, and she turned and waved Kara forward.

Kara pulled Zayeera down the path, out of the trees and into the clearing.

By the time she'd crossed the meadow to the cabin, Mika was tending to the burros. She'd found a bucket somewhere and had dumped fresh water into a trough. As soon as the water hit the wooden trough, the burros had their heads in it. The burros were thin, their coats matted and dull, and any grass in the enclosure had long since been cropped to the roots.

"Your friend?" Kara asked. She tied Zayeera up and

rummaged in the cart for the bag of feed.

"He's inside," Mika said. She took the bag from Kara. "He must have died in his sleep." She shook her head and poured some grain into a second trough. One burro stopped drinking, sputtered a bit, and then shuffled over to the grain. "It looks like it was a while ago—a month, maybe more." She ran a hand over the ribs of one burro. "It's a good thing I decided to stop in now. These two wouldn't have lasted until my return trip."

"Are there any other animals?" Kara asked.

"Not really," Mika replied. "There's some wild goats around. Terach used to catch and milk them, but they'll be fine without him."

"Terach made the cheese." She felt a little pang of loss, as though she'd known the man from eating the cheese he'd produced.

"Aye. I'll clean out any cheese that's left on my way home," Mika said.

"And the burros? Are they coming with us?"

"No," Mika replied, absently stroking one burro. "I'll give them some more grain in the morning before we leave, then I'll set them free. Burros around here are never far from being wild. These two will be fine."

Mika unhitched Zayeera and left her in the enclosure with the other burros.

"We'll want to sleep outside," Mika said. She tossed Kara's bedroll to her. "The cabin's probably not fit for us what with Terach being there for so long. But we'll look around for anything useful. Terach wouldn't have minded, as long as his things go to help an unguilded."

"He didn't like guilds?" Kara asked. She wasn't sure she wanted to enter the cabin, wasn't sure she liked the idea of taking a dead man's things, but she had so little of her own that she couldn't afford to refuse anything.

"Terach," Mika said and smiled. "He *hated* guilds. Especially Mage Guild. I never learned his story." Mika glanced over at her. "But I suspect he was Mage Guild. Always kept to himself, did Terach. He told me once if I ever brought anyone else he'd be more likely to kill me than trade with me. I believed him. I only let you come because I had a feeling something was wrong."

"And you were right," Kara said. "Let's get in the cabin before we lose the light."

Mika opened the cabin door. A few flies buzzed out, along with stale air and a hint of rotting food.

They left the door open and started their search in the kitchen.

Kara found a knife and unsheathed it. The six inch blade looked sharp enough to strip willow twigs for teas and balms. A water skin was another prize, along with a cook pot small enough for one. She spied a shelf lined with books and thought that Mika was right—Terach had been Mage Guild.

She headed to the shelf, intent on seeing what treasures had been collected over the years. As she passed the open door to the bedroom, she caught a sense of movement. She stopped, unsure if she really wanted a closer look. Animals had not gotten into the cabin, but insects would have.

She peered into the room and frowned. Wisps of grey hair were visible on the man's head, which thankfully faced away from the door. What skin she could see was dry and leathery, and the body was covered with a thin, green blanket. Terach had been an old man then, by the looks of his hair, and as Mika had said he'd died in his sleep. Except that a grey-black mist swirled around him. The grey-black of Mage Guild Secundus Valerio Valendi.

Kara bit her lip. The morning after she'd met Mika, the day Zayeera had woken them up so early—a grey-black mist had flowed over the burro, parted for Kara, and swept past Mika. Then it had gone up to the Mountain Road. Had it traveled all the way here, to this clearing? Had Terach been caught by it?

Because she knew that the mist—the *spell*—had killed this man. She shivered. If Zayeera hadn't woken her up, would she still be alive, or would she have simply slept while the mage mist killed her, dying in her sleep just like poor Terach?

"Find anything, Kara?" Mika called from the kitchen.

"Uh, just checking his books." She hurried past the bedroom door to the bookshelf. "There might be something you can surprise Allon with."

IN THE END they took very little. It had taken Terach a lifetime to accumulate everything in this cabin, but other than the books and the few items Kara claimed, Mika had only a small pile set aside to pick up on her way back from Rillidi.

"Not much of his food was still edible," Mika said, setting the stew pot onto the hot coals of the fire.

They'd built their camp close to the burro enclosure, and Terach's two huddled close to them, perhaps afraid to be forgotten again.

"The garden was picked pretty clean by animals," Kara said. "Looked like rabbits mostly, and maybe a couple of wild burros."

"That's good. When I set Terach's free, they may be able to find the wild ones."

Kara dumped some potatoes into the stew pot and sat down, staring into the flames. She hadn't told Mika about the mist—hadn't told her that her friend's death may not have been as peaceful and natural as she thought.

"Terach was a fine man, once you got to know him," Mika said. "Never would have guessed he was such a reader, though. How many books did you count again?"

"Twenty-seven," Kara replied.

"Twenty-seven," Mika repeated and shook her head. "And not one of them from me. Someone else was his book trader. I'm not sure if I'm grateful or offended."

"Be grateful," Kara said. "Some of these books would be illegal for a Mage Apprentice to own, let alone an unguilded."

One book in particular had caught her attention—a book by Santos Nimali, at one time the Mage Guild Primus. It was handwritten in a spidery script—a workbook, probably of spells—that one she was keeping. She wondered how much her mother might give to have such a book. Not that she would ever get it from Kara.

"You're right," Mika agreed. "Being caught with books only a Mage had a right to is a good way to get dead." She poked at the coals under the pot. "But there's some that will be safe enough for me to carry?"

"Oh yes. Allon will like the book on mountain plants," Kara said. "It has drawings of them and describes how to use them for healing and food. You can read them on long winter nights."

"Never thought I'd be able to read," Mika said and turned to her.

"I think I got the better part of the bargain," Kara said and smiled when Mika nodded.

"As do I," Mika replied. "Which is the best kind of trade."

THEY BROKE CAMP early, eager to leave this place of death behind. Mika gave all three burros some grain, then she freed the two that had belonged to Terach. They cropped the grass in the meadow while Kara and Mika packed the cart and harnessed Zayeera.

The burros followed them from the meadow along the road through the trees, but when Kara turned to look for them half an hour later, they were gone.

Late that afternoon they reached the track that led to Villa Salva. A mining town like Grana, it was set so high in the mountains, Mika said, that newcomers were short of breath for days. And it was cold at night, even in the height of summer. But gold was mined there, so it was worth the extra hardship.

An hour later they had to pull off the road as four Merchants, each driving a wagon pulled by a team of burros, passed them.

There were Warriors—two in front and two behind—guarding whatever was in the wagons. Gold probably, although Kara wasn't about to ask.

It was the first time she'd ever seen Warrior Guildsmen, and she tried not to stare as the hard-faced men strode past, their broadswords hanging down their backs and their leather armor creaking as they scanned the road ahead and behind.

The gaze of one Warrior flitted over her, and she had to fight the urge to run. Instead she stared at the ground and tried not to think about the book tucked away in her pack, the book that was likely full of secrets and powerful spells and incantations. Then the wagons were past them, and Mika steered Zayeera onto the road.

"We'll camp early tonight," Mika said. "There's a place to stop not far from here." Mika turned and spat into the dust. "Just as soon let them others get ahead."

"Yes," Kara agreed. She didn't want to even think about sharing a camp site with them. Not that the Warriors would allow it—she doubted they'd be willing to share anything.

IT WAS AN hour before dusk, and they'd already set up their camp. Onions and wild mushrooms simmered with dried goat meat in the stew pot.

Kara pulled a book out of the wagon and headed over to Mika, who sat with her back to a rock, staring out across the valley. The sunset had painted the tops of the mountains pink.

"We have some time to study," Kara said. She sat cross-legged beside Mika. "Is there anything you want me to go over again?"

Mika blinked. "No. I think it's best if we leave off my lessons and start in on yours."

Kara looked at her, puzzled.

"I need to tell you about Rillidi," Mika continued. "What to expect once we get to the city, who might not want us there, and about the unguilded I know. Those Merchants today reminded me that we might not always have campsites to ourselves. Can't go around talking about unguilded when Guildsmen are around."

"No," Kara said. "Especially not around Warrior Guildsmen."

"Don't worry about the Warriors."

"They didn't look friendly."

"They're not," Mika replied. "But they are professional. As long as it didn't interfere with his contract or guild, you could stick a knife into someone sitting beside a Warrior, and he wouldn't intervene. Their skills and talents are only used to honour their guild and contracts. Gyda, they'll even hire out to unguilded, as long as there's no need for them to break Guild Law."

Kara was stunned. She'd never even considered that unguilded could hire Guildsmen. "With a Guild approved contract?"

"Aye. That way they can hire out to non-Tregellans." Mika grinned. "Seyoyans like to hire Warriors."

"They do?" Kara had read that the dark-skinned, light-haired people felt at home in Rillidi, with its islands and bridges and boat travel. It reminded them of their own land, a string of islands far to the south. Some of the rarest healing herbs came from Seyoya.

"I thought Seyoyans weren't violent."

"They're not," Mika said. "But they steal from each other. Think it's a great joke. They hire Warriors to protect their goods from friends and family, but they are not allowed to kill. Any death nullifies the contract, and Warrior Guild does not get paid."

"So no one dies."

"Not for a very long time," Mika said. "And the Seyoyans hire the best Warriors. I heard they even hire Assassins, though Warrior Guild never actually admits they exist."

"Assassins who are hired not to kill," Kara said. "It seems a strange thing to do."

"Seyoyans I've met had an odd sense of humour," Mika agreed. "But they'll trade with unguilded, which is good for my business. Now, about Rillidi. The unguilded mostly keep to the original island, Old Rillidi."

"The others aren't safe?" Kara asked.

"Not as safe," Mika replied. "The rest are controlled by the guild that owns the island. Some guilds are less welcoming to unguilded than others." Mika smiled. "The Arts Guild is the friendliest and a lot more fun than other islands. But Old Rillidi Island, no one really knows who owns it."

"I thought Mage Guild owned it," Kara said. "At least that's what I've read."

"They'd like to own it," Mika said. "But the truth is it's owned by the descendants of the First Guildsman. They've been Mages for generations, but Old Rillidi is older than any guild, so ownership has remained with the family."

"But Mage Guild knows who owns it?"

"I think someone in the guild does, yes," Mika said. "Although it's been kept secret for years. In the meantime, there's no real authority on Old Rillidi."

"Is it dangerous?"

"It can be. I'll show you the places to stay away from. There's a good many unguilded there living normal lives. Those are the folks I'll introduce you to."

Chapter eight

ARABELLA LOOKED UP from the report in front of her.

"You're certain the girl was a Mage Guild runaway?" she asked the Mage who stood before the council table. A minor talent assigned to Villa Grana, the man had probably taken this news as an excuse to come to Rillidi. She might have done the same in his circumstances.

"Mason Guild believes she was," the Mage replied. "But only one Mason saw her. The other one died."

"Fell off the side of the mountain," Arabella read from the scroll. It was a copy of Mason Guild's report of the incident. They were certain enough of the facts to advise Mage Guild of the death of a runaway.

"But they are confident of the timing?"

"Yes, Master Mage," the man replied.

"Thank you," Arabella dismissed him. The man backed out of the council chamber, and Arabella set the Mason report down.

"You seemed very interested in one dead runaway," Castio drawled from across the table. "Is there something you'd like to share?" He swept a hand out, indicating the full council—eight Mages who ringed three sides of the table.

"Please do share, Master Mage," Inigo said.

Inigo was the one of the youngest council members, younger

than Arabella, and she knew he only tolerated her because he was Valerio's creature.

"I'm trying to be thorough," Arabella said. "And it happened outside of Rillidi, so yes, I am very interested."

"Ah yes," Castio nodded. "Keeping an eye on all that transpires in the country—since you yourself are . . . country."

"Yes," Arabella said. She dropped her hands to her lap, hiding her clenched fists. It was an insult of course, but since she herself had claimed that being from outside of Rillidi gave her a different—and useful—perspective, she could not very well deny it.

Castio smiled blandly before turning to other council business.

Arabella stared at the date on the Mason report. It was not the day that Valerio told her his spell had been successful—the day she'd been elevated to council—the day she had conceived—but it was close. It was possible that the Mason had mistaken the date— or even changed it to suit himself.

The date must be wrong. The girl died from Valerio's spell— she didn't think he'd lied about that. This Mason must have tossed her body off the mountain, changed the date, and claimed she'd fallen. Arabella rolled up the scroll.

The girl had died—twice, so it seemed. She didn't care about anything else, despite what she'd told Castio and the rest of the council. She had no more ties to the place of her birth, finally.

She placed a hand on her stomach. And her child—hers and Valerio's—would be born here, on Mage Guild Island.

KARA GOT HER first glimpse of the city of Rillidi three days after they'd left Terach's farm. The Mountain Road wound down to a plain, and beyond was a huge expanse of glistening blue. Pontus Bay. The dark masses of the islands, nine in total, loomed in the distance.

"It's a sight, isn't it?" Mika came up beside her. "If you look hard enough, you can see Mage Guild Island, way off in the distance. It's bigger than the rest and higher, of course."

"Because it's above the water," Kara said. "Have you been?"

"Close enough to see the underbelly of it." Mika paused, eyes wide. "That's a wonder. Boats moored to docks that have steps that disappear up into the earth." She shivered. "I didn't go under—not with a whole island, a whole city, hovering overhead.”

"But it hasn't dropped an inch since it was first created and elevated," Kara said. "At least, according to what I've been taught," she added. She had to remember that not everything the guild had taught her as fact was true.

"So they say," Mika said. "But it's not natural."

"Of course not," Kara said and laughed. "It's magic, same as all the other islands, except the first one, Old Rillidi." The island where she planned to make a home.

"But the other guild islands, they're set into the water, not above it. They *seem* more natural."

"But they aren't," Kara said. "Magic makes them possible, the same as Mage Guild Island."

"You're right," Mika said. "It would be best to remember that, wouldn't it?"

"Yes," Kara said. Mage Guild wouldn't forget, so neither should anyone else.

She gazed out at the shadow that was Mage Guild Island. Where her mother lived. Had Arabella Fonti heard about her death? More likely she'd barely spared a thought for the daughter she'd never wanted, the daughter who'd died by falling into Broken Burro Gorge.

Kara squared her shoulders. Her mother had wanted her dead—and now she was. It was time to make a new life.

THE ROAD THROUGH the valley was wide enough to allow two carts to travel abreast of each other, and almost every hour they passed a group of people or wagon heading north from the bay.

Kara was excited, and despite Mika's warning to keep her head down, her gaze was drawn to the strangers who passed them. One man had a pale yellow mist swirling about his head, while on another, deep green mist covered an arm that was strapped into a sling. They both wore guild crests, but not for Mage Guild. They'd bought spells, she decided, probably to help them heal.

The road took them straight to Rillidi Port. The small villa clung to the shore of the bay, offering access by ferry to some of the closer guild-owned islands. Wooden houses jammed up against each other, and the narrow roads were filled with mud and wagons and people. Kara took a deep breath. The salty tang in the air was almost overpowered by the smell of fish and burro dung.

Kara followed the cart as Mika slowly worked her way through the crowded streets. Eventually she led them down a quiet alley that ended at a wooden gate. Mika banged on a small door within the gate and exchanged words with someone Kara couldn't see. A moment later, the main gate swung outward. She followed Mika and the cart into a small courtyard.

"Kara, this here is Wellert," Mika said. "He owns this inn."

Kara looked past the frowning Wellert. There was a ramshackle stable and a small two-level building that must be the inn. There were no signs to indicate you could get a meal or lodging there.

"Don't never call it an inn," Wellert said.

Kara brought her gaze back to him.

"Against Guild Law for me to run an inn."

Wellert was the same height as Mika, but where Mika stood tall, Wellert seemed to hunch in on himself. Dark eyes were set deep into his pinched face. His black hair was limp and unwashed, and Kara wondered how clean the rooms he rented were.

"No, not an inn," Mika said. "'Course not. Wellert, this is Kara. She's planning to settle in Rillidi for a while. I'll be making my usual visits and introducing her around at the same time."

"Humph," Wellert grunted. "Not a good time for new unguilded."

"It never is," Mika said.

"No, but this be worse. A month or so ago the Guilds started poking around, asking about newly arrived unguilded. Mage Guild was behind it, some said. Looking fer a runaway." Wellert stared at Kara. "Heard the runaway was dead, but folk are still uneasy."

"We'll be careful," Mika said. "Come along, Kara, let's stable Zayeera and unpack the trade goods. We should be able to make the last afternoon ferry."

KARA SHIFTED THE large pack on her back, staggering slightly under its weight, before she followed Mika through the crowded streets. The noise and smells of Rillidi Port were overwhelming after the fresh mountain air.

Something plucked at the strap of her own small pack, which

she'd slung over one shoulder.

"Hey!" She batted a hand away and glared up into a grinning face. He was dark-skinned, and his long, white hair fell across his shoulders in dozens of thin braids. She glared at him, and he laughed and said something she couldn't understand before he faded into the crowd.

"Gyda-cursed Seyoyans," Mika growled. "They know unguilded can't do anything if we're robbed. Come on, stay close." Mika grabbed her hand and pulled her along.

Here the city smelled of fish, lamp oil, and fresh cut wood. And everywhere mage mist swirled. Every colour of the rainbow, it wrapped around everything—entire buildings, a woman's ring, the wheel of a cart, the shoes a of wealthy man. People, animals, foodstuffs, trade wares, at times even the road itself—mage mist was everywhere.

Mika stopped, and Kara, overwhelmed by her surroundings, almost bumped into her.

"Here's the ferry." Mika turned to her. "I'll arrange passage."

Then she was gone, leaving Kara amongst a jumble of wagons and people loaded with packs and bags.

Idly Kara shifted her small pack, keeping an eye on the people around her. A group of Seyoyans stood off to her left, and she thought she recognized the one who'd tried to steal her pack. When one of his companions nudged him, he looked over and grinned. She glared at him, angry that he'd tried to steal from her, but then he bowed elaborately, his white braids trailing the ground, and she turned away, trying not to smile.

She was surprised at how poor the people around her seemed. Rough clothing was patched and worn, and many had only meager packs slung on their backs. Children clutched the hands of women who seemed far too young to be so worn and weary.

The guilds took care of their own—that was Guild Law. But despite the guild crests sewn onto tunics and packs, these Guildsmen seemed more underfed and dispirited than anyone in Larona had been.

Then she saw the Mage—a woman shrouded in pale yellow mist. The crowd melted away from her as she passed, but when someone else wrapped in mist didn't retreat far enough, the Mage's yellow seemed to shrink in on itself. Once the Mage had passed, the trail of yellow quickly faded. Kara looked up from the mist and met the Seyoyan's surprised eyes. Quickly she turned away, wondering if he could see the mage mist too.

"We've passage on the ferry," Mika said. "Let's go."

Kara was more than happy to leave the unsettling Seyoyan behind. She followed Mika to the ferry, nervous and excited. She was almost . . . not home, at least not yet, but she *would* make a place for herself on Old Rillidi. She had to—the only other option would be to take her mother's suggestion and leave Tregella. And why would she take the advice of the woman who wanted her dead?

The crowd shuffled forward, and Kara, her pack held tight against her chest, shuffled with it. She felt it when her feet left solid land and she stepped onto a wooden gangway that was suspended over water. Mika was behind her, her own pack crushed against Kara's back. Soon the path widened, and the crowd spread out.

"This way," Mika said and steered them both to the left.

A uniformed Guildsman, the crest of Guider Guild sewn onto his left breast, stood beside a small wooden door. Mika showed him a red piece of paper, and the Guildsman opened the door. Kara followed Mika into a small cabin. The door swung shut, muffling the sounds of the crowd.

The cabin was narrow, and the long passageway was lined with wooden benches that faced each other. A squat window ran along the top of one wall, letting in some fresh air and noise, but it was too high to allow more than a view of the blue sky. No one else was in the cabin, so they walked to the far end, just in front of another door.

"This will be full soon enough," Mika said. She sat down on the bench, and Kara sat across from her, facing the window. "But it's the best an unguilded can do and a sight better than being on deck."

"Will Guildsmen travel in here too?" Kara didn't want to share such a small, cramped space with anyone from the Mage Guild.

"Not likely," Mika said. "Guildsmen that can afford cabin space were let on first. They have better quarters than this, so I've been told. Seyoyans, Wulmarians, and other unguilded, that's who'll be put in here with us."

"And all those other people, they're Guildsman?"

"Most of them, yes," Mika said. She set her pack on the floor and shoved as much of it under the bench as she could.

"But they look so poor," Kara said. "I thought the guilds had to take care of their own?"

"Shh," Mika said. "You don't want Guildsmen to hear you talking like that. The guilds don't like being called to task, especially by an unguilded."

"But it's Guild Law."

"Yes, and the guilds follow their laws when it's convenient or profitable." Mika leaned across the aisle. "And this law is neither. Guilds like cheap labour, and lots of it, so they tell a man what his station in life is and make it so he can't step out of that no matter how hard he tries. If somebody is going to be rich, then somebody has to be poor. It doesn't work any other way. And each guild has plenty of powerful, rich people wanting it to stay that way."

"It wasn't like that in my villa," Kara said. "No one lived as hard a life as these Guildsmen and women."

"Guildsmen there are lucky," Mika replied. "Maybe your villa had one or two honest folk running it. All I know is that I've been coming to Rillidi for twenty years, and it's getting worse."

"But . . ." Kara stopped speaking when the door at the far end opened.

A trail of people came through it, and the cabin quickly filled up. The last to enter was her Seyoyan and one of his companions. The Seyoyan smiled a long, slow smile and started towards her. Despite the tangled legs and packages that lined the aisle, the two Seyoyans gracefully made their way through the crowd. The one stopped, bowed low, and then squeezed in beside her on the bench. His companion settled beside Mika, who frowned and pulled her pack further away from them.

"We meet thricely," her Seyoyan said, his slight accent making him lisp. "In my country it is said that one meeting is chance, two is a coincidence, but a third is destiny."

"But you followed us," Kara said. "Does that count? Can you create your destiny?"

The Seyoyan raised his eyebrows. "Ah, a philosopher. A good question—can destiny be created? I thought Tregellans believed destiny is found—and then only within their guilds."

"Not true," Kara said before she thought about where she was and who she was speaking to.

"You disagree? Tell me." The Seyoyan leaned back, seemingly

at ease, but she felt the tension from him, almost as though he was holding his breath, waiting, daring her to say what she knew he already thought.

"One guild," she whispered. "One guild believes that if a Guildsman controls enough . . . talent, they can make their own destiny."

"Yes," the Seyoyan agreed. "They believe they can, but are they successful?"

"Not always," Kara said, thinking about her father. He'd tried to create his own future, his own destiny, but in the end he hadn't been able to control magic—not as a Mage in his own right nor by fathering a child who had magic. "And not all Guildsmen."

"No, not all Guildsmen," the Seyoyan agreed. "But which ones are successful?"

The ferry lurched, jolting Kara. She looked out the window. The sky was a brilliant blue with faint traces of fog. Except it wasn't fog—the grey-white mist eddied about the windows, but not in a way that might be caused by a breeze or the movement of the ferry. No, this mist pulsed, and each time it pulsed, she felt the ferry lurch forward.

"What do you see?" the Seyoyan asked.

He'd leaned close to her, close enough that she felt his breath on the side of her neck. A few white braids fell across her shoulder, and when she inhaled she smelled the sea and sun-warmed rocks.

"Nothing," she replied and edged away from him.

Mika frowned and glared at the Seyoyan from across the aisle.

"Leave the girl be," Mika said. "We don't even know you."

"Apologies," the Seyoyan said. "Allow me to introduce myself. I'm called Chal Honess, and my companion is Sif Shadae."

He stood and bowed, which caused some nearby passengers to snigger in amusement. His friend nodded, a small smile on his lips. As Chal settled beside her, he asked, "Will you tell me your name?"

"It's Kara," she said. "This is Mika." Mika frowned again.

"Kara, Mika," Chal nodded to each. "May the wind fill your sail."

"And abandon the sail of your enemies," Mika replied.

"Ah, you are a friend to my people already," Chal said.

"I've known a few Seyoyans," Mika said. "Not that I'd call

thieves friends."

Chal grinned. "If a Seyoyan has stolen from you, then you are indeed a friend."

"You tried to steal from me," Kara said. "And not as a friend."

"That? I was just seeing if you were paying attention. If I'd wanted something from your pack, you wouldn't even notice it was gone," he said blandly.

Kara stared at him with narrowed eyes. He'd already taken something! And from her own pack, not Mika's trade goods.

"Give it back," she said. "Whatever you took, I want it back."

It wasn't as though she had so many possessions that she could afford to lose one. She pushed her hair off her face, blinking away tears.

"Keep it," Kara said. "It's not like I've owned any of it for very long anyway."

She crossed her arms. Let him have it if it meant so much to him. There, the anger was better. That's how she'd survived so many years, that's what gave her the ability to go on.

"My sincere apologies," Chal said. "I will return it, do not worry. I fear that I cannot return it to you right now."

"What do you mean?" Mika said. "Give her back what you stole."

Chal shook his head. "I am sorry, it's not safe." His eyes bored into hers, and that's when Kara understood.

The book! He'd stolen the book of magic, the book written by a Primus of the Mage Guild. No, he could not give that to her here, in the open! Any book would be suspect, but once they found out it was a book of magic she'd be handed to Mage Guild.

"Mika," she said. "He's right. Best to be safe."

She willed Mika to agree. When the other woman nodded, Kara's shoulders slumped in relief.

Of all the things to steal from her—and how had he even stolen it? She'd buried it at the bottom of her pack, wrapped in her father's old trousers. Unconsciously she tightened her hold on her pack. No hard, book-shaped lump—just her mug, plate, and utensils. Kara's lips thinned, and she stared at the small door at the front just to keep from looking at the Seyoyan. No doubt he was laughing at her, her and her wretched pack and sad collection of possessions. She glanced his way. But he wasn't laughing. In fact, he looked quite uncomfortable. And his companion was glaring at him. No, he didn't look at all happy.

"So why did you steal from me?" Kara asked quietly. "Why me out of all the people in the crowd?"

"I thought you could afford it," Chal whispered.

She snorted. "As if you'd know."

"I am sorry. You were carrying a large pack obviously filled with trade goods. I assumed you were a reasonably well-off trader."

"But I'm not a Guildsman," Kara said.

"Neither am I," Chal replied. "And many of the Guildsmen in the crowd seemed to have less than you."

"Probably about the same," Kara said. "But they're guild, and so are better off than me."

"Are they?" Chal's voice was low and quiet. "They didn't look so to me. And I know what was taken. Do you?"

"Of course I do," Kara snapped. "It was in my pack, wasn't it?"

"Yes, it was," Chal replied. He met her gaze. "You intrigue me, Kara, unguilded."

"Don't call me that."

"You Tregellans," Chal said. "You're either obsessed by guild associations or you're embarrassed by a lack of them."

"How long have you been in Tregella?" Kara asked.

"Six months."

"Have you ever been outside of Rillidi?"

He shook his head.

"Yet you think you know my country. Don't mistake wariness for embarrassment," she hissed.

"Well said, Donna," the other Seyoyan said. "I often remind my young friend that he has much to learn." He chuckled, and Chal's dark skin flushed even darker.

Kara looked away. The Seyoyan had no idea how perilous it was to live within—or outside of—a guild. Especially Mage Guild.

The ferry shuddered and came to a stop, and Mika leaned across the aisle.

"Stay close to me and keep the pack low," she said. "We're on Merchant Guild Island, and they don't like competition."

Mika stood and nodded to the Seyoyans. Kara copied her, wrapped her arms around Mika's large pack, and slung her own over one shoulder.

Everyone else in the small cabin stood up too. The door at the front slid open, and Mika walked out into the day, Kara trailing behind her.

The crush of people almost overwhelmed her. A hand steadied her, and she threw a grateful glance over her shoulder to Chal. Mika was a step ahead, her shoulders hunched as she made her way between a set of wooden rails. The other, poorer passengers were pressed up against the rails, and Kara shrank away from them, keeping her head down. A fine, sky-blue mist coiled around the rails in a slow, undulating motion, and Kara noticed that whenever someone touched it they edged away from the railing.

Then her foot touched solid ground. Mika turned to her, and grabbed her elbow.

"Can't dally here," she said. "We need to get to the old bridge before this crowd thins out too much." Mika threaded her way through the crowd, towing Kara, who glanced back but didn't see either of the Seyoyans.

Chapter nine

THEY QUICKLY LEFT the crowds and ferry behind. When Mika turned onto a wide boulevard and slowed, Kara lifted her eyes from the cobbles under her. A few well-dressed men and women strolled by, and others, dressed plainer, scurried past with their heads down, guild marks sewn to their shirts and tunics.

Shops lined the street. Colourful signs hung over windows stuffed full of goods for sale—cloth and hats and ropes and baskets and food.

Kara's mouth watered at the smell of fresh bread, and she tightened her grip on Mika's pack as a wave of homesickness washed over her. Not for home exactly, at least not her home. But the clean, well-kept street and the sounds and smells of the bustling merchant area made her long for more comfort, more stability than what she was facing. To buy fresh bread or a crisp, tart apple, right now, right this minute, would almost be worth becoming a Mage Guild breeder. Almost.

"Kara," Mika whispered. "Be ready to run. Like we talked, yes?"

Kara's heart skipped a beat. She didn't dare look at Mika—she hardly dared breathe. Mika had told her that they might be stopped, had warned her that Merchant Guild didn't like unguilded, especially ones with trade goods. But Mika had also said it was unlikely. The unguilded trader had been traveling through Merchant Guild Island for years and had never been stopped, not as long as she went directly to Old Rillidi. Why would this year be any different? Unless Wellert, the inn keep, was right, and this year was worse for unguilded because Mage Guild had been looking for a runaway—looking for her.

Slowly, carefully, Mika set her pack down under a nearby fruit cart. Kara looked past her. Two Merchant Guildsmen, frowns on their faces, headed towards them. She was a step behind Mika, further away from the cart, so after she dropped the large pack to the ground, she had to nudge it out of the street.

"Hey, what are you doing?" It was the Guildsman manning the fruit cart, a youth with red-gold hair and just the hint of a beard. "Get away from my cart! I don't trade with the likes of you."

"Go."

Mika pushed Kara—hard—and she stumbled away from the cart, weaving through the crowd. Someone clutched at her, but she slipped away. Her shawl was stripped from her shoulders, but her small pack stayed where it was, bouncing against her back as she ran. She heard footsteps pounding the cobblestones behind her—someone was chasing her. Was it Mika?

Kara darted into an alley, not daring to look to see if Mika was behind her. They'd meet up where they'd agreed—she couldn't afford to slow down.

The alley jogged left, and she ducked around the corner and stopped, her chest heaving. It was a dead end, but the stone wall on her left had a window, fully open, and without thinking, she dove through it.

Gyda, show me a way out, she prayed, invoking Gyda as the guide, the pathfinder. She tumbled onto a smooth, tile floor and skidded across it to an open doorway. A cat, hunched over a bowl of water, looked up and raised its head at her.

Kara scrambled to her feet and darted through the doorway, gulping in huge breaths. A shadow passed outside the window. She tiptoed down a short hallway and peered around a corner. She didn't see anyone, or hear sounds of anyone inside coming to investigate the noise she'd made. The front door was just a few steps down the hall. She had it opened and was out onto the cobbles in seconds.

Right, she had to keep right in order to find the old bridge where she'd meet Mika. On the Old Rillidi side, Mika had said, if they ever got separated. Mika would meet her, she had to believe it, had to. Otherwise she was alone, just like when she'd left Larona.

Kara kept to side streets and alleys, always heading right. When there were no more streets to turn onto, she settled into a steady walk, hoping to be neither too fast nor too slow to arouse suspicion.

Large, stone houses lined the street, their walled-in grounds hidden from view except where iron or wooden gates spanned cobbled drives. Server Guildsmen, their guild patches sewn onto crisp white uniforms, hurried about their tasks, baskets and packages held tight. None of them gave her a second look, and she relaxed a little.

She followed the road as it arced around the tip of Merchant Guild Island. Once, through the wrought iron gate of a manor, she glimpsed the bay, the deep blue of the water contrasting with the grey stone of the house.

Foot traffic increased as the road looped back towards the main road, and the large estates gave way to narrow row houses, their ground floor shop windows crammed with used goods. When she spotted the main road, Kara ducked into an alley.

She peered out and scanned the street. No sign of Mika, but no sign of any pursuit either. She'd wait the few hours until dusk before crossing the bridge.

She'd passed a small, empty park a few streets back, and she went there to wait. A few roses still bloomed, their pink petals edged with brown, and the trailing limbs of the willows scraped the ground. There was a small fountain, but it was dry—brown leaves littered the basin.

Kara sat beneath a willow tree with her back against the rough bark and sipped from her water skin, careful not to drink too much. She didn't have much left, and Mika had warned her that water was hard to find on Old Rillidi, though of all the islands, it was the only one with natural springs.

As dusk approached, the road filled with people. No longer just Servers, now there were Merchant Guildsmen doubtless returning from work or school. Everyone who lived in these houses, except for the Servers, would be Merchant Guild. Husbands, wives, even the babes in arms, all were Guildsmen.

She eyed the sky through the willow branches. It was time to go—the sun was setting, and the sky had turned a deep blue.

A few people were still on the road, but they ignored her in their own haste to reach their destinations. When she finally stepped out onto the cobbled main street, most of the shops were shuttered and dark. The glow from the tops of tall lamps lit the street—mage mist swirling around them.

She walked a few blocks to the bridge—a solid-looking wooden structure.

Empty now, it was wide enough that two carts could easily pass. More lamps lit the bridge and arched away from her, off into the dark night. A pale orange mist, almost the same colour as the light, twined around each lamp. More mage mist, this time the colour of shadows, ebbed and flowed across the wooden planks of the bridge.

She gently set one foot down on the bridge. The mist puffed away before returning to lap against her shoe. When she knelt and ran a hand through the mist, it billowed away as though blown by a gentle wind. It appeared similar to the mist that had swirled around poor dead Terach, but unlike then she sensed no malevolence within this mist.

She straightened and stepped into the real shadows that surrounded the bridge. She'd wait a few minutes before she crossed, just in case Mika had made it this far and was watching.

Half an hour later it was fully dark. Only two people had passed by on the street, and neither had ventured onto the bridge. With a sigh, Kara stepped out into the light. She couldn't wait here any longer, she needed to get across and find somewhere safe to spend the night. She desperately hoped that Mika was on the other side—on Old Rillidi Island—waiting for her.

When she stepped onto the bridge, the dark mist ebbed away from her boots. Each step forward sent the mist swirling away from her, uncovering the wooden planks of the bridge beneath it. She leaned over and plunged a hand into the mist only to have it retreat from her touch.

She kicked a foot and watched a wave of mist flow out across the bridge. She imagined that wave traveling all the way to the other side, of another person standing on the bridge wondering what had caused this movement. Except no one else saw the mists. Not her mother, who had a mage mist of her own, not

Mika, not anyone else in Rillidi Port or on the ferry. She paused.

Chal Honess, the Seyoyan, had asked her what she saw when she looked out the ferry window. Did he see it too? She scowled. Whatever his talents were, he'd stolen her book. He'd promised to give it back to her, but that seemed impossible now. And now that it was gone, she realized she *had* been thinking of the book as a way to reach her mother. Her mother wanted her dead—did she really think a book would change that? She sighed and started across the bridge.

The end of the bridge was dark, but off to the right she could vaguely see the shoreline of Old Rillidi Island—an even darker mass in the night. She hesitated. Should she stay on the bridge all night? It seemed safer than heading off into the unknown. She wished Mika had told her more about where they were going, but Mika hadn't wanted to put the people she knew at risk. Instead she'd put *Kara* at risk.

She immediately felt ashamed. Poor Mika had probably been captured and sent off Merchant Guild Island, or worse, locked up in a cell somewhere. And she'd been right to keep that information from Kara, right to try to protect those who risked their lives to trade with her. Kara would just have to make her own contacts, make her own way. She could read and write—those were skills she could trade. Her mother had been correct about *that* at least.

Standing on the bridge would only make her more obvious, so she started walking. Mika had warned her that the area of Old Rillidi that surrounded the Merchant Bridge was rough—it was where Rillidians came to trade for the dangerous, illegal, exotic, and obscure items that they couldn't find anywhere else in the city.

The mist ended with the bridge, and Kara stepped off into darkness, holding her pack tight against her side. The street under her feet was uneven, and she stumbled a few times. A shadow detached from the side of the bridge, and she heard footsteps scuff the road behind her. She reached into her pack and found her knife and clutched it in her hand.

"Where're ya going?" a voice asked.

Should she answer? What if all they wanted was some sort of toll? Mika hadn't mentioned one, but it had been the better part of half a year since she'd been here.

"Visiting friends," Kara said. There, let them think she was expected.

"Yeah? Who? I know everyone."

Not a man's voice though it was male—a youth then. Who else would claim to know everyone? Maybe they'd help her?

"Friends of Mika Gianetta," she said, forcing any quaver or question out of her voice.

"Gyda's luck with that one," the voice said. He was still behind her, not coming any closer, not falling behind. "Heard Mika was caught by Merchants. He's got no friends on Old Rillidi today— least none that'd admit to it."

Kara forced herself to keep walking, putting one foot in front of the other. No help, then, not from anyone Mika knew. She really was on her own. She heard the footsteps slide away and barely had time to wonder about it before a door banged open up ahead. She stopped, her knife in her hand. A square of light splashed out onto the road, and she heard the rumble of voices. A figure stumbled to one side of the light.

"Finish yer piss and get back in here," a voice called out from the structure. "You got my money, and I'm wantin' it back."

"It's my money now," the shadow at the side of the building replied.

A few moments later, a man stepped into the light and re-entered the building. The door closed, and the street was dark again.

"You don't want to get mixed up with them," the youth said, close behind her.

Kara wheeled around, and her hand shot out, knife held high.

The youth laughed.

"That's not gonna do nothing except make people mad," he said.

The boy was a few inches shorter than her and not even as old as she'd thought. In the darkened street she couldn't give him more than thirteen or fourteen years.

"It's all I have," she said, feeling defeated. She couldn't even defend herself against a boy, what hope did she have against an adult. She turned and started to walk forward.

"Don't go that way," the boy said. "You'll be nothing but fair game and fresh meat."

"I don't have anywhere else to go," she said. "Unless you'll help me?"

He sighed, and she turned to look at him.

"You really a friend of Mika's?"

Kara nodded. "Mika was going to introduce me to someone, but we got separated after we got off the ferry. We were supposed to meet at the old bridge, but he didn't show. He's been caught?" Poor Mika. As bad as things looked for her, at least she wasn't in the hands of the guilds.

"That's what I heard. Mages are making the other guilds get tough with unguilded, and Merchants are only too happy to oblige. They've always hated unguilded traders like Mika. Don't think they'll hurt him though. I hear they take their goods and send them back to the mainland."

"Good," she said, relieved. "He'll lose some wares, but at least Mika can get Zayeera and head home."

"You do know Mika," the boy said. "Can't say I've ever met that burro, but I've heard lots of stories."

"Zayeera saved my life," she said, remembering the wild run down the mountain.

The boy laughed again. "That's a tale I wanna hear."

"I'll tell you if you help me." Kara held her breath. If he said no, she didn't know what she'd do. Probably walk right into danger.

"Yeah," was the slow reply. "I owe Mika. He's always been good to me. Come on, we gotta get out of the street before the beer runs out. I'm Vook."

He grabbed her arm and pulled her to the right, off the uneven cobbles and onto hard packed dirt.

"I'm Kara," she said, trying not to stumble in the dark.

The moon was up, a half crescent that shed pale light on the path. Wooden buildings, their walls warped and splintered, rose on either side of them.

Vook led her through shadowed alleys and empty lots, skirting any areas that emitted either sound or light. At one point a small dog trotted beside them, eerily silent as it ghosted alongside them. They left it behind when Vook and she jumped a wooden fence. Finger to his lips, Vook urged her to silence. They crept across a yard punctuated by light that streamed from two windows. At the far end, they squeezed between two buildings before they reached another cobbled street. Another turn to the left and she felt Vook relax.

"We should be safe now," Vook said. "Banditos don't come out this way, at least not at night."

"Banditos?"

"Yeah, them that cause all the trouble. Drinking, gambling, murders, fights, drugs, whores. Banditos run them all."

Vook ran a hand through his tousled hair, and Kara was struck by how world-weary he looked in that moment.

"Unguilded would be safe enough on Old Rillidi if it wasn't for them. Anyone looking for anything illegal comes here—Guildsmen, unguilded, folk from away."

"But the guilds wouldn't allow anything illegal, would they?"

"Huh," Vook snorted. "You are fresh meat. Merchant Guild backs the banditos. As long as it's not on their own islands, the guilds are happy enough to let folk kill themselves and each other. Not guild business, they say."

"But don't Guild Laws apply to Old Rillidi?"

"No. That's why us unguilded can live here. No one knows who owns this island. Lore says that a living descendent of the First Guildsman, Paolo Santonini, owns Old Rillidi, but no one knows who that is. At least not that they're talking."

"Who was the last owner?"

"Mage Primus by the name of Nimali," Vook said.

He turned down a dark alley, and she followed, almost blind.

"But he disappeared years ago," Vook continued.

"Santos Nimali?" Kara couldn't believe it. Was the last owner of Old Rillidi the same Mage who had written her book? The book that was stolen from her?

"Could be," Vook said. "Can't say as I know the first name. That last name though, I've been told it's carved onto more than a few statues around here."

"You've been told? Have you seen these statues yourself?" Kara asked.

"Sure, seen them lots," Vook said. "But I'm no mager that can read."

"Uh, no," she said. Of course Vook couldn't read. "But someone told you what it said?"

"Yeah," Vook replied. "One of them dark islanders, the ones from away."

"A Seyoyan?" Kara followed Vook out of the alley into a dark flat field.

"That's right," he said. "They come by the market sometimes, when they get tired of stealing from each other."

"What is this place?" Kara asked. The faint moonlight showed the rubble of houses and the blackened stumps of trees. A few green shoots pushed upwards, but otherwise there was devastation as far as she could see.

"This is the burn out," Vook said. "Almost a quarter of the island caught fire. Before I got here." He sniffed. "You can still smell it, though it happened almost seven years ago."

"It must have been horrible." And huge, she thought. From the little that she could see, it looked like more houses had burned than there were in the whole of Villa Larona. "Did people die?"

"I expect so." Vook shrugged and kept walking, his bare feet crunching on the debris. "Around here, most houses with more than one wall got someone calls it home."

"What caused the fire?" She couldn't believe she'd never heard of this, never once in the last seven years. Was it because the guilds didn't care?

"Dunno," Vook said. "Lots a rumours. Some say it was the magers who done it, trying to kill someone, others say it was a squatter who lit a fire and then fell asleep."

"But you don't believe either of those," Kara said. Although she did think the magers—Mage Guild— would be ruthless enough to sacrifice unguilded for their own goals.

"No." Vook met her eyes. "I think it were the mad mage. He mostly stays up on the estate, where there's water, but sometimes he wanders."

"The mad mage," Kara repeated. "Why would he do this?" She stared around at the burnt and broken houses. Why would anyone do this?

"Oh he wouldn't have meant it," Vook said. "Nor remember if he did do it. He can't control his magic."

She shuddered. A Mage who could cause this much damage would have to be very powerful.

"Who is he?" she asked.

Vook angled through the blackened landscape, and Kara followed.

"Dunno," Vook replied. "Alls I ever heard him called is the mad mage. Been here years, forever maybe."

"And he lives by himself? Mage Guild doesn't control him?" How could they let someone so dangerous live out here by themselves?

And that was the answer. Mage Guild wouldn't care what happened to anyone else on this island—unguilded, foreigners, low level Guildsmen—they wouldn't care. Easy and cheap to simply foist a mad mage onto a defenseless population, people Mage Guild would consider worthless and expendable. Gyda, how she hated them!

"The magers, they come by every few weeks," Vook said. "Hoping he's dead, I expect. I seen 'em. They leave him food and stuff."

"And the mad mage, that's what he lives off? What Mage Guild gives him?" Kara asked. Guild Law required a guild to look after any law abiding members who could no longer care for themselves. This must be how Mage Guild fulfilled its obligation. But surely they could use magic to render him safe?

"Yeah, I guess so," Vook said. "I don't know where they leave it, only that they come with packages and leave with nothin'." Vook looked back at her. "It's not like I'm gonna steal from him. Gotta be stupid to steal from a Mage, mad or not. And I ain't stupid."

"No, you're not," Kara agreed.

"Shh. Gotta be quiet for a while," Vook whispered. He slowed until she was right behind him. A road ahead was clear of debris from the fire. "Clammers sometimes come this far at night, if they run out of water."

Vook stopped and cocked his head to listen. With a nod, he stepped out into the road and ran across it. Kara hurried after him. They traveled in silence for another half an hour before they reached a line of trees. Once hidden in the trees, she inhaled deeply, glad to have the burn out behind them.

"We can talk now," Vook said. "We're real close to the docks."

"That's where we're going?" Kara asked. Until now she'd been too grateful to have Vook as her guide to even wonder about their destination. Now, she was curious—and nervous.

"Yep, the docks. Home."

Vook smiled when he said it, and she realized that he'd been tense during their trek. The dangers he'd spoken of were real—banditos, clammers, even the mad mage.

"Who do you live with? What do I need to know about them?" Kara asked, but before Vook had a chance to answer, there was a shout from their right.

Startled, she stopped. Vook surged ahead with a whoop.

"It's me," Vook yelled. "Brought a friend."

"Mika?" A girl of about twelve or thirteen edged out from behind a tree. She ducked behind the tree when she saw Kara.

"Mika's been caught," Vook said. "No doubt he's halfway home by now. This here's Kara. She was traveling with Mika." Vook turned to Kara. "That's Pilo. She don't like many people. They stare at her."

Kara nodded. All right, she'd do her best not to stare.

"What are you doing out so late?" Vook asked as they neared the tree. "Where are Harb and Lowel?"

"Over to the clammers," Pilo said. She stepped out into view with her head down and her eyes on the ground.

Kara drew in a breath. Half of the girl's face was melted, a drooping mass of scars that seemed to be sliding off her face. The scars flowed down her neck and disappeared under a dirty shirt that once might have been blue, but now was a dingy grey-brown. The shirt sleeve ended just above the wrist, where yet more scars trailed down to a hand with fingers that were partially fused together.

Kara was horrified. Not at the burns, but at that fact that nothing had been done for this child. They were practically within sight of Mage Guild Island and its Mage Healers. This child could be whole, *should* be whole, but wasn't.

She glanced away from Pilo to Vook, who stood staring at her. Her face must have given away some of her thoughts, because he relaxed and nodded.

"Pilo was caught in the fire," Vook said quietly. "Her parents survived, but never really got over it. Her pa died first, and then her ma died two years ago. Mika found her and brought her here. Pilo," he said more loudly. "When did those two idiots head to the clammers?"

"Just after you left," the girl replied. "I thought you were them. They should be back soon."

"On our way here you said you didn't want to run into clammers," Kara said as she followed Vook and Pilo. It was close to dawn, and there was enough light for her to see the large metal fence and gate that blocked the path.

"I didn't," Vook said. "And Harb and Lowel shouldn't have gone to see them. It's dangerous. I was hoping Mika could talk some sense into them."

"Why do they go?" To Kara, life seemed difficult enough without searching out trouble.

"'Cause of the women." Vook snorted in disgust. "Six months ago Harb decided he wanted a woman. Can't afford the bandito whores so he trades water to the clammers. Harb don't care that it hurts Pilo that they go." He reached over and patted Pilo's sound shoulder. She shrugged away from his touch. "Her ma ended up whoring when her pa died. She didn't last long in that life. Harb talked Lowel into it of course. Harb can talk Lowel into anything."

When they reached the gate, metal mesh with gaps big enough for a small person to slip their hands through, Pilo took a key from around her neck. She slipped her hands through the mesh and unlocked a rusty padlock.

"Mika helped us set all this up," Vook said.

Pilo slipped the padlock off.

Vook swung the door open. "The lock, the gate—keeps us pretty safe."

He ushered Kara through, and Pilo locked it again, leaving the lock on the inside.

"Come on," he whispered. "I don't want to wake the little ones up. You can meet them later." He led the way down an overgrown path.

Little ones, she thought in alarm. There were children younger than poor Pilo and Vook? How many children lived here?

A fresh breeze rustled through the treetops, and Kara took a deep breath. She'd gotten so used to the underlying smell of the burn out, that it took her a second to understand what she smelled—water, the salt water of the bay.

Suddenly the dense brush gave way, and they were at the edge of a clearing. Straight ahead, moonlight glinted off water. A few crumbling wooden buildings sagged toward the bay, and evenly spaced posts stuck straight out of the water, a couple of feet of planks still attached. It was the remnants of a dock much like the one she'd walked on to board the ferry.

"Here's where we sleep," Vook said. He headed toward an

overturned boat, ducked down, and disappeared into it.

Kara followed, her hands scraping on the splintered wood of what was once a window frame. Inside, it was dark and smelled of musty wood and stale sweat. She remained bent over, feeling as though the roof was just inches away from her head.

"This way." Vook grabbed her hand and gently tugged her forward.

Underfoot there were soft mounds of cloth, or maybe grass. Her eyes started to adjust, just a little. Then, off in the gloom, she saw a swirling mass of mist. White and light green, it shed enough light for her to see the blanket that lay beneath the mist. And beneath the blanket, two small heads crowded together, one tiny fist curled against a chin.

They were so small, *too* small to be here, living under an overturned boat. Children looking after children. Where were the adults, where were the guilds? Thanks to Mika, at least these children had a reasonably safe place to live, but how many other children were out there, living in worse conditions than this? Such bleak futures. Then she remembered that she shared their future. Her mother had sent her into this life, into this future. Well, she had some skills. And if these children let her stay, she had a fairly safe place to live. She could help make all of their lives just that little bit better.

"There, in the corner." Vook pointed towards the sleeping children. "Find a spot under the blanket if you want. Just be careful of Sidra and Mole."

He led her towards the sleeping children, and Kara realized that for Vook, there was no glow from the blanket, no radiant mist to light the way.

Kara settled down away from the blanket, her pack stuck under her head. Suddenly she was exhausted. It had been less than twenty four hours since she'd last seen Mika. She hoped the woman truly was on her way home because Kara knew she couldn't help her friend.

Chapter ten

ARABELLA PAUSED IN the doorway. Primus Rorik stood at the window of her salon, staring out into her small garden.

"Are you a fan of gardens, Primus?" she asked as she stepped into the room. "I'm afraid mine will disappoint you if you are."

"I don't often get outside," Rorik said. He turned to face her and smiled.

She had put extra effort into her appearance today; her beauty was one of her tools, after all. She strolled to the centre of the room, the silk of her skirt whispering as she walked.

"Please, sit down," Arabella gestured to the velvet settee. She settled on one end and placed her hands demurely in her lap while Rorik sat on the other end.

"I could order tea," she said. "Or wine if you'd prefer something stronger."

"Nothing, thank you," Rorik replied. "Unless of course you feel I will need something stronger."

He smiled when he spoke, but she sensed the challenge beneath his words. She should not forget that Rorik had risen through Mage Guild, no matter that she thought he was Valerio's creature now.

"No, of course not," Arabella said. "I simply thought that it would be nice to get to know each other."

"You mean it would be nice for you to know the Primus better."

"Yes," she agreed. "Although I flatter myself that I do have my own . . . charms."

"Ah." Rorik leaned back and stared at her. "I believe I will let others enjoy those charms." He fixed her with his gaze. "What do you want from me?"

"I really do want to get to know you better," Arabella said. "After all, we have much in common."

"Which is what?"

"Why our dedication to Mage Guild," she replied. And Valerio Valendi. She'd heard rumours that Valerio had engineered Rorik's ascendancy to Primus, much as he'd ensured that she was elected to the council. But she didn't know why Valerio was content to be Secundus. "And now that I'm on the council, I can help you."

"Can you?" Rorik asked.

"With your advice," Arabella said. "Yes. You know my fellow council members far better than I do—I expect that you would know *how* I should manage them in order to get the result that *you* want."

"Why?"

Arabella paused and considered the Primus. He was suspicious, as she'd expected, but she also thought that he would appreciate honesty.

"Being a woman in Mage Guild is difficult," she said. "But worse, I found my power late and did not start training until I was the age when my peers were becoming full Mages." She met Rorik's eyes. She saw understanding there, and a little pity, and she knew she would convince him. "I need allies—strong allies—if I am to survive. Who better than the Primus?"

"Why would I need *your* help?" Rorik asked. "I already have allies of my own."

"Yes," Arabella said. "But they are all known to each other. Sides were chosen years ago." Rorik nodded, and Arabella smoothed a hand across her skirt. "I'm new to council. Most of them barely know me, and since I'm a woman, they will *all* underestimate me." She gave him a half-smile. "What has always been a burden will now be an advantage. Don't you wonder which of your allies you can truly trust? Who is secretly aligned against you? I can help you find out."

"Because you're a woman?" Rorik asked.

"Yes." She nodded. "And new to council and from a small villa in the country. No one will see me as a threat. No one will suspect that I already have formidable alliances."

"They will be circling you," Rorik replied. "Trying to make you an ally."

"They've already started," Arabella said. "I've had lunch and dinner invitations, as well as invitations for more . . . intimate meetings."

"Yet you come to me."

"Yes. You are the Primus," Arabella said simply. "You have more political importance than any of the council members. And we are both allied with Valerio, in our own ways."

"Valerio," Rorik repeated. "Finally you mention his name. Did he ask you to do this? Perhaps he's using you to test my loyalty."

"He's not," Arabella replied. "I approached you of my own accord, but I can't imagine he would be unhappy that two of his allies are getting better acquainted."

"No, of course not," Rorik agreed.

Arabella met his gaze and nodded. Valerio *wouldn't* like it, of course. She had to trust that Rorik wouldn't tell Valerio—just as he had to trust that she wouldn't either.

"Then it's settled," Arabella said. "We are friends. You will let me know when you can use my help?"

Arabella closed the door after Rorik left and took a deep breath. She hoped the Primus wasn't in a rush to task her with anything—she did not want Valerio to suspect she was allied with Rorik. But after only a few weeks, she knew how deeply some council members hated Valerio. She may be carrying his child, but she could not afford to have him be her only ally. If he fell, so would she. She *would not* allow that.

"Get up."

Something tugged at her hair, and sleepily Kara swiped at it.

"I said get up."

A sharper tug.

"Hey." She clutched the hand that was grabbing her hair. "That hurts." She opened her eyes and twisted the hand.

"Ow! You whore."

The hand reared up as if to strike her, and Kara glared at the boy behind the hand.

"Don't you dare," she snapped. She scrambled to her feet, still glaring at him. He was her height and only a few pounds heavier. He shuffled a little and mumbled something.

"Harb, stop that." Vook put his smaller body between them. "This here's Kara. She's a friend of Mika's. And my guest."

Kara couldn't see the look in Vook's eyes, but from his body language *she* wouldn't assume the younger boy would back down. Or that he would be easily bested. Harb must have thought so as well because he scowled at her and then turned on his heels, stumbling as he walked away. Drunk and mad at the world. It was a dangerous combination.

"Don't know what's gotten into him," Vook said, more to himself than to Kara. "It's like he can't live in his own skin anymore." He turned to her. "You all right?"

"Yes. He just startled me," she said. She rubbed a hand over her hair. Would she be the same in a few years? So angry and hopeless that she wouldn't be able to stand her mean, miserable life? Because that's what she'd seen in Harb—the knowledge that he had nothing ahead but a hard life and no chance to make it better.

She shivered. Vook nodded to her and settled under the glowing blanket with the other, smaller children. Four heads there now—Pilo had joined them. Kara slid down to her pack. It was morning, there was light in the upside down boat, but she was still tired from her long day yesterday.

KARA WOKE SUDDENLY and found herself staring into the eyes of a boy about the same age as Osten. A pang of loneliness washed over her, and she drew in a ragged breath.

"You sad?" the boy asked. He reached out a grubby hand and awkwardly patted her hair.

Kara smiled, and he smiled back at her.

"I'm Kara," she said.

He repeated her name a few times, nodding. "Good name," he said. "I'm Mole. That's a good name too."

"It is?"

"Yep. 'Cause I see real good in the dark." He gestured around the dim structure. "Like in here. Don't like outside too much.

Least not until night."

"But a sunny day is a gift from Gyda," Kara said.

"Hurts my eyes," Mole said. "You hungry? Vook said to come get you. Pilo's made soup." Mole turned and shuffled a few steps. "Come on." He looked back at her. "Lowell will eat it all if you don't come now."

She rose and slung her pack over her shoulder, not daring to leave any of her things.

Mole ducked out of the boat, and she followed. It was dusk. The sun had just set, and the sky was streaked with pinks and golds. Vook, Pilo, and a younger girl sat around a small fire. A pot, its bottom blackened from countless fires, sat in the middle of the flames. Pilo stirred the pot with a branch stripped of bark.

"Here she is," Mole said. He sat down on a flat rock by the fire while Kara stood awkwardly a few paces away.

"Kara," Vook said. "This here's Sidra, and you met Pilo last night. We're just about to eat. Find a mug and get some soup."

Grateful, Kara retrieved her mug from her pack. She waited until all the others had their own mugs of soup before she dipped into it. She smelled fish, onions, and garlic.

She took a sip. It was good, and she was hungry. Her mug was empty very quickly. Not knowing if there was enough for another helping, she put her mug down and picked up her pack. She had some travel rations still. Her hand closed on the hard edges of a book. She peeked into the bag. Her book! The one Chal had stolen. He'd returned it after all.

"What are you smiling about?" Mole asked.

He tried to look into her pack, but Kara held it closed.

She looked up to see four sets of eyes trained on her. She hesitated, just for a moment, then she drew the book out of her pack. Mika had trusted these children so she would too.

"What is that?" Mole reached a hand out and stroked the cover of the book. "Can you eat it?"

"It's book," Pilo said. Her eyes were wide with interest. "I've seen one before. Why do you have a book?"

"Mika gave it to me," Kara said. "It belonged to a friend of his."

"Mika don't read so it makes sense he'd let you have it," Vook said, nodding.

"Mika reads now," Kara said. She stopped. What if Mika didn't want anyone to know she could read?

"Mika reads?" Pilo asked. "How?"

"I taught him to read," Kara said. "On the way here. That was our trade. Reading for a safe trip to Rillidi."

"Sounds like him," Vook said. "He don't do things for nothing. Mika helped us get set up here, where we're safe. Our part of the trade is to let him stay with us whenever he comes and to take in his friends." Vook looked at her. "Which is why I brung you here."

"And I'm grateful," Kara said, and meant it. If she hadn't met Vook, who knows what would have happened to her? "I'd like to stay." She didn't have anywhere else to go. "I'll do chores, whatever I can."

"Can you teach me to read?" Pilo asked. "If I could read, I might be able to get work. It wouldn't matter so much how I looked."

"Yes, I'll teach all of you to read, if you want," Kara said. She paused. "I might be able to help you with your scars."

Pilo glared at her, her lips drawn tight. "You can't, no one can, so don't say that. I'm ugly, and I'm gonna stay ugly."

"I can't make them go away," Kara agreed. "Only a powerful Mage could do that for scars this old. But I can make a salve that will soften them so they don't feel so tight."

"I suppose I'd let you do that," Pilo said. "What else can you do?"

"I'm good at foraging for food," Kara said. "I know a lot of plants that are good to eat—I know where to find them and how to cook them."

Pilo glared at her fiercely. Ah, that was Pilo's job. Kara needed a different task.

"I'm healer trained," she said at last.

"Healer!" Vook said. "Then you're a mager!" He stood up and backed away from her. "What do you want with us?"

"I grew up in the Mage Guild, yes," Kara said. "I have all the training any Mage Guildsman would have prior to finding their talent—but I have no magic. Which means that I'm almost useless to the guild."

"Almost?" Pilo asked quietly. "What use did they have for you?"

"They wanted me to have children—to breed me," Kara said.

She met Pilo's eyes and saw understanding there—a girl whose mother was forced to become a whore would know what *that* meant.

"So I ran away. Mage Guild thinks I'm dead."

"Why come here?" Pilo asked.

Vook sat down, but kept a wary eye on her.

"I met Mika on the road," Kara replied. "He said if I taught him how to read he'd take me to a place on Old Rillidi where I'd be safe."

"Your trade," Pilo said. "All right. Mika's the best judge of people I've ever known." Pilo looked around at the other three children. "I vote she stays."

The others all nodded their heads.

"What about Harb?" Sidra asked. She sounded afraid.

"Harb and Lowel will just have to get used to her," Pilo said. "It's us four against them two."

Kara relaxed—she'd been clutching her pack. Thank Gyda she had a place to stay. She glanced at Vook and smiled. He didn't smile back.

She opened her pack. Ah, there it was. She pulled out an oiled cloth and unwrapped it.

"It's not a lot," she said as she held the contents out. "But it won't keep so we should eat it now."

"You have bread?" Vook asked. He scooted over to her, any qualms about her being a mager forgotten in the face of a treat.

"Baked fresh yesterday morning," Kara said. "Mika had a whole loaf in his pack. I think he was bringing it for you."

She broke off the crust and handed it to Vook, who snatched it up and scrambled to his place by the fire. In moments the bread was divided up, with two pieces left for the absent Lowel and Harb. Kara rewrapped those, wishing she'd brought more bread along with some cheese. But she hadn't expected to be separated from Mika.

"Real bread," Sidra said. "I've hardly ever had it in my whole life." She was pulling off little pieces and popping them into her mouth one at a time.

"Mika always brings us some," Pilo said. "He's real good like that." She put the last of her bread into her mouth and closed her eyes while she chewed.

Only Mole seemed unimpressed by the bread. He ate it, but quickly, with none of the reverence of the other children.

Pilo served more soup, and Kara took another half a mug. She was just finishing hers when the other children tensed.

"Are you still here?"

Kara looked up. It was the youth from earlier, the one who'd woken her. His dark eyes glared at her, and his hands twitched into fists. Slowly, she set her mug down beside her pack and stood.

"Yes, still here. I'm Kara," she said. "You must be Harb." He looked younger and a lot meaner than she remembered. A second youth, older and bigger, stood behind him. "And you're Lowel?"

She smiled, and the second youth, Lowel, smiled back. Harb continued to glare at her.

"What do you want?" Harb asked.

"Kara's going to stay with us," Pilo said.

Harb's angry gaze slid from Kara to Pilo.

"Who says?"

"I say," Pilo replied. "We voted, and all four of us want her to stay."

"Who put you in charge, you scarred whore?"

Kara couldn't see Pilo's face, but she heard her sharp intake of breath.

"What's it to you?" Kara asked. "I can pull my own weight, find my own food. I have other skills that might be useful."

"What other skills?" Harb's gaze raked over her body, pausing on her breasts. "Might be I can be talked into keeping you if you make it worth my while." He leaned closer to her. "But you'll have to be real nice."

Kara suppressed a shudder. This man-child was dangerous.

"Kara knows healing," Vook said. "She's going to help Pilo."

"Pilo." Harb spat on the ground beside her. "What do I care if you help Pilo? She's never going to be pretty enough to bed."

"I wouldn't have you anyway," Pilo said. "Not after you've been with the clammers. I heard a man's thing falls off after bedding them."

"Where'd you hear that?"

Harb was still angry, but Kara heard a hint of worry in his voice.

"The whorehouse, that's where," Pilo said. "Not even whores would lie with clammers. So you're worse than a whore, Harb. You and Lowel."

"It's not true," Harb said.

Kara looked past him to Lowel, who had a look of fear on his face.

"I might be able to help," Kara said to Lowel. "With a salve."

"I want her to stay too," Lowel said quickly. "In case something happens to me on account of the clammer women."

"Shut up, Lowel." Harb turned to the bigger youth. "Nothing's going to happen to you. Pilo's lying."

"Am not," Pilo said. "Just you wait."

"Let her stay, Harb," Lowel pleaded. "I'll help her with her chores so she won't be any trouble."

"I can do my own chores," Kara said.

"See, Harb," Lowel said. "She'll work hard, just like the rest of us. Let her stay."

"All right," Harb said. He turned to stare Kara in the eyes. "But you stay out of my way."

Kara nodded, and he stomped past her.

"She better not have eaten all the food," Harb said. "Lowel and me are hungry." He looked in the pot and grunted. Vook held out the bread—Kara's bread—and Harb grunted again.

KARA SETTLED INTO the routine of the docks. They usually woke up late in the day, well past noon, and foraged for food. Vook fished off the crumbling dock, his line threaded with worms from the small garden that Pilo kept.

One night Vook left the safety of the fenced enclosure and came back with news—Mika had been sent to Rillidi Port and had last been seen leading Zayeera towards the mountains.

Kara was relieved. She'd been worried that her friend had been imprisoned—or worse—but Mika and Zayeera should make it home to Allon before the rains.

Most days Pilo and Sidra tended the garden. Lettuce, carrots, beans, and tomatoes grew in neat rows. Kara spent the afternoons in the woods inside the gate, searching for ingredients for the poultice she made for Pilo, as well as the odd handful of berries.

Harb, with Lowel trailing him, fetched water daily. It was the most dangerous task since they had to go outside the fence all the way to the edge of the mad mage's estate. They came back with tales of trees that had moved and giant flowers, evidence of the mad mage's spells. If it had been only Harb, Kara would have thought he was making things up just to scare them, but poor Lowel didn't have enough imagination to lie about this.

Harb and Lowel also visited the clammers. When they were gone, the mood of the rest of the children was noticeably lighter. But Harb usually returned drunk and surly and then the children tried to stay away from him. From what Kara could tell, Harb used to take his temper out on Pilo, but he'd transferred that anger to her, which suited her. Pilo had enough of a burden.

"I COULD PROBABLY find some wild potatoes," Kara said to Pilo. It was just over a week since she'd arrived, and the two of them were sitting by the fire pit discussing how to stock up for the coming winter. "I'd have to go outside the fence though."

"It would be worth it," Pilo said. "We could plant some in the spring too."

"Too bad there aren't any lemon trees," Kara said. "The fruit dries very well."

"The clammers have some," Vook said. He had his back against a tree, and his eyes were half closed. "Lowel said."

"Could we trade with them?" Kara asked. "We know they always want fresh water. Couldn't Lowel and Harb trade for some lemons instead of just trading for . . ." She didn't bother to finish the sentence. They all knew what Lowel and Harb traded for.

"I guess," Vook said. "Will you ask Harb?"

"Ask Harb what?"

Vook's eyes widened. Kara swiveled her head. Harb stood a few steps away, Lowel hulking behind him. Harb stared at Vook for a moment before his gaze focused on her.

"Ask Harb what?" he repeated.

"Ask Harb if he can trade with the clammers for some lemons," Kara said. Harb scowled in anger. "I'll carry the water and bring back the lemons."

"You," Harb said. "You're not big enough to carry water this far, let alone all the way to the clammers' camp."

"I'm almost as big as you." As soon as she said it, she knew it was a mistake. Harb's expression went from angry to furious.

"Think you can beat me?" he asked. His face reddened, and he loomed over her. "Do you? I'm stronger than you. I'd wager you never done a full day's work in your life, not hard labour like me."

"What hard labour?" Kara asked. She was tired of Harb

bullying everyone, pushing them around and belittling them. "You've done hardly any work around the camp since I've been here. Pilo and Vook find the food, Pilo cooks, Sidra cleans up. Even Mole does more than you. All you and Lowel do is fetch water once a day. Twice if you want to lay with the clammer women." She looked around.

Vook stared straight ahead, but Pilo grinned at her.

"At least," Kara continued, "I'm assuming you lay with the clammer *women*."

"You whore!" Harb roared. He raised his hand, and Kara scrambled to her feet.

Chest heaving, her own hands fisted, she glared at the enraged youth. She wouldn't back down, not from this lazy bully.

"If you ever want to eat my cooking again then you won't hit her," Pilo said calmly.

Harb glowered at Pilo. "Ugly girl, what do you think you're doing? I'm in charge here. Always have been, always will be."

"No," Pilo said. She rose and stood beside Kara. "You're not in charge of *me*. Besides, you're almost dead weight, you and Lowel. Don't do much around here except think we owe you. Why? Because you're saving us from the outside? I think I might be in more danger from those inside the fence. How soon before you bring the clammers here, Harb? What if they won't lie with you unless you let them come here? Based on how much water you cart them, there must be a lot of them. There can't be many clams left on that beach, what if they want our fish?"

"Harb already told them they can't have our fish," Lowel said.

"Shut up, Lowel." Harb's voice was low and angry.

"But you told 'em," Lowel repeated.

"I said shut up!"

"How long ago did they ask about the fish?" Kara asked quietly. "What did you tell them?" And how soon before the clammers were completely out of food and decided their survival depended on moving here?

"A long time ago," Harb said. "And I didn't tell them anything. And neither did Lowel."

"Lowel, is that true?" Pilo asked.

"Don't say nothing, Lowel," Harb said without looking at the other youth. "It's none of her business."

"Yes it is," Vook said. He leaned against the willow tree. "It's all of our business. The clammers leave us alone because three years ago Mika told them the mad mage wanders here. He told them that we were just kids and knew how to hide. If they don't believe that anymore, there's nothing to stop them from coming here."

"They're not coming here," Harb insisted.

"You're wrong," Kara said. "They don't have water, they're running out of food, there are more of them than there are of us, and they know there's nothing to be afraid of."

She met Vook's and then Pilo's gazes. They both looked scared. And angry.

"Gyda," Pilo swore. "Harb, what have you done?"

"I didn't do nothing," Harb screamed. "They won't come here. I told them they can't. They haven't even asked me anything for weeks."

"They asked me," Lowel said.

Harb's head turned towards the bigger youth.

"It were Lelee. She said you told her I'd answer all her questions."

"What questions, Lowel," Kara asked. "We need to know."

"She was asking how many," Lowel replied. "I told her. Didn't tell her about you though, Kara. Harb kept saying as you weren't one of us, so I didn't count you."

"What else?"

"Well, she wanted to know about the fishing. I told her I didn't know seeing as Vook here does all that. Oh and the mad mage. I told her we hadn't seen him since last summer."

Kara's heart sank. Her safe haven had just disappeared. "How many clammers are there, Harb?"

Harb glared at her. "I don't know," he said. "More than all my fingers." He held his hands up to her, fingers spread wide. "How many is that?"

"Ten," Kara replied. "Are there more than all of yours and Lowel's fingers?" Poor Harb didn't even know basic counting skills. No wonder he took what pleasure he could whenever he could.

"Yeah," he said. "I think so."

"More than twenty then," Kara said. "Against the six of us."

"The fence will keep them out though," Lowel said. "Won't it?"

"For a while," Kara replied. "But eventually they'll find a way in. We need to figure out what to do before that happens.”

“I think we should run,” Pilo said.

“They won’t come,” Harb said again. “They won’t go against me.”

“They will,” Vook said. “I’ve been hungry, Harb, so hungry I couldn’t think of anything else. If they’re like that, they *will* get in.”

“We should run,” Pilo repeated.

“Run where?” Vook asked. “Where can we go?”

“Harb still has folk over to the crossroads,” Lowel said. “We went there once to watch them.”

“They won’t help,” Harb said.

“How do you know?” Kara asked.

“They barely fed me, and I’m their blood, they won’t help strangers.”

“Then we’ll need to find somewhere else,” Kara said. “Or we can stay here and welcome the clammers.”

“No,” Pilo said. “I won’t live with clammers. They’re animals, almost.”

“They’re not that bad,” Harb said.

“They don’t wash, and they live off raw clams and bugs and rats and anything else they can catch,” Pilo said. “And when they die they eat each other. That’s why they got so many diseases. My ma told me.”

“I never saw such a thing,” Harb said. “And I’ve been going there for half a year.”

“Yeah?” Pilo said. “You ever seen one of them women big with child one week and not the next, but there’s no baby around? The whores said the clammers eat their own newborns. That’s why they’re so willing to lie with you. You give them a big belly, and they get to eat.”

“That’s not true,” Harb said. “They only want water.”

Kara shuddered. They wouldn’t know if the clammers meant them harm until they were overrun by them. Then it would be too late.

“We need to look for a new place to live,” Kara said. “Tonight. The clammers are still afraid of the mad mage—so we’ll have to move closer to him.” It was late in the season to move. They’d have to leave most of the food in their garden, and who knew if they’d find a better place to fish, but they didn’t have a choice.

Chapter eleven

ARABELLA SIPPED HER tea, waiting as Valerio's Server cleared her plate. The Secundus had invited her for supper—a rare enough event that she was worried that he'd heard about her meetings with Rorik. He'd been pleasant enough all through their meal, but with a man like Valerio that didn't signify anything. She much preferred the company of Primus Rorik, or even Castio. Both were clever men, and ambitious, but not as hard for her to read. Or as dangerous if she'd misread them.

"I have good news," she said. She wanted her news out first—hoping it would strengthen her position. "I am with child." She smiled. "Our child."

"Congratulations," Valerio said. "A child with potential. I know how important that is to you."

Arabella bowed her head. Important to her, but not to him. Valerio already had numerous children—and although none were old enough to have found their talent, he had already fulfilled his duty to Mage Guild. And now, with this child, so would she.

"But not more important than the fact that this is *your* child." She looked up and smiled again. And it *was* important that she was carrying the Secundus' child. Now that she had tasted the power of being a Councillor, she knew it wasn't enough.

"I'm flattered," Valerio said. "But it might also make you a target. I have enemies."

"I understand," Arabella said. "I will not disclose our relationship. Not yet." She'd already told Rorik, hoping that a secret between them would tie them closer. And perhaps make him feel safe enough to tell her a secret of his own, one that she and Valerio could use to remove the old man. Then she could be Secundus to Valerio's Primus.

"No, you will not," Valerio replied. "Your immediate usefulness depends on council seeing you as unaligned." He drained his wine and stood up, reaching a hand out to her. "Come, I have work to do later, but would enjoy the company of the mother of my child."

Arabella took his hand and followed him towards his bed chamber. There was no subtext to his invitation, no ulterior motive—he was simply a man who wanted to enjoy a beautiful— and willing—woman.

Valerio opened the door to his room and stepped aside, allowing her to enter first.

A woman stood in the outer sitting area, her hands knotted into the rough wool of the skirt she wore. Arabella stopped.

"What is she doing here?" Arabella asked. It was Noula, her husband's woman.

Valerio walked over to Noula and traced a hand down her face. The woman closed her eyes, trembling.

"She came to me for help," he said. "It seems your former husband didn't want to marry her after all, and the rest of the people in the villa made her leave." He smiled thinly. "The Villa Primus arranged for her to come to Rillidi."

"But why is she *here*?" Arabella asked. "In your home?"

"Noula contacted me," Valerio said. "Begged me, really, for help for her and her son. She said she would do anything." He paused. "And since you so badly wanted the girl dead, I thought it prudent to investigate a little more."

"What did you find?" Arabella asked softly. He'd done this all without her knowledge, when she thought he trusted her.

Valerio laughed. "Nothing. The girl truly had no magic." He stood in front of Arabella. "She was a failure—*your* failure—and you wanted her gone." He shrugged and walked away. "But now I know."

"What will you do with me?" Noula asked. "Will you bed me?

I've proven that I can bear boys."

"Oh please," Valerio said. "I already have one of Fonti's cast offs—I certainly don't need another." He traced a finger along her cheek. "Not even enough power to bother to extract," he murmured. He shrugged and turned to Arabella.

"I've already sent her son out to be fostered," Valerio said. "What do you think I should do with her?"

"Why would I care?" she replied, making sure her voice stayed low and calm. How dare he group her with this creature? "Although . . . she has no magic, yet she is Mage Guild—is there a particular house you would like to know more about? Servers are notoriously closed-lipped, but a minor Guildsman who owes you a debt could be very useful."

"Could you arrange it?" Valerio asked. "No one would suspect you—especially not with the existing connection you two have."

"Of course," Arabella said. "I will say that she is a distant relative from my home villa." And she would make sure that Noula understood who she owed her loyalty to.

"Excellent," Valerio waved a hand at Noula. "Find one of my Servers. Tell them to feed you and give you a place to sit while you wait for your new benefactor."

Noula hurried out of the room, closing the door behind her. Arabella fixed a smile on her face as Valerio caressed it. She would not let him see her anger over being called Banio Fonti's cast-off—but she would never forget that he'd said it.

She lifted a hand to the ties on his shirt and gently undid one.

"Come to bed," she said as she slid a hand through his shirt and rested it on his chest.

KARA HADN'T BEEN outside the fence since the night Vook brought her home. Home. The docks had felt as much like a home as any she'd ever had. Here she'd been accepted for who she was and not scorned because she didn't have magic.

Pilo re-locked the gate while Vook scouted ahead. Lowel and Harb had left an hour ago, and now the sun was low in the sky. Harb had promised to look for a new place to live, but Kara didn't trust him. He still didn't believe the clammers were dangerous.

"It's clear," Vook whispered from the shadows. "This way." He started down a path at a trot.

Kara followed with Pilo close behind. They traveled for half an hour before Vook waved them to a stop. The three of them huddled behind a fallen willow tree. A giant wedge of mushroom grew beside her knee, and Kara broke a piece off and slipped it into her pack. Vook glared at her, and she shrugged. She'd brought her pack anyway—she didn't trust Harb not to steal from her, and this mushroom could be used in a compress to reduce swelling.

"There's one of them trees Harb was on about," Vook said. "I know it wasn't like this a month ago."

A tree, probably at one time a willow, swayed in the gentle breeze. Now, instead of long strands of leaves, white feathers fluttered in the wind. A light green mage mist circled the ground underneath the branches and twisted around the trunk. The wind picked up, and a feather drifted towards them. There was a bright flash of light, and a small, brown leaf dropped to the ground.

"The mad mage did this?" Kara asked.

"Don't know who else would have," Pilo replied. "Harb said one day the tree was just changed."

"The mad mage comes this far," Kara said. "We should look around here for a place to live. Maybe even under that tree?" It might scare the clammers off, but would it really be safe? "I'm going to get a closer look."

Kara steadied her pack on her shoulders and headed towards the feathered willow. Up close it was even more beautiful. In the glow of mage mist, the feathers cast eerie shadows on the ground. She stopped just outside the range of the mist and stared at the ghostly tree. Another feather floated towards her, and she caught it. She pulled her hand in to get a better look, and a flash of heat and light startled her. She dropped the feather, and by the time it hit the ground it was a leaf.

Tentatively she stepped closer to the tree. One step, then another—the green mist eddied away from her. Finally she reached out and touched the tree.

The bark was rough. She leaned in. It looked and smelled like a normal tree. But was it as safe as a normal tree? She concentrated and let the mist settle against her. Soon she was enveloped in mist so thick that she couldn't see the tree in front of her. She must have taken a step because she no longer felt rough bark beneath her hand. She turned to call out to Pilo and Vook, and suddenly the mist was gone.

She was in a clearing—there was no tree, no mage mist, and no Pilo and Vook. Where were they?

She spun around in confusion. There, that way—she took a step.

"Pilo, Vook," she called. There was no answer. The fallen tree they'd hidden behind should have been right here, but now there was nothing but sparse, dry grass. She looked behind her. There was no sign of the feathered willow. What had happened? Where was she?

She tried to retrace her path, but the sun had set and in the shadows nothing looked familiar. Had she come through birch trees? She must have, because here they were. She parted some bushes and edged around a huge oak, only to come up against a stone wall. Covered in moss, the rough stone was cool to her touch, and the top of the wall was a foot higher than her outstretched hands. She peered along the wall—it extended as far left and right as she could see.

How to get back to Pilo and Vook?

A few steps along the wall in each direction, and overgrown bushes and brambles blocked her path. She stepped out onto a grassy area. There must be a gate somewhere, a way to get to the other side of this wall. She *felt* like she needed to be on the other side of the wall—that the docks were outside of wherever she was.

She sniffed the air hoping for the salty tang of the bay, but all she smelled was dry grass and wild flowers. Water splashed off to her left so she headed towards the sound. A shadow loomed in the darkness, and she slowed. A fountain. Moonlight sparkled off the water as it trickled from an upper bowl into a wide basin. She sat down on the edge of the basin and dipped a cupped hand into the water. It tasted cool and fresh. She took another sip. She'd been drinking water hauled by Harb and Lowel for so long that she'd forgotten how lovely cool, fresh water could be. For a moment she longed for the mountain stream that ran near Mika and Allon's cabin.

She circled the fountain, peering outward, trying to decide which way led to the docks. By the time the sky started to lighten she still she had no idea which direction to go. She perched on the edge of the fountain to wait until true daylight. If she could find the coast of the island she could follow it to the docks. As long as she went in the right direction.

She'd been staring numbly at the fountain for half an hour before she realized that softly glowing words wrapped around the upper bowl. Mage light, very faint, the faintest she'd ever seen, traced the letters.

"The waters in this fountain will run fresh and clear while an heir of the First Guildsman holds this island," Kara read aloud as she walked around the fountain. "So pledges Numa Nimali, Master Mage, heir to Paolo Santonini." A mage named Nimali. He must be related to the Mage Primus who wrote her book.

"You really can read."

Kara whirled at the sound of the voice. Harb stood in front of her, his arms crossed over his chest and an angry look on his face.

"What are you doing here, whore?" he asked.

"I got lost," Kara said. "Pilo, Vook, and I were out looking for a new place to live. It was near the feather tree." Harb at least would know the way to the docks. "Is Lowel here too?" She peered past him in the dawn light.

"No," Harb said. He smiled a dangerous, predatory smile. "We're all alone."

"But you know the way home," Kara said. If Lowel had been with him she would have felt relieved to see them, but with just Harb . . . "I can help carry the water." She gestured to the two jugs he held in his hands.

"I'm not going to the docks with this water," Harb replied.

"You said you'd stop visiting the clammers," Kara said. "It's dangerous."

"No," Harb shouted. "*You* said I'd stop visiting the clammers. *You* said it was dangerous." He dropped the jugs on the grass and took a step towards her. "I'm in charge, I say what happens, not some pathetic runaway from the backside of nowhere."

"At least I've seen some of the world," she replied. "You're a runaway from right here on Old Rillidi, you've only seen what's here on this island."

Harb took two steps towards her. "I may not have seen much of the world but I know what to do with a whore."

Angry and frightened, Kara backed away from Harb and circled the fountain, keeping it between them. Harb was madder than she'd ever seen him. She couldn't go to the docks even if she could find her way there. Harb wouldn't leave her alone, not after this. She'd never feel safe—not to sleep, not to eat, not to do chores. But neither should Harb feel safe. In her pack she had half a dozen items that could be made into poison.

"Stay away from me. You know I'm mage trained. I know a curse or two."

"You don't have any magic," Harb sneered. "That's why you're here."

"Mage Guild doesn't just teach magic."

He hesitated, and she stepped backwards, increasing the distance between them. Slowly she reached into her pack. Her hand closed around the chunk of woody mushroom, and she crushed some of it in her fist before pulling her hand out.

"Are you going to bet your life that I don't have something that can hurt you?" Kara asked.

Harb's eyes narrowed, and he took two quick steps towards her. She flung the bits of mushroom—the wind caught them and blew them into his face. Harb sputtered and lurched to his knees, cursing.

Kara ran as fast as she could, away from the fountain, away from the wall, away from Harb. Anywhere was safer than there. She risked a peek over her shoulder. Harb was only a few steps behind her.

"I'll kill you, whore!" he shouted.

Kara shivered and kept running. It was not just a threat—Harb *would* kill her if he caught her.

She ran past the overgrown symmetry of a formal garden and onto a rutted path lined with tall oaks. She rounded a bend in the road and stopped. A dilapidated manor house, one half drooping and crumpled, sat beside the curved road. Another fountain, bigger and more ornate than the one she'd just run from, was centered in front of the house. And on the ground, surrounding the fountain, filling up all of the drive between it and the house, light green mage mist writhed and twisted. Nervously she peeked behind her. Harb slowed to a trot, then to a walk, a tight smile on his face.

"I've got you now," he said. "It's me or the mad mage."

"I'll take the mad mage." She took a few steps forward, toward the house. The mist parted for her. She turned to look behind— her path had already filled in.

Harb scowled and stepped forward, one step, two steps, then he disappeared.

There was a shout from off to her left, on the far side of the fountain. Harb was on his knees, on the lawn. Kara walked up to the fountain. A marble figure of Gyda tipped clear water from a ewer into the basin.

With an oath, Harb charged directly into the mage mist. This time his yell was from further away. He shook a fist and shouted, but his words were lost to the wind. Finally he turned and stalked, back to the other fountain and his water jugs.

Relieved and puzzled, Kara sat down on the lip of the fountain. The same thing that had happened to her at the feathered willow had just happened to Harb. They'd been . . . misdirected. By a spell? She'd let the mage mist envelop her, and then she'd been somewhere else.

Mist swirled around her feet, but didn't touch her. If she let it touch her, would it send her somewhere else? She didn't dare try it. Right now she was safe from Harb—she should stay here until she was sure he wasn't going to return.

She had water at least. And Vook had said that Mage Guild left food for the mad mage. She glanced up to the front door of the manor house. It would probably be left inside. Was she willing to risk meeting the mad mage for something to eat?

Kara studied the front of the house. Although mage mist filled the space between the fountain and the house and lapped at the walls, it thinned to nothing before it reached any of the windows.

Despite the disrepair, the house was still impressive. A wide stone staircase led up to double doors that were twice her height. The wood of the doors was weathered to silver, but they were still solid Grey field stone soared above the entrance, and two rows of windows ran across the length of the entranceway. To the left and right, red-tiled roofs sloped over stone extensions that curved out along the drive. To the left, the far side of the house had been reduced to rubble and a section of the roof was missing, but the wing on the right side looked intact, right down to the white curtains that hung in each window.

She settled her pack on her shoulders. The house was big—she should be able to steer clear of the mad mage. She'd stay to the ruined part of the house; surely he never went there.

When she ascended the stone steps, mage mist twisted away from every footfall. She pushed one door, and silently it swung inward, revealing a cracked tile floor. She stepped in and closed the door, pausing to let her eyes adjust to the gloomy interior.

The entrance hall was about twenty feet across. On each side there was a set of double doors, one opening to the left and one to the right. Directly opposite from where she stood was the bottom step of a grand marble staircase—ornate iron bannisters lined stairs that swept out and up in a curve.

The doors of the ruined wing opened onto a long hallway. Tall windows that faced the curved drive cast rectangles of light that guided Kara down the marble-floored hall. She'd passed a few closed doors when, at the fifth window, a breeze teased her hair. Up ahead the wall had fallen inward, and rubble and stone blocks lay tumbled across the floor. She looked up. The roof was intact for a few more steps, but beyond that she could see the lightening sky.

Kara opened the next door, the sixth along the corridor. Windows that lined the far wall let in just enough light to allow her to navigate around two tables and a long settee. She pulled aside a dusty curtain and peered out the grime-streaked window. Scrubby bushes partially blocked her view, but out beyond them was a stretch of overgrown lawn, and past that, she saw the waters of the bay. If she could get out to the rear of the house, she could follow the shoreline to the docks.

Except for the damage to the house there was no sign of the mad mage. This destruction happened a long time ago. If the mad mage didn't come in here anymore, could they stay here for a day or two? It had to be better than waiting for the clammers to arrive. She would look around a little more before getting the rest of them. Not Harb, though, she didn't want Harb here. And Lowel would stay with Harb.

Kara drew the curtains open on all the windows in the room and opened a few casements to air the room out. She dropped her pack on a wooden bench and sat down beside it. She pulled out her almost empty waterskin and took a small sip. She should have refilled it when she was at one of the fountains, but she'd been too distracted by Harb. She'd have to retrace her steps and fill her waterskin before she returned to the docks.

She poked around the room, opening any drawers or cupboards she came across. There were a couple of spoons and a cloth that looked reasonably clean, but that was all.

She finished searching the room and went back into the hall.

She'd investigate a few more rooms before looking for a way out of the house and into the garden.

She opened a door onto a room that was mostly intact. There was a dank smell, and the walls had water marks, but she found very little of interest anywhere. The next room she checked was a mess. Only half of the ceiling remained, and timbers and tiles had fallen from the second floor into this one. A mattress, which must have come from the room above, lay in the middle of the floor. A heap of dark rags and bedding was piled high in the corner nearest to her.

And the room crawled with mage mist. The other two rooms she'd searched had been clear, but here it was everywhere. She glanced around nervously. Was this a room the mad mage frequented, or was the mage mist here because of all the damage?

Cautiously, she walked around. Light green mist ebbed away from her, so thick and dense in places that she could barely see the tiles of the floor. She drew the curtains on one window and felt better when daylight spilled into the room.

She wandered to the corner that was piled high with rags. Here, black and dark gray mage mist swirled and twined. Every once in a while a few lighter colours, including the light green that blanketed the rest of the room, were visible in the writhing mass of mist. Something about this mist was familiar. She leaned toward the mist, her hand outstretched. Then the heap of rags moved.

"Gyda!" Kara backed away from it. The rags moved again, and then, incredibly, through the mage mist she saw two blue eyes staring out at her. The mad mage! She started to run, but her pack tugged her backwards, hard. He'd grabbed her! She struggled to slip her pack from her shoulders and turned towards her attacker.

Except he hadn't grabbed her at all. The mad mage continued to stare at her with sad eyes filled with pain and despair. She gripped her pack to leave again, but it tugged her towards the mage. She opened the pack and found Santos Nimali's journal alight with the same green mage mist that filled the room. She pulled the book out of her pack and heard a grunt of surprise.

"Mine," the Mage said. He reached a hand out, and a strand of mage mist shot towards her. His mouth opened in horror. "No," he cried. "No." The despair in his voice apparent.

But the green mist forked around her. It hit the door, sparking and sizzling as it charred the wood.

"You're not hurt," the Mage said.

He shifted and stood up, mage mist and dirty rags swirling around him.

"No." She shuddered. "What was that?"

"I can't control my magic," the mad mage replied. "I don't want to hurt anyone else. You must leave."

"That was a spell?" Kara asked. He could confirm that what she saw, that mage mist, was magic.

"That was a spell," the mad mage agreed. A brief spurt of green rushed out of his mouth and floated up two floors and out the gaping hole in the roof. He looked away, careful not to point in her direction. "Where did you get my book?"

"Your book?" Kara held the journal up. Mage mist crawled all over it, disturbed only where her hand touched it. Without thinking, she brushed the mist off the book, and it stopped tugging her toward the mage. "Then you're Santos Nimali."

"I was once," was the sad reply. "Now I'm simply the mad mage."

"You don't seem mad to me." He seemed quite lucid. She felt sorry for him.

"It wasn't enough for me to be mad," he said and sighed. "I had to realize my plight and not be able to do anything about it." He looked at her sharply. "You can read. Did Mage Guild send you?"

"No," Kara said. "I'm from the docks. I got lost and ended up over here. I thought I'd see if there was anything useful."

"Ah, so you were going to steal from me."

"No, I . . ." Kara stopped. "Well yes, all right. But I didn't think you'd miss anything I found. That's why I explored the damaged part of the house."

"Damaged." The Mage laughed, a sharp bitter sound. "By me. I don't remember doing it. Perhaps I passed gas, and a spell burst forth and tore the roof off. Or maybe I did it on purpose during one of my mad periods. I'll never know."

Santos Nimali, the mad mage, took a few steps towards her. There was a thick cloud of dark grey mage mist obscuring his face, and frustrated, Kara swept a hand out. A rope of mist shrank from her and dissipated. Now she had a view of a beaked nose and bushy white brows above startled blue eyes.

"What did you just do?" Santos asked. He moved closer and peered into her face. "Just now, with your hand. Tell me!"

Kara stepped back, unnerved by intensity in his eyes. Now he looked the part of a Primus of Mage Guild, now he looked like the most powerful man in Tregella. "I, uh," she paused. How to explain? "I just wanted to see your face."

"And you couldn't before?" he asked. "Why? What do you see when you look at me?"

"I'm not sure," she replied nervously. This Santos Nimali frightened her. She'd rather deal with the madness. She tucked his journal into her pack and took another step backwards. She was only three steps away from the door. He was an old man, she could outrun him.

Santos raised a hand and pointed it right at her.

"Stop right now, and I won't hurt you," he said.

She took another step away from him. He clenched his raised fist and pursed his lips.

"Stay there," he said. He opened his fist, and a stream of green flowed towards her.

Kara stared at the mist as it circled her feet. It cinched tighter until she stood inside a ring of green mage mist that was about knee high. She looked behind. Two more steps to the door. She stepped over the mist. Eyes forward again, she met the wondering gaze of Santos.

"Can you see the spell?" he whispered.

She took the final step backwards, then pulled the door open and ducked through it.

"Wait!"

She heard him call out, but she was already halfway down the hall. Santos sane was a dangerous man, she didn't want to stay and see what changes insanity brought.

She was out the front door a few moments later, running down the curved, rutted lane past the fountain and out over the unkempt lawn. When she looked behind her, there were no sign of Santos Nimali, no signs of pursuit.

She retraced her steps to the first fountain. Thankfully Harb was gone. She dipped a hand into the stream of fresh water and drank before she refilled her water skin.

The mad mage and Santos Nimali were one and the same. She studied words that edged the fountain. Santos Nimali owned Old

Rillidi—the whole island belonged to that mad, old man. No wonder there was so much chaos and lawlessness here. He was dangerous—he'd tried to use magic on her. It hadn't affected her, but he had sent a spell her way—a spell meant to capture her.

But now she knew for certain that mage mist was magic—and each mage had a different colour mist.

Santos Nimali's spells were grass green, like most of the mage mist she'd seen on Old Rillidi. Kara slumped over her pack, feeling the square shape of Santos Nimali's journal.

Now what she'd seen on her journey to Rillidi made sense. The mist that had followed her along the road and the mist that had clung to the body of Terach—they *were* spells. And they were the same colour as the mist that surrounded Valerio Valendi—a dark grey that was almost black. He'd sent a spell to kill her, but it had killed Terach—another Mage Guild runaway.

And her mother had expected Valerio Valendi to kill her—her *problem*—a child who had no magic.

Except that she *did* have magic. Maybe she couldn't do magic, but she could see it. And *undo* it. That's what she'd done to Nimali's journal, that's what she'd done to Nimali's face. She'd waved her hand and dispersed the spell. Too excited to sit, Kara paced around the fountain.

What if she could undo magic? Could she find work? Could she join a guild? Not Mage Guild, never that. She was dead to them, and she needed to stay that way. But what about another guild?

She sat down on the edge of the fountain. There must be another guild who would want someone who could undo magic, who could use her against Mage Guild. One that would never tell her secret—Mage Guild would never let her live if they found out about her talent,

Would she be willing to become a tool in order to gain the safety and protection of a guild? Not for herself, but for Vook and the others, yes. They had no chance at a real future, and she couldn't bear to watch Vook turn into Harb, a mean, angry youth with no hope. Yes, she would become a weapon if that was required. She would do that, for the others.

According to Mika, Warrior Guild had Assassins—they would want her. But could she approach them and ask them if they could use her? Was she willing to deal with Assassins?

She sat down. She couldn't worry about that, not yet, not when she didn't understand her abilities. She'd need to figure out exactly what she could and couldn't do before she even considered offering her services to anyone, including Warrior Guild. Especially Warrior Guild.

Santos Nimali had asked her if she could see the spell. Did he know about mage gifts like hers? Should she trust him? She pulled his journal from her pack. She'd read about him—his words, his thoughts, his goals—before she decided if she could trust him, if she wanted to help him. Because she had the ability to undo the spells that surrounded him. He knew. That's why he'd tried to stop her.

What had he said to her? That it wasn't enough to be mad, he had to realize his plight and understand his own inability to change things. A terrible reality for a man who at one time was the most powerful person in all Tregella. And his madness was deliberate—someone had used magic to make him mad.

She sucked in her breath—she knew who. The mage mist had been familiar. The dark grey that twined around him and obscured his head and face was the colour of Mage Secundus Valerio Valendi's magic.

Perhaps the journal would tell her why Valerio Valendi had cursed the Mage Primus into madness. She opened it to the first page and leaned over the book.

Chapter twelve

HER STOMACH GROWLED as she squinted at the spidery script. She'd read all day, desperate to determine how dangerous the mad mage was. The moon was a sliver but the faint light of the mage mist that circled the fountain was enough for her to read by. A sound from the other side of the fountain startled her, and she almost dropped the book into the water.

Two yellow eyes peered at her from across the fountain—a cat. It sat on the edge of the lower basin and stared at her, its tail swishing angrily. Eventually it leaned in and licked at the stream of water that flowed from the upper bowl. Finished, it sat on its haunches and watched her. After a moment, it began to groom itself. Kara stared as the pink tongue lapped the grey fur, over and over again. With a trill, the cat jumped off the edge of the fountain and disappeared into the night.

Were there more animals—dangerous animals—out there? The fence at the docks kept them so safe that she'd never had to worry about it.

Water on the island was scarce. That's why Harb and Lowel came here for it, why they could trade it to the clammers for time with their women. Animals had the same limited options.

Had she waited too long? Was it too dark to find her way to the docks?

She put the book in her pack before following the path to the house.

The manor was dark except for the trails of mage mist that swirled from the base of the fountain to the door. It cast an eerie glow over the shadowed destruction, and she wondered where Nimali was—and whether he was still sane or had descended into madness.

It would be safer to wait for dawn to search for the shore line. She might have to go through the house, and she didn't want to come across the mad mage in the dark.

Kara sat down with the fountain between her and the house. The mage mist—*the magic spells*—simply flowed around her. The spells must have been set to keep people away from the house. They had kept Harb from reaching her so she hoped they kept animals away too.

She lay down and pillowed her head on her pack. It was closer to the house than she liked, but this was the safest place she could think of. The mad mage didn't want her hurt, he wanted her help. And if his mind was gone, well, she'd have to trust that her talent would keep her safe from his uncontrolled magic.

KARA ROLLED OVER and tucked her hand up by her chin. Her fingers scraped dirt, and her cheek butted up against something hard and unyielding in her pack. Her mug. She shifted her head until her cheek rested on something softer and tried to settle back into sleep.

The wind picked up, sending a spattering of water drops onto her head and face, and she opened her eyes and sat up. The base of the fountain was directly in front of her, and beyond it, beyond the roiling mage mist, was the door to the house.

The sun was low—it must be early morning. Her stomach clenched—a reminder that she hadn't eaten for a while. She rummaged in her pack and brought out the chipped porcelain mug. Two mugfuls of water from the fountain didn't ease her hunger, but at least she could think of something other than food.

Kara put the mug into her pack and walked through the mage mist. In case Santos Nimali was watching, she stayed as far away from the windows as possible as she circled the intact wing of the house to the garden.

She followed the crash of waves to the shoreline. A crumbled boathouse stood sentinel over pilings that stretched out into the bay. A few stray planks were all that was left of the deck, and no overturned boats were conveniently beached and ready for occupation. The water of the bay was a blue-green, and there was a cool breeze. No shelter, although it might be a good fishing spot for Vook. She glanced back—it might be too close to the house, though.

She skirted along the edge of the grounds as far from the house as the tangled shrubs and bushes allowed. A back door, probably to the kitchen, led out onto a bedraggled garden. Even from where she stood, she recognized peppers and the trailing vines of grapes. There were even some mountain berries growing wild beside the house. If they dared, they could replace some of what they'd be forced to leave behind in Pilo's garden. With winter approaching, they had to gather as much food as they could.

The damage to the house looked even more extensive from here. Just before she drew even with the worst of the destruction, she stopped and crouched low beside a shrub.

The large windows of the room where she'd found Santos Nimali face directly out here. She wished she'd never opened the curtains, but if she hadn't she might never have seen the mad mage—she might have stayed in the house and even now would be his captive.

Kara returned to the boat house and followed the shore away from the house. Eventually she'd find the docks and bring Vook and the rest of them here. She didn't want to think about not being able to stay here. Trusting Harb and the clammers was not an option, nor could she just leave the rest of them to that fate. So this *had* to become their safe haven.

It was so well hidden behind a thicket of willow trees and brambles and—thank Gyda—an orange tree, that she almost missed it.

It was the oranges that drew her. Birds had been at them, and the sweet, citrus scent on the wind made her mouth water. She grabbed the first whole orange she saw and tore into it, letting the sticky juice run down her chin. The orange was gone in moments, and she opened her eyes to search for another. And there, through the branches, was what she'd been looking for, more than what she'd hoped for—a cabin.

It was small, one room, maybe two, but it was intact. The dark green paint wasn't peeling, the roof didn't sag, and no shingles were missing. It blended in with the trees and foliage perfectly.

A very fine mage mist ghosted around the structure—grass green mist. Did the spell keep people out, or did it keep the structure sound? The rear and sides of the cabin had no windows, so she crept to the front, the side that faced the bay. A small door was set into the left corner, dwarfed by a large clear window that covered most of the front of the structure.

Kara peered in. A layer of dust covered the floor even though the window itself sparkled as if freshly scrubbed. More mage mist filmed across it, possibly the reason the window was unbroken and clean.

She tapped on the window, and a bird cried out from a nearby tree, but nothing moved inside. She edged over to the door and gently pushed it inward. Dusty air puffed out past her, and she wrinkled her nose. The cabin hadn't been aired in ages—no one had been here for a very long time. She toed the dust on the floor in front of the door. It might even be years since anyone had been inside.

Excited and nervous, she entered the cabin, leaving the door wide open. Sunlight spilled in, illuminating the floor tiles. She squinted to see through the dust motes that floated in the sunbeams—the floor had a faint pattern—squares inset with flowers—and a small kitchen ran along half of the rear wall. There was an open hearth for cooking, and was that a pump? She kicked up dust in her haste to get to it and coughed. More green mage mist swirled around the pump. She pulled on the handle and grinned when clear water began to flow from the spout into the basin below it.

"Gyda bless you, Santos Nimali," she whispered. Her own source of water on an island where it was the most precious thing to have and the most dangerous thing to get!

She pulled her chipped mug from her pack and filled it. The water was cool and sweet when she tasted it. They wouldn't even need Harb, not that she would allow him in here.

Except for a wooden bench that was pushed up against the far wall, the room was bare of furniture. Kara paused in front of the window. It was a spectacular view and no doubt why the cabin had been built. Through the trees she could see a rocky shoreline and beyond that, the clear blue of Pontus Bay. In the distance was another island. She could see some buildings at the edge of the land and the movement of people as they carried on with their lives.

She put her mug on the counter by the pump and opened a cupboard door at the end of the counter.

It wasn't a cupboard at all; it was a separate sleeping chamber. Nearly as big as the main room, this one had furniture. In fact, it had all the furniture for the whole cabin.

A big bed, its mattress rolled up to the head board, took up a third of the space. A small table stood beside it, and four chairs were scattered at the other end of the room. A cushioned bench and two comfortable chairs were shoved into the far corner. A big stone fireplace stretched across the wall that was directly behind the kitchen. A few split logs were stacked beside it, but there was no residue of ash in the grate.

Santos Nimali had made this cabin. At least he had used magic on it—his green mage mist was everywhere. But it didn't look lived in. Had he forgotten about it in his madness? She was willing to take a chance that he had. It was the best, most secure place to live that she could think of—right under the nose of the mad mage, yet not in his sights. And there was magic here, keeping the structure sturdy and whole, and a source of water.

She'd bring Pilo, Vook, Sidra, and Mole here—they'd move the furniture around and make it a real home.

ARABELLA LOOKED UP from her desk when Annya, her Server, announced the visitor.

"Noula," Arabella said. She didn't bother to stand as the other woman bowed.

"You asked to see me, Master Mage?" Noula asked, twisting her hands in her skirt.

Arabella waited until Annya left the room, closing the door behind her, before she put down the paper she was reading.

"Yes, I wanted to see if you were settled." She'd placed the woman in Castio's household a few days ago—a favour for a distant relative from her home Villa, she'd said when she'd pleaded for his help. She'd had to hide her amusement when he'd agreed. She'd promised to return the favour of course—and depending on where her interests lay, she might even do it.

"Yes, Donna," Noula replied. "I'm settled in. But . . . I'm sorry, I'm not actually in Mage Castio's home. I'm to help school Mage Etta's children. They're little, like my Osten."

"Etta, of course," Arabella said. She knew who the woman was, but hadn't realized how close she was to Castio. Unless . . . "And has Castio asked you to keep him informed of Etta's activities?"

"No, Donna," Noula paused. "But he did spend last night in her home."

"Ah, I see. And the children, they are Castio's?"

"I think so, Donna," Noula replied. "He seems fond of them."

"And of Etta as well, no doubt," Arabella said. She'd ask Valerio if he knew about Etta. On second thought, she'd ask Rorik. No need to give Valerio information. If Rorik already knew this, she could assume Valerio did as well. And if this was news to Rorik, it would be another secret to tie them closer.

"Noula," Arabella. "I hope that you appreciate everything both Secundus Valendi and I are doing for you."

"Yes, Donna," Noula said. "I am so very grateful for your help placing both me and my son."

"Would you like to visit your son?"

"Oh Donna, that would be beyond my expectations."

"I will arrange it," Arabella said. "If you let me know if you see or hear anything unusual."

"I promise," Noula said. "Of course I promise. When can I see my son?"

"I'll let you know in a few days," Arabella replied. She had to find out where he was. She couldn't ask Valerio, but Rorik might know.

Noula left, and Arabella returned to the papers she had been studying. She didn't expect the woman to learn anything important—at least not more important than the fact that Castio had a family—but she wanted Noula to be hers, not Valerio's.

KARA LEFT FOR the docks at dusk. And for the first time in a long time, her belly was full. She'd eaten tart apples and carrots from an overgrown vegetable garden. More vegetables—squash, potatoes, and chives—nestled between weeds, and there was evidence of small visitors everywhere. If Vook could catch a rabbit, they'd eat meat, instead of their steady supply of fish.

For over half an hour she followed the rocky shoreline,

ducking into the brush once when a boat came close to the shore. The boat, filled with stern-faced men carrying swords, rounded the tip of Old Rillidi Island and headed towards the island across the bay. She didn't move again until it was out of sight.

The stone wall that surrounded the estate had crumbled into the bay, and Kara easily scrambled over it. Dense forest edged up to an empty beach that soon gave way to tumbled rocks, and she was forced to move into the trees.

The moon was up now, but very little light filtered through the trees. Finally, after over an hour, she came across a fence made of familiar metal mesh.

She followed the fence to the corner—the gate was closed. Who had the key tonight? Pilo? Or maybe Vook? She hoped it wasn't in Harb's possession, or, even worse, the clammers.

On hands and knees she crawled alongside the fence towards the gate. There, that flickering light had to be the fire pit. She crept forward, edged behind a tree, and dropped to her stomach. She could clearly see the fire pit now.

Three figures sat around the fire. One was Harb. She watched him take a drink from a mug and hold it up to the person beside him. It was a woman—her pale skin shone ghostly in the fire light, and her hair hung down her back in dark, matted clumps. A clammer. Harb placed an arm around her bare shoulders, and she laughed, a low animal sound, and leaned into him to drink from the mug. When she leaned over, Kara got a good look across the fire. Mole sat slumped on a log, his head in his hands as he squinted against the glare of the flames.

"Fire's getting low, Mole," Harb barked without even looking at the boy.

Mole stood up, and Kara stifled a gasp. There was a collar around Mole's neck with a rope attached. Dirty-grey mage mist twisted around the collar. The clammers had magic? Mole walked until his rope was taut, and then he stretched his arms out towards a wood pile.

"I can't reach it anymore, Harb," Mole said. "You gotta untie me."

"And have you try to run away again?" Harb got up and stomped past Mole to the woodpile. He kicked the wood. "Here, now you can reach." A piece hit Mole on the knee, and the boy grunted.

"Next time get out of my way," Harb said.

He knocked into Mole on his way back to the fire, sending the boy tumbling to the ground.

"Make sure that fire is nice and bright by the time I get back." Harb reached down to the clammer woman and pulled her up. She snuggled into his side as they headed towards the boat.

Mole spent a few minutes pulling wood over to the fire before he started tugging desperately on the rope.

"Mole," Kara whispered as loud as she dared. "Mole." The boy didn't look her way.

She found a rock and tossed it over the fence. It landed with a thud near the boy.

"Mole."

This time he heard her and came as close as the rope allowed. Close enough for her to see scratches and a bruise on his face.

"Kara?" he asked.

She nodded, and his small shoulders slumped in relief.

"Harb said you were dead, that the mad mage got you."

"He lied," Kara said. "Are the others all right? Vook, Pilo, and Sidra?"

"Mostly," Mole said. "Harb tied them up on the other side of the boat. He makes Lowel watch them."

"How many clammers?"

"Just two women. One for Harb and one for Lowel." Mole made a face. "They smell bad. They take them into the boat and afterward Harb and Lowel smell bad too."

"Where's the key?" She had to get in somehow, had to free them. Just two clammers. She didn't think it would stay that way for long.

"Harb's got it. Never takes it off, not even when he's with one of them women." Mole glanced over his shoulder. "There's a way inside the fence. At the corner nearest the mad mage." He backed up towards the fire.

"You got that fire going yet?"

Harb had returned with the clammer woman in tow. His eyes shone dully in the firelight. He stretched and closed his eyes, and the clammer woman kneaded his shoulders. Harb groaned in pleasure as her hands slid over him. He shifted slightly, and Kara got a good look at the woman's face. It was feral and dangerous and full of hatred for the man she was touching. Harb opened his eyes, and she smiled sweetly up at him.

Mole stared across the fire. His gaze met Kara's for a moment, and he blinked, once. Kara nodded and slowly backed away from the fire pit. She'd head to the corner and search for the way inside the fence.

EVEN THOUGH HE'D told her where to look, Kara still had a difficult time finding the tunnel that ran under the fence—then it took her half an hour to clear out enough earth for her to fit through it. By the time she'd wriggled through the tunnel she was covered in dirt, her hair was a tangled mess, and most of her fingernails were broken. She dragged her pack out and looked up at the sky. It was almost dawn, and she was exhausted. A few steps away from the fence she wedged herself up against a fallen log and fell asleep.

Chapter thirteen

KARA WOKE SLOWLY, lifted her head off her pack, and quietly sat up. The air was still, and she could feel the heat of the sun despite the leafy canopy overhead. She'd slept longer than she'd intended—it was already late afternoon. Harb and Lowel used to sleep right until dark, before they had hostages to watch—or clammers in camp. Would they still be asleep?

She took a small sip from her water skin and rummaged for the orange she'd put in her pack yesterday. She grabbed a small packet along with the orange. Which herb was that? She smelled it. Thyme—it was good for coughs and indigestion. Too bad Harb, Lowel, and the clammer women didn't have a bad case of indigestion. She paused. What else did she have in here?

She quickly spilled the contents of her pack onto the ground and started to sort through her herbs. She sniffed, discarding one after another. She opened one packet and dipped a finger into it. She could not make a mistake, not with so much at stake. She tasted just a little and then spat it out. Squill. She stuffed the rest of the herbs back into her pack, leaving that one small packet at the top. She ate the orange—she was ready.

Now that she was inside the fence, Kara kept trees between her and the fire pit. Lowel was there. He leaned against a tree and idly watched as Pilo set a pot of water into the fire. Like Mole the night before, Pilo wore a collar that was tied to a rope. The same dirty-gray mage mist swirled around the collar.

"Is there any fish for the stew?" Pilo asked. She straightened and looked at Lowel. "Harb was pretty mad about not having any for last night."

"I'll find Vook," Lowel said. "And see what he's got. Don't want Harb mad again tonight." Lowel left his post by the tree and ambled off in the direction of Vook's favourite fishing spot.

Kara waited a minute before she crept forward on hands and knees. She peered out from behind a tree.

"Pilo."

The girl's head came up slightly, then carefully she looked behind her. She backed up a few steps until she was at Kara's tree.

"Mole said he saw you," Pilo said.

She let her hand trail down the trunk, and Kara grabbed it. Pilo sighed and leaned her head against the tree.

"I wasn't sure I could believe him."

"I'm here. I'm not leaving without you," Kara said. "All of you. The rest of the clammers will be here soon, is my guess."

"Harb still says no," Pilo said. "He and Lowel have been rutting with the clammer women so much I think they've spilled their brains out along with their seed."

"Lowel never had much in the way of brains anyway," Kara said.

Any sympathy she'd had for Lowel was gone. He wasn't very bright, but he knew right from wrong. And keeping Vook, Pilo, and the others tied up was *wrong*. Once she helped them escape the clammers could come for Harb and Lowel. Then they'd realize what they'd been leading them all into.

"Pilo, I have something I need you to add to their food," Kara said.

"I hope it's poison." Pilo's voice was hard. "I hope it kills them. I hate them. Especially the clammers. I think they really do eat their own babies. The way they look at Mole makes my skin crawl."

"Here," Kara said. She pulled the packet of dried squill from her pack. "Add it to the stew. It won't kill them, not quite." At least she hoped it wouldn't. It could make them sick enough that they'd wish they were dead, though. "Make sure none of you eat."

"Don't worry. They eat first, Harb, Lowel, and the clammers.

We get what's left. If there is anything." Pilo took the packet and slipped it into her shirt.

"I'll come back after dark," Kara said. "They should get sick right away."

Kara crept into the woods. She watched Pilo dump the packet contents into the pot. She hadn't liked the look on the girl's face when she'd been talking about killing Harb and Lowel. Even now Pilo's face was full of fury as she stirred the stew.

Kara ducked lower when Lowel returned carrying two small fish. He stood a few feet away while Pilo used a small knife to clean and gut them. Had Pilo tried to escape already? Kara had been gone for only a few days—what in Gyda's name had Harb done to them?

Pilo continued to fuss about the stew while Lowel dozed, leaning against the tree. The shadows of the trees grew longer, and Kara moved a little closer to the fire pit.

A clammer woman, one she hadn't seen before, strolled into view. She cast a disdainful look at Pilo, whose face tightened in anger, and wandered towards Lowel. She stopped in front of him, cupped her breasts, and started to undulate her hips. Lowel licked his lips and turned to face her, a slow, sleepy smile on his face.

"Yes, you enjoy yourself, Lowel," Kara whispered.

Lowel's jaw went slack as the clammer woman reached out and cupped his groin.

"This might be the last time you ever feel this good." Kara shook her head as the clammer woman dropped to her knees, pulled Lowel's trousers down and pressed her face into him.

Kara looked from the ecstatic Lowel over to Pilo. The girl franticly stirred the stew, her gaze focused on the pot in front of her. Lowel grunted once, loudly, and Kara glared at him in disgust. Had he and Harb been rutting in front of the rest of them? No wonder Pilo hated them so much.

The clammer stood up as Lowel fixed his clothes. She gave him a smile and sauntered over to Pilo. Pilo's face was as still as stone, but Kara could almost feel the fury that she held in check. The clammer grinned and touched a finger to Pilo's collar. It flared with mage mist, and Kara sucked in a breath. This clammer definitely had magic. How had they escaped the Mage Guild's notice? Or were they too depraved even for them?

Pilo's eyes widened, but she refused to acknowledge the clammer's presence. The woman simply grinned more widely and leaned over the pot and sniffed.

Gyda, don't let her eat anything yet, Kara prayed. They had to all eat together! She sighed in relief when the clammer returned to Lowel and wrapped her arms around him. Lowel leaned down and kissed her, long and deep. When he lifted his head, Kara saw another puff of mage mist around his head. The clammers were using magic on Harb and Lowel. The mist disappeared, and Lowel turned glassy eyes towards Pilo.

"Stew ready yet?" he called. "We've worked up an appetite." Sleepily, he looked down at the clammer.

"Me too." Harb walked into Kara's view, the other clammer woman pulled tight against his chest. "And it better be good tonight. I'm not in a generous mood."

Pilo edged as far away from him as the rope allowed.

Harb grabbed a mug from beside the fire and scooped out some stew. He blew on it before bringing the mug to his lips. He took a sip and grunted.

"Fish. Good." He nodded.

The clammer woman at his side picked up a second mug and dipped it into the pot. She carefully carried her mug of stew to the log and sat down. Lowel and the other woman came over and filled their own mugs. Soon all four were eating. Harb got a second helping, and the rest copied him.

Kara relaxed. Two mugs each—that should be enough to make them very ill. It wouldn't be long now.

Darkness had settled on the fire pit, and Kara started to creep closer, keeping to the shadows. The light from the fire flickered over expressions that changed from sated to uneasy.

"I don't feel so good, Harb," Lowel said. He leaned to the other side of the log and retched.

One of the clammer women copied him, clutching at her stomach.

"What have you done, whore?" Harb took an unsteady step towards Pilo. "I'll kill you."

"Not if you're dead you won't," Pilo said. She circled away from him and laughed. "That's right, Harb, you're going to die."

Harb dropped to his knees and gasped in agony. "You'll die if we die." He vomited. "No one will be here to untie you."

The last clammer was on her stomach in the dirt, her mouth open and a puddle of vomit in front of her.

Kara hurried to Pilo.

"You!" Harb grunted and tried to get to his feet. "I'm gonna kill you too."

"No you won't," Kara said. She grabbed the knife and sawed through the rope as close to Pilo's neck as she dared. "You're going to be spewing and shitting so much you won't be able to stand up for hours."

"You need the key," Harb sneered. "And I'm not going to let you have it."

"I didn't need the key to get in here, did I?" Kara said.

Pilo took the knife and ran to the boat, Kara hurrying after her. Harb's shout turned into a gag, and soon all she could hear behind her was groaning and coughing.

Pilo was already on the far side of the boat by the time Kara got there. Vook, Sidra, and Mole were tied together, mage mist swirling faintly around their collars.

She turned to Pilo. "Let me get these off you."

"No," Pilo said. She covered her collar with her hands. "If we try to untie them, they just get tighter."

"They've been spelled," Kara said. "At least one of the clammers can do magic." She lifted a hand and waved away the mage mist. "Let me see."

Pilo dropped her hands, and Kara traced her finger all the way around the collar. When no hint of mist was left, she started to untie the leather straps. The collar dropped to the ground.

"What did you do?" Pilo asked.

"I'll tell you later," Kara said. She already had her hand at Vook's neck. "Once we're safe."

"I got it," Vook said when Kara started to untie his collar. His hands made quick work of the knot, and once it was off he flung the collar into the woods. In a few more moments Sidra and Mole were free as well.

"Let's go," Kara said. "Back the way I came in." She grabbed Sidra's hand, and they started towards the fire pit. "Be quiet and don't talk to any of them."

The fire was dying, but Kara could still make out the four bodies that lay strewn on the ground. She wrinkled her nose at the smell of shit. The secondary effects of the squill had begun.

"I'm going to kill them," Pilo said. She split off from the group and headed towards one of the fallen forms. She raised her hand, and firelight glinted off the knife she held.

"Don't," Kara hissed. The knife stopped at the height of its arc. "You'll be as bad as them." The knife wavered, and then Pilo slowly lowered her hand.

"You're lucky I can't be bothered, Harb," Pilo said. She spat on his still form. "You piece of filth."

They heard a shout from the direction of the gate. One of the clammer women drew her hand across her neck and laughed.

"Run," Kara yelled. "Follow Mole, he knows the way."

The five of them took off through the trees, Kara following a few paces behind the small group. Vook slowed and dropped back beside her.

"Clammers?" he asked.

"Must be," Kara replied.

"They'll kill Harb and Lowel," Vook said. "Serves them right."

"Shhh, they'll know we've gone this way." She touched his arm and veered to the right, towards the bay. She wanted to draw the clammers off, give the younger ones time to reach the tunnel.

A few minutes later, Kara heard hurried footfalls behind them. How many were following them? She picked up a twig and gently snapped it in half. They had to follow her and Vook so the others had time to get outside the fence.

Vook found his own branch and copied her. They heard the sounds of pursuit, and they both ran as fast as they could through the darkened woods. Kara's pack snagged on a branch, and she almost lost it trying to rip it free.

There, the fence. They could follow it to the corner. She slowed to a walk and grabbed Vook's shirt. Stealth was what was needed now. She edged along the fence quietly, Vook behind her.

"They'll try to swim around the fence," a male voice said from behind them.

Kara stopped, her heart pounding. She wiped her hands on her trousers, praying to Gyda that they all went towards the bay.

"I'll set a finder on them," another voice said, this one female.

Through the trees Kara saw a glow moving towards them. Mage mist! The clammers had sent a spell after them. She grabbed a startled Vook and hugged him tight. The reddish mist drifted through the trees towards them. Concentrating, she waved a hand at the mist. It hovered and then shifted direction, moving towards the docks.

"No sign of them," the female voice said. "They must have gone to the water."

A branch snapped as the clammers moved away from them.

"Come on." Kara let go of Vook and stepped up to the fence. She trailed a hand along it as they stumbled through the brush towards the corner.

"Kara, is that you?"

She stopped and peered ahead. "Pilo?" It was too dark to see more than a few feet in front of her.

"Yeah," Pilo replied. "We're outside the fence. Hurry."

Kara knelt and stretched out a hand, searching for the tunnel.

"Vook, here." She edged away so he could get past her. "You need to crawl."

Vook disappeared, and Kara squatted on the ground. She could hear him rustling as he wriggled through the tunnel.

"I'm out," he whispered.

Kara felt for the opening in front of her and wriggled into it. The damp earth closed in on her and for a moment panic set in. Then she slowed her breathing and started to push herself through with her feet. Hands reached for her arms, and she was pulled up and out of the tunnel.

"Someone's coming," Pilo whispered. "Hurry."

Off to their left, *outside* the fence, Kara heard tree branches snapping and brush rustling.

"Mole," Kara leaned over to the small boy. "You lead." He was the smallest, so would be slow, but he could see in the dark better than the rest of them.

Kara shoved Sidra's hand into Mole's. Pilo went next, then Vook, and then Kara. As quietly and quickly as possible they headed off into the woods towards the mad mage's estate, directly away from whoever was in the woods.

Ten minutes, that was all the time they had before there was a shout from behind them.

"Go, Mole, run!" Kara called. But they could only go as fast as six year old Mole.

They gained some ground until Sidra tripped. Pilo yanked her to her feet, and they kept running. A loud thud and a curse sounded from close by. The clammers weren't doing much better than they were.

Kara scrambled over a fallen log and then halted.

"Mole, stop." Ahead was the feathered willow—mage mist illuminated the clearing. Mole stopped just in front of the edge of the mist.

"Stay close to me," Kara said. She caught up with, them and they huddled around her.

"This is where you disappeared," Vook said. "One minute you were under the tree and then next you were gone."

"Yes. There's magic here." She stepped into the mist, concentrating on keeping it away from her. When she had a spot cleared, she waved the others to her. "Keep close." She herded them forward a few steps until the mage mist surrounded them. She waved her hands to keep the mist from getting closer.

"They're all here," a voice called.

A man stood at the edge of the clearing. His long hair lay matted across his bare chest, and his rough trousers were belted with rope. Two other clammers joined him, a man and a woman.

"They're waiting all nice and quiet for us," one of them said.

Kara eased her little group further toward the tree. The clammers would have to walk into the mist, into the *spell*, in order to reach them.

"I'll get them." One of the men walked towards them. He took two steps before he disappeared.

"What did you do?" the other male clammer demanded. "Where'd you send Osai?"

"I didn't do anything," Kara replied.

As she spoke she continued to slowly shepherd the children away from the clammers. Now they were directly under the willow tree. Feathered branches fluttered in the wind.

"Let me," the woman said.

A small puff of rust red mage mist left her hand. It met the mage mist in the meadow with a bright flare. Mole cried out and hid his head against Kara's side.

"It should be fine now," the woman said.

Kara smiled as she started towards them. She got two steps past where the man had disappeared before she too was gone.

"Lelee!" the remaining clammer shouted.

"You can join them," Kara called out. She wasn't sure they'd all end up in the exact same place but she really didn't care. "Just walk towards us."

Even while she talked, Kara kept them all moving. Now they were past the feather tree, and in a few more steps they'd be out of the mage mist. She stopped the little group, and they all huddled together.

"Are we going to disappear too?" Sidra asked.

Kara stroked the girl's hair. "No, we're going to stay right here."

The last clammer looked at them uncertainly. After a few minutes, he headed left, back the way he'd come. Kara let out a deep breath. Gyda, she hoped he wasn't circling around through the woods.

"Let's go." She edged them out of the mage mist. "I've found a safe place for us."

They headed towards the shoreline, a single line of children holding hands to keep everyone together. Mole led the way, with Kara right behind, then Sidra, Pilo, and Vook.

Kara made them stop once, when she thought they were close to Harb's fountain. Vook scouted ahead, but he saw no signs of the clammers so Kara urged the little group on.

The moon was high in the night sky by the time she spotted the little cabin. It was lit by mage mist and moonlight and already looked like home.

"We're here," Kara said. "Wait."

She pulled ahead of Mole and pushed her way through some bushes and sighed. The cabin was quiet, and there were no signs it had been disturbed in her absence.

"What is it?" Pilo asked from her side. "Is there a cave or something?"

"You don't see it?" Kara asked. Pilo was frowning and squinting in the direction of the cabin. "It's right here."

She grabbed Pilo's hand and pulled her forward, placing the girl's hand on the side of the cabin.

"I can feel it," Pilo said. She bent her head to her hand. "I think I see something. Yes, I see wood." Pilo took a step back and looked up. "I see it now. Is it magic?"

"I think so," Kara said. She'd hoped that the mage mist kept the cabin whole and secret. It was good to know that the latter was true. "You can see it?"

"Now, yes," Pilo said. She trailed her hand along the side of the cabin to the corner. "I can see the whole thing. There's the door. Is it safe to go in?"

"Yes, I'll bring everyone else." She turned to find Mole, Sidra, and Vook right behind her.

"I don't need to see it," Vook said. "Not right now. I just want to be inside."

"Come on." Kara took hold of Mole and Sidra. Vook stayed close behind. In moments they were all inside the little cabin. Moonlight spilled in through the windows.

Kara rummaged in her pack, wishing she'd thought to look for a lamp or candles earlier. She had a flint but nothing to light.

"We're stuck with the dark I'm afraid," she said. "But there's water." She walked over to the kitchen and pumped enough water for everyone to have their share. Then they all settled down to sleep. The floor was hard, and her belly was empty, but they were safe.

THE PRIMUS STOOD when she entered his study.

Arabella thought the man's home was a little underwhelming. It had none of the dramatic opulence of Valerio Valendi's huge estate or even the quiet elegance of her own small house.

A scarred desk took up much of the space in the room and bookshelves lined two walls—books and scrolls overflowing the shelves.

"Ah, Arabella, so kind of you to visit," Rorik said. He wrote a few words in a small journal and waved a hand over the page before closing the book. He slid it to one side and gestured to a small wooden chair that sat beside the table. "Please, sit down."

"Thank you, Primus, but I will not detain you." She smiled and clasped her hands in front of her. She was wearing an expensive pale blue silk dress—one she wasn't going to risk damaging on the rickety chair he indicated.

"I know it's not grand," Rorik apologized. "But my study is completely shielded. We can talk freely here."

"Of course," Arabella replied, her opinion of Rorik rising. That was something she'd not thought about. "Can the shielding be detected?" A shielded room could raise the suspicions of the wrong people. In her case, Valerio Valendi.

"Probably, but this is my workroom—it's understandable that I would shield it. I wouldn't want to put anyone else at risk when

I test out new spells."

"That makes sense," Arabella replied. She would shield her own workroom as soon as she returned home. "Thank you."

Rorik inclined his head. "But that is not what you wished to see me about."

"No. I have learned that Castio keeps a family, and I was wondering if you knew the Mage involved. Her name is Etta."

"I know her, of course," Rorik replied. "Quite lovely, although she is only a minor talent. She's from a non-mage lineage—her brother is Warrior Guild. She's often part of negotiations with them."

"She's a spy?" Arabella asked, surprised.

"I wouldn't put it that way," Rorik replied. "But she was Warrior Guild until she was twelve so she knows many who are currently rising to power. I had not known about her and Castio."

He seemed sincere, but Arabella didn't know Rorik well enough to recognize if he was lying. She met his gaze, and he did not look away. "I have a spy of my own—in her household," she said, watching Rorik. His pupils dilated. *This* was news to him.

"I see," he said and nodded. "Castio spends much time there, does he?"

"So I hear," she replied. "It intrigued me. In my home villa we all live as families but here—Castio is the first Master Mage I know who does that."

"It is unusual," Rorik agreed. "But not forbidden. The Primus before me lived with a wife."

"Did he? I hadn't heard that." She hadn't heard much about Primus Nimali. No one wanted to talk about him. At least not to her. "What happened to her? When he died." As with Council Members, the Primus was appointed for life—Rorik was Primus so Nimali must be dead.

"She died," Rorik said. "Some say she was assassinated."

"What do you say?"

Rorik sighed and leaned back in his chair. "It doesn't matter what I say," he said. "She is dead, and I am Primus. Now, I appreciate your company, but I have work to do."

"Yes, of course," Arabella said.

As she made her way to her own home, she wondered about the courage of a woman who became the wife of a Primus. If she truly had been assassinated, it was not a surprising end. Without political power of her own, the wife of a Primus would be the target of his enemies. And a Primus—even one who seemed as benign as Rorik—had enemies.

Only Mages with the most magical skill and power rose to become Primus—they succumbed to their enemies otherwise. A Mage who became Primus would have spent a lifetime protecting themselves from attacks—physical or magical. But a wife—especially one who was a minor talent like Castio's Etta and perhaps Nimali's wife—would be vulnerable. She had Noula looking for such vulnerabilities, after all.

She would have to learn more about defensive spells—to ward her rooms from eavesdroppers and to keep her safe. She may not be as attached to Valerio as a wife was, but she was carrying his child and she was his ally. Once that was known, his enemies would become her enemies.

Chapter fourteen

"HOW DOES IT work?"

"Like this. Watch out!"

Water splashed close by.

"You're wasting it."

Pilo said that. Kara rolled onto her side and opened her eyes. Pilo and Sidra were frowning at Mole as he leaned on the handle of the pump.

"Stop it," Pilo said and swatted at Mole. "Stop wasting the water."

"We've got lots," Mole said. He leaned over to watch the water gush from the pump spout into the basin below it.

"How do you know?" Sidra asked quietly.

"That's right," Pilo said. "How do you know? You don't know where it comes from, so how can you know that there's lots?"

"Huh," Mole said. He pumped again, and water overflowed the basin and spilled onto the dusty floor below. "Shouldn't it go somewhere?"

"Pull the rope underneath," Kara called.

Mole looked over at her, and she pointed underneath the basin. He peered under the basin and yanked on the rope. Just like at Mika and Allon's, a wooden plug came out of the basin and the water flowed into a trough and out through the wall.

"How'd you know about that?" Vook asked. He was sitting cross-legged with his back towards the window.

Kara looked past him at the grey morning sky.

"I've seen one before," she replied. "But it was fed by a river, not by magic."

"Magic," Pilo said. "Is this magic? Is that why only I could see the cabin last night?"

"I think so," Kara said. She'd hoped that the cabin was spelled to remain hidden, but now that she knew it was, it caused other problems. Would she always have to lead them here?

"Then how did you find it?" Vook sat very still, suspicion in his eyes.

She couldn't blame him. He'd been betrayed by just about everyone he'd ever trusted.

"I can see magic," Kara said. "I've always been able to see it, I just never knew for sure what it was."

"Who told you that?" Vook didn't look any less uneasy.

"The mad mage."

The other children all stared at her.

"He was sane when I talked to him," Kara continued. "He told me that his madness comes and goes. But I saw and reacted to his magic. At least that's what he said." What he'd shouted at her as she'd run away, but she didn't need to tell them that.

"Does he know you're here?" Pilo asked. Her arms were crossed, and the scars on her face were deep red against her pale skin. "I'm not sure we're better off here with the mad mage than we were with the clammers."

"Don't be stupid," Sidra said. "The clammers were going to eat us. You said so yourself."

"The mad mage doesn't know I'm still here," Kara said. At least she hoped he didn't. What if he'd put some kind of alarm spell on the place? But if he had it would have been triggered a few days ago, giving the mad mage, Santos Nimali, plenty of time to come and investigate. She scnned the small room. Nothing had been disturbed, other than by her small group.

"He won't hurt me," Kara said. "He's not mad at all, he's been spelled. And he wants my help because I might be able to undo some of the spells."

"You would help a Mage?" Mole asked. "Why?"

"'Cause then he'd owe her," Vook said. "Maybe enough to let

us all stay here."

"Yes," Kara agreed. "Although I can't trust him completely."

Vook nodded when she said that, and seemed to relax.

"I need to find out more about him. How often the madness strikes him, where he goes, and what he does when he's mad." She paused and ran her hand through her hair. Did she so badly long to feel safe that she'd put them all at risk here? "But if he does find us, it's me he wants. And he can't hurt me, at least not with magic."

"That's how you got us away from the clammers," Pilo said. "By the tree with the feathers. There was magic there, you said."

"Yes," Kara replied. "I kept the spell away from us. But the clammers couldn't see it. One tried a spell—she barely even affected the magic under that tree."

"Clammers have magic?" Vook asked. "Harb never said."

"I don't think Harb knew," Kara said. "The women used it on Harb and Lowel, a little." Her voice turned grim. "And they used it on the collars."

Sidra's hand went to her neck and then quickly dropped down to her side. "That's why we couldn't untie them, no matter how hard we tried."

"Probably," Kara said. She got to her feet. "Who's hungry? There's a garden out back and some oranges we need to pick before the birds get them."

IT WAS LATE afternoon by the time they were finished in the garden.

Mole had clambered up the orange and apple trees and tossed the fruit down to Sidra and Pilo, while Vook and Kara dug up carrots and potatoes for supper.

Kara thought longingly of the peppers and grapes she'd seen in the garden behind the manor house. She shook her head—she might as well wish for what they'd left behind at the docks—the manor garden was just as far out of their reach. Besides, they should be grateful for what they did have. It was so much more than she had hoped to find when they'd started the search for a new home.

Only Kara and Pilo could actually see the cabin. Perhaps Pilo had some Mage blood in her, like the clammers, but no one mentioned the possibility. Kara didn't want to drive off the mage mist—the spells—that kept the cabin hidden, so they marked a path with stones for the other three. It led them to the corner of the cabin—once they touched it they could make their way to the door.

When the path was laid out, Vook set off to collect firewood, and soon a small pile was stacked just inside the door.

They sorted through the furniture in the back room and hauled what they wanted into the main room. A wooden crate tucked under the bed held bedding and some pots, as well as a real kettle. Mole and Sidra had never seen one before, so Vook started a fire in the hearth and settled the kettle near the flames. The kettle's whistle delighted the younger children, but it reminded Kara of Villa Larona and her father's house.

Kara had served tea to her father and Noula every evening, and Noula had never tired of finding fault. The tea was too cold, it had steeped too long, it hadn't steeped long enough, the milk was sour. Rarely was there a night when Kara didn't have to do something twice in order to appease her father's not-quite-wife. It would take some time before the whistle of a kettle brought her any sense of comfort, let alone the joy it gave Sidra and Mole.

They didn't have any actual tea, of course, but each of them took a mug of steaming water and sat at the table, just like any real family. There were only four chairs so Kara pulled up the small bench. It put her head at Mole's height, and he laughed. It was such an unusual sound for Mole, though her half-brother Osten had always been giggling at something or other.

"This is much nicer than the boat," Sidra said. "It's clean and there are no drafts."

"And there are no clammers," Mole said. "I hate clammers."

"They won't come this far, will they?" Pilo asked. "If they have magic, they might be able to see the cabin."

"They won't come this far," Vook replied. "I overheard the women talking. They're terrified of the mad mage."

"They *should* be," Kara said. "If Santos Nimali knew they had magic, then Mage Guild might find out."

"Would they care?" Pilo asked. "Mage Guild?"

"Yes." Kara stared out the window. The afternoon shadows were lengthening as the sun drifted lower in the sky. "When I ran away from the guild, they tried to find me." She faced the others. "I saw the spell they sent. Later, when I was traveling with Mika, we went to visit an old friend of his. He was dead—covered in that same mage mist—the spell that had been sent after me."

"It killed him?" Vook asked. "Why?"

"Because he wasn't just an old man living in the mountains." Kara went to the kitchen where she'd left her pack and pulled out the journal. "I got this book from his house." She placed the book on the table and sat back down. "And he had other books, almost thirty. A man doesn't collect so many books unless he can read."

"Only Mage Guild teaches their own to read," Pilo said. "You think he was Mage Guild, like you."

"Yes," Kara said. "I think that's why the spell killed him. Mage Guild controls all magic, and those who wield it. If the clammers have magic, Mage Guild will either find and control them, or kill them." She looked down at her hands. "From what I saw, I doubt they'd be easily controlled."

"I'll tell Mage Guild myself," Mole said. "I want them all dead!"

"Mole, don't say that!" Kara said.

"Why not? It's true." Mole crossed his arms over his chest and stared at her.

Kara looked into his belligerent face and sighed. Where was the laughing little boy from a few minutes ago?

"Because that makes you as bad as them," she said. "Besides, you don't ever want to meddle in Mage Guild business." She should take her own advice, she thought. Undoing the spells on Santos Nimali would be meddling in Mage Guild business, wouldn't it?

"I don't want Lowel dead," Sidra said quietly. "Lowel was always nice to me, before the clammers."

"Too late," Pilo said. "By now both Harb and Lowel are either slaves or dead."

"Would they eat them?" Mole asked. "They would have eaten me."

"No they wouldn't have," Vook said. "They eat food, the same as us."

"We may never know their fate," Kara said. She hoped they still were alive, but Harb had brought this on himself. Thank Gyda she'd been able to get the rest of them out. If she'd come even a couple of hours later, *all* of the clammers would have been at the docks, and there would have been no chance of rescue.

"Come on, let's finish getting that other room sorted out,"

Kara said. "I'd like to sleep in a real bed tonight."

THE BED WAS crowded with all five of them sprawled in it. Kara didn't actually get much sleep that first night. Mole, unused to sleeping in such comfort and security, fidgeted. He woke up Kara about every hour so she could confirm that they were still safe. But in a week they were all, even Mole, sleeping soundly.

Kara kept everyone close to the cabin that first week. The weather had turned, and rain lashed at the windows for three solid days. The stack of wood that was inside the door grew. It took hours for it to dry out enough to burn, but there was such a damp chill in the air that they kept the fire going all day.

The food in the garden was almost gone. There were still some oranges and apples, but they'd dug up what they could find of the wild vegetables. Vook had made himself a fishing pole and was anxious to find a place to fish, and Pilo wanted to look beyond the cabin's garden for berries and mushrooms. For Kara, it was time to search out Santos Nimali. If they wanted to stay in the cabin, she'd need to strike a bargain with him.

"STAY TOGETHER," KARA said as Vook, Pilo, Sidra, and Mole headed out the door, fishing gear and foraging baskets in hand. "If you go past the dock, you can be seen from the house."

"We've been doing this a lot longer than you," Pilo said. "We know what we're doing."

"Sorry, of course." Kara felt so responsible for the little group that she *had* forgotten that they'd been surviving without her for years. "All right. We'll meet back here before dark."

Once they'd gone, Kara stuffed her filled water skin and two oranges into her pack, alongside Santos Nimali's book.

She'd been surprised to read about her mother in the journal. Santos Nimali had been curious about Arabella Fonti. He'd called her an exceptionally promising student from an unknown strain of magical talent. He'd written of the need to explore her origins. He'd also been aware of Kara, though if he'd known her name he hadn't written it down. The last year of entries in the journal had been just before Kara turned nine—before the years of failed tests—when she'd still held so much promise.

Kara closed the pack and slung it over her shoulder. And she'd *fulfilled* that promise, though no one had recognized her magical talent.

Nimali also frequently mentioned Valerio Valendi in his journal. He'd been Nimali's Journeyman for many years, and the older man had written of him proudly, as if Valendi were his son. But she was almost certain that Valendi had caused the most harm to Nimali—much of the mage mist that twined around him was Valendi's colour.

There could be another Mage with the same colour mage mist, it was impossible to think otherwise, but the connection, the personal relationship between Nimali and Valendi, was there. And cursing someone into madness while allowing sane breaks so they knew their plight, knew they would soon go mad again, that seemed terribly personal.

She could not imagine anything justifying such unbelievable cruelty. It made her more eager to help the mad mage and not just to secure a safe place to live. He'd been wronged, horribly, and she could help.

She stepped into the tangled garden at the rear of the manor house. The house looked much the same as when she'd last seen it—the roof was blackened and caved in on the far wing, and the curtain was still open in the room where she'd confronted Nimali.

She skirted the garden bed, ignoring the onions and peppers, until she stood beside the stonework of the house. Nimali claimed he stayed in the destroyed area of the house, but that had been when he was sane. Even he didn't know what he did when he was mad.

Kara edged up to a window and peered in. The kitchen was bigger than both rooms of the secret cabin—a huge brick oven with multiple openings made her mouth water at the thought of the hot bread that once had been pulled from it. Marble counters were dull with dust, and a stack of dishes had tipped over and scattered brokenly across the floor. Directly underneath the window she peered through was a basin with two pump handles. The basin looked like it had been dry for a very long time, and she wondered where Santos Nimali got his water. Did he go to the fountain out front? She shivered. If so, then she was lucky he hadn't found her the night she'd slept under it.

A few steps past the window was a small wooden door. Only a few chips of blue paint remained, and the wood was warped and rotted in places. The door gave way with a dull squeal, and she quickly entered the room, tugging the door closed.

She rubbed her eyes against the dust and inspected the large room. Small patches of pale blue mage mist clung to the edges of the doors and windows. A fly buzzed into the mist by a window and disappeared. She looked at the door she'd entered. The blue mist lined the door frame, and she frowned. The spell hadn't kept her out. Did it keep pests away from the food and supplies? It would be a good use of magic in a kitchen.

A door that was centered in the wall directly in front of her swung inward onto a short hallway. Two open doorways branched off the hall, and a final closed door seemed to head straight to the front of the house. The first doorway led to a formal dining room. Dusty goblets and plates sat amongst tarnished silverware. Next was a small, sunny room that looked out onto the garden, the compact table and two upholstered chairs obviously meant for more intimate meals.

She eased open the door at the end of the hall. A row of paintings hung on the wall in front of her. She peered at one, recognizing the fountain at the front of the house. Three, four, five paintings and then the wall ended, and sunlight bathed the floor.

Kara peered around the corner and into the main hallway of the manor. She was behind the staircase. The front door was directly across from her. She was about to step into the main entranceway when she heard a noise at the door. She ducked around the corner, out of sight. The door opened, and a rush of fresh air swept in.

"I hate this old place," a low-pitched male voice said. "And I hate this duty."

"You say that every time," a second man said. "But it's a great honour to serve the former Mage Primus like this."

"We drop a basket off for him. That's all. We don't serve him. Gyda, we don't even see him."

"Mage Secundus Valendi's instructions are to make sure we *don't* see him. And if the Mage Secundus takes a personal interest in his former Master then we should too."

Something heavy hit the floor.

"Be careful, you'll sour the beer."

"As if the mad mage would even notice." Something was dragged across the tiles. "There. Let's go."

The wind swirled in as the door opened again.

"To think I worked so long and hard to become a Mage, and I end up doing this." The door slammed shut.

Kara slid down the wall and sat on the cool, marble floor. The food for Nimali was sent by Valerio Valendi? It was mostly his mage mist swirling about the mad mage. Was he trying to help his former Master? That didn't fit with the man she'd met in Larona.

The house had been quiet for close to an hour before she felt safe enough to creep around the corner.

A large basket sat beside the door that led to the damaged wing. And it crawled with dark grey mage mist. Kara waved the mist away and peered in.

The apples and oranges didn't tempt her, she'd had her fill of those in the last few days, but there was bread and—Gyda, were those sausages? She picked one up and sniffed, smiling at the garlicky odour. She hadn't had sausages since she'd left home over four months ago. Gently she put it back into the basket.

"You can have them if you'll help me."

Kara whirled to find Santos Nimali staring at her from the doorway to the undamaged part of the house.

"I thought you didn't go into that wing?" she asked as she backed into the opposite hallway.

"I woke up there," he said.

He looked tired and so forlorn that she stopped edging away.

"I came looking for you," Kara said. "I want to trade."

"You want to trade?" Nimali's laugh made him seem years younger. "Do you know how to bargain? It's not a skill taught to Mages."

"No, but I traveled with an unguilded trader for a while," Kara said. "I know how it works."

"What do I have that you want?"

Nimali's gaze sharpened, and Kara forced herself to keep still.

"You must know that I'll give you anything within my power to have your help."

"I know," Kara said. She paused and raised her eyes to his. "There's a small cabin on the property. I want it."

"The cabin," Nimali said. "You found it." He turned away, but not before she saw a flash of pain on his face. "It's very dear to me. Can you do what I want?"

"Yes," Kara said. "I can undo the spells. Although I'll undo the good ones as well as bad. And it might take some time."

"Thank you," Nimali said. His shoulders sagged, and he relaxed. "If you'll help me, the cabin is yours."

He smiled, a little shyly, she thought.

"It will be good to finally have someone living in the cabin," he said. "And don't worry about removing any helpful spells—no one who tried to help me made much progress."

"Good." She moved over to the basket of food. "Because I already removed the spells that Valerio Valendi had placed on your supplies."

"The food was spelled?" Nimali asked. "Are you sure it was Valendi?"

She nodded. "The mage mist was his colour, and I overheard the Mages who delivered it say that he had sent them."

"His colour," Nimali repeated. "Is that what you see, different colours? How is it you recognize his colour?"

"Each Mage seems to have their own colour of magic," Kara said. "Of what I call mage mist. And I've met Valerio Valendi. He came to my villa with my mother after I failed to find my magic at sixteen." She hesitated before she added, "My name is Kara. My mother is Arabella Fonti."

"You're the young Fonti girl? I often wondered about you."

"I know," Kara said. "I read your journal."

He glared at her, and she looked away.

"I needed to know what sort of man you were before I trusted you. I needed to know if I'd be safe with you."

"Yes, bad enough I'm mad much of the time," Nimali said. "I would be even more dangerous if I were mean and corrupt as well." He looked glanced at the basket of food. "You said you can't tell if the magic is evil or good," he said. "Maybe Valendi has been trying to help me all these years?" Nimali shook his head, and the gray-black mage mist twined tighter around him. "I can't assume that. I can't assume anything." He turned back to her. "Except that you can help me. Can we start now?"

Kara nodded. "I'd prefer to be outside."

Santos Nimali leaned against the kitchen wall and closed his eyes. Kara had been trying to untangle one thread of mage mist, but it kept wriggling away.

"I feel it tighten around my temple," Nimali said. "Is that what you see?"

"Yes," she replied. "I can make it move, but it refuses to let me cut it or disperse it or whatever it is I do that makes the spell go away." She poked her hand into the mage mist, and it shrunk away from her. "There must be something keeping it here." She stared at the strand of mist. "Turn around, please."

Nimali turned to face the wall. His shadow stretched out along the stone path that ran beside the kitchen window.

"Ah, that might be it," Kara said. There, near his shoulder, the mage mist seemed to be tied to another strand. This time when she jabbed, it clung to her. She pulled her hand away, and the mist followed in one long trail. Once it was a foot from Nimali, the mage mist thinned until it was gone.

"I felt that," Nimali said. He looked over his shoulder at her. "My head is different. I think I've lost my boat. Have you seen my boat?"

When Nimali finished speaking, he lifted a hand, and green mage mist seeped towards her.

"Santos, are you all right?" Kara waved her hand, and the mage mist dissipated.

"Who are you?" Nimali asked. "What have you done with my boat?"

Abruptly Santos Nimali got up and walked away. Kara edged towards the door into the kitchen, but Santos turned to face her.

"Listen," he said. Another wisp of green mage mist spread out from his hand. "They'll be here soon. We have to hide."

Nimali tried to grab her arm, but she shrugged away from him.

"Come with me!" Santos Nimali, the mad mage, glared at her. Despite the madness in his eyes, he was an imposing figure, one she could easily imagine giving orders to his Journeyman, Valerio Valendi.

Nimali turned away from her again, muttering to himself, and Kara crept closer to the door. She didn't feel threatened exactly, but neither did she want to stay and cause him more confusion. With one last glance at him, she slipped through the door and into the kitchen.

She hurried through the house to the front door, pausing by the basket of food. One sausage, that was all. She'd earned at least that, hadn't she? Besides, who knew how long the madness would stay with Nimali. The food might spoil in the meantime.

Oh. She stopped and stared at the basket of food. Maybe that was what the spell was for. Maybe all Valerio Valendi was doing was keeping the food fresh for his former Master. She exited the house and trotted across the yard towards the cabin.

Is that why Nimali went mad as soon as the spell was removed? Had Valendi's spell been helping? Had removing it plunged Santos Nimali into madness? Her instincts said no, there was no compassion in Valerio Valendi. He'd sent a spell after her that had killed Mika's friend, a spell that was supposed to kill her. She had to assume that any spell Valerio Valendi created was harmful.

The little cabin was empty. Kara dropped her pack on the table and wandered over to the kitchen. She put the sausage on the counter and pumped some water into her mug. She'd go to see Santos tomorrow, and every day after that, until she had rid him of the spells. If that made things worse, well, they both knew the risks. The important thing was that he'd agreed to let her have this cabin. He didn't have to know about the rest of her little group, at least not right now.

She grabbed a basket and headed out to the garden. Hopefully she could find a few onions or potatoes they'd missed to add to a stew.

"I'VE NEVER HAD anything so good in my life," Mole said. He grabbed a piece of sausage from his bowl and held it up. "It's meat?" He popped it into his mouth and closed his eyes in bliss.

"Yes, it's meat," Pilo said. "Most likely pork, mixed with spices and garlic. At least that's how my da used to make it. And the mad mage said we could stay here?"

Kara nodded. "The cabin is yours. That's exactly what he said." She ran her finger around the edge of her bowl, trying to get every last drop of liquid. One sausage didn't stretch very far for the five of them.

"Is the fish ready, Vook?" she asked. He'd caught two large bass and was frying them up alongside the mushrooms that Pilo and Sidra had foraged.

"Here." He set a plate on the table and sat down. Five arms stretched towards the food.

Kara pulled her arm in to allow the others to help themselves first. There was plenty—this would be only the second meal since being separated from Mika that she would be able to eat her fill. She leaned back and smiled. They were far better off than they had been at the docks. And with winter and the rainy season coming, this snug cabin would keep them all dry and warm. And safe.

Chapter fifteen

Despite her agreement with Santos, Kara felt too exposed to simply walk in the front door of the manor house. Instead she went in the kitchen and through to the front hallway. The basket of food was gone, which she took to be a good sign.

"Santos?" she called. "Are you here?" She stepped into the hallway of the damaged wing. "Santos Nimali? It's Kara."

"I'm here." Santos stepped out of a room. In the sunlight that streamed through the windows, the mage mist that swirled around him seemed much less dense.

She took a few steps towards him. "Do you feel any different?"

"Kara Fonti, I haven't felt this good in years." Santos bowed low to her. "My mind is clearer than it's ever been during my sane periods." He smiled. "What do you see?"

Kara walked around him, studying the mage mist. The spell she'd removed seemed to have been a major one. Loose ends of mist writhed and twisted, no longer anchored.

"I think I've removed a key spell," she said.

She waved her hand, and some of the smaller strands curled in on themselves and disappeared.

"There are a lot of smaller spells, but they no longer seem to have a focus."

Santos lifted his arms as Kara continued to walk around him, dispersing more spells. Once the smaller strands were gone, she could see another large, ropy strand twisting around him. She poked a finger into it, and he groaned and doubled over.

"I felt that," the Mage said. "My heart felt like I was being squeezed."

Alarmed, she backed away. "Could removing a spell kill you?"

"Yes," Santos said. "I devised such a spell myself, once. Don't look at me like that," he said when she frowned. "I was Mage Guild Primus. I had enemies everywhere. Apparently even in my own home." He shook his head. "Years ago Valerio Valendi was my Journeyman. I knew he was ambitious, that's one reason why I chose him, but I never would have expected him to do this to me." Santos straightened. "But I've had a lot of time to think about my failings as both Mage Guild Primus and a man over the past few years—I'm not happy with some of the things I've done. So here I am, alone, and the victim of the one man I trusted over all others."

"Do you not have any family?"

"Family," Santos snarled. "The guilds don't allow for much allegiance to family, and Mage Guild actively discourages it. They want you completely reliant on the guild." Santos paused. "But I do have children, out there somewhere. As Primus it was expected that I would pass on my abilities. But they were a duty, not a joy."

"And the mother of your children?" Kara asked softly. Bearing children to men such as the Primus, that would have been her fate, her life, if she'd stayed in the guild.

Santos laughed, a sharp bitter sound. "There was more than one mother. I learned my lesson the hard way."

He eyed her, and Kara sensed him sizing her up. He nodded, as if to confirm to himself that she could be trusted with this.

"I had a love, at one time," Santos said. "We were going to live here and have a family. We both worked on the house and grounds to make it ready." He lowered his head. "But she never lived here. My enemies hired an Assassin to kill her, and despite our magical protections, they did. I vowed to never make myself, or anyone I cared for, a target again."

"The cabin," Kara said. "That was for her."

Santos set sad eyes on her. "Yes. A small place where the two of us could shut out the rest of the world. The magic that surrounds it is my best work. I was surprised that you found it."

"It was the oranges," she said and smiled. "I could smell them, and I hadn't eaten for days. I ate my fill, and when I turned around, there it was."

"You need food?" Santos asked abruptly. "Why didn't you say so?" He brushed past her to the main hallway.

She followed him around the staircase, through the kitchen and out into the garden.

"It's sadly neglected," Santos said when she caught up to him. "But you're welcome to anything here."

Kara surveyed the overgrown garden. Peppers and grapes and a few misshapen squashes were visible, but there was probably even more she couldn't see. It was too bad she couldn't bring Pilo and Sidra over—they were tireless harvesters and better at finding food than she was. They'd had to be to survive so long on their own.

"Thank you," Kara said. "I'll take whatever I can pick. Would you like me to set some of the produce aside for you?"

"Me?" Santos seemed surprised by her offer. "No, I'll continue to eat what the guild provides." He looked over at her. "If you promise to remove any spells. It would look suspicious if all of a sudden my eating habits changed. I don't want Mage Guild to know you're here."

Kara nodded her agreement. The last thing she wanted was for the guild to know she was alive, and close by.

"Good," Santos said. "Now, if you have my journal in that pack of yours, we might find something useful in it. I wrote all of my most formidable spells in that book."

"You did?" Kara was confused. She'd read the journal cover to cover, and she hadn't come across anything that seemed like a spell, not even once.

"I've hidden them," Santos said. "With a code only I know. If I can describe the spell that can kill when it's removed, you may be able to undo it safely."

Santos was still hunched over his journal, muttering to himself, when Kara finally left, an old tablecloth heavy with vegetables slung over her shoulder. Magic had kept animals and insects out of the kitchen garden so there was plenty left to harvest. A small squash threatened to fall out of the bundle, and she stuffed it back in. The kitchen also had a good supply of jars she could use to preserve food for the winter. She smiled at the thought of the snug cabin, warm from a steady fire, jars of food stacked high in the cupboard, and the five of them in front of the window watching as a winter storm whipped the waves in the bay.

She'd need to find some spices and preservatives first though. The kitchen didn't have the right supplies, and it wasn't as though Santos could ask Mage Guild. She'd need to make a trip to the market.

It had been over a year since Vook had last been to the small Shanty Town market. The children had nothing to trade—but Kara did. Two guilders, if she dared, and her mother's jewelry. In addition to the spices, she hoped to get some clothes, maybe even some shoes, for the others.

ARABELLA SAT DOWN across from Castio and smiled. They'd just finished a council meeting, and the rest of the members had already left.

"I trust my kinswoman is working out for you?" she asked. "Her manners might be a bit rough, seeing that she's from a small villa, but she certainly has all the training you would expect a non-magical Guildswoman to have."

"Yes," Castio replied. "She's very useful."

Though a few years younger than Arabella, Castio had entered his Journeyman training the same year she had. They'd been part of a larger group who studied the archives together, but she'd become a full Mage before him. She'd worked harder than him—harder than everyone—while Castio had spent his free time socializing. At the time she'd felt superior, but he'd become a council member before her—in part due to his social connections.

"She's happy," Arabella said. "With Etta and your children."

Castio frowned. "I didn't realize you were keeping in touch with her," he said. "After all, she was your husband's lover for many years."

"A man I barely knew," Arabella replied. Noula had been talking too much. "Who is no longer my husband. Will you and Etta marry?"

"No," Castio said. "Just as you and Secundus Valendi are unlikely to marry. Or did he promise you that?"

"I just dissolved one marriage," Arabella said. "I have no wish to bind myself to anyone else."

"But you are having his child," Castio said. "Congratulations."

"Thank you," Arabella said. Had he guessed? Perhaps she would have to make her condition known. She had wanted a few more weeks—a little more time to secure her own allies before she become so publicly tied to Valerio. Because despite what she'd told Castio, her pregnancy *did* bind her to Valerio.

"I will not spoil your surprise by telling anyone your news," Castio said. He lowered his voice. "Just as I hope you will not tell anyone about Etta."

"Of course not," Arabella lied. She would tell Valerio about Etta. Castio was wrong if he thought he could bully her. Besides, her own secret made her stronger while his made him weaker.

"ARE SURE YOU don't want to come?" Kara asked Pilo.

"I never liked the market," Pilo replied. "Too many people in need of a bath."

"All right. We'll be back before dark." Kara slung her pack over her shoulder and followed Vook down the path.

"Pilo don't like the stares," Vook said softly when she caught up to him. "Because of her scars."

"Oh," Kara replied. "I didn't think of that. I actually forget about them."

"Me too," Vook agreed. "But Pilo don't forget them, ever."

No, she wouldn't, just as Kara'd never been able to forget that she had no magic. And poor Pilo's flaw was right there for everyone to see. The salve Kara made for the girl was helping, but no amount of medicines were going to remove the scars. That would take magic, and a very strong Mage. Like Santos.

She almost bumped into Vook, who had stopped behind one of the trees that lined the laneway.

"You're sure Mage Guild won't be coming here today?" Vook asked.

"I'm sure. They only come once a week, and the last time was two days ago."

Kara eyed the overgrown lane. It ran straight to the gate, and beyond that was the rest of Old Rillidi Island—and people. More people lived in Shanty Town than in all of Larona. But unlike her home villa, the people who lived here were the least fortunate in all of Rillidi: unguilded with nowhere else to go, the poorest guildsmen and women, whores, thieves, banditos. And her small group had no friends among them.

A few minutes out past the gate, the green trees and grasses gave way to the burn out. Kara had only seen it at night—in the light of day the devastation looked even worse. Blackened stone chimneys stood amid charred wooden beams and lumps of ash.

"Do people live near the burn out?" she asked Vook.

"Some. Most folk are too scared to live this close to the mad mage." Vook grinned. "And we'll make sure they stay worried about that. But there are people who'll live with a threat like that in order to stay safe from their enemies. That's why Mika brought us so far out."

"Mika found you in Shanty Town?"

"Harb, Lowel, and me," Vook replied. "Harb was good to me in those days. Kept me alive even though I was too little to be much help." Vook shook his head. "I still can't believe he let the clammers into our camp."

"Me neither," Kara said. At one point in time Harb *had* been good. What had twisted him into the angry, mean-spirited youth she'd met? "Maybe we should try to find out how they're doing? See if they are alive?"

"Yeah," Vook said. "Just because he abandoned us don't mean we should abandon him and Lowel."

"We'll go before winter," Kara said. "I promise." And maybe, just maybe, Santos would help. It meant she'd need to tell him about all of the children, but she was going to do that anyway. He was going to heal Pilo.

The burn out ended so abruptly that one moment she was beside a charred ruin and a few steps later she was looking at the weathered wood of a dilapidated cottage. It didn't look lived in, but it had escaped the fire. Another few steps and a dog growled at them from the porch of a small house. A curtain twitched, and a pale face peered out at them.

When a man and woman passed them, Vook kept his head down and shuffled out of their way. Kara peeked at the basket the woman carried, hoping for a glimpse of what the market offered, but the woman kept it tucked under her arm as though she was afraid someone would take it from her.

The small road merged with another to create a wider thoroughfare. The houses were larger and set back from the road.

Children in ragged clothes and bare feet played in front yards.

As they made their way east, people joined them on the road. Most were heading to the market with empty sacks and baskets and bottles slung over arms and shoulders, but a few looked like they were off on other, more dangerous business.

Kara clutched Vook's shirt as she trailed him through the crowd at the crossroads. She looked around at the dilapidated houses that lined the streets. Harb's people still lived here—to Kara it looked like a good place to get away from.

Once past the crowd and eastbound again, Vook steered them down a quiet side street.

"We can get to the market this way," he said as he led the way through an alley. "The more honest sellers are away from the main road anyway."

Vook helped her climb over the crumbled remains of a wall and into a small square. Water splashed in the large fountain in the centre of the square, and people thronged the edges, all manner of jugs and bottles and skins held out to catch the precious liquid as it spilled over the lip of the basin. As soon as one jug was filled and removed, another was thrust forward to take its place.

"Is this the only water source on this part of the island?" she asked. How many people relied on this one single fountain? Hundreds at least, maybe thousands, and every single one of them had to come here and fill up their water jugs. She and her small group had the luxury of the cabin with its kitchen pump and ready supply of water. They didn't even have to go outside.

"Yeah," Vook said. "It's not so crowded at night, but you have to watch out for the banditos. They bring wagons and fill up barrels so they can make beer."

"I hope to Gyda that these people don't realize what we have," Kara said.

"Don't tell them," Vook said. "Come on, I think I see a spice seller."

Vook grabbed her hand and pulled her towards a row of ramshackle huts, their wooden exteriors grayed and weathered. A few had small wisps of mage mist swirling around, and she wondered if the spells had been attached to materials that had been scavenged to make the huts, or if someone had actually paid a Mage to protect their meager belongings.

The old woman who sold spices had what she needed, but when Kara showed her a guilder, she shook her head and crossed her arms in front of her chest. Kara dug around in her pack for her mother's bracelet. She pulled it out and showed it to the spice merchant. The woman's eyes lit up, and Kara hesitated. The bracelet was expensive—her mother would never own jewelry that wasn't real gold—but preserving food for the winter was worth more. And it wasn't as though her mother had given it to her out of love.

Resigned, Kara dropped the bracelet into the woman's hand and stuffed the package into her pack. Besides the guilders, she only had her mother's broach left, and she still wanted to get clothing and shoes for them all.

"What do they use instead of guilders?" she asked Vook as they walked away. "And who do I get that from?"

"Dunno," Vook said. "It changes all the time. But only a Guildsman will touch the guilders."

Kara perused the shops until she found one that was overflowing with clothing. Much of it was dirty and ripped, but some items looked like they could be repaired. The man in the stall was dressed in clothes little better than what was on display, but there was a faded Merchant Guild patch sewn onto the front of his shirt.

"Will you take guilders for trade?" she asked softly. The Merchant turned and sized her up with a frown.

"What guild are you?"

"I'm making a purchase for a friend," she replied. "He's ill and can't travel here himself, but he gave me some guilders to purchase supplies with." She showed him two guilders.

"What guild is your friend?" The merchant still frowned, but his eyes were locked onto the guilders.

"Guider," she replied. "He travels between Rillidi and Villa Salvo, but his illness means he can't work." Kara hoped the Merchant would take pity on another struggling Guildsman. She tried not to show her relief when the Merchant finally nodded, slowly.

"Pick out your supplies, and I'll let you know what's too much."

"Thank you, Guildsman," Kara said. She waved Vook in, and the two of them rooted through the goods, piling their choices in a corner.

Finally done, Kara held the two guilders out to the Merchant. He snatched them from her and pocketed them, but when she stooped to pick up the goods, his booted foot stomped on the small pile.

"Leave them," the Merchant said.

"But I paid for them." Kara straightened to face him. "With two guilders."

"You're not a Guildsman, so you can't pay for anything with guilders." The man kicked the small pile of goods. "Now get on with ye before I get mad."

"Before *you* get mad," she said, furious. "You just stole from me."

"What did you say to me, unguilded?" The Merchant took a step towards her. "You think you can call me a thief and get away with it? I'm Merchant Guild, and that's an insult to my entire guild."

"You're the insult to your guild. You *stole* from me." Kara knew she should stop, knew she was creating a bigger problem, but not only was the Merchant a thief, but he was a liar as well. It wasn't right, it just wasn't!

"Come on, Kara." Vook took her arm and tried to pull her away, but she shook him off.

"Get out of here, Vook," she said to him.

Vook slipped out of the stall while Kara kept her eyes on the Merchant.

"I want what I paid for," she said. "Neither you nor the guilds make the rules on Old Rillidi. We had an agreement, and I expect you to fulfill your part of it."

"You'll get nothing from me," the merchant said. "And if you try to take anything, I'll name *you* a thief."

"Will you?" Kara wasn't sure who he *could* complain to. Santos owned the island, the guilds had no jurisdiction here, and no doubt this Merchant's neighbours knew how he conducted business. She was not leaving without her purchases.

She reached down and grabbed as much of the bundle as she could. The Merchant slapped her, and she grunted in pain as her head snapped backwards. She clutched the clothing to her chest and stumbled out of the stall. The Merchant followed.

"Thief!" he shouted. "I'm being robbed."

Kara continued to back out of the stall. A crowd gathered, but no one stepped in to grab her.

"I paid him, and now he won't let me take my goods," she called out.

A few faces nodded at her words, but none of them looked especially friendly.

The Merchant took a step towards her and raised his hand to strike her again. She ducked her head, and his hand smashed into her shoulder, throwing her to the ground. She scrambled away from him, and the crowd retreated to give her room.

"I would stop there, friend," a voice said from behind her.

The Merchant scowled, but stopped moving, hands at his side and his fists clenched.

"This is not your business," the Merchant said. "Foreigner." He spat on the ground.

"It is when a friend is involved," the voice said. "Kara is my friend."

At the sound of her name, Kara looked up. Chal Honess stood behind her, a grim smile on his lips. The Seyoyan's white-blond braids brushed her shoulder when he reached down to help her stand. A second man, plainer than Chal, assessed her from Chal's side. A haze of lilac mage mist wafted around him, but Kara didn't think he was a Mage. Chal's companion turned his gaze to the Merchant.

"I would do as my Seyoyan friend suggests, Guildsman," the man said in a low voice. "And stop." He nodded in Kara's direction. "I've a mind to trust the word of this one over you."

"You'd take the word of an unguilded over me, a full Guildsman?" The Merchant's eyes blazed. "How dare you! What guild are you?"

"I hope you're not suggesting that you have truth on your side simply because you are guild?" the man asked. "You might give a thought to where you are before making such claims." He gestured to the crowd.

A few in the crowd muttered angrily, and a couple of men stepped towards the Merchant. Those in the crowd with guild marks sewn to their clothing eased away.

"I'm sure that was not your intent," the man continued.

Kara looked from him to Chal, who winked at her.

"Go back to work," the man finished.

With one last glare at Kara, the Merchant returned to his stall, and the crowd, still muttering, started to wander away.

"Thank you," Kara said. She rubbed her temple where the Merchant had struck her. "Both of you." She turned from Chal and met the other man's startling blue eyes.

"You are most welcome, Kara," Chal said. "I told you we shared a destiny. This is Reo. I regret to tell you that he probably does not approve of my interference. Isn't that right, Reo?"

"Approve of it, no," Reo said. "Resigned to it, yes. Chal finds trouble wherever he goes."

"In this case I am grateful," Kara said.

"You are welcome," Reo said. "Now tell the boy who's trying to spy on us that it's safe to come out now."

Kara followed his gaze to where Vook was hiding behind a fruit wagon. She waved him over.

"I wasn't able to get everything," she said as she pushed some of the bundled goods into his arms. "We'll just have to make do."

Vook nodded and warily eyed the two men.

"Can we help?" Chal asked.

"Thank you, no," Kara replied. "You've done enough. We must get going." She wanted to be safe and secure in the cabin as soon as possible.

Reo relaxed slightly at her words, and the mage mist around him slowed as though reacting to his mood. Maybe he *was* a Mage? She fussed over the bundle in her arms, and kept her gaze off the mage mist.

Reo reached out and pushed the trailing sleeve of a coat into her arms. The mage mist retreated up his arm, away from her.

"Thank you," she said and took a quick step away from him.

The mage mist settled back along his arm. Reo sent her a puzzled look, and she smiled weakly and turned away, only to meet Chal's sharp gaze.

"What did you do?" he whispered. "To the magic?"

"Nothing," Kara stammered. She nudged Vook's arm. "We have to go." The two of them started to walk away, quickly. "Get us away from here, fast," she urged Vook, and she followed him as he plunged into the market crowd.

She thought she heard her name being called, but she ignored it, concentrating on getting as far away as quickly as possible. It was too dangerous for more people to know about her talent. On the ferry, Chal Honess had asked her what she saw because he saw it too, and knew what it was. *What did you do to the magic?* he'd asked.

Vook kept them off the road, leading them through laneways and alleys. They entered the burn out far from the main road. It was a tougher walk, and Kara stumbled a few times, once tripping over the stump of a tree covered in moss and grass, but they kept going.

Chapter sixteen

THE SUN WAS still high in the sky, and Kara could hardly believe it had only been a few hours since they'd set out from the safety of the cabin. She kept looking behind them, in case they'd been followed, but she never saw anyone.

"Want to tell me what that was about?" Vook asked.

They were in the woods that surrounded the estate.

"What do you mean?"

Vook whirled on her, and she stumbled into him.

"Don't lie to me, Kara," Vook said. "I'm not a stranger. I know some of what you can do." He glared at her, and she looked away.

"Yes, you do," she said quietly. She met his gaze. "The Seyoyan, Chal Honess? I think he sees magic, like me. But I don't think he knew about undoing magic, at least not until now. His friend had a spell on him, and it reacted when he came near me."

"And the Seyoyan noticed," Vook said.

"Yes," she agreed. "It's not the first time he's asked me about seeing spells."

"All right," he said and nodded. "We'll make sure they can't find us." He turned and started walking north through the woods, away from the lane and gate that led up to Santos' manor.

Kara settled her full pack across her shoulders, hugged the bundle of clothing to her chest, and followed.

An hour later, with the sun setting low over their shoulders, they reached the northern shore of the island.

"Does anyone live here?" Kara asked. She had no wish to meet a group like the clammers.

"Doubt it," Vook replied. "The only fresh water is back at the estate, and no one's gonna chance meeting the mad mage."

"We did," she said. "But you're probably right." She stared out across the water.

An island, Warrior Guild Island, according to Santos, was directly across from them. She could see the gray walls of their lookout towers. It was too far away to swim, thank Gyda, but any one of the sturdy boats that dotted the bay could make it across. She thought about the grim-faced Warriors she and Mika had seen on the road and hoped that the legend of the mad mage was well enough known to keep them away.

"Now what?" she asked Vook. She took a sip of water from her water skin. It was warm and stale, and the skin was almost empty.

"We follow the shoreline until we get back." Vook shaded his eyes and looked behind them. "And hope we've lost anyone who might have followed. Come on."

They stayed close to the shore as they made their way to the house. Lights and sounds drifted across the bay from Warrior Guild Island, but if there were any boats out in the night, Kara didn't see them.

Finally they stepped onto the wide expanse of lawn. The dark shape of the manor house loomed on their left. She skirted the gardens and led them to the cabin. Before her hand even reached the handle, the door opened wide, and Sidra flew into her arms.

"We were so worried," she said.

Kara entered the cabin and dumped her bundle on the floor. Vook did the same and then closed the door, shutting out the damp, cool night.

"What happened?" Pilo asked. She stood beside the table where a small lamp burned.

Heat emanated from the hearth, and Kara wearily dropped to the floor beside it. The warmth spread through her, and she sighed.

"We had some trouble with the Merchant," Kara said. "Don't worry—I got what we need to preserve the food." She dragged her pack from her shoulder and handed it to Pilo, who put it on the table.

"Kara was recognized," Vook said. He dropped into a chair at the table. "By a Seyoyan."

"A Seyoyan?" Pilo sent her a sharp look. "How do you even know one?"

"I met him on the ferry just before I got separated from Mika," Kara said. She stretched her hands out towards the fire and rubbed them together. "He and his friend helped us with the Merchant." And Gyda only knew what they were doing at the market in Shanty Town. "We took the long way home in case they decided to follow us."

"Why would they do that?" Pilo asked.

"Because the Seyoyan knows Kara can see magic," Vook replied.

Kara stared straight ahead. "And that I can affect it."

"How can he know that?"

"Because he saw it," Kara said. She met Pilo's eyes. "He sees magic, too, and he saw it react to me. We left before he could ask any questions."

"You're sure you weren't followed?"

Pilo sounded worried, and Kara couldn't blame her. If Chal found them, they wouldn't be safe, even in the cabin. He'd be able to see it, just like she could.

A FEW MORE wisps of gray faded away, and Kara dropped her hand to her lap. "The next spell layer is a big one," she said to Santos. "We should leave it for another day. How do you feel?"

Santos rolled his shoulders and shook his head.

"Clear headed," he said. "And better every time. You think the next one will send me into a mad episode?"

"Probably," Kara replied.

They'd found that removing powerful spells caused Santos to descend into madness. The episodes lasted only a few hours though, and he hadn't spontaneously gone mad in over a week.

"Another day then," Santos agreed. "It will give me time to recover."

They sat in silence for a few moments, and Kara watched the rain run down the window glass. They were in the sound wing of the house, and Santos had cleaned it using magic. The tile floor was polished, and the fabric on the sofa they shared was as bright and fresh as the day it was made.

"I'm not living in the cabin by myself," she blurted out. She kept her eyes straight ahead, afraid to look at Santos.

"I know."

She met Santos' eyes, and he smiled.

"I thought as much the day you asked me for the cabin," he said. "And since then I've become good friends with Mole."

"Mole? He's been here?" Kara asked.

Santos chuckled. "He hides in the ruined wing. He likes the dark."

"Yes he does," she agreed. She took a deep breath. "And there's Vook, Pilo, and Sidra as well."

"So Mole told me," Santos said.

"Why didn't you say anything?"

"I trusted that you'd tell me when you were ready," Santos said. "And you have."

"I know it's not part of the bargain, but I was hoping you could help us, now that you mostly have control."

"Thanks to you," Santos said.

MOLE SKIPPED AHEAD of them as Kara led Sidra, Vook, and Pilo around the rear of the house to the kitchen. The sky had cleared, and Santos sat with his back against the wall, his eyes closed against the late day sun.

"Mad mage," Mole called, and Santos opened his eyes and smiled.

"Mad mage, mad mage, mad mage." Mole danced around Santos, who stood up and brushed his hands on his trousers.

"He has a name," Kara scolded Mole. "It's Santos."

"I don't mind," Santos said. "Especially since mostly it's no longer true." He turned to the others. "And you are Sidra and Vook. Mole has told me much about you. And Pilo too."

Kara held onto Pilo's hand as Santos studied the girl's ruined face. She hadn't told Pilo anything—she hadn't wanted to get her hopes up before Santos saw her and knew whether he could help her.

Santos reached out a hand, and Pilo flinched away from it.

"Shhh, I'm not going to hurt you," Santos crooned. "But it's been a long time since I did any major healing spells, and I need to understand what's going on underneath that scar."

"He wants to help, Pilo," Kara said. "If he can."

Pilo looked at her, and Kara saw a glimmer of hope behind the fear in the girl's eyes. She trembled slightly as Santos ran a hand down her face and neck.

"I'll need to reread my journal," Santos said. "I wrote a part of a spell there, long ago." He turned towards the kitchen door, Kara and the others forgotten.

"Can you help her?" Kara asked. "Heal her?"

"Yes," Santos turned to them. "But I don't want to simply apply a spell that hides the damage, a spell that you, Kara, or someone like you, could undo. I need a spell that helps Pilo heal herself. That will take me some time to put together." He sent Pilo a sharp look. "The actual healing process will take weeks, maybe even months, and there might be some pain."

"But my scars will get better?" Pilo asked.

"Oh yes," Santos replied and smiled. "I'm quite a good Mage." He paused. "I've been afraid of my magic for a very long time because it always seemed to do damage—to my house, to people, to the grounds. But to use magic to help someone? That is a welcome gift, Kara. Thank you."

KARA AND PILO trekked to the manor house. It was the third dull, grey day in a row, and Kara was happy to be out of the cabin. They'd spent the past few days storing food, and the little kitchen was stacked with bottles of preserves.

They searched the house, calling Santos' name, finally finding him shut away in a back room that Kara had never been in before. The walls were lined with bookshelves that were bursting with books and labeled jars and pots. Santos sat at a large table, open books scattered around him and a small magical light floating in the air above.

"Santos," Kara called again. "We're here."

Santos looked up distractedly. "What? Oh good. I know just where to start. Over here, Pilo." He gestured to the girl, and she stepped nervously to his side.

Santos nudged the light until it was directly above Pilo, who looked up at it with a worried frown. The Mage either didn't notice her concern or didn't care. Instead he ran a hand down the scarred side of her face. He raised his hand again, and Kara saw a wisp of light green mage mist on his fingertips. Santos' hand ran down Pilo's scars again, this time leaving the mist in his wake. A few more passes, and half of Pilo's face was obscured by mage mist.

"That's the face," Santos said. "Now for the rest. Take your shirt off." Pilo hesitated, and he drummed his fingers on the table top. Mage mist puffed up at each touch of a finger.

"Come, child," Santos said. "I've seen more than your young hide in my day. I need to expend this magic. I've been accumulating it for days, and it wants out now."

"Go ahead, Pilo," Kara said.

Pilo ducked her head and untied the laces on her shirt. Her eyes were closed when she dropped the shirt to the floor.

Kara sucked in a breath at the extent of damage on the younger girl's torso, but Santos simply started trailing mage mist along the thick ropey scars. Soon half of Pilo's body was covered in mist.

"That's it," Santos said. "I've done all I can for now."

Pilo grabbed her shirt and pulled it back on.

"It will itch," Santos continued. "And as I said before there might be some pain. Kara, let me know when the spell has faded. I'll need to apply a second one."

"I will," Kara said.

"Thank you," Pilo mumbled. Then the girl hurried out the door.

Kara turned to follow her, but stopped and turned back to Santos.

"You said you'd been accumulating magic," Kara said. "Do you need to think about it in order to accumulate it?"

"I do now," Santos said. He waved a hand at the light, and it retreated higher overhead. "At one time I didn't have to, but when I went mad I tried not to accumulate power, hoping to keep my spells smaller and less destructive. But one of the first things a Mage is taught is how to conserve and contain their magic. Without a store of magic you cannot perform spells." He paused and ran a hand through his hair. "Unless you take it from someone else, of course. But that requires very advanced skill that only a very few Mages can master."

"Does the magic need to be given?" Kara asked.

"No," Santos replied. "But to take without it being offered is such a grave offense that you will be expelled from Mage Guild and could even be put to death. Only the most foolish or desperate Mage would flaunt Guild Law so blatantly."

Kara hovered while Santos rearranged some books on his table. She recognized the journal she had carried with her from the mountains, and it reminded her of Chal Honess.

"Santos, I might need you to keep watch for someone," Kara said. She traced a finger along the edge of the table, running her hand over the journal. "With magic." She lifted her eyes to his. "Vook and I went to the market at Shanty Town a few days ago, and I met someone there, a Seyoyan, and I think he knows what I can do."

"A Seyoyan," Santos repeated. "There were rumours that a few of them see magic." He pulled a stool up and sat down, a thoughtful look on his face. "Even as Mage Guild Primus, I was never able to confirm it. Warrior Guild keeps the Seyoyans very close. I've heard that they work with Assassins, although Warrior Guild claims Assassins do not exist."

"But they do, don't they," Kara said. "You said one killed your wife."

"Yes." Santos sent her a sharp look. "It would not be good for them to know about you."

"It might be too late." She shivered, suddenly chilled. "Do you think that a Seyoyan who can see magic would travel with an Assassin?" Chal's mysterious friend had acted like he was a Guildsman, but he hadn't been wearing a patch.

"Have you seen one?" Santos asked.

"Maybe," Kara said. "His name is Reo."

Santos shook his head. "It's not a name I'm familiar with, but I've been mad for the better part of seven years, and Assassins have notoriously brief lives."

"Can you guard against them?" Kara asked. She almost wished she hadn't started this conversation. If she hadn't, she'd be a little worried about Chal Honess and his friend Reo, but she wouldn't have this knot of fear clutching at her gut.

"I can create some spells," Santos agreed. "But not to maim or kill. Even the mad mage can't kill an Assassin and not expect consequences." He shook his head. "You'd be very valuable to an Assassin."

"They don't know where I am," Kara said, thankful that she and Vook had come home the long way.

"They know you're on Old Rillidi," Santos replied. "I don't want to alarm you, but Assassins are trained to uncover secrets, and they are very, very good at it. And your abilities would be so useful that I'm not sure one would *ever* stop looking for you."

"They could earn guilders with my skills?" she asked.

"Yes," Santos replied. "I'm sure there would be a way."

"Could I bargain with one? My talents for their protection?"

"It's possible," Santos said. "But dangerous."

"Why? You said they could earn guilders with me."

"And they could," Santos replied. "If they chose to. But more importantly, you could help an Assassin stay alive. As I said, they don't live long. What would another year or two of life be worth to a man trained to take the lives of others?"

EVEN WITH EXTRA protection from Santos' magic, for the next few weeks Kara only left the cabin to undo the spells cursing him. She told the others that she didn't care for the cold, rainy weather, or that she wanted to make sure their stores were put away so nothing would spoil, or that she didn't feel very well. In reality, she was terrified that an Assassin was looking for her.

So she wasn't surprised when he found her.

"Kara."

She turned at the sound of Vook's voice, and the smile slid off her face. Chal Honess and Reo stood in the doorway behind Vook, each one with a tight grip on the boy's shoulders. She straightened her shoulders and met Reo's blue eyes.

"Let him go," Kara said. "It's not your fault, Vook."

Reo nodded and lifted his hand off Vook's shoulder. Chal let go too.

"Get the others and take them to Santos," she told him calmly. Santos would keep them safe—the Assassin only wanted her.

The two men stepped aside, and Vook squeezed past them. He sent Kara a worried look before he sprinted away.

"Close the door," Kara said. She turned her back on them, closed her eyes, and sent a prayer to Gyda. When she heard the door shut softly, she walked over to the table and sat down.

When Chal and Reo sat across from her, there was no trace of mage mist on Reo.

"Santos would be Santos Nimali, the mad mage," Reo stated.

"Yes," Kara said. "You are no longer spelled."

"No, it was a temporary protective spell." Reo and Chal exchanged glances. "And quite fortunate for me that I had it when we met."

"Fortunate," Kara said. "Not the word I would use."

"You don't seem very surprised to see us, Donna Kara," Chal Honess' voice was almost a caress.

"Santos has told her what to expect," Reo said. "Isn't that right?"

"Yes," Kara agreed. "He said I would be far too valuable for an Assassin to walk away from."

Reo leaned back and watched her through lidded eyes. Even sitting still he exuded an air of unleashed power. He reminded her of snakes she'd seen near Larona. They'd curl up and sun themselves on a rock, but at the smallest sound they could launch themselves in the air and strike a target four feet away.

"Santos is correct," Reo said finally. "But how is it that you have conversations with the mad mage? I hear that he can barely function."

"He's not mad anymore," Kara said. She hoped he might be afraid of a capable Mage of Santos' skills, but Reo simply nodded. "I've been helping him. Undoing the spells that made him go mad."

Reo sat up. "He was spelled? Another Mage made him go mad?" He looked over at Chal before he leaned back again. "But you have confirmed Chal's assumption. You *can* affect spells."

"Yes," Kara said. "Just as you've confirmed that you are an Assassin."

Reo smiled. "I like you, Kara. I think we will work well together."

"Do you?" she asked, bitterness creeping into her voice. "A few months ago I was foolishly thinking of approaching Warrior Guild with just such an offer, but now that I don't have a choice, I want you to leave me alone. Except you know I exist, so you'll either use me or kill me to make sure I can't be used against you." She met his eyes with a steady gaze. Eventually he looked away.

Reo shrugged and stared at her again. "We all do what we must to survive. But it doesn't mean we can't be pleasant to each other."

"Is that what you say to the people you kill?" As soon as she said it she wanted to take it back. Why was she provoking this

Assassin?

Chal glowered at her, and Reo's eyes darkened for just a moment.

"As a matter of fact, it is," Reo said. "I've been guild-trained since I was a boy. I know no other life, and frankly, I've lived longer than I expected to. There is no point in living or dying in fear and anger. It's much better to accept your fate."

"I'm not sure I believe in fate," Kara replied. If she'd believed in fate she never would have left her home in Larona, never would have traveled with Mika, never would have understood her talents, or been able to save the group from the clammers.

She looked at Chal. "Or destiny."

SHE SPENT HOURS answering Reo's questions—where she grew up, what happened when she'd reached sixteen without magic, what other skills she had. For the most part Kara answered as truthfully as she could, but she told him that her name was Kara Banio and said nothing about Arabella Fonti being her mother. Reo would be angry if he found out she'd lied to him, but that secret seemed too big and too dangerous. She would rather risk the wrath of an Assassin than have her mother know she was living on Old Rillidi.

It was dark before Reo finally let her get some fresh air. Not alone of course; Chal shadowed her as she strolled through the almost bare garden.

"How did you find me?" Kara asked. She and Vook had been so careful.

"People living down near an old dock told us," Chal replied. "Odd, pale people with a small amount of magic."

"Clammers," Kara said. "That's where we were living. Then they moved in, and we moved here." When she said it like that, it sounded so easy. Not the harrowing escape through the forest in the dark, not the feral looks on the faces of the clammers when they thought they weren't being watched. She shivered.

"Clammers," Chal repeated. "They weren't very friendly, but Reo has his ways."

"Did he kill them?"

When he spoke, Chal's voice was full of humour. "You want the answer to be yes, don't you?"

"Did he?" she asked again. "It would be doing everyone a great service.”

“No, he didn’t kill them,” Chal replied. “But a couple of men with them were more than eager to tell Reo all about you.”

“Harb and Lowel,” Kara said. “So they’re still alive.”

“Probably wish they weren’t,” Chal said. “They were slaves, and not being treated very kindly. But that’s neither mine nor Reo’s concern.”

“So you left them?”

“We left them,” Chal agreed. “Are they friends of yours? They didn’t have a very high opinion of you.”

“Not friends,” Kara said. “But not enemies either. They’re just stupid boys who made mistakes.” She felt sorry for them, Lowel especially. He didn’t deserve that kind of life.

“I could go and get them,” Reo said from behind them. “If you asked me to.”

Kara stopped. She hadn’t heard Reo come outside, hadn’t heard the door to the cabin close, or the sound of his footsteps. She sighed and turned around. Pale moonlight bathed one side of his face. She stared at him, searching for answers in the set of his jaw, the angle of his head.

“Why would you do that?” she asked.

“We *will* work together,” he said. “I’d prefer you as a willing partner. I could do much for you, Kara.”

“What is it you think I want?”

“I can give every unguilded person you care about guild status,” he said.

Kara sucked in her breath. “I’m not sure I want them all in the Warrior Guild.”

Reo shrugged. “I can arrange to have them join other guilds,” he said.

Could he do that? She met his eyes and saw only confidence. He probably could. He must be very good to be able to so casually offer what would be coveted by so many unguilded. Then she thought about Mika and Allon, who wouldn’t thank anyone to belong to a guild. And what of Pilo, Vook, Sidra, and Mole? Would a guild really give them a future? So many Guildsmen she’d seen since coming to Rillidi seemed worse off and with less hope than her small group. She would hate to agree and then later find out she’d sent them into servitude.

“No guilds,” she said. “I’d not send people I care about into that life."

Chal smiled at her, and Reo nodded his head once.

"Then I can offer some protection from the guilds," Reo said. "Not from the Mage Guild, I'm afraid. They are beyond my influence at the moment. But the others, yes."

"What am I giving up in return?" Kara asked.

"One year," Reo said. "One year during which you will help me in any way I ask."

"As long as it does not put me or those I care about at risk," she said. Could she do it? Could she survive a year being at the beck and call of an Assassin? And was it worth it to have all but Mage Guild leave them alone?

Reo stared at her for a moment before he spoke. "I cannot guarantee you will not be at risk," he said. "It is the nature of my profession. But I will promise to minimize the danger to you as much as I can, even if it increases my own risks."

"That's fair." She nodded. "Now I need you to tell me what's so important to you that you had to hunt me down. What is that *you* want, Reo?"

They stared at each other for a few moments. Reo's gaze flickered, and Kara was sure he was going to lie to her, that he would smile and say something convincing and half true but not *the truth*. Instead, he looked at her and shrugged.

"I'm twenty-four years old—an age few Assassins reach." He shook his head. "An age no Assassin *should* reach. Because, Kara, I'm old enough to know that I want more. More life, more years, more time. But I'm a liability to my guild—I know too many secrets. Who would you hire to kill an Assassin?"

"A Mage," she said. There was no one else who *could* do it.

"Yes," Reo agreed. "I occasionally buy protective spells, like the one I had when we met, but it's dangerous to let a Mage, even one I have paid, know even that much about me. I am fortunate enough to have Chal, but there are places where a Seyoyan would not be welcome. Places where a well-educated young Guildswoman *would* be."

"And not be suspected of being able to see magic," Kara said.

Reo grinned, and his face transformed from a serious, dangerous Assassin to a carefree young man. "Or to affect it. Even the Mage Guild doesn't know your ability exists," he said. "No one will suspect you of anything."

"I only need to help you for one year?" she asked. She didn't see how one year would make the difference. In her experience, Mage Guild didn't stop chasing someone until they were dead.

"One year," Reo agreed. "After that, I will either be safely retired or dead."

ARABELLA EASED OUT of bed and pulled her robe on. She sighed at the way the silk slid under her hand. When he'd given it to her, Valerio had said that the fabric was from Seyoya.

"Leaving already?" Valerio said from the bed behind her.

"You've exhausted me," she replied. She looked over her shoulder and smiled. "I need my rest, and if I stay, I don't believe I will get any." She remembered feeling tired during her first pregnancy, but not this heavy weariness. Even her magical abilities seemed to be suffering, although she would never admit that to anyone.

"Come back to bed," Valerio said.

Arabella closed her eyes. It hadn't been a request. She would love to tell him no, but she didn't have the energy for that. She still needed Valerio's good will. She would cancel her morning appointments and stay in her quarters tomorrow.

"Yes," she turned and let the robe drop to the floor. "Maybe one day I will learn to say no to you." She smiled to take the sting out of her words, but vowed that one day she would have the power to say no.

"You can tell me no," Valerio said as he reached for her. "But I will only ever hear yes."

Arabella let herself be pulled into his arms. He rolled on top of her and wedged a knee between her legs.

"I hear you had a visit with your friend from Larona," Valerio said, his breath warm on her neck.

"Yes," Arabella replied. She ran her hands along the smooth skin of his back. "She is very grateful."

"As she should be. She's been put in an interesting household."

Valerio must know about Castio's family with Etta. Arabella shifted and wrapped her legs around his waist. "She's been placed with a family," she said. If he was testing her, she could not fail. "A Mage by the name of Etta, do you know her?"

"I know everyone," Valerio said. "She's the mother of Castio's children. Does he visit often?"

"He's there most nights," Arabella said.

"So I have been told," Valerio replied, and Arabella had to concentrate on not reacting to his words.

He *was* testing her. Did he know about her visit with Rorik? She closed her eyes and found his lips with her own. She must not let him doubt her, not even for a moment. With more desperation than passion, she strained towards him. He must not doubt her.

IF SHE NEEDED proof that Reo was both serious and powerful, she got it with the swiftness that he arranged everything.

One week after she'd agreed to help Reo, two men led Lowel and Harb, filthy and battered, past the main house. Neither of the youths lifted their heads, but a note was left saying that they would enter Maker Guild, and from there it was up to them to find their own way.

Two days later Chal knocked on the door of the cabin. He carried a long, dark cloak for Kara and waited impatiently while she stuffed a few items into her pack and said her goodbyes.

Chal led her to a small boat that was tied up at Vook's fishing pier. Mage mist glowed as the small craft silently raced across the bay towards Warrior Guild Island. She kept her gaze forward, toward their destination. She was leaving again. Just when she'd started to feel like she had a home, she was leaving again.

"YOUR ROOMS ARE to your liking?"

Reo leaned against the door jamb, his arms crossed over his chest, a lazy smile on his lips. Kara stepped away from the doorway, and he straightened and entered her rooms, closing the door behind him.

"They are lovely," she said.

And they were. She'd thought Santos' manor house wonderfully lush and luxurious, but it was almost rough compared to the rich silks and exquisitely carved furniture in the rooms that Reo had provided her on Warrior Guild Island. She could easily imagine her mother living in this type of splendor, but for her, it was a prison. Two days she'd been here, and not once had she been allowed outside of her rooms, not even into the hallway. There was a small terrace, and this morning she had at least felt the warmth of the sun on her face, but the terrace was completely walled with a view of only the sky.

"Good," Reo said. "You need to be comfortable in this type of setting."

"Why?" She took a seat on the sofa, the silk of her dress whispering against the silk covering she sat on.

"Because a woman with your background would be," he said. "At least the woman you will be portraying—the only child of a wealthy Merchant who has spent all of her life in Seyoya. But your beloved father died, and now you've come home to Rillidi." Reo sat on a chair across from her. "Sadly you have no ties with Merchant Guild. Other than your father, the only true Guildsmen you know are the Warriors who were hired to protect your father's greatest treasures."

"That's why I've chosen to stay on Warrior Guild Island rather than make my way to Merchant Guild Island?"

"Yes. And because your lover is Warrior Guild."

"Ah, and that would be you," Kara said. Reo gave a little nod, and she picked at the hem on her dress. "Won't you be recognized?"

"Not by anyone who would betray me."

"Will my story be believed?" Now she understood the etiquette lessons—the indulged daughter of a very wealthy Merchant would know what Kara was being taught.

"Yes," Reo said. "It's all true. Except the woman whose identity you are using died last year of the same fever that took her father."

"How do you know this?"

"There really were Warriors with the family. Although I don't believe any of them became her lover." He grinned at her. "The Warriors were old men who all stayed in Seyoya."

"And what is the purpose of this?" She still couldn't figure out what her role was, how she could help Reo stay alive until he could retire.

Reo leaned back in his chair and studied her for a moment. "There are two truths known by those who hire Assassins," Reo said. "The first is that Warrior Guild will deny that Assassins exist. The second is that Assassins die young, and their secrets go to their graves with them. But I plan on becoming visible—an aging Assassin who knows too many secrets."

"Everyone who has ever hired you will feel threatened," Kara said. "Isn't it easier to simply leave Rillidi, leave Tregella?"

"Simpler, yes," Reo said. "Safer, no. Better to stay here and flush out anyone who wishes me dead."

"Will they hire other Assassins?"

"That's the crucial question," Reo said with a nod. "Will my own guild allow a fellow Assassin to be hired to kill me? I'm not only one of their own, but I'm one of their best, one who has served Warrior Guild exactly as I've been trained to." He shook his head. "I am very interested to know if they will accept such a commission."

"You don't think they will," Kara said.

"No, I don't. I can't think of one Assassin who would be willing to take this contract. And Warrior Guild has too much to lose if they allow it. They will hope my former patrons succeed in killing me, but they will not aid them."

"They'll hire Mages."

"They will hire Mages," Reo agreed. "There is no other choice. It will be very expensive, and Mage Guild will make them pay in ways they don't yet understand, but some will be foolish or desperate enough to bargain with them anyway."

"That's why you need me." She nodded. It made sense now. She would protect him from spells meant to kill him. "Will I be a target of Assassins?" What if someone found out what she was doing for Reo?

"No."

She shivered at the coldness in his voice.

"I will make it clear that I will consider any attempt on your life to be the same as an attempt on my own." He smiled a cheerless, feral smile. "If they kill you, then they *must* kill me."

Kara swallowed. She could easily believe that Reo was one of the most dangerous men in all of Rillidi. Who would be brave enough to try to kill him? "Will one year be enough time?" she asked.

"Yes," Reo replied. "Those with enough guilders to hire a Mage will do so early and exhaust their fortunes. If I'm still alive after a year, and have not spilled any secrets, the others will choose to forget that I am a threat." He smiled his cold smile again. "Most of the people who hired me did so for financial gain. None of them want to part with their guilders."

"Do I really need to pretend to be a rich Merchant?"

All Kara had done was learn—etiquette, fashion, history, Seyoyan, politics, gossip, needlework. She hated the needlework more than anything. She'd rather try taming a wild burro, and Gyda knew she had no talent for *that*.

"Yes."

Reo and Chal answered at the same time, and Kara groaned.

Chal was teaching her about Seyoyan customs. She didn't think she would ever truly understand how the act of stealing from one another conveyed honour and regard, but according to Chal it did.

For the past two weeks Reo had sat in on all her lessons, although he usually read a book or wrote in a small leather bound journal. Initially, Kara had been caught off guard that a Warrior knew how to read and write, but the more time she spent in Reo's company the less surprised she was by his knowledge. He was extremely intelligent, something she hadn't expected from a man who killed for a living.

"It's the best role for what I need," Reo said. "As a beautiful, rich Guildswoman who's led an exotic, yet tragic life you will be the most sought after guest in all of Rillidi. You've chosen an Assassin as your lover—which makes you even more fascinating—and as your escort I will be able to socialize with the wealthiest, most connected, and ruthlessly ambitious people in all of Rillidi. Some of whom will be nervous to be in the same room as me because they have secrets—secrets *I* know because they hired me." Reo put his book down and leaned forward. "I want my presence to make them nervous enough to act quickly and rashly."

"And spend their money right away," Kara said.

"Yes." Reo nodded. "And you need to be seen as rich because I don't want anyone to speculate about my wealth. People know that Assassins are at work in this city, and being at a party with one might give them a bit of a thrill. But I don't want them wondering how I acquired my wealth. Who paid me for which deaths."

"Or worse, that the dead man might have paid for his own assassination," Chal said.

"You've let someone do that?" Kara asked. "Pay you after they've acquired the victim's possessions?"

"Not every heir is content to wait for their inheritance," Reo said. "And they know the consequences of their failure to pay."

"You kill them too?"

"Ah, Kara," Reo said. "You must think me evil to believe I kill so indiscriminately." He leaned back in his chair, a hint of sadness in his eyes. "I am a professional. I do not kill for joy, I do not kill out of anger, I do not kill on impulse. I am contracted, and I fulfill my obligations. That is all I do." He sighed.

"What I meant," Reo continued, "is that those who contract an assassination risk the same exposure that any Guildsman risks if they fail to live up to their contractual obligation."

"Oh." She looked at the floor. Breaking a contract without the agreement of the other party was punishable by expulsion from the guild. And a contract was a contract, even if it was about a death.

"But," Reo said, "though I've earned my fortune legitimately, as I said, the size of it might attract unwanted attention and speculation."

"So I'm a rich Merchant," Kara said.

"You're a rich Merchant," Reo agreed. "Hopefully that will take some of the focus off of me."

And put the focus directly on her. Reo may want to live out in the open, but that was the last thing that she wanted. She sat back in her chair and watched Chal and Reo talking softly, planning the future. All she wanted was the snug little cabin on Santos Nimali's estate. Would she ever have that again?

Chapter seventeen

KARA WAS NERVOUS. Reo had finally decided that she was ready for her first public appearance. She'd had only Chal and Reo for company for so long that, despite her apprehension, the thought of doing something—anything—was appealing.

It was Founders Day, the day all of the guilds celebrated the creation of the First Guild, and Kara was attending Warrior Guild's celebration with Reo. It was the first day of the last month of the year, and she'd already spent two months reading and studying and wishing the days would go by fast so her year could be over.

Reo had sent her a dress. The silk rustled when she moved, and when she'd looked in the mirror, she almost hadn't recognized herself. The blue set off her dark hair, and the bodice of the dress was cut very low. The large emerald pendant Reo had given her nestled between breasts that Kara felt were far too exposed, but the green of the stone was the exact same colour as her eyes. The woman in the mirror looked like Arabella Fonti's daughter.

When Reo joined her in front of the mirror, she'd been stunned at their reflection. Alone each of them was striking, together they were dazzling.

Reo wore a slim-fitting, black jacket over a shockingly white shirt and black trousers. His vest was the same emerald as her eyes, just as the blue of her dress matched his.

And while her eyes sparkled, Reo's were incandescent—he looked as though he could see through doors, walls, even into her heart. She turned away, not wanting him to see her anxiety. Not at the task tonight, although she was apprehensive about that. No. Suddenly she was nervous about the man standing beside her. Always confident, tonight he exuded power and ease and mystery. Kara had never been to an event like this before, but she knew that Reo was somehow *more* than the other guests could ever hope to be.

Warrior Guild was ablaze with mage lights that did nothing to ward off the chill in the hallways. Reo escorted Kara through the walkways and stone passageways of the Guildhall, her silk wrap pulled close.

"Will other guilds be here?" she asked. Her stomach tightened. Would her mother be here?

"Yes," Reo said. "Although it's unlikely we'll meet the Primus or Secundus from any of the other guilds. They usually spend Founders Day in their own halls."

"In my villa, everyone goes to the upper square," Kara said. "They build a big fire, and Makers roast three or four goats. The Villa Mage Primus leads the Guildsmen and women in the recitation of the Amicitia to renew their oaths for the coming year."

"No one will be leading the Amicitia," Reo said. He paused to look at her. "Is that what's bothering you?"

"I'm not a Guildswoman," Kara said. "I've never been through the ceremony nor have I ever taken the oath, the Amicitia."

"No one will expect you to do that tonight," Reo said. "Founders Day or not, few attending this party will want to be reminded that they are bound to their guild." He smiled. "Come, let's make our entrance."

REO GUIDED KARA down a wide staircase. She heard murmurs and whispers, and many heads turned to watch them descend. Kara knew that this was what Reo had planned, this excitement and mystery and curiosity, but she couldn't help feeling flattered that she was the one he was escorting. Reo was an attractive man—a dangerous man—and he was with her.

Guildsmen milled at the base of the staircase, but the crowd parted as Reo led her into their midst. One after another she was introduced to people whose names and ranks she immediately forgot. Reo's hand gently gripped her elbow, keeping her steady through the constant introductions. Merchants, Warriors, Mages, Guiders, Masons, Artists—she was presented to Guildsmen from every guild.

A weathered Guildsman, a Guider, she thought, asked her a question in Seyoyan, and without thinking she answered him in the same language. Reo squeezed her elbow, and she knew he was pleased. Eventually the crowd thinned, and they were able to make their way to a less crowded part of the room.

Despite being almost overwhelmed, Kara kept a smile on her face as she surveyed the room. So much mage mist! Some of it was so dense that many of the guest's faces were almost obscured by it. The most interesting thing was that the few Mages in attendance had far less mist surrounding them than some of the other guests.

"What in Gyda's name have these people done to themselves?" she whispered in Reo's ear. "They are absolutely covered in magic."

"Really?" Reo said. "Tell me who has the most spells."

"The woman in the ghastly yellow-green silk dress," Kara said. "There is so much mage mist around her face that I can't even see what she looks like."

"Ah, Donna Rualla," Reo said. "She's the wife of the Warrior Guild Secundus. She's never been known as a great beauty, but I have heard that lately she's become obsessed with looking younger. Perhaps she's bought some spells to help?"

"You could be right," Kara said. She scanned the crowd. Many of the older women had the same pale pink mage mist swirling about their heads.

"They've all been spelled by the same Mage." Kara spotted pink wisps of mist trailing behind a woman. "That must be her." The woman stopped, and a cloak was draped over her shoulders. When she lowered her head to allow her hood to be pulled over her hair, Kara found herself staring directly into the familiar eyes of Noula, her father's not-quite wife from Villa Larona.

"Step in front of me," she urged Reo. "Now." She grabbed his arm, and he swung around until he blocked her view. "Someone who knows me is here."

Reo bent to whisper in her ear. "Which way should we go?"

"Behind me."

Keeping his body between her and Noula, Reo turned her around and maneuvered them through the crowd towards a hallway. Once in the hallway he shut the door.

After the noise of the crowd, Kara realized that her breathing was ragged and shallow. Of all people, why Noula?

"Do I need to worry?" Reo asked softly.

"No, I don't think so," Kara said. "I don't think she got a good look at me. I think she was here to attend the Mage."

"She is Server Guild then?"

"No," Kara replied. She wished Noula was Server Guild, then she'd have taken an oath of silence. Servers did not gossip, ever. "She's Mage Guild, but without magic. She could be assigned many duties."

"If she recognized you, will she tell anyone?" Reo asked.

"I doubt she has anyone to tell," Kara said.

She felt Reo relax and wondered what he would have done if she'd answered that Noula was a threat. Would Noula have mysteriously died in the next few days?

"Good," Reo said. "I'll take you back to your rooms. We've made our debut, and leaving early may even increase the curiosity about us."

Arabella frowned and stopped. Noula. What was she doing here? The other woman hid her face until Castio had passed her.

Arabella waited just inside the doors to the council chamber until the room was empty. Then she stepped into the hallway.

"This better be important," Arabella whispered to Noula.

Noula clutched her hands together and nodded. "It is, Master Mage, but I want a promise."

"You want to negotiate with me?" Did Noula know what a dangerous game she was playing? "What is it you want?"

"I want to see my son," Noula said. "You told me you'd arrange, it but you haven't, even though I've done everything you've asked of me for weeks."

Arabella sighed. "I am tired of hearing you complain about it. All right." She met Noula's eyes, and the other woman flinched and looked away. "But if your news is not sufficiently important, both you and your son will regret it."

Noula paled, but she lifted her eyes to Arabella's and nodded.

"Come with me," Arabella said.

"You are risking much for so little," Arabella said. They were sitting in her workroom—at least *she* was sitting; Noula stood in front of her. She'd taken all precautions with this room—just as Rorik had done with his own workroom— and she was confident that Noula's news would not be overheard.

"I'd risk my life to see my son," Noula said.

"And so you have," Arabella replied. "And risked his as well. Tell me."

"Kara Fonti is in Rillidi."

"What? Are you sure?" The girl was dead—Valerio had confirmed that his spell had been activated, and Mason Guild reported that she fell into Broken Burro Gorge.

"She's a little older," Noula said. "And she was dressed very fine, but I had that girl in my house for eight years. It was her."

"Where did you see her?"

"I attended Mage Etta at Warrior Guild last night," Noula said. "For Founders Day. Kara was there, I saw her as we were leaving."

"Do you know why she was there?" Arabella gripped the arms of the chair she was sitting in. Alive! And why Warrior Guild?

"I only saw her for a moment." Noula paused. "She recognized me too. She left the room quickly in the company of a man."

"You may go," Arabella said. If the girl had left because she'd seen Noula, then it must be her. Had she become the bedmate of a Warrior? Is that who she'd been with? She wasn't Arabella's equal, but the girl was pretty enough.

She looked up. "You're still here," she said to Noula. "Why?"

"My son," Noula said. "When can I see him?"

"When I have proof that you really did see Kara. Now go."

Alive—how was that possible? Because even though she'd told Noula she needed proof—deep down she knew that Kara Fonti was alive. And at Warrior Guild!

She took a deep, steadying breath. She should tell Valerio. It was his spell that failed, after all, he would want to know. And then he could teach *her* to create a killing spell. *She* wouldn't fail.

He would not like being told that he'd been unsuccessful in stopping the girl—again—nor would he like anyone knowing of his failure. Could it turn him against her? Would he withhold his support of her as she rose through the council? Or . . . she sucked in a breath. Would he see this as enough of a threat to his reputation that he had to silence her permanently?

She'd grown to know Valerio Valendi since their trip to Larona—enough to know that if she threatened his plans, he would not hesitate to kill her. No, she would have to take care of this herself—make sure the girl died—herself.

She smiled. Kara Fonti had been seen within Warrior Guild's walls—she would have Warrior Guild do her work for her. Rorik would know who their best Assassin was.

A WEEK LATER, Kara still wondered about Noula. Why was she in Rillidi? Had she and Banio Fonti parted ways? It was what her mother had thought would happen. And what about Osten—was he in Villa Larona with Papa, or was he here with Noula?

She'd felt the sting of Noula's bitterness too many times to feel sorry for her, but Osten was just a little boy. He had little chance of having magic, so she hoped Mage Guild had let him stay in Larona—life there would be far kinder to him than Rillidi would be, though his own father would find him of no use.

Every few days Reo came to test her memory of the Founders Day celebration. The first few times she'd tried, really she had, but the fourth time he'd asked her to describe every non-Mage who'd been spelled, she exploded with frustration.

"I told you all this already! I don't see the point in going over it again."

She was sitting on the sofa. Reo perched calmly in front of her on a long low table, and Chal lounged in a chair off to her left, a smirk on his face.

"And don't you laugh," she said and glared at the Seyoyan. "It's not funny."

"It is to me," Chal said. "He did the same thing to me when I first came to work with him."

"Chal."

Reo spoke so softly that even Kara, sitting close to him, barely heard. But Chal nodded and left the room. She glared at him as he left.

"Better?" Reo asked in that soft voice.

Kara nodded. "I still don't see the point."

"The point," Reo said and slid into the seat beside her, "is to see if you remember anything differently as time goes by. For instance, the first time you described Warrior Guild Secundus and Donna Rualla, you only mentioned that *she* was covered in mage mist. Pale pink you said. Yesterday you remembered that he also had a few strands of mist, and that it was a totally different colour."

"You're right," Kara said. "It was a dirty brown colour for him. It was on his left shoulder. Is that significant?"

Reo shrugged and smiled. "Significant, yes, important, who knows? What it tells me is that both husband and wife pay for magic—but they deal with different Mages. What do you make of that?"

"Well," Kara said. "Each of them must have access to sizable amounts of guilders. Mages are expensive. It also makes me wonder if Warrior Guild Secundus Rualla knows his wife is spending on a Mage. If she's doing it to keep herself looking young, she may not want him to know."

"Yes, that was my thought also. I also wonder if she's trying to stay young for her husband or if she's taken a younger lover."

"Would she dare?" Kara asked. "Her husband is very powerful."

Reo laughed. "That would make her even more attractive to some of my colleagues," he said. "To seduce the wife of the Guild Secundus? That Assassin would be remembered for a very long time."

"Is that important?" Kara asked. "To be remembered?" She tried to read his expression, but he faced away from her, gazing out the window.

What would it be like to know that you would probably only live a few more years? Would it make you reckless, or would you become more cautious?

"For some," Reo eventually said. "We are separate even within the guild, and there are only a handful of years to build a reputation. Once we start our training, we are dead to our families. It's very easy to die unnoticed when you're an Assassin. Any memory left behind is better than being forgotten."

His words were bitter and his tone harsh, but instead of scaring her, Kara felt relief. Reo had feelings after all. She placed her hand on his arm. His muscles tensed up under her hand, then relaxed.

"That's the real reason why you want my help," she said. "You don't want to be unnoticed anymore, to be just another Assassin who died young."

Reo pulled his arm out from under her hand and ran his hand through his hair. Then he grinned at her.

"There are times when being unnoticed is very useful," he said. He sighed and relaxed into the sofa.

"That I understand," Kara replied. "I wish I'd not been noticed that day in Shanty Town."

"Do you?"

She met his eyes and nodded solemnly. "My life would have been much simpler," she said.

"But boring," Reo replied. "You're too young to settle for boring. Why did you run away from your guild if not to escape the boring, predictable future?"

Because my mother urged me to leave and now I believe she simply wanted me out of the way—either dead or in another country.

"I didn't run from boring," Kara replied. "I ran from having no choice. Right now I'd choose safe, stable, boring."

Reo eyed her for a long moment. A small smile twitched at his lips. "You would choose boring, would you?"

Reo leaned towards her, and her heart sped up. His eyes darkened and half-closed.

"Choose boring, Kara." His breath feathered the hair around her ears.

His mouth barely touched her neck, but she felt his heat spread from his lips along her neck until her skin tingled all over.

"Have I told you how exquisitely beautiful you are?"

Warm lips trailed down her neck to her shoulder, and all she could do was lean into him. Why was she letting him kiss her like this? Why didn't she stop him?

Because she felt safe. Reo wanted her, *needed* her alive and well. He wouldn't hurt her.

Gently, he cupped her chin and turned her head to face him. He waited until she lifted her eyes to his. Their gaze locked for a few moments, and then he smiled.

"I knew you wouldn't choose boring." Then his lips met hers, and she was lost in a haze of warmth and want and desire.

She'd never really been kissed before, not by a man. His stubbled cheek was rough against her skin, and his mouth was sure and confident against hers and oh so different from the few times a boy in her villa had tried to kiss her. Reo looped one arm around her waist and pulled her onto his lap without breaking the kiss. She leaned into his shoulder, eyes closed, marveling at the heat that was coursing through her. She opened her eyes and touched his face, feeling his smile with both her lips and her hand. She pulled back and stared into his eyes for a moment before she smiled at him.

She felt Reo's low laughter along the length of her body where she was pressed against him.

"You are more than expected, Kara," he said. Then he bent his head to kiss her again, and she sank deeper into him.

"Are you sure?" Reo asked.

"Yes," Kara said. She lifted her arms and slowly started to pull the pins from her hair. Soon her hair hung past her shoulders. She eased off his lap, gently pushed him until he was flat on the sofa, and then she lay on top of him.

Reo wrapped his arms around her, and she dropped her lips to his. His hands fumbled at her back, and then she felt him tug, hard. Fabric ripped, and she heard the soft skitter of buttons hitting the stone floor.

"The man who gave me this dress will be very angry," she said.

"The man who gave you this dress will never again give you clothing so difficult to get you out of," Reo replied. His hands pushed her dress down past her shoulders until her bare breasts pressed against his chest. Reo gently cupped each breast before he tugged at his shirt.

More buttons popped off, and Kara giggled. Then she felt the warm silkiness of his bare skin against her own, and she forgot to breathe.

They were both naked by the time he carried her into the bedroom. Reo laid her gently on the bed and knelt beside her. Soft kisses burned a path from her foot, past her knee, and up along one hip. His lips drifted across her hip, and she trembled when he breathed in the heat between her legs. His mouth found her belly button and then the hollow between her ribs. First one nipple, then the other was gently sucked into his mouth, and Kara whimpered with need. Finally his lips met hers. When his tongue snaked into her mouth, she sucked on it, hard. She felt his knee nudge her legs apart, and Reo steadied himself on his arms. She wrapped her arms around him, and he plunged into her. There was a brief, sharp pain, and then her need took over, and she rocked her hips up to meet his downward thrusts. Her breath ragged, she dropped her head to his shoulder as their pace increased. Pleasure washed over her as she arched towards him. Dimly she heard Reo laugh before his body stiffened, and he plunged into her once more, hard. Kara clung to him, taking him in as deep as she could before they both stilled and then relaxed.

Reo rolled off her, one arm slung over her heaving chest. Shyly, she closed her eyes and nestled her head into his shoulder. Her body felt languid and boneless and totally alive, and she didn't want to move, ever. She felt cool air on her chest when Reo lifted his arm to twitch her hair away from her face.

"Definitely more than expected," Reo said against her hair.

He pulled her close until she lay along his side, their skin damp where they touched. Her head lay on his shoulder, one hand tucked under her chin, resting on his chest. She flattened her hand and rubbed it across smooth skin sprinkled with a few coarse hairs. She felt the muscles of his arm flex as he tightened his grip on her shoulder.

Was this feeling—this languid sense of bliss—was this what Harb had been chasing with the clammers? Kara could better appreciate his motives, although she could never forgive him for putting them all at risk.

Reo's heart beat steadily beneath her hand. Had she put herself at risk? Reo needed her help, she knew that. He wouldn't do anything to hurt her until she'd given him her year. But would sharing his bed make it worse or better? She didn't know, maybe could never know. What had happened between them hadn't been planned, hadn't been thought out in advance, it had simply happened. Reo was an attractive man, and in the eyes of the guilds, she was a grown woman. Long past time for her to be wed, let alone bedded. And she was grateful that her first time had been of her choosing—not everyone was so fortunate. She wouldn't have been if she'd let Mage Guild decide her fate.

Kara stretched. Her body was sore and stiff in some unusual places, but she wasn't tired, not really. She smiled and rubbed her palm across Reo's nipple.

"What are you doing?" he asked sleepily.

"Nothing," she replied. She smiled again and let her hand wander down his chest to the flat muscles of his stomach. Her choice. Her hand dipped lower, and Reo grabbed her wrist.

"That doesn't feel like nothing," he growled.

Kara tilted her head and met his eyes. He smiled, and she grinned at him.

"How about this?" she asked. She tugged her hand loose from his grasp and trailed it down past his hips. His eyes darkened when she grasped him, and she felt a sense of satisfaction at the immediate effect she had on him. Reo Medina, a man who had assassinated countless people, trembled and gasped when she touched him here and here and here.

"My turn to do nothing to you," Reo said gruffly. His hand slipped between her thighs, and it was her turn to tremble and gasp.

Chapter eighteen

KARA STRETCHED UNDER the linen bed covering. She was sore, but pleasantly so. Reo was gone. She ran a hand across the bed beside her. It was cool, so he must have left a while ago. She rolled over onto her side and stared at where he'd lain last night.

More than expected, he'd said to her. She could say the same about him. An Assassin trained to kill since childhood, yet those same hands that killed had been gentle and teasing and had given her tremendous pleasure. She stretched again. She should get up. Judging by the light that was filtering in around the curtain, it was well past noon. Maybe, she grinned, if she stayed in bed Reo would come and check on her, and she could entice him to join her. No. He would have things to do, he always did. Chal was the one who'd come to find her. She didn't yet have the words to explain this to Chal. Not yet, not when it was so fresh and new.

A few minutes later, dressed in a soft white shirt and dark blue skirt, Kara eased the bedroom door open. She spied the book Chal wanted her to read, and she stepped over to the dresser to pick it up. Another history of Seyoya. It took her forever to read the language since Seyoyan used a very different alphabet. She shook her head and returned to the door.

"I told you to go slow, Reo."

It was Chal's voice, and he sounded angry. Kara edged closer to the partially open door.

"I should have bedded her before last night," Reo said. "I told you I didn't want to be out in public with her until I had."

She clutched the book to her chest. What did he mean? Last night was planned? And Chal had known?

"Then you should have waited for that as well," Chal said.

"I don't have time," Reo replied. "I need her out. She needs to be invited to parties and dinners so I can go with her. You know that. I've already lost two months to all of this training."

"Her safety depends on this training," Chal said. "What if she's not ready? For you or the invitations?"

"She seemed ready last night," Reo said.

Kara sucked in her breath. He sounded so smug! What had made her want him in her bed in the first place? Had he planned to seduce her? She'd been so sure it had been her choice. She'd choose differently from now on, no matter what Reo Medina wanted.

"Be careful, Reo," Chal said. "She's not like the women you're used to."

"What, because she's chaste and demure?" Reo said. "You know she's not demure, and, Chal, I wasn't her first."

Kara shrunk in on herself. He was her first, he was wrong about that, but she'd never tell him, not now, not when he was so arrogant about bedding her, about planning it and then actually doing it.

"I think you're wrong," Chal said quietly.

"I was there," Reo said. "I know what I'm talking about."

"Maybe," Chal replied. He sighed. "Ah well, what's done is done. Have you given any thought to how to proceed?"

"I thought I should move here from my own rooms," Reo said. "Now that Kara and I . . ."

"Now that Kara and I are what?" Kara asked as she entered the room. "Bedmates? Lovers? What exactly did you plan, and how long ago was it?"

"Kara!" Reo jumped to his feet.

He made a motion to kiss her, but she stepped around him and settled herself on a chair opposite the sofa he'd been sitting on. The sofa they'd been on when it had all started last night.

"You're angry," Reo said.

A smile hovered around his mouth, and Kara's anger

deepened.

Did he think this was amusing? "I'm angry," she acknowledged. "No woman likes to learn she's been seduced according to a weeks-old plan. Answer one question, and then we'll never have to discuss this again." She smoothed her skirt, relieved to see that her hand was calm. She looked up at him and concentrated on keeping any emotion out of her voice and face. "Why?"

He met her gaze for a moment before he answered. Meeting his eyes and covering up her hurt and disillusionment was one of the hardest things she had ever done.

"We have to be believable," Reo said eventually. "As lovers. A woman carries herself differently around a man she's bedded."

"And people notice?" Kara asked.

"*I notice*," Reo said. "I have to assume others will too. It's for our safety."

"Oh, it's to keep me safe, keep us both safe," Kara said. "Why didn't you discuss this with me? Did you think I wouldn't be interested in being safer?"

"I didn't think . . ."

"No you didn't think, did you? Instead you made a decision and took away my choice."

"You did choose," Reo said defiantly. "Last night."

"An uninformed choice isn't really a choice at all." She took a deep breath and slowly exhaled. "So now I will choose. Don't bother moving from your rooms, I won't be sharing my bed with you again. I trust people will still be able to tell I've bedded you by the way I carry myself when I'm around you?"

Reo nodded. His jaw clenched, and she knew he was furious. Well so was she!

"Please leave," she said to Reo. "You too, Chal. Don't think I'm not angry at you as well. By not telling me what to expect, you played your own part in this."

Reo's anger was palpable as he walked past her. Chal simply regarded her with sad eyes and shrugged.

"And, Reo?" Kara said. "I'll do one assignment with you, to help introduce you, and that's it."

Reo turned to her, his body so tightly controlled that Kara wondered if she'd gone too far. Too late—she wasn't backing down now.

"We had a bargain," Reo said. "I expect you to keep your end of it."

"No," she said. "I can't trust you."

"We had a bargain," Reo repeated.

"Fine," Kara said. "Perhaps I'll simply step aside when I see a spell heading your way."

He paled, and she smiled sweetly.

"One assignment. Your choice and your timetable, but after that I *will* leave."

Reo glared at her, his fists clenching and unclenching as she stood as straight and steady as she could. It was Chal who broke their stalemate. He slipped a hand under Reo's elbow and gently ushered him to the door. The door closed after them, and she was alone in her rooms.

Kara rubbed at her face, wiping away a few stray tears. She would not cry—she would *not* let Reo Medina affect her so much. She'd been foolish and naïve, and he'd taken advantage of that, but she wouldn't allow him to do that to her again. One assignment, she'd told him, and then she would return to Santos' cabin, *her* cabin, and try to make a life. And when she looked out the cabin window at Warrior Guild Island, she would *not* think about Reo Medina.

CHAL VISITED THE next day, his face serious as he set some books on her sitting room table.

"You made him very angry," Chal said softly. "I've never seen him like this."

"He made me angry too," Kara replied. Idly she picked up one of the books and flipped a few pages. It was another history of Seyoyan navigation, complete with star charts and maps of islands. She set it down with a sigh. "Why does everyone think I can't make my own choices?"

"Would you have bedded him if he'd explained it?"

"Probably," Kara said. "If he'd explained why and asked nicely." Her face flushed when she remembered how he had asked her to choose and she had chosen him. But she hadn't known it was to help them both be safe, she'd thought it was because . . . because why? Had she thought Reo Medina was in love with her? No, but she'd thought he'd respected her, enjoyed her company, *liked* her. And all along it was simply something he had to do to prepare them for their tasks. No different than making sure she learned Seyoyan navigation.

"It would be nice to be treated as an adult," she said. "To be allowed to make my own informed choices."

"Not so different from what Reo wants for himself," Chal said.

"What do you mean?" Kara asked. "He's making all the decisions."

"No, he too is constrained by his guild and the expectations they have for him." Chal shook his head. "Unfortunately, in his resolve to free himself, Reo has robbed you of your own freedom."

KARA DIDN'T SEE Reo for more than two weeks, although Chal continued to tutor her. Eventually he declared her Seyoyan respectable enough for a foreigner. The language still felt odd rolling off her tongue, and she had a long way to go before she could read it fluently, but she wasn't concerned about that. Few Tregellans could read their own language half as well as she could read Seyoyan.

"Maybe I should go and live in Seyoya," Kara mused in Seyoyan. "Do you think I could make a living for myself?"

"Yes." Chal lounged on the sofa, a book on guild history in his hands. Kara had started to teach him all she knew about the guilds, Mage Guild in particular, and he'd spent hours reading and asking her questions, always in Seyoyan. "Every trader needs to learn Tregellan, and many would pay for your knowledge of the political history."

"So I could teach," she said. Just as her mother had suggested—had she ever expected her daughter to live long enough to do it?

"What would you like to do?" Chal asked quietly. He set his book down.

Kara leaned across the desk and met his gaze.

"I want to help my friends on Old Rillidi—Vook, Pilo, Sidra, and Mole. And Santos," Kara added. And she wanted to fit in with them again. Reo had changed her—educating her, refining her manners—but she could fit in again. It would take a little time, that's all. Reo had yet to choose her one and only assignment, and she hoped he wasn't going to make her wait too long. She wanted, no needed, to return to her cabin and start making a life for herself.

There was a quick knock, and the door to her apartment swung open.

"Put this on." Reo tossed a dark bundle onto the sofa beside her. He crossed his arms and ran his gaze over her. "What you're wearing will do," he said.

Kara felt her face flush, and she smoothed a hand along her woolen skirt to cover her nervousness.

"Are we attending a party?" she asked. Her skirt and vest were dark blue and her blouse was a pale silvery grey—good quality, but by no means suitable attire for a social function.

"No," Reo replied. "Make sure you wear sturdy footwear. We leave in half an hour." He turned and left the room as abruptly as he'd entered it.

Chal followed him out, stopping briefly to give Kara a questioning look.

Kara unfolded her legs from under her skirt and set her book on the table in front of the sofa. She grabbed the cloth Reo had tossed to her and shook it out. It was a cloak—dull, black wool with a deep, cowled hood. She stood and held it up. It would cover her completely. She peered out the window.

The sky was already a deep indigo, and the moon was a sliver on the horizon. In half an hour it would be dark. They were going in secret then. Was Reo still angry enough with her that he would lead her away and kill her? Kara shook her head. No, if he'd wanted to kill her, he wouldn't have waited so long. This was something he wanted her help with—this was her assignment, her mission. Boots, that's what she needed. Sturdy footwear indeed.

ARABELLA PACED HER workroom. She'd sent the request days ago, and still there was no firm reply. They had acknowledged the request—they couldn't do otherwise for a Mage of her standing. She was on the council—she'd made certain they understood that. But still no firm contract, even though she was offering a substantial number of guilders.

The girl had to die—she'd known it as soon as she arrived in that pitiful mountain town all those months ago. Unconsciously she rubbed her belly—and it wasn't just because Valerio had seemed interested in the girl. No, she had at least a dozen years before this child would be expected to display magical abilities—

by then she would be so entrenched in the Guild power structure that the shame of not producing talented offspring would no longer matter.

She sat heavily in the chair, suddenly feeling drained. This pregnancy would be her last—it was too exhausting.

Valerio had proven to be far too shrewd for her to manipulate into showing her how to create a killing spell. And as for Primus Rorik . . . though he was her confidant these days, a spell of this kind was beyond his skill level.

Arabella wiped a stray hair from her neck. As tired as she was, she may not have the strength to create such a spell even if she knew how.

Warrior Guild must accept her contract—the girl had to die.

Chapter nineteen

REO WAS STILL furious with her. Kara followed his stiff-backed figure through dark, dank tunnels as they decended into the fortifications of Warrior Guild Island. His anger radiated from him, and he'd barely spoken to her since he'd fetched her from her rooms. *Let him stew.* She was still angry too. He'd coerced her into helping him originally, and then he'd had the nerve to use her.

Reo stopped abruptly, and she bumped into him. He glared at her before he pulled a key from inside his jacket and unlocked the door in front of him. When he pulled the door open, the salty odour of the bay wafted out. Reo pulled something else from his jacket, and mage mist swirled around his hand. He held a mage light up, and she preceded him through the door.

After being cooped up within her rooms for so long, even this dank place was a welcome change. A stone jetty extended out a dozen feet, and a few small boats were tied up beside steep staircases that were chiseled into the rock. Multi-coloured mage mist swirled over each of the boats.

"What is this place?" she asked, her voice hushed in the watery cavern.

"It's where the Assassins' boats are kept," Reo said.

The door shut, and she glanced over to see him relocking it

from the inside.

"But they're spelled."

"Of course." Reo stepped down towards the boat. "They are powered by magic and spelled to be silent and unseen."

"How come we can see them here?"

Reo held up his mage light. "This allows the boat to be seen. Once we are on our way, we won't have any light. And when we leave the boat, without this light we'll struggle to find it again."

"Have you ever lost one?" Kara asked. "A boat, I mean."

For a moment she thought he would answer, but then his eyes hardened.

"Time to leave," he said.

He held out a hand and awkwardly helped her down the steps and into the boat.

"Cover up with your cloak." He stepped lightly into the boat and seated himself in the stern, one hand on the tiller. "In case we run across Seyoyans." He reached over and slipped a rope from an iron post driven into the rock face. "Or a Mage with your skills."

Kara lurched as the boat started to move. She huddled into her cloak, suddenly chilled. She glanced at Reo, but he sat stock still, only the hand on the tiller uncovered. The shadows his hood cast were too dark for her to penetrate; she couldn't see his eyes. Then the mage light went out, and they ghosted silently through the cavern.

She felt the air change. A cool breeze blew towards them, carrying the scent of fish and the autumn night. The mouth of the cavern showed the lighter night sky, and once they were out in the open, the pale moon sparkled on the water of the bay. The hulking mass of Warrior Guild Island was behind them, lights streaming through the many windows. Sentries paced along the tops of the walls as they sped away unnoticed.

She sighed and breathed in the tangy salt air. She'd missed being outside. Even Reo's dour presence and the worry of their unknown destination couldn't keep her from smiling.

She sat up. On her right was Old Rillidi Island and the point near Santos' estate. Was Pilo gazing across the water, wondering if she really was seeing the hazy boat? Reo was right, they needed the cloaks. How many others like Pilo were out there? People who could see through magic, but didn't understand what they were seeing? It would give Mage Guild nightmares if they knew about it—if they knew about her.

Kara stared at the shoreline. Somewhere along here was the little cabin. She pictured the rows of food they'd set aside for the winter and smiled, wondering if any of the apples they'd preserved were still uneaten. Pilo would have a hard time keeping Mole away from them, he'd loved them so much.

They passed near the docks, and she strained to see it in the dark. Was that the hulk of the overturned boat? Off in the woods she thought she saw the flickering of a fire, but then they were past, following the coast and rounding a wide, silvery beach. *Probably where the clammers had lived*, she thought.

Lights blazed up ahead, and Kara pulled her cloak tighter. It was a bridge, the one she'd crossed alone after she'd been separated from Mika. The mage lights sparkled on the water, and she held her breath as a few people hurried from Old Rillidi to Merchant Guild Island. She shivered. She'd been lucky that Vook had found her that first night. She could have ended up with the banditos. She peered out from under her hood at Reo. What the Assassin had requested of her seemed reasonable compared to what life with the banditos would have been like. But it didn't mean she'd forgiven him.

A second bridge loomed ahead, and Kara tried to remember her geography lessons. Mason Guild Island, of course, she knew it as soon as she saw the cut stone of the bridge. Reo motioned, and she ducked. If she reached out, she could touch the stone that arched above her head. Mage mist faintly outlined each block, and she wondered if Masons unconsciously used magic. If Pilo and the clammers had magic—so could others.

When they emerged from under the bridge, Kara sat up and stifled a gasp.

Ahead the sky was bright with mage mist. It flowed and swirled in every colour and hue—blues, greens, white, purples.

None of the books, none of the descriptions she'd read, had prepared her for her first real look at Mage Guild Island.

Turrets and towers stretched up into the sky. The mage mist that blanketed the city varied in density, and in places she was able to see through it to the actual buildings. A sweet perfume drifted across the bay, and she sighed at the lovely smell of roses and sunshine and honey.

As they got closer to the dark shadow that stretched out below Mage Guild Island, she shivered. They were going underneath it. She knew that the island floated, but the realization that the huge mass would soon be above her was unnerving. She pulled her cloak tight and concentrated on not letting the mage mist react to her. What if her mere presence was enough to interfere with the magic that held the island aloft? Had Reo even considered that when he'd decided to bring her here?

Why *had* he brought her to Mage Guild Island? Did he plan to assassinate a Mage? Did he expect her to protect them both from magical attack? Or maybe Reo was doing a Mage a favour, and Kara would be asked to remove a curse or two? But if so, it would expose her talent to a Mage, something Reo had said he didn't want to do. Unless that was his revenge for withdrawing her help.

They slowed as they entered the shadow. Mage mist eddied against the sides of the boat, and mage lights twinkled on the underside of the island, illuminating patches of earth. Wooden docks, many with small boats tethered to them, dotted the water as far as she could see. Staircases attached to the docks led up into the earth itself. She didn't smell dirt or fish or sea, instead there was just the sweet floral scent, which seemed more cloying than pleasant now.

The boat took them further and further under the island, and Kara turned to watch Reo's profile, hoping to get a sense of what he was thinking, but he stared straight ahead.

Finally the boat glided up to a small dock attached to a set of stairs. She glanced around nervously. Mage lights dotted the underside of the island as far as she could see, and around everything rainbows of mage mist eddied. Her mouth felt dry, and she licked her lips. The stairs they stopped beside seethed with mist.

"Come," Reo said. He stood and held out a hand to her.

Kara grabbed it and let him steady her as she stepped onto the small dock.

Reo joined her, keeping a hand firmly on her waist. The lit staircase led up to a closed door. Reo urged her forward, and she climbed the steps.

The door was covered in more mage mist. Kara squinted, trying to see beyond the mist. Reo reached the top step, and she moved aside.

"Is there magic?" he asked. His voice was quiet, almost a whisper, and Kara wondered if he was as nervous as she was.

"Yes," she replied. "Everywhere."

He frowned and glanced around, and again she wondered what he had planned, what would bring him here, with her as his only protection.

Reo reached out and rapped twice on the door. The sound of his knock was so muffled that Kara barely heard it, yet the door swung open immediately. An old woman, the crest of the Server Guild sewn onto her blouse, stepped aside so that they could enter.

"You are expected," she said and quickly closed the door behind them.

Reo pushed his hood off his face and reached out to pull Kara's down. She passed a hand through her hair and turned to look at him, but he had already turned away.

They followed the Server through hallways lit by mage lights. After a few turns, their surroundings changed—the hallways were larger, and the ceilings were higher. The Server stopped in front of two large, ornately carved doors, bowed low to them, and backed away.

Kara looked at Reo, but he kept his gaze averted, and an uneasy feeling settled over her. Had he brought her here to have her killed because she'd defied him?

The doors cracked open, and a swirl of mage mist flowed out. Before she could react, it skipped past her and swept over Reo. Briefly he clenched his hands and then opened them wide, leaving them to dangle at his side.

He felt the magic. Maybe that was the point of the spell. The mist quickly faded, and Reo turned to face the open door.

"Enter," came the order.

"Behind me," Reo said.

She slipped behind him as he walked through the door.

"That's far enough, Assassin," a voice said. A woman's voice.

Kara felt the sweat chill on her skin. The mage mist that had greeted them was a vaguely familiar purple. She peeked over Reo's shoulder and sucked in her breath.

"Reo, what have you done?" she whispered, horrified to see her mother, Arabella Fonti, staring down at them from the front of the room.

Purple mage mist swirled around Arabella's cloaked figure, and mage lights hovered overhead, creating a spotlight that shone directly on her. Arabella Fonti peered out into the darker end of the room. One hand gestured, and a mage light flew towards Kara and Reo.

"Be quiet," Reo whispered. "She doesn't know I brought you." The mage light stopped and hovered over them, illuminating the fury on Reo's face. "She wants you dead."

"I know," Kara said. And she had known, but this *proved* it.

Her mother had never believed she'd survive long enough to find her way to another country—to live a happy, safe life. And Reo didn't know who he was dealing with. Her mother wanted her own daughter dead—she wouldn't hesitate to kill the Assassin she'd hired to do it.

"What are you whispering about, Assassin?" Arabella Fonti asked. She made another hand gesture, and a wisp of mage mist flowed their way.

Before it reached them, Kara stepped out from behind Reo and into the light.

"What are you doing?" He grabbed her arm just as she swept the mage mist aside.

"Making sure that the spell she just released doesn't touch you," Kara said. She shook his hand off and took a step forward.

"Hello, Mother," Kara said.

From behind her she heard Reo's sharp intake of breath, while at the front of the room, her mother glared down at her.

"Why did you bring her?" Arabella said.

"Reo's angry with me and trying to prove a point," Kara replied.

Reo stepped up beside her, and she glanced over at him.

"You once told me that when an Assassin starts their training they are dead to their family. But at least your family hasn't tried to kill you. That's twice now, isn't it, Mother?"

"I told you to never call me that," Arabella said. "I may have given birth to you, but you are *not* my daughter."

"Yes, I've learned that the hard way," Kara replied. Now that she was actually confronting her mother, she felt calm. "It was Noula, wasn't it? She's the one who told you I was alive and in the city."

"Noula, yes." Arabella's voice was full of contempt. "She's

pathetic. She'll do anything for that brat of hers. As if Banio Fonti's child is of any interest to me."

"Where is he?" Kara asked, worried. Her mother wouldn't care what happened to Osten.

"Why should you care?" Arabella sneered. "Oh, of course, he's your half-brother." She smiled a slow, dangerous smile. "That's a nice touch. I'll have to thank the Assassin for that. Your last thoughts will be about the horrible existence that child will have because of your failure. You should have died on the road, like you were supposed to."

"Sorry I couldn't oblige you, Mother."

"I haven't taken the commission," Reo said. "Nor will I."

"I understand that," Arabella replied. Her gaze swept over the two of them. "Well, that is interesting." She leaned forward a little. "I suppose I must give the girl a tiny bit of credit for bedding one of Rillidi's best Assassins. I'm not sure what you see in her, but it does not matter to me. You have saved me a considerable amount of expense and trouble. You don't think you can walk out of here alive, do you?"

"As a matter of fact I do," Kara replied. She took hold of Reo's arm. "Stay close," she whispered. "Don't take a step unless I tell you to."

"It's sad, really," Arabella said. "Killing you won't even be a challenge, and the Assassin won't get close enough to pose any real danger." She eyed Reo. "A shame too. He is lovely."

Arabella formed a ball of mage mist and hurled it towards them. When it was close, Kara raised her arm and—as though she was ridding Santos of a curse—swept it aside. It spun towards the stone wall and hit it with a burst of sparks.

Arabella frowned and sent another spell, and Kara deflected it, too. Her mother's spells came faster, but Kara waved her hands and sent them spinning away from her and Reo.

"What are you doing?" Arabella asked.

The mage mist was less and less dense—the power of each spell weakening—until a wisp of magic she sent their way dissipated even before it reached them.

"You're tired, Mother," Kara said. "Your spells are losing power." She squinted and frowned. A thin band of dark grey and purple mage mist trailed away from her mother and out under a closed door.

"I have more than enough power to destroy you," Arabella said.

"No," Kara said. "Someone is draining your power. Can't you feel it?"

"No one would dare," Arabella said. "Not from me."

"I can see it," Kara said. "I have a talent after all—I can see magic."

"That's impossible," Arabella said. "And even if you can, it doesn't sound very useful."

"You'd be surprised how useful it is," Reo said.

"You believe her." Arabella settled back against the desk. "Do you think avoiding spells is enough to get you off Mage Guild Island safely?"

"I can do more than see magic, Mother," Kara replied.

Reo tightened his grip on her hand, and she winced. *What was he doing?*

"I can tell whose magic it is. I met the person who's draining your magic when you both came to Villa Larona. Valerio Valendi is siphoning off your power."

"He would never," Arabella said.

Kara could see the doubt in her mother's eyes even from where she stood. Then Arabella laughed.

"If Valerio's magic is near me, it's no doubt because I'm carrying his child." She pulled the fabric of her robe tight across her bulging belly. "We already expect our child to have great power—perhaps it will also be able to see magic."

"Were you jealous of me?" Kara asked. Santos had admitted to being curious about her—*their*—bloodline. Was that something Valerio Valendi shared?

"Jealous of you?" Arabella laughed. "An insignificant, untalented, villa girl? Not likely."

"Yes, you were," Kara said. "That's the real reason I was a problem, wasn't it? Why I was *your* problem. Valerio Valendi thought I might have some latent talent that I could pass on to a child—*his* child—but you wanted to be the one to bear it. When I had no magic, you didn't think enough about me to care whether I lived or died. Until you thought I would be in your way."

"Now that won't matter," Arabella said. "You'll never leave here alive."

"Do you want her to die?" Reo asked.

Kara paused. Did she want her mother to die?

"You, kill me?" Arabella's laugh rang out in the room. "You realize where you are, don't you?"

"Yes," Reo replied, his mouth tight. "But Kara has said that your magic is weakening." He turned to Kara. "I am truly sorry. I will do everything I can to get you to safety, though I fear even giving my life won't be enough."

"How touching," Arabella drawled. "I didn't realize Assassins were so dramatic. You should die just for that." She flicked her fingers, and a wisp of mage mist sped towards him.

Kara stepped in front of Reo and waved it off.

"How are you doing that?" Arabella asked. Another smaller cloud of mage mist left her hand and trailed behind her, then drifted under the door.

"Who have you sent for?" Kara asked. "The spell you just sent off, who are you hoping will respond?"

"How are you deflecting my spells?" Arabella asked.

"Kara," Reo said. "Tell me now if you want her to die. Otherwise we must leave—now—before more Mages come."

Kara studied the woman who had given birth to her, but had never wanted to be her mother. She was mean and vindictive and jealous, and she'd tried to hire someone to kill her own daughter. Did Kara want Reo to kill her? She shook her head.

"Let's go," she said. "She's not worth your life, Reo." She turned and pulled him with her through the door.

ARABELLA WATCHED THE two slip out the door.

"You will not get away!" she called after them. She clutched at the table and gasped. She'd exhausted her magic—she could feel it—and the girl had not even seemed tired. Was it a new form of magic? She could not trust anyone with this knowledge.

Not Valerio—because despite what she'd told the girl she *did* believe her. She'd put it down to the pregnancy, but her exhaustion wasn't natural—it hadn't responded to any spells from the healer, and no matter how much rest she got she never felt recovered. She had to admit that Valerio was most likely stealing her power—making her weaker—even while she carried his child.

"Arabella. I came as soon as I received your summons."

"Rorik, good." She let him lead her to the chair. "There are enemies of Mage Guild on the island, but we need to be discreet. One of them is an Assassin, and I asked him here . . . you know how that causes questions."

"Of course," Rorik replied. "I will send for a few trusted guards." He waved a hand towards the door. "They should be here soon. Who is the Assassin with?"

"A girl—a Mage Guild runaway," Arabella said.

"Does she have magic?"

Arabella shook her head. She wasn't going to tell him that the girl had somehow managed to evade the many spells she'd tried to kill her with—or that it was *her* child. No one needed to know that. And once the girl and the Assassin were dead—no one would.

A guard slipped into the room, and Rorik whispered instructions to him. He bowed quickly, then left.

"A tracker will be set on them," Rorik said. "They won't get far."

"Who won't get far?"

Arabella turned in time to see Valerio shut the door. He strode up to her and Rorik.

"My dear, you look a bit . . . tired," he said.

When she met his eyes, there was a hint of humour in them. Had he noticed the decline in her power through his feed from her? She nodded, but didn't smile. She wouldn't accuse him—there was no way she would win that battle even though it was a serious offence.

"And you look very vigorous," she replied. She continued to meet his eyes until his humour dissipated, and he looked away. Not a victory—but he knew she *knew*.

"I repeat my first question," Valerio said. He turned to Rorik. "Who won't get far?"

"An Assassin and a runaway."

"A girl?" Valerio asked.

He glanced at Arabella, and she dropped her eyes to her lap.

"Yes," she replied. "A female Mage Guild runaway." She felt it when his insolence turned to anger. She met his gaze and slowly nodded.

"How is it possible?" Valerio said.

"Arabella brought the Assassin in," Rorik interjected. "Although we want to keep that quiet. For some reason the girl was with him.”

“For some reason,” Valerio replied. “How?”

“I don’t know how!” Arabella said. “It shouldn’t be possible—is in fact impossible—yet there she was.”

“I’m sure she came with the Assassin,” Rorik said.

“I will take care of this,” Valerio said.

“I’ve already assigned guards,” Rorik said. “They are efficient and will keep this to themselves. If the Secundus joins in the search, it will garner far more attention than we want.”

“I will go alone,” Valerio said. “They will not elude me.” He nodded to Arabella and left.

She heaved herself to her feet. She needed food—and rest—some way to recover some energy. Valerio would find them—but she wanted to be there, too. She needed to see the girl die—needed proof that it was finally done.

ARABELLA FONTI’S SHOUT followed them as they hurried down the hallway, away from whoever was approaching, away from their boat, away from the only way out that Kara knew. Mage lights twinkled all along the hall, and Kara squeezed Reo’s hand, trying to reassure him.

“Stay close,” she whispered. “I need to keep the mage mist away from us.”

He nodded and settled in next to her, his body almost pressed against her side. Step by step, she tried to hurry through the eddies of multicoloured mist that writhed along the hallway. Another turn, and then another, and she had no idea which direction they were heading in, but they were further away from any sounds of pursuit. A passage intersected the corridor they were in, branching off in two more directions and she stopped, unsure of which way to go.

“What’s wrong?” Reo asked in her ear.

“I don’t know the way out,” Kara said. “Should we go straight, left, or right? I’ve gotten us lost.”

“Right,” Reo said. “That’s south. They’ll be less likely to look for us that way.”

“South,” Kara repeated. “How do you know?”

“I always know.” Reo shook his head and grimaced. “Assassins are trained to always know which direction we face. And they won’t expect us to go south because it’s the most unlikely choice—

straight through the heart of Mage Guild Island." He laughed bitterly. "A lunatic's choice."

"Sometimes they work," Kara said, thinking about her own choice to run away from Villa Larona. A lunatic's choice, yes, since she'd been so badly prepared. "Sometimes they have to since the alternative is worse."

Reo laughed again—this time with genuine pleasure.

"Then let's be lunatics," he said. "And make the choice no one would expect."

"I do count the mad mage among my friends you know," Kara said. "South it is." She tugged on Reo's arm as she headed down the corridor.

Chapter twenty

REO LED THE way at a quick pace, and Kara did her best to keep up, but she tripped over her skirts and stumbled into him. He gently steadied her before they rounded a corner. She grabbed him and stopped.

"Stay still," she whispered. "And keep close. There's mage mist ahead."

Reo nodded, stepped behind her, and wrapped his arms around her. Facing forward, she had to admit that she welcomed his warmth—the amount of mage mist that swirled and coiled in the corridor ahead of them frightened her. Slowly she walked them forward.

Like the day the clammers had chased her small group, she concentrated on letting the mist eddy past. But on that other day, the mage mist had been benign—these spells were malevolent, purposeful, and searching for *them*. Most of it was the familiar dark grey of Valerio Valendi.

Kara continued to inch them down the corridor until they were finally out of the mage mist. She nodded to Reo—he grabbed her hand, and they trotted down the hall.

"I DON'T SEE anyone," Reo said as he slid down the wall to sit beside her. "What about magic?"

Kara grabbed the stone sill of the window, pulled herself up, and peered outside. It was dark, well after midnight, and the grounds of the little park were shadowed. Mage mist lit up the odd flower or tree, simple spells to make them grow and bloom, she supposed. None of the crawling grey-black clouds of Valerio Valendi or the purple swirls of her mother.

"It seems clear," she said and sat down beside Reo.

"Good. The building on the other side looks like a school of some sort. Let's hope it's empty at this time of night." He crouched, but kept his eyes on the park. "We'll wait an hour before we cross the park. That should be long enough for any guard to come by." He glanced down at her. "Why don't you try to sleep? It may be a while before you have another chance."

"What about you?"

"I'll be fine," he replied. He gazed out the window again. "This time of night is when I usually work."

She shivered as she lay down on the floor. Reo was an Assassin—she shouldn't forget that, ever. He was dangerous, yes, but he wasn't infallible. Why had he brought her here to confront the woman who wanted to hire him to kill her? Why had he allowed himself to be so angry that he'd walked them both into danger? Her mother would never have let him leave alive. How had he not realized that? Had he expected her to get them out safely? Or had he even thought that far? When they were safe, *if* they were safe, she'd ask him.

"Kara."

She felt her shoulder being shaken, and groggily she opened her eyes. In spite of the thoughts that had been running through her head, she had actually fallen asleep.

"We need to go," Reo said.

She sat up and stretched. "I'm ready," she said and stifled a yawn.

"Good. There's been no sign of a watch or guard. Can you check again for magic?"

She poked her head up past the window sill.

"Nothing's changed," she said.

"Let's go."

Reo edged over to the open window, and Kara followed. The night was still warm, but the air was slightly damp, and she was chilled from sleeping on the stone floor. She rubbed her hands against her arms, trying to warm herself up.

"Keep low," Reo said. He swung his legs over the sill and eased through it.

Kara leaned out, and Reo grabbed hold of her waist and pulled. Her skirt snagged, and she heard the fabric tear, and then she was out and in Reo's arms. She breathed in his scent—clean and musky with an undercurrent of salt air, then he dropped his arms and turned away. Kara wrapped her arms around herself. She was angry with him, and hurt by what he'd done tonight, but she still felt safe in his arms.

He was willing to die for her. He'd made that promise many weeks ago, but tonight, when he'd told her that in front of her mother, she'd felt it in her soul. He was willing to die for her. It was a huge responsibility—she could make a choice that would send him to his death. She hadn't been willing to make that choice earlier, didn't think she'd ever be able to make it.

"Stay close," Reo whispered.

He turned, and she met his eyes, cool and shadowed in the moonlight. Kara nodded, and Reo squeezed her arm before he turned to view the garden again.

He tensed and then he was off, a low, dark blur against the hedges and bushes. Kara picked up her skirts and followed. He didn't stop until he was flat against the far building. As she scrambled towards him, he looked past her, scanning for danger. She hunched against the cold, stone wall, trying to be quiet as she gulped in air. She was nervous and scared, and her heart was pounding after that mad dash across the park.

Reo peered out at the garden for a few minutes more. Finally he turned to her.

"Stay here," he said. "While I go inside."

"Don't you want me to look for mage mist?" she asked.

"Not this time," Reo replied. He studied the open space around the door. "If I'm not back in half an hour, don't come after me. Keep heading for the southern edge of the island."

He opened the door to the building and entered it. Kara shivered. If he didn't come back, she'd have to manage—she'd keep to their plan and make her way to the south part of the island. Then she'd find a boat and try to get to Old Rillidi.

The door to the building finally opened again. Reo beckoned her forward, and she sighed with relief.

"All clear?" she asked once she was inside.

"It is now," Reo said. "This way." He set off down a corridor.

Kara smelled it first. A tangy, iron odour mixed in with the smell of urine. A door along the corridor was slightly ajar, and a long, dark smear led from another closed door straight to it. As she passed by, she peered in. Bodies—three that she could see—lay tumbled over one another. One face stared up at her, the man's mouth open in an O of surprise. She looked away and found herself staring directly into Reo's eyes.

"Are you all right?" she asked.

Something—she thought it was relief—flashed across his face.

"I'm fine," he replied. "We need to keep moving."

Kara followed as he rounded a corner and strode through an open door. Stairs led down, and she could smell the floral scent that masked the salty smell of the bay. Reo opened a small wooden door, and for Kara, the bottom stairs were illuminated by the glow of mage mist.

"It will be dawn soon, and too bright for us to stay above ground," Reo said. "We'll take a boat and try to find a quiet place where we can stay until dark."

"Can we take the boat all the way to the southern edge of the island?" Kara asked.

"No," Reo said. "We'll be too exposed. We're being looked for, and a moving boat can be seen for miles down here. Even this late at night, I don't dare row." He crawled down a few steps, crouched, and leaned over until his eyes were below the bottom of the island. Reo shifted around until he'd scanned every direction.

"I don't see anyone," he said when he came back up. "Is there magic?"

"Lots," Kara replied. "I'll keep it away from us."

Reo helped her into a small boat before he shrugged out of his cloak, took off his boots, and tossed them into the bottom of the boat. Then he untied the boat and slipped into the dark water.

Reo's hands gripped the gunwale, and his head bobbed beside her.

"Keep the magic away from us and stay as low in the boat as possible," he said. "I'll tow you until we find a safe place to hide for the day."

"We should leave the boat," Kara replied. "Why don't we both swim?"

"No, the water is too cold," Reo said. "I've trained for this, and even I can't do it for very long." His head disappeared, and the boat jerked forward. His head surfaced. "Can you swim?" he asked.

"No," Kara said. She'd waded into her share of rivers and streams, but always with her feet on the bottom.

Reo smiled. "Then it's not a valid offer anyway. I can do this for about half an hour, maybe more, then I might need your help getting back into the boat. Now you get out of sight."

Kara lay down in the bottom of the boat and concentrated on letting the mage mist swirl past them. She was grateful for the small reminders that Reo was still with her—his hand on the gunwale, a sharp intake of breath every once in a while. Soon the stairs they had descended were left behind as Reo navigated them through the waters beneath Mage Guild Island.

Mage lights lit their way, almost as bright as day, and for Kara, the added glow of mage mist meant that she had to keep her eyes closed against the glare. Then the light changed, and they were beneath a shadowed section. There were no mage lights here, and when she peeked over the gunwale, a small dock was bare of mage mist.

Kara reached out and placed her hand on top of Reo's. His head swiveled towards her.

"This dock is different." She pointed. "There's no magic."

Reo tugged the boat to the dock and heaved himself up onto it.

"Then this is where we stop," he said. He quickly tied the boat up.

Kara tossed him his cloak, and he swept it over his shoulders, pulling the hood over his head. He reached for his boots and pulled them on. Only when he stopped moving did she notice how much he was shivering.

"Are you all right?" She'd been asking him that a lot in the last few hours. And it wasn't simply because she needed his help to get out of this situation. *He is willing to die for me.* And tonight, he'd killed for her.

"I'm fine." Reo's voice came out in a whispery shudder. "Just need to warm up. You're sure there's no magic?"

"None," Kara said. "I think it's abandoned. See, all the other docks are brightly lit and in good repair, but this one is dark and run-down."

"You don't think anyone lives here."

"No," Kara replied. "Not for a long time."

Reo frowned and looked around. "I can't see a better place to try to hide. I can't swim any further—not without rest—and it will be daybreak soon. We need to be off the water now.

"Careful." Reo steadied her as she stepped onto the dock. He untied the boat and shoved it away. "Let's go."

Carefully, Kara followed him along the rickety dock and up the stairs. After seeing such huge amounts of mage mist, the absence of any left her blind. Wood scraped against wood, and a dusty breeze puffed down the stairs.

"Be careful on the fourth step," Reo called softly.

Kara felt around, and her hand caught on jagged wood. She relaxed a little—no one had used these stairs in years—and scrambled past the broken step.

A faint, natural light highlighted Reo against the doorway. Dawn had arrived. As soon as she was through the door, he swung it closed, shoving it hard. The wood groaned, and the door wedged shut.

They were in a hallway. A high window let in pink-tinged sunlight, and dust motes floated in the air. More dust layered the floor in front of them, and a few bare patches of floor showed through where their feet had scuffed the yellowed tiles. She'd thought that Santos' house on Old Rillidi had been in disrepair, but this was far worse. If magic had ever kept this place clean, it had long since faded. Just as on the dock below, there was no trace of mage mist.

"I doubt we'll run into anyone," Reo said. He drew a finger across the handle of a half-open door, and a thick film of dust clung to him. "But there could still be magic."

Reo took her hand and peered around the door before he pushed it completely open. Swaths of yellowed fabric draped lumps that must have been furniture.

"There's no mage mist," Kara said. "None. Which is odd."

"Could it have run out?" Reo asked. "Do spells fade with time?"

She frowned. "I'm not sure." She walked around the room. Something about it felt familiar. She spun around. The furniture was placed the same as the Old Rillidi estate. "I think this house may belong to Santos."

Reo looked over at her. "Is there a spell?"

"No," she said. "I don't *know*—but the room—it's almost as though it's an echo of his estate on Old Rillidi." She shrugged. "Not that it matters, but it feels like him."

"It makes sense," Reo said. "They left him on Old Rillidi, and his house on Mage Guild Island is intact. Does he have any living relatives?"

"None that he's talked about," she said.

"Good," Reo said. "No one to suddenly appear."

It took them just over half an hour to search the house, then Reo led the way to the workroom.

"We'll stay here until it's dark," he said.

The room had two doors, one that led to the kitchen and a second that probably led outside. Daylight filtered in through a window set high up in the same wall as the second door.

"Get some sleep," Reo said. He gently tugged a cloth off a bench and wrapped it up, dusty side in. He set the bundle down in a corner and gestured to Kara.

"You too," she said. She huddled into her cloak and sat on the floor near the cloth. She stifled a sneeze as the dust settled.

"Later," Reo said. "Once I'm sure we haven't been followed."

She stared at him for a moment before she lay down and closed her eyes, content to let Reo watch over her. She pulled the hood of her cloak tight around her face, blocking out the light. She shouldn't trust him, not after he'd taken her to her mother, the person who had tried to hire him to kill her. But everything he'd done since then, every look he'd given her, everything he'd said, even the way he held himself, all told her that he hated himself for what he'd done and that he would do everything within his power to get her out safely.

The arrogant Assassin who had manipulated her into his bed and then been furious when she'd refused to co-operate was gone. And this new Reo, this apologetic, considerate Reo, she trusted. But now she worried that he was almost too calm. Had he already decided that she was the only one that would come out of this alive?

Arabella sat motionless, trying not to let her fatigue

overwhelm her. She wasn't positive, but it felt as though the weariness she was experiencing now was natural—a result of the mostly sleepless night spent creating spells to find the girl and the Assassin—and not because Valerio was stealing her energy.

"This one should do it," Valerio said. His eyes were dull and his movements slow—proof that he too was suffering from overextending his power.

"So you said the last time." Arabella was too tired to keep the reproach out of her voice, and the Secundus winced.

"Yes. There is no reason why that spell failed, and yet it did."

No reason. Arabella hadn't told him about her own futile attempts to use magic against the girl—or about the girl's claim that she could see and manipulate spells—she'd said that her own exhaustion had made her spells too weak. He'd seemed uneasy at her words. She wondered if he felt any guilt over using— *stealing*—her power. He should.

"I have no idea why, but I've been unable to find your daughter."

This time it was Arabella's turn to wince—she hated that she'd given birth to the girl, and he knew that.

"This spell targets the Assassin. There can only be a few dozen Warriors on the island—I don't care if they all die today, as long as the Assassin dies."

"Warrior Guild will not be happy," Arabella commented. She didn't care about a few Warriors either, but she was interested in how he thought he could manage their guild.

"*I'm* not happy," Valerio said. "A Warrior Guildsman is helping a Mage Guild runaway escape capture. Even Warrior Guild cannot deny our right—our obligation—to uphold Guild Law. When they learn of this, losing a few Guildsmen will seem a small price to pay. Come. Rorik will be awake by now. I need an update from the guards he sent out."

Silently, Arabella followed Valerio out of his workroom and into the hall of his home. She was beginning to see the pattern in how Valerio managed his affairs. He never seemed to care, and he was always able to find a way to minimize his own responsibilities by attacking how poorly others had managed theirs. In this case—it would work.

Chapter twenty-one

"KARA."

A hand grasped her shoulder and shook it gently.

"Time to go."

She pulled her hood off her head and blinked open her eyes. Reo crouched in front of her.

"Did you sleep?" she asked.

"Some," he replied and moved away from her.

"Good." Kara stretched her left arm over her head. It tingled a little as the circulation returned. "We both need to be rested if we're going to get out of this."

She stood up, smoothing out her skirt.

"Now what?" she asked.

"The door leads to a small laneway," Reo said. "I checked while you were asleep. Once we're outside, we'll make our way south."

"To the far side of the island," Kara said.

"To the far side," Reo agreed. "Ready?"

"Yes."

Reo opened the door, and a breeze wafted through it. She smelled flowers and damp earth and grass. She took a deep breath before she followed Reo out into the night. He gently pushed the door shut behind them, grabbed her hand, and tugged her after him down a short alley.

They made their way through alleys and streets that were bright with mage mist. At times Kara pulled Reo to a stop to let clouds of magic sweep past them. Sometimes it was her mother's purple mist, but most of it was the familiar dark grey-black of Valerio Valendi.

Had Reo known who the Mage was who'd wanted to hire him? Had he known that she counted the Mage Guild Secundus as an ally? Perhaps. But he hadn't known that Arabella wanted him to assassinate her own daughter, and so he might have underestimated her resolve. And for that, Kara had to shoulder some of the responsibility. Reo hadn't told her someone wanted her dead, but neither had she told him that her mother was a powerful Mage. They'd both made mistakes, and now they were both in danger.

Reo found a fountain in a small park, and Kara knelt and scooped water up with cupped hands. Too soon, Reo pulled her to her feet, and they set off again, keeping to the narrow, twisting alleys as much as they could.

Reo stopped and bent towards her. "We should start looking for a place to hide for the day," he said, the first words he'd spoken to her all night.

Startled, she glanced around. The mage mist was so thick and glowed so brightly that she'd lost all track of time.

"Everything's covered with mage mist," she said. "It's coating all the buildings and streets. Even the trees and flowers."

Reo nodded. "Let me know when you see a place, any place, that has a little less magic." He set off down another alley way, heading south, always south.

They'd gone a few more blocks when she tugged on Reo's hand and pointed towards a small roof that barely poked above a rough, wooden fence.

"No magic," she said. "Just a little on the fence."

Reo nodded, and they stopped beside the fence.

"Stay here," he said. "In the shadow." He took off his cloak and bundled it into her arms. "I'll be back soon."

Reo grabbed the top of the fence and slowly pulled himself up high enough to look over it. A few moments later, he dragged himself up and over.

Kara slid down to a crouch, leaning against the fence. Reo had told her that she was in shadow, but she felt exposed. Light from mage mist swirled around the alley and flowed along the side of the building across from her. A few wisps of yellow and green mist trailed along the bottom of the fence, and idly she poked her finger into it, watching as the mist curled away from her. She didn't even have to concentrate—mage mist simply passed by her. When her mother had attacked them, all she had done was redirect the magic as it recoiled from her.

So much hate from a woman who, by all rights, should love her more than anyone else in the world. Gyda, she was tired of being alone. Maybe when she and Reo got off this island, she'd head back into the mountains—she could build a cabin near Mika and Allon. The few weeks that she'd spent there had been the most serene of her life. She'd have to visit Santos and Vook and the others before she left. Could she take them with her? Would they want to leave Rillidi? She'd only known them for a few months, and already they were more important to her than her own flesh and blood.

She rubbed her eyes. What had Arabella said about Noula and Osten? That the child had been sent somewhere. She remembered the smiles and bright laughs when he was young, before he was old enough to follow Noula's lead and treat Kara with disdain. She hoped he . . . what? What did she hope for him? That he survived and lived a horrible life filled with pain and misery or that he sickened and died quickly? That he lived, she decided. As long as Osten lived there was hope—hope for a better life, hope for some small joys. Hope. That's what she was clinging to as well.

"Kara, throw me both cloaks," Reo's whisper drifted over the wall.

She tossed Reo his bundled cloak and quickly pulled off her own. The cool night breeze lifted the edge of her skirt. She wadded up her cloak and threw it over the fence.

Reo tossed them down on the other side of the fence and reached for her. She stretched her arms up, and he gripped her left forearm. She copied him, feeling his warm flesh beneath her hand, their wrists fitting together like a puzzle. He heaved her up, and she grabbed the top of the fence and swung her legs over it. Reo dropped into shadows and caught her as she slid over the fence.

"Thanks," Kara said. "Sorry I'm not better at this." She

steadied herself against his warm chest.

"Not to worry," Reo whispered into her ear. "You have other talents that make up for it."

For a moment she wondered if he was referring to the night they'd bedded, but no, he would be thinking about her ability to see and avoid magic. That's what he'd wanted from her all along.

Reo guided her to a small hut.

"Anything?" he asked.

She shook her head. There was not a trace of mage mist around this small building. The door was half off its hinges, and the wood was worn and splintered. Other than Santos' house, this was the only structure she'd seen in all of Mage Guild Island that was devoid of magic.

Reo pushed open the door, and she stepped past him. It was dark inside. She shuffled her feet along the floor, stubbing her boot into something solid. Her hand went out, and she felt what seemed to be a stack of wooden planks. There was a scuffling sound in front of her, and she froze.

"It's just mice," Reo whispered.

"Mice?" Kara sighed with relief. "That means no one comes here."

"My thought as well," Reo agreed. "There's a spot where we can put the cloaks down and get some rest." His arm brushed hers as he passed.

She rubbed her arm where he'd touched her. In the dark, only hearing and feeling him, she was more aware of Reo than before. Even now she could hear him breathe, smell his musky scent, feel his movements as he spread both cloaks on the floor.

"You first," he whispered. "I need to be closest to the door, in case."

Kara shuffled towards him, and she felt him move aside. She knelt and crawled across the cloaks. She didn't need to be *told in case of what*. Reo had piled the cloaks against the wood of the wall, so she stretched out on her side, her back against the cushion of the cloaks. Reo shifted in alongside her. His back bumped into her, and he mumbled an apology. For a long time she simply stared at him, at where she knew he was, could feel where he was, but couldn't see. She didn't think he was asleep.

"Reo," she whispered. "We should talk."

He sighed, but didn't turn around. "Later," he said. "When

you're safe. Then we can talk."

"I don't blame you."

"You should." Even in a whisper his voice was harsh with self-recrimination. "Get some sleep."

She sighed and closed her eyes. At least she'd told him the truth. She *didn't* blame him. She was actually lucky that he was the Assassin who'd been contacted by her mother because otherwise she'd be dead. Reo's only mistake was in taking her to see the woman who wanted her dead, rather than asking her about it. As if he was the only one with enemies. She was the one who hadn't told him about Arabella Fonti. It was *her* mother who wanted them dead, *her* mother who had recruited other Mages to help. None of that was Reo's doing. And if they didn't make it off Mage Guild Island alive, that wouldn't be Reo's fault either.

SHE TIGHTENED HER arm and snuggled into the warmth, trying to counter the chill at her back. She shifted slightly, and then the warmth withdrew, and her arm dropped to the ground. Kara opened her eyes to see Reo sitting up, his back to her. She pulled her arm against her chest. She knew by the coolness she felt along the front of her body that she'd been sleeping huddled up against Reo, her arm slung across him. She'd slept soundly, as he must have for him to allow that closeness, even in sleep.

Reo walked over to a stack of planks and sat down. Kara thought he was deliberately not looking at her. She rolled over and stretched, trying to work the kinks out of her right shoulder. Daylight filtered in through small cracks and gaps in the wooden walls.

"Will we make it to the sea tonight?" she asked.

"If all goes well," Reo replied. "We still have a few hours before we can move. Try to sleep some more. It will be a long night."

She rolled over onto her side, facing away from him. He obviously didn't want to talk to her. She closed her eyes and tried to ignore her empty stomach and dry, cracked lips. Would he think her weak if she asked him to find them some water? Or some food? She thought of the jars of preserves that lined the wall of the cabin. When she, Pilo, and Vook had filled that wall, she'd thought that she'd never go hungry again, but here she was, without even water to fill her belly. She sighed and drifted off to sleep with the quiet sounds of Reo moving around the small hut.

SHE OPENED HER eyes to darkness.

"It's time," Reo said.

"You should have woken me up." Had they lost time because of her? She slowly got to her feet, pulling the two cloaks with her. In the dark she couldn't tell which was hers and which belonged to Reo. She bundled them under her arm and shuffled towards his voice.

"I'll take those," Reo said, and she felt his hands grab the cloaks from her. "It's only now dark enough to leave."

Reo wrestled with the cloaks for a moment before he reached for her hand and led her to the door. She felt the wind on her face, and then she was outside. They stood within a patch of darkness, but the glow of mage mist surrounded them.

Reo pointed forward and left, towards an overgrown garden path that ran beside the fence. "We need to go that way," he said. "Is there magic?"

Mage mist shone on the other side of the fence, but along the path, nothing. "No," she said. "Not on this side of the fence."

She followed Reo down the path, her skirt brushing the plants on either side.

She almost walked into him, he stopped so suddenly. His hand flashed behind his back, gesturing for her to duck. Kara sank into the dirt of the path. She felt a rock under her hand and grabbed it, thinking that she could throw it if she had to. Reo crouched in front of her, silent and still. After a few minutes, he straightened and waved her forward. She dropped her rock and stepped up beside him.

"There was a guard on the street," he said.

She followed his gaze out beyond a thicket of bushes to a wide street, lit by both mage mist and mage lights.

"There's magic there," she said.

Reo nodded and clasped her arm. "We'll need to go together then," he said. "I need to get us off that street as soon as I can."

After the dark confines of the hut and the faintly lit garden, she felt exposed when they stepped onto the street. Reo steered them across the open area as mage mist swirled around them. Finally there was grass under her feet, and they ducked into a narrow lane that ran between two buildings.

FOR HOURS REO kept them moving, always in the same direction, south. Kara had long ago forgotten about her hunger, but her mouth felt like cotton, and she could barely swallow. She heard the sounds of a fountain and tugged on Reo's arm.

"I need water," she croaked.

He turned and looked into her face, and she saw a hint of apology there. He cocked his head for a moment, then led them off in the direction of the splashing sounds of water.

It wasn't a park so much as a statue. The figure of a man held an open book, his eyes fixed on the stone page in front of him. Beside each carved boot, water tumbled over three stone steps. Kara brushed the mage mist away and dropped to her knees, scooping up mouthfuls of cool, clear water.

"What have we here," a voice said.

Kara stopped drinking, her heart in her throat. She turned and slowly got to her feet. The man in front of her was big, at least a head taller than her, and his dark uniform had the Mage Guild symbol sewn over his heart. Her own heart sank when she saw the trails of mage mist drifting from his fingertips.

"You fit the description," the man said. "The guild will reward—" His voice cut off in a gurgle, and he clawed at his throat.

She stepped back as he stumbled towards her. Reo clung to the guard, his face blank as he pulled something tight against the guard's throat. The guard fell to his knees, still clawing at his throat, his eyes bulging with fear. Reo was on his feet now, behind the guard. Each hand held the end of a black cord, and the muscles in his arms flexed as he pulled. A black line dug into the skin of the guard's throat until blood suddenly spurted towards her. She scrambled further away and huddled against the base of the statue.

The guard toppled onto his face with a sickening crunch, and still Reo pulled on the cord. After a few moments, he relaxed his hands. He loosened the cord and placed two fingers behind the guard's ear. He nodded and lifted the guard's head off the pavement. Kara recoiled. The man's nose was smashed, and his face was covered in blood. His eyes were wide open, still echoing the fear he'd felt in his last moments.

Casually, Reo unwrapped the cord from around the man's neck, bits of flesh coming away as he pulled it from the wound.

Once the cord was free, he dragged the guard over to some bushes and rolled the corpse as far under the foliage as he could.

"Have you finished drinking?"

All Kara could do was nod. He knelt by the lowest pool of water and dipped both hands and the black cord into it. A pink cloud bloomed in the water. Reo pulled the cord out and wound it around one fist before he tucked it into a pocket.

"Let's go," he said and held one damp hand out to her.

She stared at it, afraid to take it, afraid to touch the hand that had just killed a man, right in front of her.

"You know what I am, Kara." Reo's whisper was harsh and bitter.

She did know what he was—he'd been honest about that from the start. Reo was an Assassin, a paid killer. It had almost sounded romantic. But now she *knew* what that meant, to be an Assassin. Now she'd seen him kill. And everything was different. She looked up and met his gaze. An Assassin. And he'd killed to save her life. She took his hand, the hand that had so recently choked the life out of another man, and got to her feet.

"A GUARD HAS been found—murdered." Rorik swept past her and straight into her sitting room.

Arabella followed, tying her robe. It was early—too early for her Server even, and she'd answered the pounding door herself.

"Can I get you something to drink?" she asked.

"No," Rorik replied. He paced the room twice before he stopped in front of her. "I won't be able to keep this quiet."

"Are you sure it was done by the ones we're looking for?"

Arabella closed her eyes. Valerio leaned against the door frame that led to the kitchen. Why couldn't he just stay in her bedchamber—as she'd asked? Rorik knew about their relationship—but she'd been trying to make him think it was in the past.

"Yes." Rorik looked from Valerio to Arabella and back to Valerio, as if trying to determine who had the power in this situation. "His throat was cut—by a garrote."

"Ah, a professional's tool," Valerio said.

"Where was he found?" Arabella asked. A man was dead—but they at least knew where the two fugitives had been. It was more information than they'd had in two days of searching—magically and otherwise.

"At the Santonini statue," Rorik said. "The guard was found an hour ago, but he was killed in the middle of the night."

"That's on the south side of the island," Arabella said. "Why would they go there? Without a bridge or a ferry they have no way to get off the island."

"They might not know that," Rorik said. "They might assume there's a ferry."

"An Assassin would not assume anything," Arabella said. Could they have planned this? Or did they have help? "Rorik, would Warrior Guild be able to hide a boat somewhere on Mage Guild Island?"

"It would be very dangerous for them to do that."

"But useful if they could," Valerio added.

"I don't think their current Primus or Secundus would take that big of a risk," Rorik said.

"They hate us," Arabella said. "They would risk it."

"I agree." Valerio nodded in her direction, and she had to stifle the pleasure she felt at his approval.

"Besides," he continued, "they could blame it on some rogue Assassin. Who knows, that might even be the truth."

"So they are headed somewhere," Arabella said. "We need to find them before they reach their destination."

KARA COULD SMELL the sea. *Not far now*, she thought as Reo led them through yet another yard. They'd left the large estates and fine parks behind and were in a poorer part of Mage Guild Island. The houses were small and close together, and very little mage mist swirled around the homes here. The narrow streets were still covered in it though, and Kara and Reo walked side by side, he scanning for people, she deflecting magic.

She looked up—dawn was approaching. It was hours since they'd left the body of the guard in the bushes, and she still saw his eyes, the fear and panic in them as he made futile attempts to dislodge the cord from around his throat. Would he have been more afraid if he'd known that he was struggling against a Master Assassin? Yes. He would have understood the futility of his struggle. And Reo. She shuddered. The guard had been all emotion, but Reo had shown none. No sorrow, no pain, no joy— not even satisfaction. She eyed him as he walked beside her. He'd told her that, too, weeks ago. He killed without emotion, without passion. It was a job, a task, nothing more.

"Wait," Kara whispered and grabbed Reo's arm. "Mage mist, a lot of it."

Grey-black mist drifted towards them, filling the street. She glanced behind her. Stone walls rose up on both sides of the alley, leaving them no place to hide. A figure stepped into the mouth of the alley a block behind them. Light blue mage mist trailed from his fingertips.

At Reo's sharp intake of breath, Kara whipped her head forward. Another figure was silhouetted in front of them. She didn't need the mage lights to show her who it was—the tell-tale grey-black mage mist identified him.

"Assassin, you've made a fatal error," Valerio Valendi said. "Give me the girl, and I'll make sure your death is quick and painless."

"I don't plan to die today," Reo drawled. "And who are you to pass sentence on me?"

"I am Mage Secundus Valerio Valendi," was the haughty reply. "And I withdraw my offer. I will take the girl, and you will die slowly and in great pain." Valendi waved a hand, and a dark trail of mist sped towards them.

Kara made a sweeping gesture, and it went past them before it thinned and faded. She re-focused on Valendi; he was frowning at her.

"My mother kept something from you," she said. "She used all her power trying, but she couldn't stop us." She studied Valendi until she finally spotted the slight trail of purple mist. "Although she doesn't have as much magic since you are stealing it." She smiled when his eyes widened, startled. "And that's against Guild law."

"No one will know," Valendi said with a shrug. "You'll both be dead." He threw his hands forward, and a stream of mage mist hurtled towards them.

Kara stepped in front of Reo and *willed* the magic around them. There was a scream from behind, and Reo, who had his back pressed to hers, laughed harshly.

"He killed his own man," Reo said.

Kara nodded. One less Mage to worry about.

Valendi took a step towards them and let loose another stream of magic. This time it weaved and twisted as it came towards them. Kara, her arms circling, waved the magic past them. Valendi continued to advance, still attacking magically.

She edged herself and Reo back a step. Their only escape was through the end of the alley.

Valerio Valendi had a lot of power, some of it not his. A purple mist was now visible, entwined with his dark grey. Arabella Fonti must be able to feel her power draining, and Kara wondered if *now* her mother believed her.

"How are you doing this?" Valendi asked. He was now only a few steps away.

"Tell me how to stay away from his spells, and I'll kill him," Reo said from over her shoulder.

"There's no clear path." She shook her head. "He has too much power, too much magic."

She felt Reo shrug, but then she realized he was loosening his shoulders, getting ready to attack.

"No," she said. "He'll kill you."

Reo turned around and put his arms around her waist. "Let him get close enough, and I will kill him too."

"No."

"I promised you," Reo said. "That if necessary I would spend my life to save yours."

She twisted her head slightly to look at him. He was staring over her shoulder at Valendi. She felt Reo tense, and then he jumped out to the side.

"No!" she screamed. Grey-black mage mist streamed towards Reo. With another shout, she *pushed* the mage mist away from Reo, *willed* it back on itself and forced it to return to where it had come from. The mist paused and hovered for a split second, suspended over the dark alley. Reo leapt towards Valendi, a knife in his hand, but the mage mist retracted, sped back to its source, and caught Valendi square in the chest.

With a blast and a flash of light, the Mage was blown out of the alley. Reo landed where the Mage had last stood, and Kara collapsed in a heap. Reo ran down the alley. Mage lights illuminated him as he lifted the knife over the black mass that was slumped at the alley's edge. His knife hand dropped to his side, and one foot toed the lump. He trotted back to her.

"He's dead," he said when he reached her. "I didn't know you could do that.”

“Neither did I.”

She was so exhausted she simply let Reo pull her to her feet and usher her down the alley. He tried to shield the body from her view, but she shook him off. She’d killed a man, she should know what it looked like.

She held her breath against the stench of charred flesh, and leaned over the mass of black, and searched for a hood, a head, anything that would tell her that this blackened lump used to be a man. She touched what she thought was a cloak and recoiled, pulling her hand away.

“He’s melted,” she said in horror. The stench hit her again, and she staggered away and retched.

Reo followed and gently helped her to her feet.

“It’s what he was trying to do to us,” he said quietly.

He wrapped an arm around her shoulder and guided her down the street.

“I know,” Kara said. “It doesn’t make me like it.”

“No, it doesn’t,” Reo replied. “That’s a good thing.”

Was it? Was it a good thing? To know that you’ve escaped by dealing your enemy the horrible death he was trying to give you? She’d killed her mother’s lover, the father of her unborn half sibling. She felt hysterical laughter bubbling up from her chest, but she clamped her mouth shut. She couldn’t give way to her feelings now, not until they were safe. She glanced at Reo, who sensed her looking at him and squeezed her shoulder. He’d killed for her tonight, more than once. And it had changed things between them. Now she’d killed for him. And that changed things again.

Chapter twenty-two

ARABELLA STAGGERED AND almost fell as a burst of energy flowed through her. *What happened?*

"Where's Valerio?" She grabbed Rorik's arm and spun him around. "Where is he?"

"He doubled back away from the shoreline," Rorik said. "Why? What's wrong?"

"Nothing." *Everything.* Arabella let her hands slip from Rorik's arm and fell in behind him. They were bookended by guards—two ahead and two behind—as they searched the streets and alleys near the southern tip of the island for the fugitives.

She felt energized—more so than she had all during her pregnancy—which meant only one thing. Valerio was no longer drawing power from her. Had the girl somehow severed the connection? Or was Valerio injured—or dead? She followed Rorik down an alley. The waters of the sea glinted at the far end, where the road ended.

Should she make Rorik turn back to find Valerio? Though not healers, she and Rorik were powerful enough to cure any injury short of death, if they arrived in time. But then the girl and the Assassin would escape.

If Valerio was injured and survived, he would have no reason to suspect she would have known he was in trouble—not without admitting that he was stealing her power. He would never admit that, not even to her—especially not to her. That would give her a measure of influence over him—some control—and he would never live with that.

And if he was dead? She rolled the thought around in her mind. If he was dead, then trying to find him would allow the girl to escape—and that *she* could not live with. And really, it might be better for her if he *was* dead. She stared at Rorik's back. He'd chosen Valerio as Secundus—could she convince Rorik to choose her? He had few friends on council—Valerio had seen to that—and she had been cultivating him as a mentor for months. Who else would he choose?

"Primus!"

The guards behind her drew their swords and spread out in front her. They relaxed as another guard ran into view.

"Primus! The fugitives, they've killed the Secundus. You must come!"

The new guard's clothes were blackened, and he was out of breath.

"Are you certain?" Arabella asked.

"I saw it myself," the guard replied. "And the body afterwards."

Rorik drew up beside her, and she gripped his arm. "Gyda!" she said. "This is terrible." She forced a few tears from her eyes and smiled when Rorik patted her arm.

"I must go," the Primus said. "I must see for myself."

"I . . ." she trailed off, and Rorik patted her arm again.

"I'm so sorry," he said. "I know how close you were. There is no need for you to see him this way."

"Thank you, Rorik." She bowed her head. "I will continue with these three guards. It's even more important that we stop these fugitives."

"If you're up to it, my dear."

She lifted her head to meet his eyes. She blinked, and a tear trailed down her cheek. "I will not let them get away with this. I will avenge Valerio!"

"Yes, of course." Rorik turned to the guards. "Nothing can happen to her—or you will answer to me."

They nodded, and with one last look, Rorik strode down the alley.

Arabella ducked her head and smiled. Some of the other councilors had been fawning over Valerio for years with the assumption that Rorik would die first and Valerio would choose one of them as Secundus when he became Primus. She would dearly love to see their reactions when they learned that Valerio was dead and *Rorik* would choose another Secundus. She must make sure he chose her.

JUST AFTER DAWN, the bells started ringing. The lightening sky illuminated the rundown neighbourhood Kara and Reo were walking through. Drowsy people came out of the dilapidated huts and shacks, thin robes clutched to even thinner bodies. A few glanced at her and Reo as they crowded together.

"Who's it this time?" a woman asked her neighbour. "The Primus ain't old enough for a natural death."

"It's for the Secundus," Reo whispered in her ear. "Just keep walking."

"Like any of them die a natural death," another woman replied. She spit on the roadway. "Gyda help us, we don't need another fight amongst the Council."

Reo kept them at a steady pace as they moved through the streets. They passed throngs of people heading in the opposite direction, towards the centre of the island. One or two eyed them, but no one stopped them or asked who they were. Guild symbols were sewn onto rough woolen tunics and mended cloaks—the faces above were gaunt and haggard.

These were not prosperous Guildsmen, these people who lived on the southern edge of the island. Kara wondered if they would even care that she was the one who'd killed the Mage Guild Secundus. Yes, she decided, but only because it meant they had to start their day earlier than usual.

SOON THE CROWDS were behind them. The roads were more like footpaths, and the structures—she couldn't really think of them as houses—were more dilapidated and run down. She smiled when she saw an overturned boat, much like the one she'd lived in at the docks, a line of drying clothes strung up beside it. Her smile faltered when she realized that *Guildsmen* lived this way. Mage Guild was the richest in all of Tregella—why did its people live like this?

"We're almost there, Kara," Reo said. "Just a few more streets." He turned to her and smiled, the first genuine smile she'd seen on his face for a very long time. Then he grunted and stumbled into her.

"Get off the path." He pulled her down into the dirt beside a crumbling fence. Reo covered her head with his arms, and something thudded into the wood above their heads.

"I'm grateful that Mages have terrible aim," Reo said. He grimaced and looked over her shoulder.

Kara craned her head and saw two armed guards trotting down the path towards them, crossbows pointing their way. Beyond them purple mage mist swirled.

"My mother's here," she said.

"She must know how the Secundus died," Reo said. "That's why they aren't using magic." He peered at the guards for a moment. "Keep your head down and her magic away from me."

Before she could protest, Reo was gone. She sucked in her breath when she saw the pool of blood beside her. A short arrow stuck out of the back of his thigh, and he limped as he ran, but he was still fast enough to reach the guards before they could react.

Reo grabbed the first guard's crossbow and shoved the man off balance. A crossbow bolt burrowed into the ground while the guard struggled to stay on his feet. Reo's left hand snapped out, and the second guard grunted. Another punch caught him in the throat, and the guard gasped for breath as he dropped to the ground, his crossbow falling from his hands.

Reo wrestled with the first guard, pulling him down on top of him. A ball of purple sped down the lane, and Kara stood up and *willed* it away. It hit the fence, and the wood splintered. Reo glanced over at her before he twisted and rolled, pulling the guard with him. When he came up, he was straddling the guard. Reo flattened his hand and slammed it into the guard's nose. Bone crunched sickeningly, and the guard went still. Reo looked over at the other guard, who had finally found his breath and his feet.

"Kill him," Arabella shouted from down the lane.

Another ball of purple hurtled towards them, and Kara waved a hand, sending it crashing into the fence. The fence exploded, and the guard, wide-eyed, stared past her and Reo towards her mother. A third guard hulked in the entrance to the laneway.

"Come on," Reo said. He grabbed Kara's hand, and they ran

back the way they'd come.

She looked over her shoulder. The last guard had joined the first one. Instead of crossbows, now they both wielded swords. Her mother was nowhere to be seen.

They rounded the corner at a dead run, and Kara stepped on the hem of her long skirt. She would have fallen if Reo hadn't grabbed her arm, keeping her on her feet. They passed two more lanes before they ducked into the mouth of an alley. Reo stopped, and she collapsed against him, her chest heaving as she tried to catch her breath. Reo peered around the corner.

"I don't see them," he said. "Do you?"

She peered past his shoulder. A wave of purple mage mist roiled down the lane.

"My mother has sent a spell," she said. "It's about thirty paces behind us."

"The guards won't be far behind it," Reo said. He eyed her. "That skirt is slowing us down—we need to find you something else to wear."

"What about you?" She gestured to the arrow that was still sticking out of his thigh. "Should we do anything?"

"I'll be fine," Reo assured her. "I'll cut the shaft when I get a chance."

Taking her arm, he guided her down the alley, south, towards the shoreline. Despite his limp, Reo kept them moving at a steady pace.

He steered them through dusty yards and empty lanes. One narrow alley ended at the door of a small weathered shed and instead of going around it, Reo led them inside.

No one was in the single room, but there was a patched pair of trousers on a hook by the bed. Reo gestured to her, and she removed her skirt and pulled on the trousers. They were stained and dirty, but at least they wouldn't trip her up. She tucked her blouse into the waistband and tied a rough rope around her waist.

She turned to find Reo sitting on the floor, his left leg raised in the air. The fabric of his trousers was wet with blood. He held the arrow in his left hand, and with his right, he sawed at the wooden shaft with a knife. The arrow fell to the floor, and he sighed and squeezed his eyes shut.

"Are you all right?" Kara asked.

"I'll do," Reo said. He opened his eyes, gingerly rolled over, and stood up. He stepped down on his left leg and winced. "Let's go."

Reo studied the squalid yard through the one small window before he eased himself through it. She scrambled after him, thankful for the trousers. A scrubby bush spanned the back of the yard, and Reo plunged into it, wrestling the branches aside so that Kara could push through. With the addition of a few scratches, she was in another yard. This one was slightly better tended, with a few rows of vegetables lined up along the back wall of a shack.

They crept around the side of the structure and paused for a few seconds while Reo scanned the front yard. Finally, he grabbed her, and they trotted forward.

The blue expanse of the sea stretched before them, surprising her. She'd smelled it for blocks, but she'd expected to hear the sounds of the surf. Then she remembered that Mage Guild Island floated *above* the water—there was no shoreline for waves to crash against.

"Let's see if we can find a dock," Reo said. He walked to the edge of the island and peered over.

Kara took a hesitant step towards the edge as well.

Fifty feet below her, the waters of the bay flowed out of sight beneath the island. The white sails of ships were visible further south, out on the water. The closest one flew the blue and green flag of Seyoya. She searched island's edge, but didn't see anything that resembled a dock.

"Let's try east," Reo said. "Your mother should still be west of us."

She nodded and followed his limping form.

A shout came from behind them. There, west, as Reo had said, were her mother and two guards. Arabella stopped and threw her hands forward. A ball of purple mage mist hurtled towards them. It brushed one of the guards as it passed, and he collapsed. The other guard continued running towards them, his sword drawn.

Reo stopped and turned, partially shielding Kara with his body. She waved the mage mist away, and it sped out into the sea.

"Swim or fight?" he said. "Your choice."

She met his eyes. Even if they did fight, they still had to get off the island. There was no boat in sight, and based on the ramshackle huts they'd been traveling amongst, they were unlikely to find one.

"Swim," she said and lifted her chin. He knew she didn't know how to.

Reo nodded. "We'll get as far away as we can." He waved towards the ships in the distance. "We'll head towards the ships."

"That's what we'll do," Kara said. They wouldn't make it that far, of course. Reo was hurt, and the water was cold. No matter how good a swimmer he was, he'd had little sleep in the past few days, less food, and was wounded. But she'd rather die out in the sea than here at the hands of her mother.

Reo took her hand, and they ran off the edge of the island.

She hit the water feet first. The impact slowed her descent, but she almost inhaled at the cold. With arms flailing, she tried to move up, towards the bright light of the sun. Then she felt a tug at her waist. She twisted her head and saw Reo, one hand stuck into her rope belt, swimming upwards. They broke the surface, and Kara sucked in a deep breath.

"Gyda, that's cold," she said. She struggled to keep her head above water, but waves swept over her head every few seconds.

"Try to take deep, slow breaths," Reo said.

She breathed in deeply, once, then again, until her breathing evened out. She followed Reo's gaze to the shadow underneath the island.

"No boats," he said. "At least not close enough to see." He looked over at her. "It was a faint hope anyway. Out to sea we go." He smiled sadly—they both knew they were swimming to their deaths.

"Show me how to swim." She stared up at the lip of the island. They'd drifted a little further away from it, but she recognized the figure who stepped up to the edge. A purple ball of mage mist swept towards them.

"Reo, get behind me," Kara said. She felt him grab one of her shoulders, and then the mist was there. She flung an arm out, and it sped off under the island. Kara would have slipped under the water then if Reo hadn't held her up.

"Relax," he said. "I'll tow you, and you keep the spells away." She nodded, and he wrapped an arm around her waist. He leaned back and drew her with him until she was almost on top of him. His first kick tangled in her legs, but then she figured out how to keep them near the surface and out of his way. Reo headed away from Mage Guild Island, out towards the distant ships, and Kara stared at the figure of her mother, standing at the edge of the island.

Five, seven, ten times, purple mage mist hurtled towards them, and each time Kara deflected it. They'd been in the water for almost an hour, and Kara could feel Reo faltering. His kicks weren't as strong, and his breathing was more and more laboured. They were both shivering, and the only part of her that felt warm was where Reo held her against him. Kara's teeth chattered as she swept aside yet another wave of mage mist.

"Someone's coming for us," Reo said. "Hold on."

"What?" His words penetrated the numbness that had enveloped her. Someone was coming? She'd given up on that, had in fact forgotten that Reo was actually swimming towards something. Kara had forgotten everything except the need to keep her mother's spells from them. "Who?"

"Seyoyans," Reo gasped. This time his kick was stronger, as though his energy was renewed by hope.

"We'll be safe?" Kara asked. She couldn't believe that anyone was going to pluck them out of the sea, especially since they'd jumped from Mage Guild Island. She didn't think even Seyoyans would dare to make enemies of a Mage.

"Not safe, exactly," Reo replied. "They could still let us drown. Or they might hand us over to Mage Guild."

She heard a shout, and she craned her head to look past Reo. A small boat was about two hundred feet away, and four men rowed, their backs to her. Another man sat in the prow, staring across the bay at them.

"Hello," she called out in Seyoyan. "Help us, please." She saw the look of surprise on the Seyoyan's face, and then he pointed.

"Watch out," he called, and she turned to find another wave of mage mist bearing down on them.

She waved her hand, and it spun towards Mage Guild Island. There was a shout of surprise behind her, and she turned to find the Seyoyan staring at her. He muttered to the rowers, and the boat surged towards them.

Kara kept her eyes on the shoreline in case her mother attacked again. Reo slipped one hand off her shoulder, and when she glanced around, he was holding onto the prow of the dory. She looked up into the bright blues eyes of the Seyoyan, and then

Reo was pulling her towards the man's waiting hands.

"Are any spells coming?" Reo asked.

She shook her head, and at the same time the Seyoyan said no. He hauled her into the boat. Shivering and dripping, she scrambled away in order to make room for Reo. He grunted and rolled into the bottom of the boat, clutching his thigh. A trickle of blood seeped from the wound where the broken arrow shaft protruded.

The Seyoyan gave a command, and the rowers started to turn the boat around.

"I must ask you to keep watch," the Seyoyan said to Kara in perfect Tregellan. "It seems you have a talent that I myself do not."

Kara nodded, almost too tired to speak, and then she shivered. The Seyoyan draped a blanket over her, and she knelt and peered towards Mage Guild Island. A mass of purple mage mist flowed slowly towards them. She didn't wait for it to get closer; she pulled one cold hand out from beneath the blanket and waved it back towards the island.

"I would very much like to know how you do that," the Seyoyan said. "But I know you are tired. Once we get you aboard our ship, we will sail to safety." He too looked out towards the island. "I will warn the other ships as well. I suspect that the Mage responsible for these attacks will continue for some time."

"Yes," Reo said.

He shuffled up beside her and put an arm around her shoulder. She lifted the blanket, and Reo settled underneath.

"She's very determined. Helping us will put you in danger."

"What I have seen with my own eyes makes me believe that you are worth it," the Seyoyan replied.

Kara peered towards Mage Guild Island. They were far enough away that she could no longer make out the figure that must still be standing at the edge. Purple mage mist sped their way twice more, but she easily deflected it. The mist seemed less dense, but was it because her mother was depleting her magic or was she sending different spells? Thankfully no other Mages joined in the attack. Had Valerio Valendi been her mother's only ally? Would the Mage Guild leave them alone? No, she'd killed the Mage Secundus, the guild could not allow that to go unpunished.

ARABELLA CLUTCHED HER fists to her side and watched as the small boat pulled into the shadow of a ship. *Seyoyans.* She'd need to talk to Rorik about this. The thieving foreigners could not be allowed to steal the girl and the Assassin away from her. Her eyes narrowed. Seyoyans were closer to Warrior Guild than any other—even the Merchants who sailed to their lands—could this ship have been waiting for them? Was this why they'd come south—away from any bridges or ferries?

"They're gone," she said to the guard still at her side. "I must return to the council. There is much for me to do."

She looked towards the centre of Mage Guild Island. The sun sparkled on the now quiet bell tower. She wished Rorik had waited for her return before having them rung—now the news was known. The Secundus was dead, and no doubt her fellow council-members were already scheming. She had to get to Rorik now—had to make herself absolutely necessary to him.

She took a deep breath. Her magic was depleted, but she would have to find the energy to hurry. She rushed down the street, the guard trailing her. At a crossroad, she slowed.

Let them wait for her. She was the one who'd been trying to avenge Valerio's death, she was the one who had been closest to him—she was the one who had been with Rorik when he received the terrible news of Valerio's death. And she was the one with information about his killers. She would make them *all* wait for her—make them realize that nothing would happen until she was ready.

She calmed as the guard fell in behind her. It would have been better—so much better—if she'd been able to tell them that she'd avenged Valerio—that she'd killed his murderers. She smiled— and so she would.

She turned onto a lane that led towards the edge of the island. No one was around—every Guildsman had responded to the summons of the bell. After travelling a few minutes she felt some of her power returning. Just enough to allow her to suck the breath out of her companion. She let him fall—she'd blame his death on the girl and the Assassin—no one would know anything different.

Arabella tousled her hair and ripped her skirt before heading towards the centre of the island.

She'd arrive disheveled and alone—but victorious. The

fugitives had managed to kill the guards, but she'd been able to force them to jump into the sea to try to escape her attack. She had waited until she was certain they'd drowned before returning to report to the council.

Once she was Secundus, she would have the political power to find the Seyoyan ship and take it apart.

THE DORY SLOWED, and Kara peered over her shoulder. They were less than ten feet from the side of the ship.

A rope ladder was lowered, and the Seyoyan in the prow of the dory seized it. Kara grabbed the Seyoyan's outstretched hand, and he pulled her over to the ladder. Reo was right behind her, steadying her as she gripped the rope rungs. She scrambled up, and the dark-skinned hands of Seyoyans helped her over the gunwale. She took a shaky step, then another, and then Reo was at her side again, pulling her into his warmth.

"I will take you to a cabin," the Seyoyan said. "And I will have a healer look at your leg."

Kara followed the Seyoyan through a small wooden door and down some steep steps, clutching at the thick rope railing as the ship pitched and rolled. The Seyoyan opened another small door and gestured for her to enter.

"In the cabinet, you will find dry clothes that should fit well enough," the Seyoyan said. "Although they are not very fashionable."

She plucked her bedraggled trousers and blouse. "They can't be worse than what I have on."

"Now we shall see to your friend," the Seyoyan said.

Kara had a brief glimpse of Reo's wan face before the door closed.

The room was small and quiet. A narrow bunk stretched across the far wall, a grey woolen blanket carefully folded and placed on one end of it. The only other piece of furniture was the cabinet. It was tucked along the wall to the left of the door, directly across from a small round window. She reached into the cabinet and pulled out a pair of soft black trousers, so worn in spots that the fabric showed grey, and a long green shirt that had been patched many times with neat, compact stitches.

With numb hands, she stripped off her wet clothes and tugged the black trousers on, threading the damp rope through the belt loops to keep them up. She sighed as the dry, green shirt slid over her damp skin.

Kara piled her wet clothes into the corner by the door and barefoot, padded over to the bunk. She wrapped the blanket around her shoulders, tucked her feet under her, and leaned against the cabin wall.

She should be worried. Reo was gone, and these Seyoyans were strangers. For all the time she'd spent with Chal, she didn't know very much about his people—their politics, their loyalties. All she really knew was that they had elaborate customs surrounding stealing—and that she was grateful that they'd agreed to help.

The Seyoyan had seen what she could do with mage mist, with magic—and he wanted to know more. Which meant that Chal hadn't told them about her. Would they know of Reo? That he worked with a Seyoyan? Would they help him because of that history, or would they try to keep him from her so they could find out what else she could do?

She pulled the blanket tighter. She'd see Reo again—he'd taken his vow to save her very seriously. They'd have to kill him to keep him from her—which would not be easy—so she would see him.

And then what? If she asked, would they take her to Seyoya? Her mother would be glad to see the last of her, although Kara thought she'd rather see her daughter dead than gone. Did she want to go to Seyoya? It had been one of her mother's suggestions—to live in another country and teach. Now that she could speak Seyoyan, she really *could* do that. But did she want to?

There was a sharp knock at the door.

"Kara, it's me," Reo called. "May I come in?"

"Yes."

He ducked through the doorway, closing the door behind him, and crossed the small space to stand in front of her.

"How are you?" he asked.

"Fine," she replied. The blanket slipped a little, and she pulled it back up. "A little cold still."

"That should pass soon." Reo sat down on the bunk beside her.

For a moment she thought he would wrap his arms around her, but then he dropped his hands to his thighs and looked away.

"Are we safe?" Kara asked. "How's your leg?"

Reo stretched his left leg out. "Good." He met her gaze. "We're safer than I'd hoped. The Seyoyan who plucked us from the bay is in charge."

"Is he the ship's captain?"

"No, but Javan Losi can see magic."

"Like Chal," Kara said.

"Like Chal," Reo agreed. "That talent is a little more rare and important than I knew."

"Chal kept things from you."

"So it seems." Reo gave her a crooked smile. "But I kept things from him as well."

She laughed. Of course he had. Reo didn't trust his own guild, of course he wouldn't trust a Seyoyan. For the first time since they'd been pulled from the water, she felt as though they might actually have a real chance to be safe.

"What did Javan Losi have to say about me?"

"Not very much," Reo said. "I think he's going to ask you himself. We're to wait here for something to eat and drink, and then he'll come see us."

"Are we prisoners?"

"Not exactly," Reo said. "I think Javan Losi has already decided that he will help us. I think he wants as few witnesses to our rescue as possible because they'll have to answer Mage Guild's questions."

"Mage Guild *will* ask them," Kara said. Her mother would not give up so easily.

"The Mage Guild Secundus was killed," Reo said softly. "They will ask."

She shuddered and huddled into her blanket. She hadn't meant to kill Valerio Valendi, she'd only been protecting Reo, but he was dead, and by her hand. Mage Guild would put all of their considerable power behind the search for Valendi's killer.

"Maybe I should go to Seyoya," she mused out loud.

"If that's what you want, then we can ask the Seyoyans," Reo replied in a tight voice.

When she looked over at him, he was staring down at his bare feet.

"It's not what I want," she said. "But it may be the best way to stay alive."

Reo gazed into her eyes. "Tell me what you want, and I'll do my best to make it happen. I owe you so much, Kara, I've done you so many wrongs, let me try to make things right."

Reo's eyes held such sorrow and regret that she found she couldn't look away. She took a deep breath.

"I want what I've always wanted. A place I can call home with people who I consider family. For me that's Old Rillidi with Santos and Vook and Pilo and the rest of them."

Reo smiled and squeezed her shoulder beneath the blanket. "Then that's what I'll get for you," he said.

She frowned and shook her head. How was that possible when she'd killed the Mage Guild Secundus?

Chapter twenty-three

FOOD ARRIVED—A spicy fish soup that warmed her to her toes and dry journey bread that she and Reo soaked in the soup to soften. After eating, her eyes drooped. She barely noticed when Reo took her mug from her and helped her stretch out on the bunk.

She woke to murmurs. She opened her eyes and yawned, covering her mouth with the blanket. Reo's eyes darted in her direction, and his mouth twitched in a soft smile.

"Ah, you are awake."

Again the Seyoyan spoke Tregellan. He smiled broadly at her, his light blue eyes contrasting with his dark skin. His white hair was cropped short, and a gold chain dangled from his right earlobe.

"I hope you are comfortable."

He took a step towards her, but Reo blocked his path. The Seyoyan shook his head.

"Where are my manners? I am Javan Losi, at your service." He bowed, and Kara pulled herself up to a sitting position.

"Javan Losi," she repeated. "Hello," she said in Seyoyan. "I am Kara, and I owe you a great deal of thanks."

"In Tregellan please," Javan said. "Most of the crew does not speak it."

He glanced at Reo, who smiled, a tight, warning smile, and

stepped aside. Javan crossed the floor to stand by the bunk.

"The fewer who know you are here the better."

"Didn't they see me come aboard?" Kara asked.

"They saw someone, yes," Javan said. "We will tell them it was the Assassin."

"Yes," Reo agreed. "That should work." He looked at her. "Warrior Guild will protect me. I will tell them that it was a commission." Reo smiled slowly. "Let Mage Guild prove it wasn't."

"My mother knows we came aboard your ship," Kara said. "She won't stop looking for me."

"No, she won't," Reo agreed. "But Mage Guild will, if they believe you are dead." He looked at Javan. "If the Seyoyans all swear that only I came aboard and I swear that you drowned, Mage Guild will have to stop their search."

"But you must make it worth my while," Javan said. "Lying to Mages carries considerable risk."

"You would have the satisfaction of knowing that you had stolen something of great value from Mage Guild," Kara said. "Would that not be a great reward?"

Javan's blond eyebrows arched up, and he smiled. "And what would I have helped to steal from them?"

"Me," Kara said. "I'm Mage Guild born, but I ran away. They want me back. The guild doesn't understand what I am, what I can do, but my mother, Arabella Fonti, does."

"And what is it that you can do?" Javan asked.

"I see magic." Kara nodded at him. "Like you. But I can also manipulate it. I can divert it, as you saw, I can send it back to its source, as Mage Guild Secundus discovered too late—and I can *unmake* spells."

"Unmake spells?" Javan repeated. "How?"

"It depends on the spell," Kara said. She wasn't about to admit she didn't understand her talent, not with so much at stake. "Some I simply touch and they disappear, others I need to unwind slowly." She looked up at Javan and then over at Reo. "Given enough time, I think I could unmake Mage Guild Island."

Javan sucked in his breath. Slowly a smile spread across his face. "Kara, daughter of Arabella Fonti, you are indeed a worthwhile prize to be stolen from Mage Guild. I will help. My crew will be saddened to hear that a young woman perished before we could reach her, that the Assassin was the only one we were able to pull from the sea."

"Mage Guild will use magic to question them," Reo said. "Will they be able to resist?"

"No, of course not," Javan said. "This is why the few men who know she is aboard will leave the ship as soon as possible. As for me, I will be able to dodge the spells, and thus my lie will seem like truth." He regarded Reo. "Will *you* be able to resist?"

"No," Reo said. "I will make sure that they do not question me." He looked directly at Kara. "I promised that you would be safe no matter the cost to me. If they come for me, I will kill myself."

Kara frowned. "Gyda! Will you stop staying things like that? We'll get a spell to counteract anything Mage Guild uses on you. Besides, it would look suspicious if you died right before being questioned." She glared at Reo.

He blushed and ducked his head.

"I want to stay dead this time."

"I doubt any Mages will be willing to go against their guild so directly," Javan said. His amused gaze swept between Kara and Reo. "And you say that you have been dead before."

"Yes," Kara said. "Until a few days ago Mage Guild and my mother thought I was dead." She tugged on the blanket. "And all of us were very happy with that situation."

"I see," Javan said.

He nodded his head, but Kara could still see questions in his eyes.

"But that still doesn't help you buy or coerce a Mage to go against their guild."

"Then we won't ask anyone in the guild," Kara replied. "Can you take us to Old Rillidi? There's an old manor house at the northeast tip." She smiled at Reo. "Santos will help."

Reo nodded, and his shoulders relaxed.

Javan left to give his crew instructions, and Kara sat on the bunk, leaning against the wall. Reo stood by the door, his body stiff, as though he was expecting her to order him out of the room.

They would leave the ship after dark, Javan had said. In just a few hours, she would be back on Old Rillidi Island with Santos, Pilo, and Vook. Would they be happy to see her? Would she be welcome at the little cabin? After months of living in her own suite of rooms on Warrior Guild Island, she wasn't sure she'd be able to share that small space with all the children.

"I forgive you," she said.

Reo shrugged. "I have not forgiven myself."

"I'm at fault as well," Kara said. "I should have told you who my mother was." She shook her head. "Especially after Noula saw me at Founders Day."

"It is *not* your fault," Reo said, his eyes boring into hers. "It was my doing."

"Why did you do it?" Kara asked softly. "Why did you take me to see the woman who wanted you to kill me?"

Reo ran a hand through his hair and sighed. "I was not thinking clearly," he said finally, staring at the floor. "I was angry—*furious*—and I reacted." He smiled ruefully. "Assassins are taught to perform without emotion because emotions get in the way of reason, as I found out. Somehow I thought that taking you to see the woman who wanted you dead would prove how much you needed me."

"Because I refused to go along with your plans," Kara said.

"Yes. But you also refused *me*." Reo met her eyes and looked quickly away. "I told myself that bedding you was necessary in order to reinforce our story and keep us both safe. But the truth is I desperately wanted you. You were willing to do anything within your power to keep those you care about safe. I've never in my life had anyone willing to fight for me in that way. I wanted that for myself." He lifted his gaze to hers. "I am sorry."

Kara was the first to look away. The yearning in Reo's eyes was disconcerting. Was that because she had wanted what he had offered that night? Did she still want it?

"I know you're sorry," she said. "And I did *do anything within my power* to keep you safe." She met his eyes again. "I killed a man for you."

His face froze, and he hurried to her side.

"Gyda," he said. He sat down on the bunk and wrapped her in his arms. "I forgot. And you are not used to killing."

Kara leaned into him and closed her eyes. "I can still see him," she said. "I can still *smell* him." Would she always be haunted by the smell of burnt flesh? A part of her wished she'd listened to Reo and not looked, even though she felt it was necessary to acknowledge what she had done.

"It's not something you forget," Reo murmured. "I still remember the first man I killed. All Assassins do. At least all the ones I've talked to."

"I don't want to remember," she said. "I want it out of my head. He was my mother's lover—the father of my unborn half brother or sister."

"And he was trying to kill us," Reo said. "You saved me, saved us both."

"I know," Kara said. "But I hadn't meant to kill him."

"You reacted," Reo said. "And that was a good thing for us."

"If you hadn't charged him, I wouldn't have had to react," Kara said.

"Perhaps we'd both be dead," Reo replied calmly. "Or I would be dead, and you would be a prisoner."

She shivered. The man who had cursed Santos would have kept her captive and forced her to bear his children—unless her mother killed her out of jealousy.

"I'll always remember?" Kara whispered.

"That is not a bad thing," Reo said.

She opened her eyes and looked up into his gaze.

"Taking another's life should not be a casual act, there should always be a cost."

"Even for an Assassin?" she asked.

"Even for an Assassin."

She closed her eyes again and let the steady beat of Reo's heart lull her to sleep.

ARABELLA WORRIED THAT it had been too easy. Rorik had believed her—even defended her against other council members who had asked a few too many questions. Like why an Assassin was even on Mage Guild Island.

She stepped into the tub and let the warm water seep into her. She sighed and sank lower.

Rorik had insisted that she take care of herself. She'd objected of course, but the Primus had insisted. She wasn't going to against his wishes—at least not yet.

And the others! How they'd fawned over Rorik. But she hadn't—she'd acted as his equal, his collaborator in the search for justice for Valerio, someone strong who he could count on.

A few of them had understood—two had even been solicitous of her—because they knew what she knew. At this moment she was Rorik's choice for Secundus. All she had to do was have him formally select her.

She rose and let the water sluice off her, and grabbed the cloth that hung beside the tub.

Once dry, she padded into her bedchamber and threw open her closet.

What to wear . . . not black. She wasn't in mourning—at least not officially. Ah—there. Purple—a powerful colour—a strong colour.

A few minutes later, she headed down to the corridors that crisscrossed the island.

The halls were busy—Servers and Mages hurrying to complete their tasks before the formal ceremony to mark the passing of the Secundus.

Arabella strolled, taking her time. Rorik had promised that the ceremony would not start until she was ready. She breathed in a deep breath. They were waiting on her—they were *all* waiting on *her*.

She knocked at the door to Rorik's estate, and a Server opened it.

"The Primus is in his salon," he said and bowed. Arabella followed him up a set of stairs to an open set of double doors. Quiet voices—male voices—drifted out into the hall.

"Master Mage Fonti," the Server announced before stepping out of the way.

Rorik hurried to her side. "My dear, we didn't expect to see you so soon, I trust you are rested?"

"Primus, I am refreshed, but I could not sleep. There is so much to do, and I wish to help."

"Yes, of course," Rorik said. "Your help will be greatly appreciated. Inigo has also offered his help."

Arabella looked past Rorik and met Inigo's gaze. As a council Mage, he had been fully bound to Valerio. She smiled wanly.

"How kind of you," she said. She stepped past Rorik and sat down on the settee beside Inigo. Was he maneuvering for Secundus? He wasn't simply offering to help—no one in this room believed *any* of them were here for that, despite what they said.

"We are all shocked at Valerio Valendi's sudden death," Inigo said. "It must be doubly wretched for you. You were very close to him, I hear."

"Yes." She patted her belly, and Inigo's eyes widened. In a few hours, the whole council would know she was carrying Valerio's child. "As was Rorik."

"Yes," Rorik agreed. "In the past few months, we three became a good team."

"And now we are two," Arabella said sadly. "But we must set aside our grief for the good of the guild."

"Are you sure you are well enough to do this?" Rorik asked her.

"I have to be—I have no choice." Arabella folded her hands in her lap. "And being active will keep me from dwelling on my loss."

"All of Mage Guild mourns the loss of Valerio Valendi," Inigo said.

"Of course," Arabella replied. "I did not mean to imply that my loss was greater than yours."

"But it is," Rorik interjected. "You've lost not only a friend and mentor, but the father of your child." He clasped her shoulder briefly before stepping away.

"Inigo," Rorik said. "While I appreciate your offer, I do think that Arabella and I can handle any tasks still to be done."

"Of course, Primus," Inigo said. "I will leave you to them."

Arabella nodded as Inigo made his farewells. As he left the study he glanced over at her—his face was blank, but there was fury in his eyes. She ducked her head to hide her smile. Had Inigo petitioned Rorik to become Secundus? He had been Valerio's ally—had he really expected that to be enough to secure the position? He had underestimated her, but she doubted he would make that mistake again. Once Rorik named her Secundus, she would have to be careful. It seemed she had made an enemy.

"Shall I order something to eat?" Rorik asked when he returned.

"Something light would be nice," she replied. "I fatigue so quickly these days and now with . . ." She let her voice trail off. In truth she had more energy now that Valerio was dead—but Rorik would never know that.

He called his Server, and she smiled, trying to portray a sense of gratitude.

"Thank you. I do not know what I would do without such a

good friend." She paused as Rorik sat down beside her. "But I worry about my child," she said. "Mine and Valerio's child."

"That is natural," Rorik replied. "A mother is always concerned about her children. How can I help?"

"I feel vulnerable, exposed politically. I will have some protection since I am on the council, but I fear that Valerio's enemies will harm our child. You know what happens to the offspring of dead Mages." It wasn't an idle worry—even now Valerio's children were probably being eliminated. No one wanted children with potential to grow up and exact revenge on their parent's enemies.

"I do." Rorik's face darkened. "It's a horrendous practice." He clasped her hands in his. "Again, how can I help?"

"Make me Secundus. Not for me, but for my child. No one will dare touch him if I am Secundus to your Primus."

Rorik dropped her hands and leaned back. "What will you give me in return?"

Arabella dropped her eyes. Based on Rorik's response, Inigo *had* been lobbying to be appointed Secundus. "I will give you what I have always given you," she said. "Loyalty, friendship, and someone you can trust."

"Can I trust you?"

"Yes. You know my secrets."

"Ah yes, the daughter and the Assassin." He paused. "I'll do it. Gyda knows I can't trust any of the others. I will make you Secundus—but only if you tell me what really happened."

"It's all true," she said, meeting his eyes. She hadn't planned on telling anyone—but somehow Rorik suspected. And becoming Secundus was worth anything, including this last secret. "Except I did not see them drown. They were picked up by a Seyoyan vessel, which makes me suspect that Warrior Guild is behind this."

"Warrior Guild!" Rorik exclaimed. "If they were responsible for the death of a Mage Guild Secundus, they will pay dearly."

"Once I am Secundus, I can help," Arabella said.

"Yes. I will make the announcement today and arrange the official appointment as soon as possible."

He left her just as her meal arrived. Arabella picked up a fork and speared some salad. She'd known that Rorik disliked Warrior Guild—that was why she'd blamed them—but she hadn't realized how much he hated them. He'd been so focused on them that he hadn't even asked her why she'd lied to the council. If she could keep Rorik focused on Warrior Guild, she could manage the council.

"KARA, WAKE UP."

Her arm was being prodded, but she was too tired to open her eyes. She sighed and burrowed deeper against the warmth.

"Kara."

That voice again. She frowned. Couldn't they leave her alone?

"Kara."

She opened her eyes. She was pressed against Reo and she edged away from him. Nervously she looked at him—*what must he think of her, sleeping curled up against him?* He met her gaze with a tenderness that made her heart falter.

"We need to get moving." He eased his arm out from between her back and the wall and stretched.

Kara smoothed her green shirt down over her ill-fitting trousers and stood up. She hadn't meant to fall asleep, and certainly not in Reo's arms, but she'd been warm, finally, and she'd felt safe. She glanced at him from the corner of her eye. He smiled at her shyly, and she smiled back.

"Are we leaving the ship?" she asked.

"Yes," Reo replied. "Javan came by a few minutes ago. We're off the coast of Old Rillidi. Just a little north of the old docks where I found those two boys you knew."

"Harb and Lowel," Kara said with a nod. "We're close to Santos' estate. How long was I asleep?" What she wanted to know was how long he'd let her nestle against him.

"A few hours—it's around midnight. There's enough moonlight to let us find our way."

Reo stood up, and suddenly she felt crowded in the little cabin. She moved towards the door. There was a sharp knock, and she jumped.

"We're ready," someone called softly in Seyoyan.

Kara followed Reo out into the narrow hallway. A single lamp hung from a wooden beam, the flame sputtering as it swung. She hadn't noticed the rocking of the ship, but now she had to steady herself by trailing a hand along each wall of the passageway. She climbed a short flight of stairs to the deck where a salty breeze whipped her hair around her face.

Reo leaned in. "Come," he whispered, taking hold of her arm and steering her towards one side of the ship.

A Seyoyan scrambled over the railing and disappeared from view. Another one waved her forward. Kara took two unsteady steps and grabbed a thick rope that trailed over the side. A rope ladder led down to a dory that bobbed in the moonlight. She slipped over the edge and stepped down two rungs—then hands reached for her, gently guiding her into the prow of the boat. Soon Reo huddled beside her, and two Seyoyans rowed them away from the ship.

She peered forward—the shore was faintly outlined in mage mist. Light green—Santos' colour.

"Santos has a spell in place," Kara said softly to Reo.

"Do you know what it does?" he asked.

Kara shook her head. "No." She turned to the rowers. "We need to stop here," she said in Seyoyan.

The Seyoyans looked at her before digging their oars in the water—the dory lurched and slowed. Water slapped against the wooden sides of the boat, and a cool wind blew them towards the mage mist that swirled a few feet away.

"We need something to throw." She stared at the mage mist. "I can get us through it, but it I would like to know what kind of spell it is." She paused. "Whether it just keeps intruders away or is something more dangerous."

Reo leaned over and grabbed a rope that was coiled in the bottom of the boat. A knife flashed in his hands, and he handed her a six inch length of rope.

"Do you think they've been attacked?" he asked her quietly.

Kara took the rope. "I hope not. That would mean my mother and Mage Guild know I lived here." And *that* would mean she'd put her friends at risk.

She leaned out over the prow and tossed the rope through the mage mist—it arced halfway through the green and then it disappeared. She heard a splash behind them.

"It's a relocation spell," she said, relieved. "It's a basic spell to keep anyone from landing here. It probably pushes them out into the bay. I'll make it go around us."

"Is it to defend against attack?" Reo asked.

"No." She focused on the mage mist. "Santos can create this

type of spell in his sleep." She glanced at Reo. "If they were attacked I'd expect something stronger than this—something more damaging." She looked at the Seyoyans. "We can land," she said to the Seyoyans.

The boat moved forward, and the mist parted to let them through. She still didn't like that there was a spell. Why had Santos cast it?

"You're worried," Reo said.

"Yes," Kara replied. "Santos didn't want anyone to know that he was sane and capable of magic again."

Reo nodded. "That spell reveals that there's a practicing Mage close."

The boat slowed as it got close to the rocky shore. One of the Seyoyans crept past them to the prow and scrambled over the side with the rope in his hand. Half walking, half swimming, he towed them until a rock scraped against the bottom of the boat.

Reo stepped out first, motioning for Kara to stay back.

"They might know someone is here," he said. "I'll take a look." He waded towards shore, the moon glinting off the ripples he made in the water.

Kara gazed out to sea. The mage mist swirled unbroken just off the coast. The only thing that comforted her was the knowledge that it was Santos Nimali's spell. What had changed that he felt the need to safeguard his estate? She looked in the direction of the buildings—the damaged estate and the small cabin she'd felt so at home in. Even though the trees were mostly bare she was still too far away to see any lights.

"Clear," Reo called in a hushed voice.

A Seyoyan helped her step out of the boat. Her foot slipped on a wet rock as she scrambled up to Reo. Absently he pulled her close.

"Any magic?" he asked.

She shook her head.

"Good. I'll have the men wait for me. Hopefully Santos will help, and I can leave before dawn."

Reo turned to talk to the crew, and Kara stared into the dark woods. A few months ago it had been her home, but now, with mage mist hugging the shore, the island felt foreign. Would they want her back? Had she become so different that she'd no longer fit in? She'd killed a man—a Mage—was she too dangerous to live here now? It had been her safe haven once—she wanted, *needed,* it to be that again.

Reo touched her arm and nodded. She took the hand he offered and followed him into the woods. A few minutes later they emerged from the trees into a small clearing.

Kara frowned. She hadn't spent much time roaming the woods, but the estate wasn't that big. This clearing was new. She tightened her grip on Reo's hand.

"Stop!"

The voice came from their left. She sucked in her breath and froze. Reo's shoulders tensed for a moment, and then he relaxed, ready to fight.

"Stay there, where I can see you."

A light flared, a torch with flame, and Kara squinted in the glare.

"Kara? Is that you?"

She tried to peer past the torch. The voice was familiar, but she couldn't quite place it.

"Vook, get that light out of her eyes, the poor girl's blinded."

"Sorry, Mika."

"Mika," Kara said. "I didn't expect you."

She stepped past Reo and wrapped her arms around the trader.

"And Vook. I'm so happy to see you." She ruffled his hair. She had to reach up to do it—he'd grown a few inches since she'd last seen him and put on a few pounds.

"Reo," Kara turned around. "This is Mika Giannetti, the trader I traveled with in the summer. You know Vook."

Mika eyed Reo and nodded.

"I can't believe it's you!" Mika said. "We heard just today that you were dead." Mika squeezed her against her side. "I'm awfully glad it's not true. Come on up to the house. Santos will be so relieved."

"He's awake?" Kara asked.

Mika nodded.

"We need his help."

Kara and Reo followed Mika through another small stand of trees to the house. Lights glowed in a few of the windows, and it looked warm and inviting.

"He fixed it," Kara said. "The damage." The house was

magnificent now, truly befitting the Mage Guild Primus that Santos had been.

"Yeah," Vook said. "Santos hired folk down by Shantytown. Dozens of men and boys have been crawling all over this place for the last month. Said the house was built without magic so it shouldn't be repaired with magic."

"People know about him?" Kara asked.

"Santos said it was Mage Guild that wanted him kept a secret," Mika said. "But he got worried when we heard you'd been killed." She looked at Reo. "And that you were in trouble with Mage Guild."

"That's why he put a spell along the shore," Kara said.

"Yeah," Vook replied. "Just in case Mage Guild knew you'd come from here."

Light streamed from the windows of the kitchen along the rear of the house. Mika pushed open the door.

"Look who we found," Mika called.

"Kara?" Santos said. He was standing in the doorway to the hall, a puzzled look on his face. "Kara." He smiled. "It *is* you."

She rushed to him, and his thin arms encircled her.

"It's good to be back," she said.

Santos pulled away and studied her. "You're home for good?"

Kara glanced at Reo, who nodded, his mouth tight.

"Yes," she said and then she smiled. "I'm home."

"What about Reo?" Santos asked. "I thought . . ."

"I have released Kara from any further obligations," Reo said. "Considering what I've put her through, I'm grateful for any good will she has for me."

"What you put her through?" Santos asked, frowning.

"I'll tell that tale later," Kara said. "Right now I need a favour." She looked at Reo again. "*We* need a favour."

IT WAS ALMOST dawn. Reo had left with the Seyoyans, and Kara was exhausted, but she needed to tell Santos everything. She wanted him to make his decision tonight—she didn't think she could endure being asked to leave once she'd settled back into the cabin.

She'd told Santos and Mika everything, except the one thing that she thought would change their minds about her. She stared down at her empty tea cup and took a deep breath.

"I'm the one who killed Valerio Valendi," she said.

"You did?" Santos asked. "I assumed it was Reo. Tell us what happened."

"Reo and I were trying to get away," Kara said. "Valendi had us trapped. He was at the front of the alley, and his men were behind us." She paused for a moment, seeing the mage-mist enshrouded figure again. "He started launching spells at us." She looked up and met Santo's gaze. "Bad ones. We avoided the first one, but it struck and killed one of his men. After that I deflected the spells, but Valendi kept coming. When he was close, Reo rushed him, hoping to kill him. Valendi sent one last spell. It would have killed Reo so I . . . I pushed his spell back onto him and he died."

"It was his spell," Mika said. "Sounds like the Mage killed himself."

"No, I did it," Kara said. "I'm a killer."

"Hush," Santos said. "You were defending yourself and Reo. You said yourself Valendi would have killed both of you." Santos covered one of her hands with his. "Besides," he continued. "He's the one who cursed me. You've saved me some trouble."

"What do you mean?" she asked.

"You don't really think that Valerio Valendi would have let me live once he heard that I was sane, do you? My former Journeyman would need to get rid of me, permanently this time."

"He would dare? Even if you didn't trouble him?"

"He'd have to," Santos said. "I know far too much and am far too powerful for him to feel safe while I'm alive. I've been meaning to create some safeguards spells around the estate to protect against any magical attacks." He smiled sadly. "I hadn't thought it urgent until we heard that you had died."

"How did you learn that?" Kara asked.

"Reo's Seyoyan friend," Mika said. "Chal came by boat this afternoon. You were dead, and Reo was wanted for questioning by Mage Guild. He said that he'd heard it from the Mage Guild Primus himself."

"Good. That's what we want everyone to think," she said. Reo's task would be much easier if Mage Guild already thought she was dead.

"That's the official version," Santo's said. "It's hard to say what the Primus really believes, or knows, but Mage Guild can't afford to let anyone think that the death of their Secundus has gone unpunished.”

“Will they come here?” Kara asked. “Have I put you at risk?” She paused. “Should I leave?”

“Leave? Absolutely not,” Santo said. “This island belongs to me. *I* say who is welcome or not. Mage Guild has no power here. Besides,” he grinned. “I *am* the Mage Guild Primus. It’s a title held for life, and I am still alive.”

“What about the current Primus?” Mika asked.

“He’s the acting Primus,” Santos said. “Although he probably does not feel that way.” He waved his hand. “No matter. I don’t want the position, he does, so we should be able to come to an agreement.”

“My mother won’t agree,” Kara said. There was no way Arabella Fonti would let her daughter live, not after she’d killed Valendi.

“She’ll have no choice,” Santos said his voice hard. “I am the Mage Guild Primus. Now, time to find you a place to sleep. Everyone else has moved into the house so the cabin is empty. It’s yours if you want it, or you can stay here. There are plenty of rooms.”

Kara didn’t even have to think about it. “The cabin.” It was home.

“Then it’s yours,” Santos said. “But the house is always open to you—just come over when you feel like company.”

Mika walked with her to the cabin, carrying two small lamps to light their way. Kara’s eyes were almost closed by the time she turned the corner and saw the front door.

“I’ve been in it, so I know it’s there,” Mika said, handing her a lamp. “But I can’t see it, so you’ll need to visit me before I head home in a few days.”

“I will,” Kara said. She gave her friend a quick hug and entered the cabin. The rows of preserves, considerably depleted, were still stacked in the small kitchen, the glass glinting in the lamplight. She sighed, content to be home.

Chapter twenty-four

KARA SETTLED BACK into her cabin. In the mornings she gazed out the window at the waters of the bay. Winter was here and the wind-whipped waves crashed against the rocks, white spray sparkling in the sun. After enjoying her solitude, she ventured to the main house, where she would make lunch for Vook, Sidra, or Santos, or the many workers from Shantytown still at work on the interior of the house.

Pilo's scars were almost gone, although the girl was still shy around people she didn't know. She'd quietly help Kara, setting out cups and keeping the kettle full for the constant request for tea.

Vook was in his element. He'd attached himself to the crew boss, a former Mason, and was eagerly learning everything the man was willing to teach. The thought that Vook would have made a fine apprentice made her sad until she realized that he already was one.

Sidra spent most of her time with Mika. After living so long with the threat of hunger, the girl seemed determined to gather and store enough food to keep them fed for years. The garden was going to be much expanded come spring. A few new beds were being cleared, including the one that she and Reo had walked through the night they arrived.

Kara rarely saw Mole but he seemed healthy and growing, and Santos said he'd taken to prowling the estate at night. One evening after she'd settled into her cabin, he came in and sat down. He didn't say much, but Mole never had—and he left after a few quiet hours.

Mika departed with the promise that she'd return in the spring. Kara watched her go, glad that her friend was heading back to Allon and their home in the mountains, but she would miss her. Kara wasn't much older than Vook, but her months with Reo had changed her, forced her to grow up, and she craved the adult company that Mika had provided.

Santos was completely free of all of the spells that had cursed him. He kept to his workroom, and a part of Kara worried that since he no longer needed her help, he didn't want to spend time with her. But a few days after Mika left, he stopped her on her way to her cabin.

"Will you be ready to start in the morning?" Santos asked.

Kara paused and turned to him. His arms were crossed over his chest, and a small half smile played on his lips.

"Start what?"

"Your training, of course," Santos said. "I want you to be my Apprentice." He frowned. "Unless you're not interested."

"Of course I am," she replied. "But I can't do magic." She dropped her gaze to the ground, filled with the familiar feelings of failure and disappointment.

"Yes, you can," Santos said. "You do the most extraordinary magic. You just can't create spells. I'm fascinated and want to find out exactly what you can do."

She looked up into his bright gaze. Santos' smile widened, and she returned his smile.

"We'll start in the morning then," Kara said.

Santos nodded and turned away.

She watched him go. She hadn't even hoped for that. She felt lucky—Gyda-blessed—to have a safe home and friends. But to have someone willing—*eager*—to work with her and help her develop her talents? That was a dream she'd given up years ago.

ARABELLA PLACED HER open palm against her heart. "By Gyda's light I pledge to uphold Guild Law. As Mage Guild Secundus I put the guild above all, even myself, and promise to use all my talents to further the guild and its Guildsmen."

"I, Primus Rorik, appoint you Secundus Fonti."

Arabella met Rorik's eyes and nodded. It was done. The appointment had taken longer than she'd expected, but finally she was Secundus and none of the Mages who stood as witnesses could undo it. She was safe—and in power—for the rest of her life.

"Thank you, Primus," she nodded. She turned to the crowd—every single council member was in attendance, of course—along with an assortment of lesser Mages, Journeymen, Apprentices, and other Guildsmen and women. Warrior Guild had sent a minor official. She chose not to be offended, although she could tell by the set of Rorik's shoulders that he was. He had been pressing Warrior Guild rather hard about their involvement in Valerio's death. She hadn't been able to make Rorik wait until she was appointed—otherwise she would have been there when the Assassin was interviewed.

Rorik had used magic on him, and he was confident that he'd told the truth—that the girl was dead. But Arabella had heard of her death far too many times to truly believe it. She would need to see her body with her own eyes.

"Enjoy your reception, Arabella," Rorik said as he led her down from the dais. "But meet me later. We have much to talk about."

"Such as?"

"There are reports that Santos Nimali is no longer mad. I need you to find out if there is any truth to this." He looked out across the room. "Someone here knows something. They will tell you, if you ask nicely."

"I will do my best to make new friends and strengthen old alliances."

"I'm sure you will." Rorik bowed and left her to the crowd that waited for her.

"The worst news, Primus," Arabella said. Gratefully, she dropped into the chair he gestured to. Her reception had ended a few moments ago, and she'd headed straight to Rorik's quarters.

"More than just Santos Nimali has been spotted on Old Rillidi."

"The Assassin?" Rorik asked. "Warrior Guild promised he

would not be a problem."

"The girl." She had no idea how she'd managed to live, but the half-brother—Noula's son—had been taken from his fostering—who else would want the brat? "Even though the Assassin said she was dead."

"I used a spell on him," Rorik said. "He could not have lied!"

"Unless another Mage spelled him first." It was the only thing that would have worked.

"Who? Nimali? But he's been mad for years."

"And yet he is no longer mad," she replied.

Rorik paled. "Are you certain?"

"There are too many reports. He's hired labourers—*unguilded*—from that island of his to repair his house." Though if he was as powerful as everyone said, she couldn't understand why he wouldn't just use magic.

"That is his way," Rorik mused. "Santos always liked things to be made by workers, rather than be created with magic. His entire estate was built by Masons."

"That would take so long," Arabella said. "And there would be imperfections."

"I never agreed with him," Rorik said. "But it was his way. We need to see him."

"And bring the girl to justice." The Assassin was out of reach, but the girl? Arabella wanted to see her die.

Chapter twenty-five

"WHAT DO YOU feel," Santos said. "Close your eyes and concentrate on what you feel from the spell."

After making sure that her hand was still thrust into the grass green mage mist that swirled around the top of the worktable, Kara closed her eyes. They'd been attempting this same test for three days, and she still couldn't feel anything except the slight damp she always felt when she touched mage mist. But Santos was confident that this could be done by someone with her unique magical talents, so she'd kept trying.

"I don't feel anything," she said.

"How about now," Santos said.

"Nothing."

She shivered despite the warmth of the sun streaming through the workroom window. Suddenly she had the urge to snatch her hand away from the mist, as though something terrible would happen if she kept it there. Was that feeling coming from the spell?

"I feel danger," she said. "Or a threat of some kind." She frowned as the feeling grew stronger. Her hand itched, and she pulled it towards her chest. She opened her eyes. The spell continued swirling, the same as before, but now she clearly felt the underlying malice.

"Excellent," Santos said. "I put as much ill will into that spell as I could safely do, and you felt it."

"Eventually," she said. "But how useful will this be if it has to be that malicious?"

"It would have been nice to know if the food was spelled to help or harm," Santos said.

With Kara gone, Santos hadn't felt comfortable eating the food Mage Guild left. After the death of Valerio Valendi, and with the obvious signs that the *mad mage* was in the process of fixing his manor house, the Mages had stopped bringing it. But Kara knew Santos would always wonder if his former Journeyman had kept him mad by cursing his food.

"All right," she agreed. "There is a use for it. Will it always be so decisive? Can't a spell be cast that isn't meant to harm, but does anyway?"

"Yes," Santos said. "You might only feel the intent of the Mage when they cast the spell, and not whether they are incompetent or foolish."

"Kara," Pilo called from the garden. "Reo's here."

Reo! The door swung open, and he stood in the doorway, and Kara's heart skittered for a moment. He looked tired and worn down. Empty.

"Reo," Kara said. "What are you doing here?"

His mouth tightened, and she stopped speaking.

"I mean, is it safe for you to come here?"

"Safe?" Reo said. "No, probably not. There's no danger to you, but there's no safe place in Rillidi for a former Assassin. We have some unfinished business, you and I. I have to right a wrong that happened because I forced you to work with me."

"I told you," Kara said. "I forgive you."

Santos came up beside her and took her arm as she faced Reo. She didn't invite him in, nor did he step inside the house.

"So you said. But I have not forgiven myself," Reo said.

His eyes met hers, and Kara was shocked at the bleakness in them.

"I have a gift that I hope will allow you to remember me with some admiration."

"But I do . . ."

Reo stepped aside, and a small worried face peered up at her.

"Osten," Kara breathed. Her younger brother was frightened

and thin and dirty, but he also appeared unhurt. "Thank Gyda you're safe."

Osten, wary and nervous, stared at her.

"Osten," she said. "Come here. You're safe now." Slowly the boy crossed to her and gave her an awkward hug.

"I promise. You're safe."

"But mama was never nice to you," Osten said.

"No, but that wasn't your fault." Kara looked up and met Reo's gaze. "Thank you, Reo. This is a gift beyond my expectations. How did you find him?"

Reo smiled then, not quite the carefree smile from before their trip to Mage Guild Island, but it lightened her heart just the same.

"Arabella Fonti likes her people to know what happens to those who displease her," he said. "I found one willing to tell me what happened to your brother." His smile faltered. "He was not being treated well."

"Reo killed my master," Osten said. His face twisted into a scowl. "And I'm glad. I wish I was bigger so I could have killed him."

Shocked, Kara stared at Osten. The innocent, laughing little boy he'd been just this past spring was gone, replaced by this angry child with hurt eyes.

His chin jutted out, and he glared at her. "I would have killed him if I could have," Osten declared.

Kara's chest constricted. What had been done to her poor brother?

"Thank you again, Reo," she said. "I almost wish I'd let you kill her," she said, thinking about when Reo asked her if she wanted him to kill her mother. Arabella Fonti had known exactly what life she was delivering her brother into.

"Don't thank me just yet," Reo said. He stepped out of the doorway to let a young boy in. No more than nine, he was thin and pale. "He was there as well, and not likely to have any friends left now."

Kara walked over to the boy, Osten at her side.

"Hello," she said. "I'm Kara." He had to be. The eyes, the colouring, the arch of the nose. This boy was Valerio Valendi's child.

"I'm Giona," was the soft reply.

"He's my friend," Osten stated. "I told *him*," he gestured to

Reo, "that I wasn't leaving Giona behind."

"Did you now," Kara said.

She met Reo's eyes and smiled. For all that Osten was two or three years younger than Giona, he clearly was the fighter.

"Giona, you are most welcome here. As you can see, it's a big house with plenty of room."

"I'll work hard," Giona said. "I know how."

"That's good to know," Kara replied gently. "We'll let you get settled, both of you, then we'll decide. I think schooling will be required." It was something that she'd meant to start, and with two more students, she couldn't put it off any longer.

Reo declined the offer to stay overnight, but he agreed to at least stay for a meal.

Pilo and Vook took the newcomers on a tour of the house. They returned in time for dinner, chattering about the rooms they'd selected. Kara had wondered if she should ask Osten to stay with her in the cabin, but he didn't seem likely to leave Giona. The children ate quickly and bolted to their new rooms with Pilo, who promised to make them bathe, trailing behind them.

"He looks a great deal like Valendi," Santos said. He filled Kara's and Reo's cups with tea.

"Yes," Reo agreed. "He was treated slightly better, no doubt because his master was afraid of the Secundus. At least he didn't have to share the man's bed."

A wave of anger flashed through Kara. "Despicable ruffiano," she spat. "I'm glad he's dead."

"Yes, but that's not why I killed him," Reo said. "He saw me, so he was a liability. That's also why I brought Giona, although young Osten did say he wasn't coming without him."

"You did the right thing," she said.

"Do you think he knows who his father was?" Santos asked.

"No," Reo replied.

"I'm not surprised," Santos said. "Mages often don't acknowledge a child until they know if they have magic. But this child might have significant power." Santos smiled. "At least I hope so. As lovely an Apprentice as you are, Kara, it would be good to be able to teach someone who can use what I know."

"And not fumble and guess at answers?" She turned to Reo. "We heard Mage Guild interrogated you about my disappearance."

Reo frowned. "All they wanted was confirmation that you died as they suspected." He nodded at Santos. "The spell you set on me seems to have worked. At least the Primus seemed convinced."

"And my mother?" Kara asked.

"I didn't see her," Reo replied. "Although I've heard she's been appointed Secundus."

Kara stared at her tea for a moment as they all fell silent.

"And what about you?" she asked Reo softly. "What will you do now?"

Reo's sharp laugh was full of bitterness. "Me? I suppose I'll return to Warrior Guild and perform my duties for the rest of my life."

"Stay here," Kara blurted out.

Santos raised an eyebrow, but she ignored him. Reo wouldn't live long, not now that he'd helped her escape her mother. And Arabella Fonti would consider Kara's death an escape. Reo had only been trying to make a life for himself. Not much different from what she'd been trying to do.

"I can't," Reo said flatly.

"Why not? There's plenty of room. You can stay here in the house or even build your own place if you want."

She looked at Santos, and he nodded.

"Besides, we should try to have at least one person from each guild here, to share knowledge."

"And train a few Assassins?" Reo asked.

She met his bitter gaze. He'd killed *for her*, she *would not* hold that against him.

"It would be prudent to train some of the residents of Old Rillidi to protect themselves," Santos said. "And teaching all guild-held skills would lessen the guilds' collective power."

"See," Kara said. "Santos thinks it's a good idea too." She covered Reo's hand with her own, afraid he'd say yes, even more afraid that he wouldn't.

There was a glimmer of hope in his eyes, then it was gone, replaced with flat despair.

No," Reo said. "Warrior Guild will never let me leave." He pulled his hand from beneath hers and dropped a clenched fist to his side.

"We'll trade," Santos said. He nodded thoughtfully. "Soon

we'll have something they will want very, very much. Something that *all* the guilds will want, except maybe one."

"It doesn't matter," Reo said. "It's never been done, no Assassin has ever left the guild."

"But that's what you were trying to do," Kara said. "You were going to be the first."

"And I was a fool to think it possible," Reo said.

"I say that it *is* possible," Santos said. When he glared at Reo, he *was* the Mage Primus, the most powerful man in Tregella.

Reo saw it too—he unclenched his fist and placed his hand flat on the table.

"What is it?" Reo asked. "It would have to be something extraordinary."

"Yes," Santos said. "It's Kara. Or rather, it's what Kara can do. Tell me," he leaned towards Reo. "What would Warrior Guild pay to have their Guildhall rid of any spells cast with malice, anything that hinted at anger, or revenge, or spite. What would they pay for that?"

Reo leaned back in his chair. His eyes darted to Kara. "You can do that?"

She nodded, and he expelled the breath he'd been holding.

"They would pay any price," Reo said. "To know that Mage Guild couldn't overhear or influence their decisions, they would pay anything." He looked over at her again. "You would do that for me?"

"Yes," she said.

Reo smiled a real smile—full of hope and perhaps a little bit of promise.

"I'm not sure I'm ready, but I'm sure Santos can bargain with Warrior Guild Primus."

Santos nodded. "One can always bargain when one has something others want. We'll go tomorrow, Reo. You and I."

Reo nodded. "I will accept your offer of a place to stay tonight after all."

THOUGH KARA WAS at the main house early the next day, Santos and Reo had already left by the time she arrived. She'd wanted to see them before they left to wish them Gyda's luck, and to, well, to make sure that Reo knew he was welcome here, after.

She went to the kitchen, pulled out a pot, and filled it with water and oats. The children filed in, Osten peppering poor Vook with questions about the house construction. Sidra grabbed some bowls and spoons from the shelf near the back door while Giona simply sat at the table, looking bewildered.

"Is there anything I can help you with, Donna," Giona asked Kara in a quiet voice.

"You can help eat the porridge," she said and smiled.

"I can do chores to earn my keep," the boy said.

Her smile faltered when she saw his hands tremble.

"Giona," Kara said gently. "There will be plenty of time for you to figure out how and what you want to contribute. There's no rush."

He looked up and then quickly looked away.

"I know what my master did to Osten," Giona whispered. "I couldn't help him, no matter what I did. Tell me what I can do to help now? I don't want you to hurt him."

"No one's going to hurt him," she said. "And certainly not like that."

"But he said his mama was mean to you," Giona said. "Like my master was mean to me. I thought you'd be angry."

"That wasn't his fault," Kara said.

"You're not going to hurt him?"

"Of course not—he's all the family I have."

There was a shout from the front of the house. Kara glanced around the kitchen. All the children had frozen.

"Kara!" Pilo ran into the kitchen from the front hallway, her eyes wide with fear. "There's a man and a woman out front—Mages." Her voice was shaky. "Looking for you. They don't seem friendly."

"Can you still find the cabin?" Kara asked.

Pilo nodded.

Kara let out a breath. "Good, take everyone and hide there."

Pilo nodded again, and she, Vook, and Sidra ushered the other two boys out the back door.

Kara wasn't really surprised that her mother had found her, here, on Old Rillidi. Had she followed Reo when he'd brought Osten and Giona? It didn't matter, really. Despite what Reo and Santos had said, she hadn't believed that her mother would give up so easily.

She brushed her skirt and looked around the kitchen. The cozy family atmosphere of a few moments ago was gone now. Half empty bowls and cups littered the table and counters where the children had left their breakfasts. When would her mother simply leave her alone? She squared her shoulders and strode to the front door.

Kara closed her eyes and concentrated on pushing away any magic that might be near the door. She eased it open and stepped out onto the front step. Waves of purple and tan mage mist eddied at the base of the steps. Even from a few feet away, she could sense the malevolence in the magic.

"Mother," Kara drawled. "Even you might have the decency to talk before attacking." Kara crossed her arms over her chest.

Arabella Fonti glared at her from a few yards away.

"You must be the Mage Guild Primus," Kara said to the man at her mother's side.

Her mother's hands flew up, and a wave of mage mist flew towards her.

Kara waved a hand, and it soared up into the sky.

"Will you make the same mistake Valerio Valendi did?" Kara asked. "I turned his own spell on him."

Her mother shuddered, and Kara suppressed the urge to do the same. She was doing her best to keep the tremor out of her voice, but her knees could give out at any moment.

"Mage Guild Primus," Kara said. "What can I do for you?"

"Mage Guild demands justice," he said. He looked to be about Santos' age, but an easy life had allowed him to overindulge, leading to a thick waist and a ruddy face. Thin lips were tight with anger.

"That's not my concern," Kara said. "I'm unguilded and do not recognize guild authority."

"You donnina," Arabella snapped. "You *are* Mage Guild. My daughter."

Kara laughed. "All these years, Mother, all these years and now you decide to acknowledge me as your daughter? You're too late."

Her mother flung another spell, and Kara's hands flashed up, sending it back towards them. It exploded two feet in front of them, and both the Mage Guild Primus and her mother jumped back in alarm.

"I warned you," Kara said. "I may not be able to create spells, but I can redirect them."

She frowned at the Primus. Tan mage mist was thickening at his feet. "I wouldn't," she said to him. "I can feel the intent of that spell. This one I *will* send back. I saw Valendi's body. Did you?"

The Primus blanched slightly and took a step away, dropping his arms. The tan mist swirled around his feet for a moment more before dissipating.

"You killed a high ranking Guildsman," the Primus said.

"Who was trying to kill me," Kara said.

"His actions did not violate Guild Law," the Primus said. "Yours did."

"Your Guild Laws do not apply to me," Kara said. "And you have no right to be on this island." The Primus glared at her but he finally nodded. There was a flicker of movement, and Kara raised her hand. An ugly wall of purple mist hung suspended in front of her.

"I should send this spell back to you," Kara said. She pushed the spell until it hovered in front of Arabella and the Primus. The Primus took another step back, but her mother continued to glare at her, her hands fisted.

"You would kill your own mother?" Arabella asked. "And your unborn brother or sister?" She turned to the Primus. "She has threatened the Mage Guild Secundus in front of you. You *must* act."

"It's your spell," Kara said. "I have no idea what it will do but apparently you're trying to kill me." She looked from her mother's angry face to the Primus. "Old Rillidi is not under Guild control. You will leave now."

"Yes," the Primus agreed.

"No!" Arabella said. "She cannot be allowed to live."

"Arabella," the Primus said. "Come. This is not finished." He met Kara's eyes. "We will send spells from Mage Guild Island."

"No. I need to see her die," Arabella said. "I've been lied to before. I need to see it."

Kara felt the blood drain from her face. Any fear she'd had turned to fury. She took a breath to calm herself, remembering Reo's warning. She would not kill in anger. But she would kill them if she had to. She closed her hand and the spell—her mother's killing spell—compressed into a pulsating ball.

"You will not threaten me or my home again," Kara said. "Or I will spend every ounce of energy I have taking Mage Guild Island apart, spell by spell." She smiled when the Primus blanched.

"She could you know."

It was Reo. Kara turned as he and Santos exited the house. Reo, his eyes on the two hostile Mages, stopped beside her, his shoulder brushing hers, and she exhaled in relief. She opened her hand and let the spell she'd been holding disperse.

"You must pay," Arabella hissed. "I will not allow you to get away with murder!"

"Murder. Is that what you call it when a Mage is killed by his own spell?" Santos asked. He took a step forward. "And Rorik, though you've become comfortable in your role, you do not have full authority to speak for Mage Guild."

"Of course he speaks for the guild," Arabella said. "He's Primus."

"There can only be one Primus," Santos said.

Arabella's face went white. "No," she said. "You went insane and were relieved of the title. Primus Rorik, tell him!"

Rorik shook his head. "It's a title held until death." He bowed to Santos. "Primus."

"No!" Arabella yelled. "He's mad, everyone knows that. The mad mage."

"Yes, I was," Santos said. "Thanks to Valerio Valendi's curses. It took Kara's unusual gifts to untangle the spells."

"Valendi cursed you?" Primus Rorik asked, clearly horrified. "Are you sure?"

"Kara is sure, and that's enough for me," Santos said.

"He was draining power from my mother as well," Kara said.

"He would never," Arabella said. Her hand automatically went to her rounded stomach.

Chin lifted, Kara met her mother's eyes. And sucked in her breath. The hatred there was frightening. She felt Reo's shoulder touch hers again, and she leaned into him, just a little. She wished she didn't care, wished that after all this time she could forget her mother, but this venomous hatred was almost more than she could bear. For the first time in her life Kara was actually glad she'd been raised by her indifferent father and his mean-spirited wife. Noula's envy had been petty and harmless compared to Arabella Fonti's hate.

"He would and he did," Kara said. "Valerio Valendi was

siphoning your power even as your body nurtured his unborn child."

"This is where this ends," Santos said. "Valendi is dead, Mage Guild has appointed a replacement, and I, as Primus, am satisfied that there is no need to discuss this further. Rorik?"

"Agreed," Primus Rorik said. "This is finished."

"We are not agreed," Arabella said. "If you will not kill her," she glared at Rorik, "I will."

"As Primus, I can revoke your rank and exile you if I wish to," Santos said calmly. "Both of you."

"But you're not really Primus," Arabella said. "You've been gone years. You have no allies, no political power within the guild. The council will expel you."

"No," Rorik said. "This is finished."

"But . . ."

"I said no!" Rorik repeated. "There would be a war within the guild. Santos *will* have allies, once the truth about Valendi is known. And *his* crimes, if they become known, will taint both you and your unborn child. Is that what you want?"

Arabella glared at the Primus again. Finally, she stepped aside, her back stiff. Kara almost felt sorry for her mother, until she remembered what she'd done to Osten.

"Our business is done," Santos said. "But understand that if Mage Guild or any of its Guildsmen takes any further action against Kara, Reo, or anyone else on Old Rillidi, I will consider it defying a direct order from the Primus."

"You have my word that Mage Guild will not condone any further interference with Old Rillidi, Kara Fonti, or Reo," Rorik said. He nodded and turned, towing an angry Arabella Fonti after him.

"Are you all right?" Reo asked her.

Kara nodded and took a shaky breath.

"I think so," she replied. "I'm grateful that you returned when you did. I'm not sure what I would have done."

"You would have kept those you care about safe," Reo said. "You always do."

She met his gaze. She saw compassion and understanding there.

"Yes. And I would have had to live with the fact that I'd killed my mother." And she would have always regretted the loss of her unborn sibling.

"Then it's good that Warrior Guild Primus was so agreeable," Santos said. "It took a few minutes for him to understand what was being offered, but once he grasped it, he couldn't agree to our terms fast enough."

"You're free?" Kara asked Reo. "Truly free of the guild?" He grinned, and she hugged him, squeezing tight.

"I'm free," Reo said into her hair. "Free to stop killing, free to live where I want, free to grow old."

"We'll need to keep working on your skills, Kara," Santos said.

She stepped away from Reo and nodded.

"But that can wait for another day." Santos grinned at her. "Welcome home to both of you."

Acknowledgements

This book first saw the light of day in SLS Lithuania. Thanks to Antanas Sileika and everyone in his morning workshop and to later critiquers Sandra and Andrew. Every comment has helped me make this book better.

Much thanks also goes to my Editor, Margaret Curalas, and not only for her hard work on this book. Margaret's interest in an earlier story gave me the confidence to forge ahead with this one. As did Nalo Hopkinson, my excellent mentor at The Humber School for Writers.

I have found that in writing – as in life – the best (and often most difficult) thing is to show up and keep doing. But good things happen when you make good things happen.

Jane Glatt

Author Biography

Jane Glatt is an IT professional from Southern Ontario with a passion for writing fantasy.

She has a BA in Sociology from Western University and a Certificate in Marketing from Ryerson which she puts to good use dreaming up the worlds and characters she writes about.

An avid cyclist, Jane loves to pedal along the shores of Lake Ontario and has even taken her cycling as far afield as Ireland, Austria and Hungary.

Most days Jane can be found in her ergonomic chair in front of her computer with her Norwegian Forest cat on her lap.